THE BISHOP MURDER CASE

The Earth is a Temple where there is going on a Mystery Play, childish and poignant, ridiculous and awful enough in all conscience — *Conrad*.

THE BISHOP MURDER CASE

A PHILO VANCE STORY

S. S. VAN DINE

THORN[illegible] PRESS • THORNDIKE, MAINE

Library of Congress Cataloging in Publication Data:

Van Dine, S. S.
The Bishop murder case.

1. Large type books. I. Title.
[PS3545.R846B5 1984] 813'.52 83-18024
ISBN 0-89621-501-6

Large Print edition available through arrangement with Charles Scribner's Sons.

Cover design by Holly Hughes

CONTENTS

I.	"Who Killed Cock Robin?"	11
II.	On the Archery Range	28
III.	A Prophecy Recalled	51
IV.	A Mysterious Note	69
V.	A Woman's Scream	89
VI.	" 'I,' Said the Sparrow"	105
VII.	Vance Reaches A Conclusion	124
VIII.	Act Two	142
IX.	The Tensor Formula	157
X.	A Refusal of Aid	172
XI.	The Stolen Revolver	186
XII.	A Midnight Call	206
XIII.	In the Bishop's Shadow	227
XIV.	A Game of Chess	244
XV.	An Interview with Pardee	262
XVI.	Act Three	280
XVII.	An All-Night Light	296
XVIII.	The Wall in the Park	310
XIX.	The Red Note-Book	326
XX.	The Nemesis	338
XXI.	Mathematics and Murder	350
XXII.	The House of Cards	367

XXIII. A Startling Discovery 385
XXIV. The Last Act 400
XXV. The Curtain Falls 415
XXVI. Heath Asks a Question 437

CHARACTERS OF THE BOOK

PHILO VANCE

JOHN F.-X. MARKHAM

District Attorney of New York County.

ERNEST HEATH

Sergeant of the Homicide Bureau.

PROFESSOR BERTRAND DILLARD

A famous physicist.

BELLE DILLARD

His niece.

SIGURD ARNESSON

His adopted son: an associate professor of mathematics.

PYNE

The Dillard butler.

BEEDLE

The Dillard cook.

ADOLPH DRUKKER

Scientist and author.

MRS. OTTO DRUKKER

His mother.

GRETE MENZEL

The Drukker cook.

JOHN PARDEE

Mathematician and chess expert: inventor of the Pardee gambit.

J. C. Robin

Sportsman and champion archer.

Raymond Sperling

Civil Engineer.

John E. Sprigg

Senior at Columbia University.

Dr. Whitney Barstead

An eminent neurologist.

Quinan

Police Reporter of the *World*.

Madeleine Moffat

Chief Inspector O'Brien

Of the Police Department of New York City.

William M. Moran

Commanding Officer of the Detective Bureau.

Captain Pitts

Of the Homicide Bureau.

Guilfoyle

Detective of the Homicide Bureau.

Snitkin

Detective of the Homicide Bureau.

Hennessey

Detective of the Homicide Bureau.

Emery

Detective of the Homicide Bureau.

BURKE

Detective of the Homicide Bureau.

CAPTAIN DUBOIS

Finger-print expert.

DR. EMANUEL DOREMUS

Medical Examiner.

SWACKER

Secretary to the District Attorney.

CURRIE

Vance's valet.

CHAPTER I

"WHO KILLED COCK ROBIN?"

(Saturday, April 2; noon)

Of all the criminal cases in which Philo Vance participated as an unofficial investigator, the most sinister, the most bizarre, the seemingly most incomprehensible, and certainly the most terrifying, was the one that followed the famous Greene murders. The orgy of horror at the old Greene mansion had been brought to its astounding close in December; and after the Christmas holidays Vance had gone to Switzerland for the winter sports. Returning to New York at the end of February he had thrown himself into some literary work he had long had in mind – the uniform translation of the principal fragments of Menander found in the Egyptian papyri during the early years of the present century; and for over a month he had devoted himself sedulously to this thankless task.

Whether or not he would have completed the

translations, even had his labors not been interrupted, I do not know; for Vance was a man of cultural ardencies, in whom the spirit of research and intellectual adventure was constantly at odds with the drudgery necessary to scholastic creation. I remember that only the preceding year he had begun writing a life of Xenophon – the result of an enthusiasm inherited from his university days when he had first read the *Anabasis* and the *Memorabilia* – and had lost interest in it at the point where Xenophon's historic march led the Ten Thousand back to the sea. However, the fact remains that Vance's translation of Menander was rudely interrupted in early April; and for weeks he became absorbed in a criminal mystery which threw the country into a state of gruesome excitement.

This new criminal investigation, in which he acted as a kind of *amicus curiae* for John F.-X. Markham, the District Attorney of New York, at once became known as the Bishop murder case. The designation – the result of our journalistic instinct to attach labels to every *cause célèbre* – was, in a sense, a misnomer. There was nothing ecclesiastical about that ghoulish saturnalia of crime which set an entire community to reading the "Mother Goose Melodies" with fearful apprehension;* and no one of the name of Bishop was, as far as I know, even remotely connected with the monstrous events which bore that appellation. But, withal, the word "Bishop" was appropriate, for it was an *alias* used by the murderer for the grimmest of purposes. Incidentally it was this name that eventually led Vance to the almost incredible truth, and ended one of the most ghastly multiple crimes in police history.

The series of uncanny and apparently unrelated events which constituted the Bishop murder case and drove all thought of Menander and Greek monostichs from Vance's mind, began on the morning of April 2, less than five months after the double shooting of Julia and Ada Greene. It was one of those warm luxurious spring days which sometimes bless New York in early April; and Vance was breakfasting in his little roof garden atop his apartment in East 38th Street. It was nearly noon – for Vance worked or read until all hours, and was a late riser – and the sun,

*Mr. Joseph A. Margolies of Brentano's told me that for a period of several weeks during the Bishop murder case more copies of "Mother Goose Melodies" were sold than of any current novel. And one of the smaller publishing houses reprinted and completely sold out an entire edition of those famous old nursery rhymes.

beating down from a clear blue sky, cast a mantle of introspective lethargy over the city. Vance sprawled in an easy chair, his breakfast on a low table beside him, gazing with cynical, regretful eyes down at the treetops in the rear yard.

I knew what was in his mind. It was his custom each spring to go to France; and it had long since come to him to think, as it came to George Moore, that Paris and May were one. But the great trek of the post-war American *nouveaux riches* to Paris had spoiled his pleasure in this annual pilgrimage; and, only the day before, he had informed me that we were to remain in New York for the summer.

For years I had been Vance's friend and legal advisor – a kind of monetary steward and agent-companion. I had quitted my father's law firm of Van Dine, Davis & Van Dine to devote myself wholly to his interests – a post I found far more congenial than that of general attorney in a stuffy office – and though my own bachelor quarters were in a hotel on the West Side, I spent most of my time at Vance's apartment.

I had arrived early that morning, long before Vance was up, and, having gone over the first-of-the-month accounts, now sat smoking my pipe idly as he breakfasted.

"Y' know, Van," he said to me, in his emotionless drawl: "The prospect of spring and summer in New York is neither excitin' nor romantic. It's going to be a beastly bore. But it'll be less annoyin' than travelin' in Europe with the vulgar hordes of tourists jostlin' one at every turn. . . . It's very distressin'."

Little did he suspect what the next few weeks held in store for him. Had he known I doubt if even the prospect of an old pre-war spring in Paris would have taken him away; for his insatiable mind liked nothing better than a complicated problem; and even as he spoke to me that morning the gods that presided over his destiny were preparing for him a strange and fascinating enigma – one which was to stir the nation deeply and add a new and terrible chapter to the annals of crime.

Vance had scarcely poured his second cup of coffee when Currie, his old English butler and general factotum, appeared at the French doors bearing a portable telephone.

"It's Mr. Markham, sir," the old man said apologetically. "As he seemed rather urgent, I took the liberty of informing him you were in." He plugged the telephone into a baseboard switch, and set the instrument on the breakfast table.

"Quite right, Currie," Vance murmured, taking off the receiver. "Anything to break this deuced monotony." Then he spoke to Markham. "I say, old man, don't you ever sleep? I'm in the midst of an *omelette aux fines herbes.* Will you join me? Or do you merely crave the music of my voice –?"

He broke off abruptly, and the bantering look on his lean features disappeared. Vance was a marked Nordic type, with a long, sharply chiselled face; gray, wide-set eyes; a narrow aquiline nose; and a straight oval chin. His mouth, too, was firm and clean-cut, but it held a look of cynical cruelty which was more Mediterranean than Nordic. His face was strong and attractive, though not exactly handsome. It was the face of a thinker and recluse; and its very severity – at once studious and introspective – acted as a barrier between him and his fellows.

Though he was immobile by nature and sedulously schooled in the repression of his emotions, I noticed that, as he listened to Markham on the phone that morning, he could not entirely disguise his eager interest in what was being told him. A slight frown ruffled his brow; and his eyes reflected his inner amazement. From time to time he gave vent to a murmured "Amazin'!" or "My word!" or "Most extr'ordin'ry!" – his favorite expletives – and when at the end of several minutes he spoke to Markham, a curious excitement marked his manner.

"Oh, by all means!" he said. "I shouldn't miss it for all the lost comedies of Menander. . . . It sounds mad. . . . I'll don fitting raiment immediately. . . . *Au revoir.*"

Replacing the receiver, he rang for Currie.

"My gray tweeds," he ordered. "A sombre tie, and my black Homburg hat." Then he returned to his omelet with a preoccupied air.

After a few moments he looked at me quizzically.

"What might you know of archery, Van?" he asked.

I knew nothing of archery, save that it consisted of shooting arrows at targets, and I confessed as much.

"You're not exactly revealin' don't y' know." He lighted one of his *Régie* cigarettes indolently. "However, we're in for a little flutter of toxophily, it seems. I'm no leading authority on the subject myself, but I did a bit of potting with the bow at Oxford. It's not a passionately excitin' pastime – much duller than golf and fully as complicated." He smoked a while dreamily. "I say, Van; fetch me Doctor Elmer's tome on archery from the library –

there's a good chap."*

I brought the book, and for nearly half an hour he dipped into it, tarrying over the chapters on archery associations, tournaments and matches, and scanning the long tabulation of the best American scores. At length he settled back in his chair. It was obvious he had found something that caused him troubled concern and set his sensitive mind to work.

"It's quite mad, Van," he remarked, his eyes in space. "A mediæval tragedy in modern New York! We don't wear buskins and leathern doublets, and yet – *By Jove!*" He suddenly sat upright. "No – no! It's absurd. I'm letting the insanity of Markham's news affect me. . . ." He drank some more coffee, but his expression told me that he could not rid himself of the idea that had taken possession of him.

"One more favor, Van," he said at length. "Fetch me my German diction'ry and Burton E. Stevenson's 'Home Book of Verse.' "

When I had brought the volumes, he glanced at one word in the dictionary, and pushed the book from him.

"That's that, unfortunately – though I knew it all the time."

*The book Vance referred to was that excellent and comprehensive treatise, "Archery," by Robert P. Elmer, M.D.

Then he turned to the section in Stevenson's gigantic anthology which included the rhymes of the nursery and of childhood. After several minutes he closed that book, too, and, stretching himself out in his chair, blew a long ribbon of smoke toward the awning overhead.

"It can't be true," he protested, as if to himself. "It's too fantastic, too fiendish, too utterly distorted. A fairy tale in terms of blood – a world in anamorphosis – a perversion of all rationality. . . . It's unthinkable, senseless, like black magic and sorcery and thaumaturgy. It's downright demented."

He glanced at his watch and, rising, went indoors, leaving me to speculate vaguely on the cause of his unwonted perturbation. A treatise on archery, a German dictionary, a collection of children's verses, and Vance's incomprehensible utterances regarding insanity and fantasy – what possible connection could these things have? I attempted to find a least common denominator, but without the slightest success. And it was no wonder I failed. Even the truth, when it came out weeks later bolstered up by an array of incontestable evidence, seemed too incredible and too wicked for acceptance by the normal mind of man.

Vance shortly broke in on my futile speculations. He was dressed for the street, and seemed impatient at Markham's delay in arriving.

"Y' know, I wanted something to interest me – a nice fascinatin' crime, for instance," he remarked; "but – my word! – I wasn't exactly longin' for a nightmare. If I didn't know Markham so well I'd suspect him of spoofing."

When Markham stepped into the roof garden a few minutes later it was only too plain that he had been in deadly earnest. His expression was sombre and troubled, and his usual cordial greeting he reduced to the merest curt formality. Markham and Vance had been intimate friends for fifteen years. Though of antipodal natures – the one sternly aggressive, brusque, forthright, and almost ponderously serious; the other whimsical, cynical, debonair, and aloof from the transient concerns of life – they found in each other that attraction of complementaries which so often forms the basis of an inseparable and enduring companionship.

During Markham's year and four months as District Attorney of New York he had often called Vance into conference on matters of grave importance, and in every instance Vance had justified the confidence placed in his judgments. Indeed, to Vance almost entirely belongs the credit for solving the large number of major crimes which occurred during Markham's four years' incumbency. His knowledge of human nature, his wide reading and cultural attainments, his shrewd sense of logic, and his *flair* for the hidden truth beneath misleading exteriors, all fitted him for the task of criminal investigator – a task which he fulfilled unofficially in connection with the cases which came under Markham's jurisdiction.

Vance's first case, it will be remembered, had to do with the murder of Alvin Benson; and had it not been for his participation in that affair I doubt if the truth concerning it would ever have come to light. Then followed the notorious strangling of Margaret Odell – a murder mystery in which the ordinary methods of police detection would inevitably have failed. And last year the astounding Greene murders (to which I have already referred) would undoubtedly have succeeded had not Vance been able to frustrate their final intent.

It was not surprising, therefore, that Markham should have turned to Vance at the very beginning of the Bishop murder case. More and more, I had noticed, he had come to rely on the other's help in his criminal investigations; and in the present instance it was particularly fortunate that he appealed to Vance for only through an intimate knowledge of the abnormal psychological manifestations of the human mind, such as Vance possessed, could that black, insensate plot have been contravened and the perpetrator unearthed.

"This whole thing may be a mare's-nest," said Markham, without conviction. "But I thought you might want to come along. . . ."

"Oh, quite!" Vance gave Markham a sardonic smile. "Sit down a moment and tell me the tale coherently. The corpse won't run away. And it's best to get our facts in some kind of order before we view the remains. – Who are the parties of the first part, for instance? And why the projection of the District Attorney's office into a murder case within an hour of the deceased's passing? All that you've told me so far resolves itself into the uttermost nonsense."

Markham sat down gloomily on the edge of a chair and inspected the end of his cigar.

"Damn it, Vance. Don't start in with a mysteries-of-Udolpho attitude. The crime – if it is a crime – seems clear-cut enough. It's an unusual method of murder, I'll admit; but it's certainly not senseless. Archery has become quite a fad of late. Bows and arrows are in use to-day in practically every city and college in America."

"Granted. But it's been a long time since

they were used to kill persons named Robin."

Markham's eyes narrowed, and he looked at Vance searchingly.

"That idea occurred to you, too, did it?"

"Occurred to me? It leapt to my brain the moment you mentioned the victim's name." Vance puffed a moment on his cigarette. " 'Who Killed Cock Robin?' And with a bow and arrow! . . . Queer how the doggerel learned in childhood clings to the memory. – By the by, what was the unfortunate Mr. Robin's first name?"

"Joseph, I believe."

"Neither edifyin' nor suggestive. . . . Any middle name?"

"See here, Vance!" Markham rose irritably. "What has the murdered man's middle name to do with the case?"

"I haven't the groggiest. Only, as long as we're going insane we may as well go the whole way. A mere shred of sanity is of no value."

He rang for Currie and sent him for the telephone directory. Markham protested, but Vance pretended not to hear; and when the directory arrived he thumbed its pages for several moments.

"Did the departed live on Riverside Drive?" he asked finally, holding his finger on a name he had found.

"I think he did."

"Well, well." Vance closed the book, and fixed a quizzically triumphant gaze on the District Attorney. "Markham," he said slowly, "there's only one Joseph Robin listed in the telephone direct'ry. He lives on Riverside Drive, and his middle name is – Cochrane!"

"What rot is this?" Markham's tone was almost ferocious. "Suppose his name *was* Cochrane: are you seriously suggesting that the fact had anything to do with his being murdered?"

" 'Pon my word, old man, I'm suggesting nothing." Vance shrugged his shoulders slightly. "I'm merely jotting down, so to speak, a few facts in connection with the case. As the matter stands now: a Mr. Joseph Cochrane Robin – to wit: Cock Robin – has been killed by a bow and arrow. – Doesn't that strike even your legal mind as deuced queer?"

"No!" Markham fairly spat the negative. "The name of the dead man is certainly common enough; and it's a wonder more people haven't been killed or injured with all this revival of archery throughout the country. Moreover, it's wholly possible that Robin's death was the result of an accident."

"Oh, my aunt!" Vance wagged his head reprovingly. "That fact, even were it true, wouldn't help the situation any. It would only make it queerer. Of the thousands of archery enthusiasts in these fair states, the one with the name of Cock Robin should be accidentally killed with an arrow! Such a supposition would lead us into spiritism and demonology and whatnot. Do you, by any chance, believe in Eblises and Azazels and jinn who go about playing Satanic jokes on mankind?"

"Must I be a Mohammedan mythologist to admit coincidences?" returned Markham tartly.

"My dear fellow! The proverbial long arm of coincidence doesn't extend to infinity. There are, after all, laws of probability, based on quite definite mathematical formulas. It would make me sad to think that such men as Laplace* and Czuber and von Kries had lived in vain. – The present situation, however, is even more complicated than you suspect. For instance, you mentioned over the phone that the last person known to have been with Robin before his death is named Sperling."

"And what esoteric significance lies in that fact?"

*Though Laplace is best known for his "Méchanique Céleste," Vance was here referring to his masterly work, "Théorie Analytique des Probabilités," which Herschel called "the ne plus ultra of mathematical skill and power."

"Perhaps you know what *Sperling* means in German," suggested Vance dulcetly.

"I've been to High School," retorted Markham. Then his eyes opened slightly, and his body became tense.

Vance pushed the German dictionary toward him.

"Well, anyway, look up the word. We might as well be thorough. I looked it up myself. I was afraid my imagination was playing tricks on me, and I had a yearnin' to see the word in black and white."

Markham opened the book in silence, and let his eye run down the page. After staring at the word for several moments he drew himself up resolutely, as if fighting off a spell. When he spoke his voice was defiantly belligerent.

"*Sperling* means 'sparrow.' Any school boy knows that. What of it?"

"Oh, to be sure." Vance lit another cigarette languidly. "And any school boy knows the old nursery rhyme entitled 'The Death and Burial of Cock Robin,' what?" He glanced tantalizingly at Markham, who stood immobile, staring out into the spring sunshine. "Since you pretend to be unfamiliar with that childhood classic, permit me to recite the first stanza."

A chill, as of some unseen spectral presence,

passed over me as Vance repeated those old familiar lines:

> "Who killed Cock Robin?
> 'I,' said the sparrow.
> 'With my bow and arrow.
> I killed Cock Robin.' "

CHAPTER II

ON THE ARCHERY RANGE

(Saturday, April 2; 12.30 p.m.)

Slowly Markham brought his eyes back to Vance.

"It's mad," he remarked, like a man confronted with something at once inexplicable and terrrifying.

"Tut, tut!" Vance waved his hand airily. "That's plagiarism. I said it first." (He was striving to overcome his own sense of perplexity by a lightness of attitude.) "And now there really should be an *inamorata* to bewail Mr. Robin's passing. You recall, perhaps, the stanza:

"Who'll be chief mourner?
'I,' said the dove,
'I mourn my lost love;
I'll be chief mourner.' "

Markham's head jerked slightly, and his

fingers beat a nervous tattoo on the table.

"Good God, Vance! There *is* a girl in the case. And there's a possibility that jealousy lies at the bottom of this thing."

"Fancy that, now! I'm afraid the affair is going to develop into a kind of *tableau-vivant* for grownup kindergartners, what? But that'll make our task easier. All we'll have to do is to find the fly."

"The fly?"

"The *Musca domestica,* to speak pedantically. . . . My dear Markham, have you forgotten? –

"Who saw him die?
'I,' said the fly,
'With my little eye;
I saw him die.' "

"Come down to earth!" Markham spoke with acerbity. "This isn't a child's game. It's damned serious business."

Vance nodded abstractedly.

"A child's game is sometimes the most serious business in life." His words held a curious, far-away tone. "I don't like this thing – I don't at all like it. There's too much of the child in it – the child born old and with a diseased mind. It's like some hideous perversion." He took a deep inhalation on his cigarette, and made a slight gesture of repugnance. "Give me the details. Let's find out where we stand in this topsy-turvy land."

Markham again seated himself.

"I haven't many details. I told you practically everything I know of the case over the phone. Old Professor Dillard called me shortly before I communicated with you –"

"Dillard? By any chance, Professor Bertrand Dillard?"

"Yes. The tragedy took place at his house. – You know him?"

"Not personally. I know him only as the world of science knows him – as one of the greatest living mathematical physicists. I have most of his books. – How did he happen to call you?"

"I've known him for nearly twenty years. I had mathematics under him at Columbia, and later did some legal work for him. When Robin's body was found he phoned me at once – about half past eleven. I called up Sergeant Heath at the Homicide Bureau and turned the case over to him – although I told him I'd come along personally later on. Then I phoned you. The Sergeant and his men are waiting for me now at the Dillard home."

"What's the domestic situation there?"

"The professor, as you probably know, resigned his chair some ten years ago. Since then he's been living in West 75th Street, near the Drive. He took his brother's child – a girl of fifteen – to live with him. She's around twenty-five now. Then there's his protégé, Sigurd Arnesson, who was a classmate of mine at college. The professor adopted him during his junior year. Arnesson is now about forty, an instructor in mathematics at Columbia. He came to this country from Norway when he was three, and was left an orphan five years later. He's something of a mathematical genius, and Dillard evidently saw the makings of a great physicist in him and adopted him."

"I've heard of Arnesson," nodded Vance. "He recently published some modifications of Mie's theory on the electrodynamics of moving bodies. . . . And do these three – Dillard, Arnesson and the girl – live alone?"

"With two servants. Dillard appears to have a very comfortable income. They're not very much alone, however. The house is a kind of shrine for mathematics, and quite a *cénacle* has developed. Moreover, the girl, who has always gone in for outdoor sports, has her own little social set. I've been at the house several times, and there have always been visitors about – either a serious student or two of the abstract sciences up-stairs in the library, or some noisy young people in the drawing-room below."

"And Robin?"

"He belonged to Belle Dillard's set – an oldish young society man who held several archery records. . . ."

"Yes, I know. I just looked up the name in this book on archery. A Mr. J.C. Robin seems to have made the high scores in several recent championship meets. And I noted, too, that a Mr. Sperling has been the runner-up in several large archery tournaments. – Is Miss Dillard an archer as well?"

"Yes, quite an enthusiast. In fact, she organized the Riverside Archery Club. Its permanent ranges are at Sperling's home in Scarsdale; but Miss Dillard has rigged up a practice range in the side yard of the professor's 75th-Street house. It was on this range that Robin was killed."

"Ah! And, as you say, the last person known to have been with him was Sperling. Where is our sparrow now?"

"I don't know. He was with Robin shortly before the tragedy; but when the body was found he had disappeared. I imagine Heath will have news on that point."

"And wherein lies the possible motive of jealousy you referred to?" Vance's eyelids had drooped lazily, and he smoked with leisurely but precise deliberation – a sign of his intense interest in what was being told him.

"Professor Dillard mentioned an attachment between his niece and Robin; and when I asked him who Sperling was and what his status was at the Dillard house, he intimated that Sperling was also a suitor for the girl's hand. I didn't go into the situation over the phone, but the impression I got was that Robin and Sperling were rivals, and that Robin had the better of it."

"And so the sparrow killed Cock Robin." Vance shook his head dubiously. "It won't do. It's too dashed simple; and it doesn't account for the fiendishly perfect reconstruction of the Cock-Robin rhyme. There's something deeper – something darker and more horrible – in this grotesque business. – Who, by the by, found Robin?"

"Dillard himself. He had stepped out on the little balcony at the rear of the house, and saw Robin lying below on the practice range, with an arrow through his heart. He went downstairs immediately – with considerable difficulty, for the old man suffers abominably from gout – and, seeing that the man was dead, phoned me. – That's all the advance information I have."

"Not what you'd call a blindin' illumination, but still a bit suggestive." Vance got up. "Markham old dear, prepare for something rather bizarre – and damnable. We can rule out accidents and coincidence. While it's true that ordin'ry target arrows – which are made of soft wood and fitted with little bevelled piles – could easily penetrate a person's clothing and chest wall, even when driven with a medium weight bow, the fact that a man named 'Sparrow' should kill a man named Cochrane Robin, *with a bow and arrow,* precludes any haphazard concatenation of circumstances. Indeed, this incredible set of events proves conclusively that there has been a subtle, diabolical intent beneath the whole affair." He moved toward the door. "Come, let us find out something more about it at what the Austrian police officials eruditely call the *situs criminis.*"

We left the house at once and drove up-town in Markham's car. Entering Central Park at Fifth Avenue we emerged through the 72nd-Street gate, and a few minutes later were turning off of West End Avenue into 75th Street. The Dillard house – number 391 – was on our right, far down the block toward the river. Between it and the Drive, occupying the entire corner, was a large fifteen-story apartment house. The professor's home seemed to nestle, as if for protection, in the shadow of this huge structure.

The Dillard house was of gray, weather-darkened limestone, and belonged to the days when homes were built for permanency and comfort. The lot on which it stood had a thirty-five-foot frontage, and the house itself was fully twenty-five feet across. The other ten feet of the lot, which formed an areaway separating the house from the apartment structure, was shut off from the street by a ten-foot stone wall with a large iron door in the centre.

The house was of modified Colonial architecture. A short flight of shallow steps led from the street to a narrow brick-lined porch adorned with four white Corinthian pillars. On the second floor a series of casement windows, paned with rectangular leaded glass, extended across the entire width of the house. (These, I learned later, were the windows of the library.) There was something restful and distinctly old-fashioned about the place: it appeared like anything but the scene of a gruesome murder.

Two police cars were parked near the entrance when we drove up, and a dozen or so curious onlookers had gathered in the street. A patrolman lounged against one of the fluted columns of the porch, gazing at the crowd before him with bored disdain.

An old butler admitted us and led us into the drawing-room on the left of the entrance hall, where we found Sergeant Ernest Heath and two other men from the Homicide Bureau. The Sergeant, who was standing beside the centre-table smoking, his thumbs hooked in the armholes of his waistcoat, came forward and extended his hand in a friendly greeting to Markham.

"I'm glad you got here, sir," he said; and the worried look in his cold blue eyes seemed to relax a bit. "I've been waiting for you. There's something damn fishy about this case."

He caught sight of Vance, who had paused in the background, and his broad pugnacious features crinkled in a good-natured grin.

"Howdy, Mr. Vance. I had a sneaking idea you'd be lured into this case. What you been up to these many moons?" I could not help comparing this genuine friendliness of the Sergeant's attitude with the hostility of his first meeting with Vance at the time of the Benson case. But much water had run under the bridge since that first encounter in the murdered Alvin's garish living-room; and between Heath and Vance there had grown up a warm attachment, based on a mutual respect and a frank admiration for each other's capabilities.

Vance held out his hand, and a smile played about the corners of his mouth.

"The truth is, Sergeant, I've been endeavorin' to discover the lost glories of an Athenian named Menander, a dramatic rival of Philemon's. Silly, what?"

Heath grunted disdainfully.

"Well, anyhow, if you're as good at it as you are at discovering crooks, you'll probably get a conviction." It was the first compliment I had ever heard pass his lips, and it attested not only to his deep-seated admiration for Vance, but also to his own troubled and uncertain state of mind.

Markham sensed the Sergeant's mental insecurity, and asked somewhat abruptly: "Just what seems to be the difficulty in the present case?"

"I didn't say there was any difficulty, sir," Heath replied. "It looks as though we had the bird who did it dead to rights. But I ain't satisfied, and – oh, hell! Mr. Markham . . . it ain't natural; it don't make sense."

"I think I understand what you mean." Markham regarded the Sergeant appraisingly. "You're inclined to think that Sperling's guilty?"

"Sure, he's guilty," declared Heath with over-emphasis. "But that's not what's worrying me. To tell you the truth, I don't like the name of this guy who was croaked – especially as he was croaked with a bow and arrow. . . ." He hesitated, a bit shamefaced. "Don't it strike you as peculiar, sir?"

Markham nodded perplexedly.

"I see that you, too, remember your nursery rhymes," he said, and turned away.

Vance fixed a waggish look on Heath.

"You referred to Mr. Sperling just now as a 'bird,' Sergeant. The designation was most apt. *Sperling,* d' ye see, means 'sparrow' in German. And it was a sparrow, you recall, who killed Cock Robin with an arrow. . . . A fascinatin' situation – eh, what?"

The Sergeant's eyes bulged slightly, and his lips fell apart. He stared at Vance with almost ludicrous bewilderment.

"I said this here business was fishy!"

"I'd say, rather, it was avian, don't y' know."

"You *would* call it something nobody'd understand," Heath retorted truculently. It was his wont to become bellicose when confronted with the inexplicable.

Markham intervened diplomatically.

"Let's have the details of the case, Sergeant. I take it you've questioned the occupants of the house."

"Only in a general way, sir." Heath flung one

leg over the corner of the centre-table and relit his dead cigar. "I've been waiting for you to show up. I knew you were acquainted with the old gentleman up-stairs; so I just did the routine things. I put a man out in the alley to see that nobody touches the body till Doc Doremus arrives,* – he'll be here when he finishes lunch. – I phoned the finger-print men before I left the office, and they oughta be on the job any minute now; though I don't see what good they can do. . . ."

"What about the bow that fired the arrow?" put in Vance.

"That was our one best bet; but old Mr. Dillard said he picked it up from the alley and brought it in the house. He probably gummed up any prints it mighta had."

"What have you done about Sperling?" asked Markham.

"I got his address – he lives in a country house up Westchester way – and sent a coupla men to bring him here as soon as they could lay hands on him. Then I talked to the two servants – the old fellow that let you in, and his daughter, a middle-aged woman who does the cooking. But neither of 'em seemed to

*Heath was referring to Doctor Emanuel Doremus, the Chief Medical Examiner of New York.

know anything, or else they're acting dumb. – After that I tried to question the young lady of the house." The Sergeant raised his hands in a gesture of irritated despair. "But she was all broke up and crying; so I thought I'd let *you* have the pleasure of interviewing her. – Snitkin and Burke" – he jerked his thumb toward the two detectives by the front window – "went over the basement and the alley and back yard trying to pick up something; but drew a blank. – And that's all I know so far. As soon as Doremus and the finger-print men get here, and after I've had a heart-to-heart talk with Sperling, then I'll get the ball to rolling and clean up the works."

Vance heaved an audible sigh.

"You're so sanguine, Sergeant! Don't be disappointed if your ball turns out to be a parallelopiped that won't roll. There's something deuced oddish about this nursery extravaganza; and, unless all the omens deceive me, you'll be playing blind-man's-bluff for a long time to come."

"Yeh?" Heath gave Vance a look of despondent shrewdness. It was evident he was more or less of the same opinion.

"Don't let Mr. Vance dishearten you, Sergeant," Markham rallied him. "He's permitting his imagination to run away with him." Then with an impatient gesture he turned toward the door. "Let's look over the ground before the others arrive. Later I'll have a talk with Professor Dillard and the other members of the household. And, by the way, Sergeant, you didn't mention Mr. Arnesson. Isn't he at home?"

"He's at the university; but he's expected to return soon."

Markham nodded and followed the Sergeant into the main hall. As we passed down the heavily-carpeted passage to the rear, there was a sound on the staircase, and a clear but somewhat tremulous woman's voice spoke from the semi-darkness above.

"Is that you, Mr. Markham? Uncle thought he recognized your voice. He's waiting for you in the library."

"I'll join your uncle in a very few minutes, Miss Dillard." Markham's tone was paternal and sympathetic. "And please wait with him, for I want to see you, too."

With a murmured acquiescence, the girl disappeared round the head of the stairs.

We moved on to the rear door of the lower hall. Beyond was a narrow passageway terminating in a flight of wooden steps which led to the basement. At the foot of these steps we came into a large, low-ceilinged room with a door giving directly upon the areaway at the west side of the house. This door was slightly ajar, and in the opening stood the man from the Homicide Bureau whom Heath had set to guard the body.

The room had obviously once been a basement storage; but it had been altered and redecorated, and now served as a sort of clubroom. The cement floor was covered with fibre rugs, and one entire wall was painted with a panorama of archers throughout the ages. In an oblong panel on the left was a huge illustrated reproduction of an archery range labelled "Ayme for Finsburie Archers – London 1594," showing Bloody House Ridge in one corner, Westminster Hall in the centre, and Welsh Hall in the foreground. There were a piano and a phonograph in the room; numerous comfortable wicker chairs; a varicolored divan; an enormous wicker centre-table littered with all manner of sports magazines; and a small bookcase filled with works on archery. Several targets rested in one corner, their gold discs and concentric chromatic rings making brilliant splashes of color in the sunlight which flooded in from the two rear windows. One wall space near the door was hung with long bows of varying sizes and weights; and near them was a large old-fashioned tool-chest.

Above it was suspended a small cupboard, or ascham, strewn with various odds and ends of tackle, such as bracers, shooting-gloves, piles, points of aim, and bow strings. A large oak panel between the door and the west window contained a display of one of the most interesting and varied collections of arrows I had ever seen.

This panel attracted Vance particularly, and adjusting his monocle carefully, he strolled over to it.

"Hunting and war arrows," he remarked. "Most inveiglin'. . . . *Ah!* One of the trophies seems to have disappeared. Taken down with considerable haste too. The little brass brad that held it in place is shockingly bent."

On the floor stood several quivers filled with target arrows. He leaned over and, withdrawing one, extended it to Markham.

"This frail shaft may not look as if it would penetrate the human breast; but target arrows will drive entirely through a deer at eighty yards. . . . Why, then, the missing hunting arrow from the panel? An interestin' point."

Markham frowned and compressed his lips; and I realized that he had been clinging to the forlorn hope that the tragedy might have been an accident. He tossed the arrow hopelessly on a chair, and walked toward the outer door.

"Let's take a look at the body and the lie of the land," he said gruffly.

As we emerged into the warm spring sunlight a sense of isolation came over me. The narrow paved areaway in which we stood seemed like a canyon between steep stone walls. It was four or five feet below the street level, which was reached by a short flight of steps leading to the gate in the wall. The blank, windowless rear wall of the apartment house opposite extended upwards for 150 feet; and the Dillard house itself, though only four stories high, was the equivalent of six stories gauged by the architectural measurements of to-day. Though we were standing out of doors in the heart of New York, no one could see us except from the few side windows of the Dillard house and from a single bay window of the house on 76th Street, whose rear yard adjoined that of the Dillard grounds.

This other house, we were soon to learn, was owned by a Mrs. Drukker; and it was destined to play a vital and tragic part in the solution of Robin's murder. Several tall willow trees acted as a mask to its rear windows; and only the bay window at the side of the house had an unobstructed view of that part of the areaway in which we stood.

I noticed that Vance had his eye on this bay

window, and as he studied it I saw a flicker of interest cross his face. It was not much later that afternoon that I was able to guess what had caught and held his attention.

The archery range extended from the wall of the Dillard lot on 75th Street all the way to a similar street wall of the Drukker lot on 76th Street, where a butt of hay bales had been erected on a shallow bed of sand. The distance between the two walls was 200 feet, which, as I learned later, made possible a sixty-yard range, thus permitting target practice for all the standard archery events, with the one exception of the York Round for men.

The Dillard lot was 135 feet deep, the depth of the Drukker lot therefore being sixty-five feet. A section of the tall ironwork fence that separated the two rear yards had been removed where it had once transected the space now used for the archery range. At the further end of the range, backing against the western line of the Drukker property, was another tall apartment house occupying the corner of 76th Street and Riverside Drive. Between these two gigantic buildings ran a narrow alleyway, the range end of which was closed with a high board fence in which had been set a small door with a lock.

For purposes of clarity I am incorporating in

this record a diagram of the entire scene; for the arrangement of the various topographical and architectural details had a very important bearing on the solution of the crime. I would call attention particularly to the following points: – first, to the little second-story balcony at the rear of the Dillard house, which projects slightly over the archery range; secondly, to the bay window (on the second floor) on the Drukker house, whose southern angle has a view of the entire archery range toward 75th Street; and thirdly, to the alleyway between the two apartment houses, which leads from Riverside Drive into the Dillard rear yard.

The body of Robin lay almost directly outside of the archery-room door. It was on its back, the arms extended, the legs slightly drawn up, the head pointing toward the 76th-Street end of the range. Robin had been a man of perhaps thirty-five, of medium height, and with an incipient corpulency. There was a rotund puffiness to his face, which was smooth-shaven except for a narrow blond moustache. He was clothed in a two-piece sport suit of light gray flannel, a pale-blue silk shirt, and tan Oxfords with thick rubber soles. His hat – a pearl-colored felt fedora – was lying near his feet.

Beside the body was a large pool of coagulated blood which had formed in the shape of a huge pointing hand. But the thing which held us all in a spell of fascinated horror was the slender shaft that extended vertically from the left side of the dead man's breast. The arrow protruded perhaps twenty inches, and where it had entered the body there was the large dark stain of the hemorrhage. What made this strange murder seem even more incongruous were the beautifully fletched feathers on the arrow. They had been dyed a bright red; and about the shaftment were two stripes of turquoise blue – giving the arrow a gala appearance. I had a feeling of unreality about the tragedy, as though I were witnessing a scene in a sylvan play for children.

Vance stood looking down at the body with half-closed eyes, his hands in his coat pockets. Despite the apparent indolence of his attitude I could tell that he was keenly alert, and that his mind was busy co-ordinating the factors of the scene before him.

"Dashed queer, that arrow," he commented. "Designed for big game; . . . undoubtedly belongs to that ethnological exhibit we just saw. And a clean hit – directly into the vital spot, between the ribs and without the slightest deflection. Extr'ordin'ry! . . . I say, Markham;

such marksmanship isn't human. A chance shot might have done it; but the slayer of this johnny wasn't leaving anything to chance. That powerful hunting arrow, which was obviously wrenched from the panel inside, shows premeditation and design –" Suddenly he bent over the body. "Ah! Very interestin'. The nock of the arrow is broken down, – I doubt if it would even hold a taut string." He turned to Heath. "Tell me, Sergeant: where did Professor Dillard find the bow? – not far from that club-room window, what?"

Heath gave a start.

"Right outside the window, in fact, Mr. Vance. It's in on the piano now, waiting for the finger-print men."

"The professor's sign-manual is all they'll find, I'm afraid." Vance opened his case and selected another cigarette. "And I'm rather inclined to believe that the arrow itself is innocent of prints."

Heath was scrutinizing Vance inquisitively.

"What made you think the bow was found near the window, Mr. Vance?" he asked.

"It seemed the logical place for it, in view of the position of Mr. Robin's body, don't y' know."

"Shot from close range, you mean?"

Vance shook his head.

"No, Sergeant. I was referring to the fact that the deceased's feet are pointing toward the basement door, and that, though his arms are extended, his legs are drawn up. Is that the way you'd say a man would fall who'd been shot through the heart?"

Heath considered the point.

"No-o," he admitted. "He'd likely be more crumpled up; or, if he did fall over back, his legs would be straight out and his arms drawn in."

"Quite. – And regard his hat. If he had fallen backwards it would be behind him, not at his feet."

"See here, Vance," Markham demanded sharply; "what's in your mind?"

"Oh, numberless things. But they all boil down to the wholly irrational notion that this defunct gentleman wasn't shot with a bow and arrow at all."

"Then why, in God's name –"

"Exactly! Why the utter insanity of the elaborate stage-setting? – My word, Markham! This business is ghastly."

As Vance spoke the basement door opened, and Doctor Doremus, shepherded by Detective Burke, stepped jauntily into the areaway. He greeted us breezily and shook hands all round. Then he fixed a fretful eye on Heath.

"By Gad, Sergeant!" he complained, pulling his hat down to an even more rakish angle. "I only spend three hours out of the twenty-four eating my meals; and you invariably choose those three hours to worry me with your confounded bodies. You're ruining my digestion." He looked about him petulantly and, on seeing Robin, whistled softly. "For Gad's sake! A nice fancy murder you picked out for me this time!"

He knelt down and began running his practiced fingers over the body.

Markham stood for a moment looking on, but presently he turned to Heath.

"While the doctor's busy with his examination, Sergeant, I'll go up-stairs and have a chat with Professor Dillard." Then he addressed himself to Doremus. "Let me see you before you go, doctor."

"Oh, sure." Doremus did not so much as look up. He had turned the body on one side, and was feeling the base of the skull.

CHAPTER III

A PROPHECY RECALLED

(Saturday, April 2; 1.30 p.m.)

When we reached the main hall Captain Dubois and Detective Bellamy, the finger-print experts from Headquarters, were just arriving. Detective Snitkin, who had evidently been watching for them, led them at once toward the basement stairs, and Markham, Vance and I went up to the second floor.

The library was a large, luxurious room at least twenty feet deep, occupying the entire width of the building. Two sides of it were lined to the ceiling with great embayed book-cases; and in the centre of the west wall rose a massive bronze Empire fireplace. By the door stood an elaborate Jacobean side-board, and opposite, near the windows which faced on 75th Street, was an enormous carved table-desk, strewn with papers and pamphlets. There were many interesting *objets-d'art* in the room; and two diagrammatic Dürers looked down on us from the tapestried panels beside the mantel. All the chairs were spacious and covered with dark leather.

Professor Dillard sat before the desk, one foot resting on a small tufted ottoman; and in a corner near the windows, huddled in a sprawling armchair, was his niece, a vigorous, severely tailored girl with strong, chiselled features of classic cast. The old professor did not rise to greet us, and made no apology for the omission. He appeared to take it for granted that we were aware of his disability. The introductions were perfunctory, though Markham gave a brief explanation of Vance's and my presence there.

"I regret, Markham," the professor said, when we had settled ourselves, "that a tragedy should be the reason for this meeting; but it's always good to see you. – I suppose you will want to cross-examine Belle and me. Well, ask anything you care to."

Professor Bertrand Dillard was a man in his sixties, slightly stooped from a sedentary studious life: clean-shaven, and with a marked brachycephalic head surmounted with thick white hair combed pompadour. His eyes, though small, were remarkably intense and penetrating; and the wrinkles about his mouth held that grim pursed expression which often comes with years of concentration on difficult problems. His features were those of the dreamer and scientist; and, as the world knows, this man's wild dreams of space and time and motion had been actualized into a new foundation of scientific fact. Even now his face reflected an introspective abstraction, as if the death of Robin were but an intrusion upon the inner drama of his thoughts.

Markham hesitated a moment before answering. Then he said with marked deference:

"Suppose, sir, you tell me just what you know of the tragedy. Then I'll put whatever questions I deem essential."

Professor Dillard reached for an old meerschaum pipe on the stand beside him. When he had filled and lighted it he shifted himself more comfortably in his chair.

"I told you practically everything I know over the telephone. Robin and Sperling called this morning about ten o'clock to see Belle. But she had gone to the courts to play tennis, so they waited in the drawing-room down-stairs. I heard them talking there together for half an hour or so before they went to the basement club-room. I remained here reading for perhaps an hour, and then, as the sunshine looked so pleasant, I decided to step out on the balcony at the rear of the house. I had been there about five minutes, I should say, when I chanced to look down on the archery range; and to my horrified amazement I saw Robin lying on his back with an arrow-shaft protruding from his breast. I hastened down as quickly as my gout would permit, but I could see at once that the poor fellow was dead; so I immediately telephoned to you. There was no one in the house at the time but old Pyne – the butler – and myself. The cook had gone marketing; Arnesson had left for the university at nine o'clock; and Belle was still out playing tennis. I sent Pyne to look for Sperling, but he was nowhere about; and I came back to the library here to wait for you. Belle returned shortly before your men arrived, and the cook came in a little later. Arnesson won't be back until after two."

"There was no one else here this morning – no strangers or visitors?"

The professor shook his head.

"Only Drukker, – I believe you met him here once. He lives in the house at our rear. He often drops in – mostly, however, to see Arnesson: they have much in common. He's written a book on 'World Lines in Multidimensional Continua.' The man's quite a genius in his way; has the true scientific mind. . . . But when he found that Arnesson was out he sat for a while with me discussing the Brazilian expedition of the Royal Astronomical Society. Then he went home."

"What time was this?"

"About half past nine. Drukker had already gone when Robin and Sperling called."

"Was it unusual, Professor Dillard," asked Vance, "for Mr. Arnesson to be away on Saturday mornings?"

The old professor looked up sharply, and there was a brief hesitation before he answered.

"Not unusual exactly; although he's generally here on Saturdays. But this morning he had some important research work to do for me in the faculty library. . . . Arnesson," he added, "is working with me on my next book."*

There was a short silence; then Markham spoke.

"You said this morning that both Robin and Sperling were suitors for Miss Dillard's hand. . . ."

"Uncle!" The girl sat upright in her chair and turned angry, reproachful eyes upon the

*The book referred to by Professor Dillard was the great work which appeared two years later. "The Atomic Structure of Radiant Energy," a mathematical emendation of Planck's quantum theory refuting the classical axiom of the continuity of all physical processes, as contained in Maximus Tyrius' Ουδε ενταυθαη φυοες μετατηδα αθποως

old professor. "That wasn't fair."

"But it was true, my dear." His voice was noticeably tender.

"It was true – in a way," she admitted. "But there was no need of mentioning it. You know, as well as they did, how I regarded them. We were good friends – that was all. Only last night, when they were here together, I told them – quite plainly – that I wouldn't listen to any more silly talk of marriage from either of them. They were only boys . . . and now one of them's gone. . . Poor Cock Robin!" She strove bravely to stifle her emotion.

Vance raised his eyebrows and leaned forward. " 'Cock Robin'?"

"Oh, we all called him that. We did it to tease him, because he didn't like the nickname."

"The sobriquet was inevitable," Vance observed sympathetically. "And it was rather a nice nickname, don't y' know. The original Cock Robin was loved by 'all the birds of the air,' and they all mourned his passing." He watched the girl closely as he spoke.

"I know," she nodded. "I told him that once. – And every one liked Joseph, too. You couldn't help liking him. He was so – so good-hearted and kind."

Vance again settled back in his chair; and

Markham continued his questioning.

"You mentioned, professor, that you heard Robin and Sperling talking in the drawing-room. Could you hear any of their conversation?"

The old man shot a sidelong glance at his niece.

"Does that question really matter, Markham?" he asked, after a moment's hesitation.

"It may have some very vital bearing on the situation."

"Perhaps." The professor drew on his pipe thoughtfully. "On the other hand, if I answered it I may give an erroneous impression, and do a grave injustice to the living."

"Can you not trust me to judge that point?" Markham's voice had become at once grave and urgent.

There was another short silence, broken by the girl.

"Why don't you tell Mr. Markham what you heard, uncle? What harm can it do?"

"I was thinking of you, Belle," the professor answered softly. "But perhaps you are right." He looked up reluctantly. "The fact is, Markham, Robin and Sperling were having some angry words over Belle. I heard only a little, but I gathered that each regarded the other as being guilty of playing unfair – of standing in each other's way. . . ."

"Oh! They didn't mean it," Miss Dillard interpolated vehemently. "They were always ragging each other. There *was* a little jealousy between them; but I wasn't the real cause of it. It was their archery records. You see, Raymond – Mr. Sperling – used to be the better shot; but this last year Joseph beat him at several meets, and at our last annual tournament he became the club's Champion Archer."

"And Sperling thought, perhaps," added Markham, "that he had correspondingly fallen in your estimation."

"That's absurd!" the girl retorted hotly.

"I think, my dear, we can leave the matter safely in Mr. Markham's hands," Professor Dillard said mollifyingly. Then to Markham: "Were there any other questions you cared to ask?"

"I'd like to know anything you can tell me about Robin and Sperling – who they are; their associations; and how long you have known them."

"I think that Belle can enlighten you better than I. Both boys belonged to her set. I saw them only occasionally."

Markham turned inquiringly to the girl.

"I've known both of them for years," she said promptly. "Joseph was eight or ten years older than Raymond, and lived in England up to five years ago, when his father and mother both died. He came to America, and took bachelor quarters on the Drive. He had considerable money, and lived idly, devoting himself to fishing and hunting and other outdoor sports. He went about in society a little, and was a nice, comfortable friend who'd always fill in at a dinner or make a fourth hand at bridge. There was nothing really much to him – in an intellectual way, you understand. . . ."

She paused, as if her remarks were in some way disloyal to the dead, and Markham, sensing her feelings, asked simply:

"And Sperling?"

"He's the son of a wealthy manufacturer of something or other – retired now. They live in Scarsdale in a beautiful country home, – our archery club has its regular ranges there, – and Raymond is a consulting engineer for some firm down-town; though I imagine he works merely to placate his father, for he only goes to the office two or three days a week. He's a graduate of Boston Tech, and I met him when he was a sophomore, home on vacation. Raymond will never set the world afire, Mr. Markham; but he's really an awfully fine type of American young man – sincere, jolly, a little bashful, and perfectly straight."

It was easy to picture both Robin and Sperling from the girl's brief descriptions; and it was correspondingly difficult to connect either of them with the sinister tragedy that had brought us to the house.

Markham sat frowning for a while. Finally he lifted his head and looked straight at the girl.

"Tell me, Miss Dillard: have you any theory or explanation that might, in any way, account for the death of Mr. Robin?"

"No!" The word fairly burst from her. "Who could want to kill Cock Robin? He hadn't an enemy in the world. The whole thing is incredible. I couldn't believe it had happened until I went and – and saw for myself. Even then it didn't seem real."

"Still, my dear child," put in Professor Dillard, "the man was killed; so there must have been something in his life that you didn't know or suspect. We're constantly finding new stars that the old-time astronomers didn't believe existed."

"I can't believe Joseph had an enemy," she retorted. "I won't believe it. It's too utterly absurd."

"You think then," asked Markham, "that it's unlikely Sperling was in any way responsible for Robin's death?"

"Unlikely?" The girl's eyes flashed. "It's impossible!"

"And yet, y' know, Miss Dillard," – it was Vance who now spoke in his lazy casual tone – "*Sperling* means 'sparrow'."

The girl sat immobile. Her face had gone deathly pale, and her hands tightened over the arms of the chair. Then slowly, and as if with great difficulty, she nodded, and her breast began to rise and fall with her labored breathing. Suddenly she shuddered and pressed her handkerchief to her face.

"I'm afraid!" she whispered.

Vance rose and, going to her, touched her comfortingly on the shoulder.

"Why are you afraid?"

She looked up and met his eyes. They seemed to reassure her, for she forced a pitiful smile.

"Only the other day," she said, in a strained voice, "we were all on the archery range downstairs; and Raymond was just preparing to shoot a single American Round, when Joseph opened the basement door and stepped out on the range. There really wasn't any danger, but Sigurd – Mr. Arnesson, you know – was sitting on the little rear balcony watching us; and when I cried 'He! He!' jokingly to Joseph, Sigurd leaned over and said: 'You don't know what a chance you're running, young man. You're a Cock Robin, and that archer's a sparrow; and you remember what happened to your namesake when a Mr. Sparrow wielded the bow and arrow' – or something like that. No one paid much attention to it at the time. But now! . . ." Her voice trailed off into an awed murmur.

"Come, Belle; don't be morbid." Professor Dillard spoke consolingly, but not without impatience. "It was merely one of Sigurd's ill-timed witticisms. You know he's continually sneering and jesting at realities: it's about the only outlet he has from his constant application of abstractions."

"I suppose so," the girl answered. "Of course, it was only a joke. But now it seems like some terrible prophecy. – Only," she hastened to add, "Raymond *couldn't* have done it."

As she spoke the library door opened suddenly, and a tall gaunt figure appeared on the threshold.

"Sigurd!" Belle Dillard's startled exclamation held an undeniable note of relief.

Sigurd Arnesson, Professor Dillard's protégé and adopted son, was a man of striking appearance – over six feet tall, wiry and erect, with a head which, at first view, appeared too large for his body. His almost yellow hair was unkempt, like a schoolboy's; his nose was aquiline; and his jowls were lean and muscular. Though he could not have been over forty, there was a net-work of lines in his face. His expression was sardonically puckish; but the intense intellectual passion that lighted his blue-gray eyes belied any superficiality of nature. My initial reaction to his personality was one of liking and respect. There were depths in the man – powerful potentialities and high capabilities.

As he entered the room that afternoon, his searching eyes took us all in with a swift, inquisitive glance. He nodded jerkily to Miss Dillard, and then fixed the old professor with a look of dry amusement.

"What, pray, has happened in this three-dimensional house? Wagons and populace without: a guardian at the portals . . . and when I finally overcame the Cerberus and was admitted by Pyne, two plainclothes men hustled me up here without ceremony or explanation. Very amusing, but disconcerting. . . . Ah! I seem to recognize the District Attorney. Good morning – or rather, afternoon – Mr. Markham."

Before Markham could return this belated greeting Belle Dillard spoke.

"Sigurd, please be serious. – Mr. Robin has been killed."

" 'Cock Robin,' you mean. Well, well! With such a name what could the beggar expect?" He appeared wholly unmoved by the news. "Who, or what, returned him to the elements?"

"As to who it was, we don't know." It was Markham who answered, in a tone of reproach for the other's levity. "But Mr. Robin was killed with an arrow through the heart."

"Most fitting." Arnesson sat down on the arm of a chair and extended his long legs. "What could be more appropriate than that Cock Robin should die from an arrow shot from the bow of –"

"Sigurd!" Belle Dillard cut him short. "Haven't you joked enough about that? You *know* that Raymond didn't do it."

"Of course, sis." The man looked at her somewhat wistfully. "I was thinking of Mr. Robin's ornithological progenitor." He turned slowly to Markham. "So it's a real murder mystery, is it – with a corpse, and clews, and all the trappings? May I be entrusted with the tale?"

Markham gave him a brief outline of the situation, to which he listened with rapt interest. When the account was ended he asked:

"Was there no bow found on the range?"

"Ah!" Vance, for the first time since the man's arrival, roused himself from seeming lethargy, and answered for Markham. "A most pertinent question, Mr. Arnesson. – Yes, a bow was found just outside of the basement window, barely ten feet from the body."

"That of course simplifies matters," said Arnesson, with a note of disappointment. "It's only a question now of taking the finger-prints."

"Unfortunately the bow has been handled," explained Markham. "Professor Dillard picked it up and brought it into the house."

Arnesson turned to the older man curiously.

"What impulse, sir, directed you to do that?"

"Impulse? My dear Sigurd, I didn't analyze my emotions. But it struck me that the bow was a vital piece of evidence, and I placed it in the basement as a precautionary measure until the police arrived."

Arnesson made a wry face and cocked one eye humorously.

"That sounds like what our psychoanalytic friends would call a suppression-censor explanation. I wonder what submerged idea was actually in your mind. . . ."

There was a knock at the door, and Burke put his head inside.

"Doc Doremus is waiting for you downstairs, Chief. He's finished his examination."

Markham rose and excused himself.

"I sha'n't bother you people any more just at present. There's considerable preliminary routine work to be done. But I must ask you to remain upstairs for the time being. I'll see you again before I go."

Doremus was teetering impatiently on his toes when we joined him in the drawing-room.

"Nothing complicated about it," he began, before Markham had a chance to speak. "Our sporty friend was killed by an arrow with a mighty sharp point entering his heart through the fourth intercostal space. Lot of force behind it. Plenty of hemorrhage inside and out. He's been dead about two hours, I should say, making the time of his death around half past eleven. That's only guesswork, however. No signs of a struggle – no marks on his clothes or abrasions on his hands. Death supervened most likely without his knowing what it was all about. He got a nasty bump, though, where his head hit the rough cement when he fell. . . ."

"Now, that's very interestin'," Vance's drawling voice cut in on the Medical Examiner's staccato report. "How serious a 'bump' was it, Doctor?"

Doremus blinked and eyed Vance with

some astonishment.

"Bad enough to fracture the skull. I couldn't feel it, of course; but there was a large hæmatoma over the occipital region, dried blood in the nostrils and the ears, and unequal pupils, indicating a fracture of the vault. I'll know more about it after the autopsy." He turned back to the District Attorney. "Anything else?"

"I think not, Doctor. Only let us have your *post-mortem* report as soon as possible."

"You'll have it to-night. The Sergeant's already phoned for the wagon." And shaking hands with all of us, he hurried away.

Heath had stood glowering in the background.

"Well, that don't get us anywheres, sir," he complained, chewing viciously on his cigar.

"Don't be downhearted, Sergeant," Vance chided him. "That blow on the back of the head is worthy of your profoundest consideration. I'm of the opinion it wasn't entirely due to the fall, don't y' know."

The Sergeant was unimpressed by this observation.

"What's more, Mr. Markham," he went on, "there wasn't any finger-prints on either the bow or the arrow. Dubois says they looked as though they'd both been wiped clean. There were a few smears on the end of the bow where the old gentleman picked it up; but not another sign of a print."

Markham smoked a while in gloomy silence.

"What about the handle on the gate leading to the street? And the knob on the door to the alley between the apartment houses?"

"Nothing!" Heath snorted his disgust. "Both of rough, rusty iron that wouldn't take a print."

"I say, Markham," observed Vance; "you're going at this thing the wrong way. Naturally there'd be no finger-prints. Really, y' know, one doesn't carefully produce a playlet and then leave all the stage props in full view of the audience. What we've got to learn is why this particular impresario decided to indulge in silly theatricals."

"It ain't as easy as all that, Mr. Vance," submitted Heath bitterly.

"Did I intimate it was easy? No, Sergeant; it's deucedly difficult. And it's worse than difficult: it's subtle and obscure and . . . fiendish."

CHAPTER IV

A MYSTERIOUS NOTE

(Saturday, April 2; 2 p.m.)

Markham sat down resolutely before the centre table.

"Suppose, Sergeant, we overhaul the two servants now."

Heath stepped into the hall and gave an order to one of his men. A few moments later a tall, sombre, disjointed man entered and stood at respectful attention.

"This is the butler, sir," explained the Sergeant. "Named Pyne."

Markham studied the man appraisingly. He was perhaps sixty years old. His features were markedly acromegalic; and this distortion extended to his entire figure. His hands were large, and his feet broad and misshapen. His clothes, though neatly pressed, fitted him badly; and his high clerical collar was several sizes too large for him. His eyes, beneath gray, bushy eyebrows, were pale and watery, and his mouth was a mere slit in an unhealthy puffy face. Despite his utter lack of physical prepossession, however, he gave one the impression of shrewd competency.

"So you are the Dillard butler," mused Markham. "How long have you been with the family, Pyne?"

"Going on ten years, sir."

"You came, then, just after Professor Dillard resigned his chair at the university?"

"I believe so, sir." The man's voice was deep and rumbling.

"What do you know of the tragedy that occurred here this morning?" Though Markham put the question suddenly, in the hope, I imagine, of surprising some admission, Pyne received it with the utmost stoicism.

"Nothing whatever, sir. I was unaware that anything had happened until Professor Dillard called to me from the library and asked me to look for Mr. Sperling."

"He told you of the tragedy then?"

"He said: 'Mr. Robin has been murdered, and I wish you'd find Mr. Sperling for me.' – That was all, sir."

"You're sure he said 'murdered,' Pyne?" interjected Vance.

For the first time the butler hesitated, and an added astuteness crept into his look.

"Yes, sir – I'm sure he did. 'Murdered' is what he said."

"And did you see the body of Mr. Robin when you pushed your search?" pursued Vance, his eyes idly tracing a design on the wall.

Again there was a brief hesitation.

"Yes, sir. I opened the basement door to look out on the archery range, and there I saw the poor young gentleman. . . ."

"A great shock it must have given you, Pyne," Vance observed drily. "Did you, by any hap, touch the poor young gentleman's body? – or the arrow, perhaps? – or the bow?"

Pyne's watery eyes glistened for a moment.

"No – of course not, sir. . . . Why should I, sir?"

"Why, indeed?" Vance sighed wearily. "But you saw the bow?"

The man squinted, as if for purposes of mental visualization.

"I couldn't say, sir. Perhaps, yes; perhaps, no. I don't recall."

Vance seemed to lose all interest in him; and Markham resumed the interrogation.

"I understand, Pyne, that Mr. Drukker called here this morning about half past nine. Did you see him?"

"Yes, sir. He always uses the basement door;

and he said good-morning to me as he passed the butler's pantry at the head of the steps."

"He returned the same way he came?"

"I suppose so, sir – though I was up-stairs when he went. He lives in the house at the rear –"

"I know." Markham leaned forward. "I presume it was you who admitted Mr. Robin and Mr. Sperling this morning."

"Yes, sir. At about ten o'clock."

"Did you see them again, or overhear any of their remarks while they waited here in the drawing-room?"

"No, sir. I was busy in Mr. Arnesson's quarters most of the morning."

"Ah!" Vance turned his eyes on the man. "That would be on the second floor rear, wouldn't it? – the room with the balcony?"

"Yes, sir."

"Most interestin'. . . . And it was from that balcony that Professor Dillard first saw Mr. Robin's body. – How could he have entered the room without your knowing it? You said, I believe, that your first intimation of the tragedy was when the professor called you from the library and told you to seek Mr. Sperling."

The butler's face turned a pasty white, and I noticed that his fingers twitched nervously.

"I might have stepped out of Mr. Arnesson's room for a moment," he explained, with effort. "Yes – it's quite likely. In fact, sir, I recall going to the linen-closet. . . ."

"Oh, to be sure." Vance lapsed into lethargy.

Markham smoked a while, his gaze concentrated on the table-top.

"Did any one else call at the house this morning, Pyne?" he asked presently.

"No one, sir."

"And you can suggest no explanation for what happened here?"

The man shook his head heavily, his watery eyes in space.

"No, sir. Mr. Robin seemed a pleasant, well-liked young man. He wasn't the kind to inspire murder – if you understand what I mean."

Vance looked up.

"I can't say that I, personally, understand exactly what you mean, Pyne. How do you know it wasn't an accident?"

"I don't, sir," was the unperturbed answer. "But I know a bit about archery – if you'll pardon my saying so – and I saw right away that Mr. Robin had been killed by a hunting arrow."

"You're very observin', Pyne," nodded Vance. "And quite correct."

It was plain that no direct information was to

be got from the butler, and Markham dismissed him abruptly, at the same time ordering Heath to send in the cook.

When she entered I noticed at once a resemblance between father and daughter. She was a slatternly woman of about forty, also tall and angular, with a thin, elongated face and large hands and feet. Hyperpituitarism evidently ran in the Pyne family.

A few preliminary questions brought out the information that she was a widow, named Beedle, and had, at the death of her husband five years before, come to Professor Dillard as the result of Pyne's recommendation.

"What time did you leave the house this morning, Beedle?" Markham asked her.

"Right after half past ten." She seemed uneasy and on the alert, and her voice was defensively belligerent.

"And what time did you return?"

"About half past twelve. That man let me in" – she looked viciously at Heath – "and treated me like I'd been a criminal."

Heath grinned. "The time's O. K., Mr. Markham. She got sore because I wouldn't let her go down-stairs."

Markham nodded non-committally.

"Do you know anything of what took place here this morning?" he went on, studying the woman closely.

"How should I know? I was at Jefferson market."

"Did you see either Mr. Robin or Mr. Sperling?"

"They went down-stairs to the archery-room past the kitchen a little while before I went out."

"Did you overhear anything they said?"

"I don't listen at keyholes."

Markham set his jaw angrily and was about to speak when Vance addressed the woman suavely.

"The District Attorney thought that perhaps the door was open, and that you might have overheard some of their conversation despite your commendable effort not to listen."

"The door might've been open, but I didn't hear anything," she answered sullenly.

"Then you couldn't tell us if there was any one else in the archery-room."

Beedle narrowed her eyes and gave Vance a calculating look.

"Maybe there was some one else," she said slowly. "In fact, I thought I heard Mr. Drukker." A note of venom came into her voice, and the shadow of a hard smile passed over her thin lips. "He was here to call on Mr. Arnesson early this morning."

"Oh, was he, now?" Vance appeared surprised at this news. "You saw him perhaps?"

"I saw him come in, but I didn't see him go out – anyway, I didn't notice. He sneaks in and out at all hours."

"Sneaks, eh? Fancy that! . . . By the by, which door did you use when you went a-marketing?"

"The front door. Since Miss Belle made a club-room out of the basement, I always use the front door."

"Then you didn't enter the archery-room this morning?"

"No."

Vance raised himself in his chair.

"Thanks for your help, Beedle. We won't need you any more now."

When the woman had left us Vance rose and walked to the window.

"We're expending too much zeal in irrelevant channels, Markham," he said. "We'll never get anywhere by ballyragging servants and questioning members of the household. There's a psychological wall to be battered down before we can begin storming the enemy's trenches. Everybody in this ménage has some pet privacy that he's afraid will leak out. Each person so far has told us either less or more than he knows. Disheartenin', but true.

Nothing that we've learned dovetails with anything else; and when chronological events don't fit together, you may rest assured that the serrated points of contact have been deliberately distorted. I haven't found one clean joinder in all the tales that have been poured into our ears."

"It's more likely the connections are missing," Markham argued; "and we'll never find them if we don't pursue our questionings."

"You're much too trustin'." Vance walked back to the centre-table. "The more questions we ask the farther afield we'll be taken. Even Professor Dillard didn't give us a wholly honest account. There's something he's keeping back – some suspicion he won't voice. Why did he bring that bow indoors? Arnesson put his finger on a vital spot when he asked the same question. Shrewd fella, Arnesson. – Then there's our athletic young lady with the muscular calves. She's entangled in various amat'ry meshes, and is endeavoring to extricate herself and her whole coterie without leaving a blemish on any one. A praiseworthy aim, but not one conducive to the unadulterated truth. – Pyne has ideas, too. That flabby facial mask of his curtains many an entrancin' thought. But we'll never probe his cortex by chivyin' him with questions. Somethin' rum, too, about his matutinal labors. He says he was in Arnesson's room all morning; but he obviously didn't know that the professor took a sunnin' on Arnesson's verandah. And that linen-closet alibi – much too specious. – Also, Markham, let your mind flutter about the widowed Beedle's tale. She doesn't like the over-sociable Mr. Drukker; and when she saw a chance to involve him, she did so. She 'thought' she heard his voice in the archery-room. But did she? Who knows? True, he might have tarried among the slings and javelins on his way home and been joined later by Robin and Sperling. . . . Yes, it's a point we must investigate. In fact, a bit of polite converse with Mr. Drukker is strongly indicated. . . ."

Footsteps were heard descending the front stairs, and Arnesson appeared in the archway of the living-room.

"Well, who killed Cock Robin?" he asked, with a satyr-like grin.

Markham rose, annoyed, and was about to protest at the intrusion; but Arnesson held up his hand.

"One moment, please. I'm here to offer my exalted services in the noble cause of justice – mundane justice, I would have you understand. Philosophically, of course, there's no such thing as justice. If there really were justice we'd all be in for a shingling in the cosmic wood-shed." He sat down facing Markham and chuckled cynically. "The fact is, the sad and precipitate departure of Mr. Robin appeals to my scientific nature. It makes a nice, orderly problem. It has a decidedly mathematical flavor – no undistributed terms, you understand; clear-cut integers with certain unknown quantities to be determined. – Well, I'm the genius to solve it."

"What would be your solution, Arnesson?" Markham knew and respected the man's intelligence, and seemed at once to sense a serious purpose beneath his attitude of sneering flippancy.

"Ah! As yet I haven't tackled the equation." Arnesson drew out an old briar pipe and fingered it affectionately. "But I've always wanted to do a little detective work on a purely earthly plane – the insatiable curiosity and natural inquisitiveness of the physicist, you understand. And I've long had a theory that the science of mathematics can be advantageously applied to the trivialities of our life on this unimportant planet. There's nothing but law in the universe – unless Eddington is right and there's no law at all – and I see no sufficient reason why the identity and position of a criminal can't be determined just as

Leverrier calculated the mass and emphemeris of Neptune from the observed deviations in the orbit of Uranus. You remember how, after his computations, he told Galle, the Berlin astronomer, to look for the planet in a specified longitude of the ecliptic."

Arnesson paused and filled his pipe.

"Now, Mr. Markham," he went on; and I tried to decide whether or not the man was in earnest, "I'd like the opportunity of applying to this absurd muddle the purely rational means used by Leverrier in discovering Neptune. But I've got to have the data on the perturbations of Uranus's orbit, so to speak – that is, I must know all the varying factors in the equation. The favor I've come here to ask is that you take me into your confidence and tell me all the facts. A sort of intellectual partnership. I'll figure out this problem for you along scientific lines. It'll be bully sport; and incidentally I'd like to prove my theory that mathematics is the basis of all truth however far removed from scholastic abstractions." He at last got his pipe going, and sank back in his chair. "Is it a bargain?"

"I'll be glad to tell you whatever we know, Arnesson," Markham replied after a brief pause. "But I can't promise to reveal everything that may arise from now on. It might work against the ends of justice and embarrass our investigation."

Vance had sat with half-closed eyes, apparently bored by Arnesson's astonishing request; but now he turned to Markham with a considerable show of animation.

"I say, y' know'; there's really no reason why we shouldn't give Mr. Arnesson a chance to translate this crime into the realm of applied mathematics. I'm sure he'd be discreet and use our information only for scientific purposes. And – one never knows, does one? – we may need his highly trained assistance before we're through with this fascinatin' affair."

Markham knew Vance well enough to realize that his suggestion had not been made thoughtlessly; and I was in no wise astonished when he faced Arnesson and said:

"Very well, then. We'll give you whatever data you need to work out your mathematical formula. Anything special you want to know now?"

"Oh, no. I know the details thus far as well as you; and I'll strip Beedle and old Pyne of their contributions when you're gone. But if I solve this problem and determine the exact position of the criminal, don't pigeon-hole my findings as Sir George Airy did those of poor Adams when he submitted his Neptunean calculations prior to Leverrier's. . . ."

At this moment the front door opened, and the uniformed officer stationed on the porch came in, followed by a stranger.

"This gent here says he wants to see the professor," he announced with radiating suspicion; and turning to the man he indicated Markham with a gesture of the head. "That's the District Attorney. Tell him your troubles."

The newcomer seemed somewhat embarrassed. He was a slender, well-groomed man with an unmistakable air of refinement. His age, I should say, was fifty, though his face held a perennially youthful look. His hair was thin and graying, his nose a trifle sharp, and his chin small but in no way weak. His eyes, surmounted by a high broad forehead, were his most striking characteristic. They were the eyes of a disappointed and disillusioned dreamer – half sad, half resentful, as if life had tricked him and left him unhappy and bitter.

He was about to address Markham when he caught sight of Arnesson.

"Oh, good-morning, Arnesson," he said, in a quiet, well-modulated voice. "I hope there's nothing seriously wrong."

"A mere death, Pardee," the other replied carelessly. "The proverbial tempest in a teapot."

Markham was annoyed at the interruption.

"What can I do for you, sir?" he asked.

"I trust I am not intruding," the man apologized. "I am a friend of the family, – I live just across the street; and I perceived that something unusual had happened here. It occurred to me I might be of some service."

Arnesson chuckled. "My dear Pardee! Why clothe your natural curiosity in the habiliments of rhetoric?"

Pardee blushed.

"I assure you, Arnesson –" he began; but Vance interrupted him.

"You say you live opposite, Mr. Pardee. You have perhaps been observing this house during the forenoon?"

"Hardly that, sir. My study, however, overlooks 75th Street, and it's true I was sitting at the window most of the morning. But I was busy writing. When I returned to my work from lunch I noticed the crowd and the police cars and also the officer in uniform at the door."

Vance had been studying him from the corner of his eye.

"Did you happen to see any one enter or leave this house this morning, Mr. Pardee?" he asked.

The man shook his head slowly.

"No one in particular. I noticed two young men – friends of Miss Dillard – call at about ten o'clock; and I saw Beedle go out with her market basket. But that's all I recall."

"Did you see either of these young men depart?"

"I don't remember." Pardee knit his brows. "And yet it seems to me one of them left by the range gate. But it's only an impression."

"What time would that have been?"

"Really, I couldn't say. Perhaps an hour or so after his arrival. I wouldn't care to be more specific."

"You recall no other person whatever either coming or going from the house this morning?"

"I saw Miss Dillard return from the tennis courts about half past twelve, just as I was called to lunch. In fact, she waved her racket to me."

"And no one else?"

"I'm afraid not." There was unmistakable regret in his quiet response.

"One of the young men you saw enter here has been killed," Vance told him.

"Mr. Robin – *alias* Cock Robin," supplemented Arnesson, with a comic grimace which affected me unpleasantly.

"Good Heavens! How unfortunate!" Pardee

appeared genuinely shocked. "Robin? Wasn't he the Champion Archer of Belle's club?"

"His one claim to immortality. – That's the chap."

"Poor Belle!" Something in the man's manner caused Vance to regard him sharply. "I hope she's not too greatly upset by the tragedy."

"She's dramatizing it, naturally," Arnesson returned. "So are the police, for that matter. Awful pother about nothing in particular. The earth is covered with 'small crawling masses of impure carbohydrates' like Robin – referred to in the aggregate as humanity."

Pardee smiled with tolerant sadness, – he was obviously familiar with Arnesson's cynicisms. Then he appealed to Markham.

"May I be permitted to see Miss Dillard and her uncle?"

"Oh, by all means." It was Vance who answered before Markham could reach a decision. "You'll find them in the library, Mr. Pardee."

The man left the room with a polite murmur of thanks.

"Queer fellow," commented Arnesson, when Pardee was out of hearing. "Cursed with money. Leads an indolent life. His one passion is solving chess problems. . . ."

"Chess?" Vance looked up with interest. "Is he, by any chance, John Pardee, the inventor of the famous Pardee gambit?"

"The same." Arnesson's face crinkled humorously. "Spent twenty years developing a cast-iron offensive that was to add new decimal points to the game. Wrote a book about it. Then went forth proselytizing like a crusader before the gates of Damascus. He's always been a great patron of chess, contributing to tournaments, and scurrying round the world to attend the various chess jousting-bouts. Consequently was able to get his gambit tested. It made a great stir among the infra-champions of the Manhattan Chess Club. Then poor Pardee organized a series of Master Tournaments. Paid all the expenses himself. Cost him a fortune, by the way. And of course he stipulated that the Pardee gambit be played exclusively. Well, well, it was very sad. When men like Doctor Lasker and Capablanca and Rubinstein and Finn got to combating it, it went to pieces. Almost every player who used it lost. It was disqualified – even worse than the ill-fated Rice gambit. Terrible blow for Pardee. It put snow in his hair, and took all the rubber out of his muscles. Aged him, in short. He's a broken man."

"I know the history of the gambit," murmured Vance, his eyes resting pensively on the ceiling. "I've used it myself. Edward Lasker* taught it to me. . . ."

The uniformed officer again appeared in the archway and beckoned to Heath. The Sergeant rose with alacrity – the ramifications of chess obviously bored him – and went into the hall. A moment later he returned bearing a small sheet of paper.

"Here's a funny one, sir," he said, handing it to Markham. "The officer outside happened to see it sticking outa the mail-box just now, and thought he'd take a peep at it. – What do you make of it, sir?"

Markham studied it with puzzled amazement, and then without a word handed it to Vance. I rose and looked over his shoulder. The paper was of the conventional typewriter size, and had been folded to fit into the mail-box. It contained several lines of typing done on a machine with élite characters and a faded blue ribbon.

The first line read:

Joseph Cochrane Robin is dead.

*The American chess master – sometimes confused with Doctor Emanuel Lasker, the former world champion.

The second line asked:

Who Killed Cock Robin?

Underneath was typed:

Sperling means sparrow.

And in the lower right-hand corner – the place of the signature – were the two words, in capitals:

THE BISHOP.

CHAPTER V

A WOMAN'S SCREAM

(Saturday, April 2; 2.30 p.m.)

Vance, after glancing at the strange message with its even stranger signature, reached for his monocle with that slow deliberation which I knew indicated a keen suppressed interest. Having adjusted the glass he studied the paper intently. Then he handed it to Arnesson.

"Here's a valuable factor for your equation." His eyes were fixed banteringly on the man.

Arnesson regarded the note superciliously, and with a wry grimace laid it on the table.

"I trust the clergy are not involved in this problem. They're notoriously unscientific. One can't attack them with mathematics. 'The Bishop'. . . ," he mused. "I'm unacquainted with any gentlemen of the cloth. – I think I'll rule out this abracadabra when making my calculations."

"If you do, Mr. Arnesson," replied Vance seriously, "your equation, I fear, will fall to pieces. That cryptic epistle strikes me as rather significant. Indeed – if you will pardon a mere lay opinion – I believe it is the most mathematical thing that has appeared thus far in the case. It relieves the situation of all haphazardness or accident. It's the *g*, so to speak – the gravitational constant which will govern all our equations."

Heath had stood looking down on the typewritten paper with solemn disgust.

"Some crank wrote this, Mr. Vance," he declared.

"Undoubtedly a crank, Sergeant," agreed Vance. "But don't overlook the fact that this particular crank must have known many interestin' and intimate details – to wit, that Mr. Robin's middle name was Cochrane; that the gentleman had been killed with a bow and arrow; and that Mr. Sperling was in the vicinity at the time of the Robin's passing. Moreover, this well-informed crank must have had what amounted to foreknowledge regarding the murder; for the note was obviously typed and inserted in the letter-box before you and your men arrived on the scene."

"Unless," countered Heath doggedly, "he's one of those bimboes out in the street, who got wise to what had happened and then stuck this paper in the box when the officer's back was turned."

"Having first run home and carefully typewritten his communication – eh, what?" Vance shook his head with a rueful smile. "No, Sergeant, I'm afraid your theory won't do."

"Then what in hell does it mean?" Heath demanded truculently.

"I haven't the foggiest idea." Vance yawned and rose. "Come, Markham, let's while away a few brief moments with this Mr. Drukker whom Beedle abhors."

"Drukker!" exclaimed Arnesson, with considerable surprise. "Where does he fit in?"

"Mr. Drukker," explained Markham, "called here this morning to see you; and it's barely possible he met Robin and Sperling before he returned home." He hesitated. "Would you care to accompany us?"

"No, thanks." Arnesson knocked out his pipe and got up. "I've a pile of class papers to look over. – It might be as well, however, to take Belle along. Lady Mae's a bit peculiar. . . ."

"Lady Mae?"

"My mistake. Forgot you didn't know her. We all call her Lady Mae. Courtesy title. Pleases the poor old soul. I'm referring to Drukker's mother. Odd character." He tapped his forehead significantly. "Bit touched. Oh, perfectly harmless. Bright as a whistle, but monominded, as it were. Thinks the sun rises and sets in Drukker. Mothers him as if he were an infant. Sad situation. . . . Yes, you'd better take Belle along. Lady Mae likes Belle."

"A good suggestion, Mr. Arnesson," said Vance. "Will you ask Miss Dillard if she'll be good enough to accompany us?"

"Oh, certainly." Arnesson gave us an inclusive smile of farewell – a smile which seemed at once patronizing and satirical – and went up-stairs. A few moments later Miss Dillard joined us.

"Sigurd tells me you want to see Adolph. He, of course, won't mind; but poor Lady Mae gets so upset over even the littlest things. . . ."

"We sha'n't upset her, I hope." Vance spoke reassuringly. "But Mr. Drukker was here this morning, d' ye see; and the cook says she thought she heard him speaking to Mr. Robin and Mr. Sperling in the archery-room. He may be able to help us."

"I'm sure he will if he can," the girl answered with emphasis. "But be very careful with Lady Mae, won't you?"

There was a pleading, protective note in her voice, and Vance regarded her curiously.

"Tell us something of Mrs. Drukker – or Lady Mae – before we visit her. Why should we be so careful?"

"She's had such a tragic life," the girl explained. "She was once a great singer – oh, not just a second-rate artist, but a prima donna with a marvelous career before her.* She married a leading critic of Vienna – Otto Drucker† – and four years later Adolph was born. Then one day in the Wiener Prater, when the baby was two years old, she let him fall; and from that moment on her entire life was changed. Adolph's spine was injured, and he became a cripple. Lady Mae was heartbroken. She held herself to blame for his injury, and gave up her career to devote herself to his care. When her husband died a year later she brought Adolph to America, where she had spent some of her girlhood, and bought the house where she now lives. Her whole life has been centred on Adolph, who grew up a hunchback. She has sacrificed everything for him, and cares for him as though he were a baby. . . ." A shadow crossed her face. "Sometimes I think – we all think – that she still

*Mae Brenner will still be remembered by Continental music lovers. Her début was made at the unprecedented age of twenty-three as *Sulamith* in "Die Königin von Saba" at the Imperial Opera House in Vienna; although her greatest success was perhaps her *Desdemona* in "Otello" – the last rôle she sang before her retirement.

†The name was, of course, originally spelled Drucker. The change – possibly some vague attempt at Americanization – was made by Mrs. Drukker when she settled in this country.

imagines he's only a child. She has become – well, morbid about it. But it's the sweet, terrible morbidity of a tremendous motherlove – a sort of insanity of tenderness, uncle calls it. During the past few months she has grown very strange – and peculiar. I've often found her crooning old German lullabies and kindergarten songs, with her arms crossed on her breast, as if – oh, it seems so sacred and so terrible! – as if she were holding a baby. . . . And she has become frightfully jealous of Adolph. She's resentful of all other men. Only last week I took Mr. Sperling to see her – we often drop in to call on her: she seems so lonely and unhappy – and she looked at him almost fiercely, and said: 'Why weren't you a cripple, too?' . . ."

The girl paused and searched our faces.

"Now don't you understand why I asked you to be careful? . . . Lady Mae may think we have come to harm Adolph."

"We sha'n't add unnecessarily to her suffering," Vance assured her sympathetically. Then, as we moved toward the hall, he asked her a question which recalled to my mind his brief intent scrutiny of the Drukker house earlier that afternoon. "Where is Mrs. Drukker's room situated?"

The girl shot him a startled look, but

answered promptly:

"On the west side of the house – its bay window overlooks the archery range."

"Ah!" Vance took out his cigarette case, and carefully selected a *Régie*. "Does she sit much at this window?"

"A great deal. Lady Mae always watches us at archery practice – why I don't know. I'm sure it pains her to see us, for Adolph isn't strong enough to shoot. He's tried it several times, but it tired him so he had to give it up."

"She may watch you practising for the very reason that it does torture her – a kind of self-immolation, y' know. Those situations are very distressing." Vance spoke almost with tenderness – which, to one who did not know his real nature, would have sounded strange. "Perhaps," he added, as we emerged into the archery range through the basement door, "it would be best if we saw Mrs. Drukker first for a moment. It might tend to allay any apprehensions our visit might cause her. Could we reach her room without Mr. Drukker's knowledge?"

"Oh, yes." The girl was pleased at the idea. "We can go in the rear way. Adolph's study, where he does his writing, is at the front of the house."

We found Mrs. Drukker sitting in the great bay window on a sprawling old-fashioned chaise-longue, propped up with pillows. Miss Dillard greeted her filially and, bending over her with tender concern, kissed her forehead.

"Something rather awful has happened at our house this morning, Lady Mae," she said; "and these gentlemen wanted to see you. I offered to bring them over. You don't mind, do you?"

Mrs. Drukker's pale, tragic face had been turned away from the door as we entered, but now she stared at us with fixed horror. She was a tall woman, slender to the point of emaciation; and her hands, which lay slightly flexed on the arms of the chair, were sinewy and wrinkled like the talons of fabulous bird-women. Her face, too, was thin and deeply seamed; but it was not an unattractive face. The eyes were clear and alive, and the nose was straight and dominant. Though she must have been well past sixty, her hair was luxuriant and brown.

For several minutes she neither moved nor spoke. Then her hands closed slowly, and her lips parted.

"What do you want?" she asked in a low resonant voice.

"Mrs. Drukker," – it was Vance who answered – "as Miss Dillard has told you, a tragedy occurred next door this morning, and since your window is the only one directly overlooking the archery range, we thought that you might have seen something that would aid us in our investigation."

The woman's vigilance relaxed perceptibly, but it was a moment or two before she spoke.

"And what did take place?"

"A Mr. Robin was killed. – You knew him perhaps?"

"The archer – Belle's Champion Archer? . . . Yes, I knew him. A strong healthy child who could pull a heavy bow and not get tired. – Who killed him?"

"We don't know." Vance, despite his negligent air, was watching her astutely. "But inasmuch as he was killed on the range, within sight of your window, we hoped you might be able to help us."

Mrs. Drukker's eyelids dropped craftily, and she clasped her hands with a kind of deliberate satisfaction.

"You are sure he was killed on the range?"

"We found him on the range," Vance returned non-committally.

"I see . . . But what can I do to help you?" She lay back relaxed.

"Did you notice any one on the range this morning?" asked Vance.

"No!" The denial was swift and emphatic. "I

saw no one. I haven't looked out on the range all day."

Vance met the woman's gaze steadily, and sighed.

"It's most unfortunate," he murmured. "Had you been looking out of the window this morning, it's wholly possible you might have seen the tragedy. . . . Mr. Robin was killed with a bow and arrow, and there seems to have been no motive whatever for the act."

"You know he was killed with a bow and arrow?" she asked, a tinge of color coming into her ashen cheeks.

"That was the Medical Examiner's report. There was an arrow through his heart when we found him."

"Of course. That seems perfectly natural, doesn't it? . . . An arrow through the Robin's heart!" She spoke with vague aloofness, a distant fascinated look in her eyes.

There was a strained silence, and Vance moved toward the window.

"Do you mind if I look out?"

With difficulty the woman brought herself back from some far train of thought.

"Oh, no. It isn't much of a view, though. I can see the trees of 76th Street toward the north, and a part of the Dillard yard to the south. But that brick wall opposite is very depressing. Before the apartment house was built I had a beautiful view of the river."

Vance looked for a while down into the archery range.

"Yes," he observed; "if only you had been at the window this morning you might have seen what happened. Your view of the range and the basement door of the Dillards' is very clear . . . . Too bad." He glanced at his watch. "Is your son in, Mrs. Drukker?"

"My son! My baby! What do you want with him?" Her voice rose pitifully, and her eyes fastened on Vance with venomous hatred.

"Nothing important," he said pacifying. "Only, he may have seen some one on the range –"

"He saw no one! He couldn't have seen any one, for he wasn't here. He went out early this morning, and hasn't returned."

Vance looked with pity at the woman.

"He was away all morning? – Do you know where he was?"

"I always know where he is," Mrs. Drukker answered proudly. "He tells me everything."

"And he told you where he was going this morning?" persisted Vance gently.

"Certainly. But I forget for the moment. Let me think. . . ." Her long fingers tapped on the arm of the chair, and her eyes shifted uneasily.

"I can't recall. But I'll ask him the moment he returns."

Miss Dillard had stood watching the woman with growing perplexity.

"But, Lady Mae, Adolph was at our house this morning. He came to see Sigurd –"

Mrs. Drukker drew herself up.

"Nothing of the kind!" she snapped, eyeing the girl almost viciously. "Adolph had to go – downtown somewhere. He wasn't near your house – I *know* he wasn't." Her eyes flashed, and she turned a defiant glare on Vance.

It was an embarrassing moment; but what followed was even more painful.

The door opened softly, and suddenly Mrs. Drukker's arms went out.

"My little boy – my baby!" she cried. "Come here, dear."

But the man at the door did not come forward. He stood blinking his beady little eyes at us, like a person waking in strange surroundings. Adolph Drukker was scarcely five feet tall. He had the typical congested appearance of the hunchback. His legs were spindling, and the size of his bulging, distorted torso seemed exaggerated by his huge, domelike head. But there was intellectuality in the man's face – a terrific passionate power which held one's attention. Professor Dillard had called him a mathematical genius; and one could have no doubts as to his erudition.*

"What does all this mean?" he demanded in a high-pitched, tremulous voice, looking toward Miss Dillard. "Are these friends of yours, Belle?"

The girl started to speak, but Vance halted her with a gesture.

"The truth is, Mr. Drukker," he explained sombrely, "there has been a tragedy next door. This is Mr. Markham, the District Attorney, and Sergeant Heath of the Police Department; and at our request Miss Dillard brought us here that we might ask your mother whether or not she had noticed anything unusual on the archery range this morning. The tragedy occurred just outside the basement door of the Dillard house."

Drukker thrust his chin forward and squinted.

"A tragedy, eh? What kind of tragedy?"

"A Mr. Robin was killed – with a bow and arrow."

The man's face began to twitch spasmodically.

"Robin killed? *Killed?* . . . What time?"

*He gave me very much the same impression as did General Homer Lee when I visited him at Santa Monica shortly before his death.

"Some time between eleven and twelve probably."

"Between eleven and twelve?" Quickly Drukker's gaze shifted to his mother. He seemed to grow excited, and his huge splay of fingers worried the hem of his smoking-jacket. "What did you see?" His eyes glinted as he focussed them on the woman.

"What do you mean, son?" The retort was a panic-stricken whisper.

Drukker's face became hard, and the suggestion of a snear twisted his lips.

"I mean that it was about that time when I heard a scream in this room."

"You didn't! No – no!" She caught her breath, and wagged her head jerkily. "You're mistaken, son. I didn't scream this morning."

"Well, some one did." There was a cold relentlessness in the man's tone. Then, after a pause, he added: "The fact is, I came up-stairs after I heard the scream, and listened at the door here. But you were walking about humming 'Eia Popeia,' so I went back to my work."

Mrs. Drukker pressed a handkerchief to her face, and her eyes closed momentarily.

"You were at your work between eleven and twelve?" Her voice now rang with subdued eagerness. "But I called you several times –"

"I heard you. But I didn't answer. I was too busy."

"So that was it." She turned slowly toward the window. "I thought you were out. Didn't you tell me – ?"

"I told you I was going to the Dillards'. But Sigurd wasn't there, and I came back a little before eleven."

"I didn't see you come in." The woman's energy was spent, and she lay back listlessly, her eyes on the brick wall opposite. "And when I called and you didn't answer I naturally thought you were still out."

"I left the Dillards' by the street gate, and took a walk in the park." Drukker's voice was irritable. "Then I let myself in by the front door."

"And you say you heard me scream. . . . But why should I scream, son? I've had no pains in my back this morning."

Drukker frowned, and his little eyes moved swiftly from Vance to Markham.

"I heard some one scream – a woman – in this room," he iterated stubbornly. "About half past eleven." Then he sank into a chair and gazed moodily at the floor.

This perplexing verbal intercourse between mother and son had held us all spellbound. Though Vance had stood before an old eighteenth-century print near the door, regarding it with apparent absorption, I knew that no word or inflection had escaped him. Now he swung about and, giving Markham a signal not to interfere, approached Mrs. Drukker.

"We're very sorry, madam, that we've had to trouble you. Forgive us, if you can."

He bowed and turned to Miss Dillard.

"Do you care to pilot us back? Or shall we find our own way down?"

"I'll come with you," the girl said; and going to Mrs. Drukker she put her arm about her. "I'm so sorry, Lady Mae."

As we were passing out into the hall Vance, as if on second thought, paused and looked back at Drukker.

"You'd better come with us, sir," he said, in a casual yet urgent tone. "You knew Mr. Robin, and you may be able to suggest something –"

"Don't go with them, son!" cried Mrs. Drukker. She was sitting upright now, her face contorted with anguish and fear. "Don't go! They're the enemy. They want to hurt you. . . ."

Drukker had risen.

"Why shouldn't I go with them?" he retorted petulantly. "I want to find out about this affair. Maybe – as they say – I can help them." And with a gesture of impatience he joined us.

CHAPTER VI

" 'I,' SAID THE SPARROW"

(Saturday, April 2; 3 p.m.)

When we were again in the Dillard drawing-room and Miss Dillard had left us to rejoin her uncle in the library, Vance, without preliminaries, proceeded to the business in hand.

"I didn't care to worry your mother, Mr. Drukker, by questioning you in front of her, but inasmuch as you called here this morning shortly before Mr. Robin's death, it is necessary – as a mere routine procedure – that we seek whatever information you can give us."

Drukker had seated himself near the fireplace. He now drew in his head cautiously, but made no answer.

"You came here," continued Vance, "about half past nine, I believe, to call on Mr. Arnesson."

"Yes."

"By way of the archery range and the basement door?"

"I always come that way. Why walk around the block?"

"But Mr. Arnesson was out this morning."

Drukker nodded. "At the university."

"And, finding Mr. Arnesson away, you sat for a while in the library with Professor Dillard, I understand, discussing an astronomical expedition to South America."

"The expedition of the Royal Astronomical Society to Sobral to test the Einsteinian deflection," amplified Drukker.

"How long were you in the library?"

"Less than half an hour."

"And then?"

"I went down to the archery-room, and glanced at one of the magazines. There was a chess problem in it – a *Zugszwang* end-game that came up recently between Shapiro and Marshall – and I sat down and worked it out. . . ."

"Just a moment, Mr. Drukker." A note of suppressed interest came into Vance's voice. "You're interested in chess?"

"To a certain extent. I don't spend much time at it, however. The game is not purely mathematical; and it's insufficiently speculative to appeal to a wholly scientific mind."

"Did you find the Shapiro–Marshall position difficult?"

"Not so difficult as tricky." Drukker was watching Vance shrewdly. "As soon as I discovered that an apparently useless pawn move was the key to the impasse, the solution was simple."

"How long did it take you?"

"Half an hour or so."

"Until about half past ten, shall we say?"

"That would be about right." Drukker settled deeper into his chair, but his covert alertness did not relax.

"Then you must have been in the archery-room when Mr. Robin and Mr. Sperling came there."

The man did not answer at once, and Vance, pretending not to notice his hesitancy, added: "Professor Dillard said they called at the house about ten and, and after waiting a while in the drawing-room here, went down to the basement."

"Where's Sperling now, by the way?" Drukker's eyes darted suspiciously from one to the other of us.

"We expect him here any minute," Vance replied. "Sergeant Heath has sent two of his men to fetch him."

The hunchback's eyebrows lifted. "Ah! So Sperling is being forcibly brought back." He pyramided his spatulate fingers and inspected them musingly. Then he slowly lifted his eyes to Vance. "You asked me if I saw Robin and Sperling in the archery-room. – Yes; they came down-stairs just as I was going."

Vance leaned back and stretched his legs before him.

"Did you get the impression, Mr. Drukker, that they had – as we euphemistically say – been having words?"

The man considered this question for several moments.

"Now that you mention it," he said at length, "I do recall that there seemed to be a coolness between them. I wouldn't however, care to be too categorical on that point. You see, I left the room almost immediately after they entered."

"You went out the basement door, I think you said, and thence through the wall gate into 75th Street. Is that correct?"

For a moment, Drukker seemed loath to answer; but he replied with an effort at unconcern.

"Quite. I thought I'd take a stroll along the river before going back to work. I went to the Drive, then up the bridle path, and turned into the park at 79th Street."

Heath, with his habitual suspicion of all statements made to the police, put the next question.

"Did you meet any one you knew?"

Drukker turned angrily, but Vance quickly stepped into the breach.

"It really doesn't matter, Sergeant. If it's necess'ry later on to ascertain that point, we can take the matter up again." Then to Drukker: "You returned from your walk a little before eleven, I think you said, and entered your house by the front door."

"That's right."

"You saw nothing, by the by, that was in the least extr'ordinary when you were here this morning?"

"I saw nothing except what I've told you."

"And you're quite sure you heard your mother scream at about half past eleven?"

Vance did not move as he asked this question; but a slightly different note had crept into his voice, and it acted on Drukker in a startling manner. He heaved his squat body out of his chair, and stood glaring down on Vance with menacing fury. His tiny round eyes flashed, and his lips worked convulsively. His hands, dangling before him, flexed and unflexed like those of a man in a paroxysm.

"What are you driving at?" he demanded, his voice a shrill falsetto. "I tell you I heard her scream. I don't care a damn whether she admits it or not. Moreover, I heard her walking in her room. *She was in her room,* understand, *and I was in my room,* between eleven and twelve. And you can't prove anything different. Furthermore, I'm not going to be cross-examined by you or any one else as to what I was doing or where I was. It's none of your damned business – do you hear me? . . ."

So insensate was his wrath that I expected any minute to see him hurl himself on Vance. Heath had risen and stepped forward, sensing the potential danger of the man. Vance, however, did not move. He continued to smoke, languidly, and when the other's fury had been spent, he said quietly and without a trace of emotion:

"There's nothing more we have to ask you, Mr. Drukker. And really, y' know, there's no need to work yourself up. It merely occurred to me that your mother's scream might help to establish the exact time of the murder."

"What could her scream have to do with the time of Robin's death? Didn't she tell you she saw nothing?" Drukker appeared exhausted, and leaned heavily against the table.

At this moment Professor Dillard appeared in the archway. Behind him stood Arnesson.

"What seems to be the matter?" the professor asked. "I heard the noise here, and came down." He regarded Drukker coldly. "Hasn't

Belle been through enough to-day without your frightening her this way?"

Vance had risen, but before he could speak Arnesson came forward and shook his finger in mock reprimand at Drukker.

"You really should learn control, Adolph. You take life with such abominable seriousness. You've worked in interstellar spatial magnitudes long enough to have some sense of proportion. Why attach so much importance to this pin-point of life on earth?"

Drukker was breathing stertorously.

"These swine –" he began.

"Oh, my dear Adolph!" Arnesson cut him short. "The entire human race are swine. Why particularize? . . . Come along. I'll see you home." And he took Drukker's arm firmly and led him downstairs.

"We're very sorry we disturbed you, sir," Markham apologized to Professor Dillard. "The man flew off the handle for some unknown reason. These investigations are not the pleasantest things in the world; but we hope to be through before long."

"Well, make it as brief as you can, Markham. And do try to spare Belle as much as possible. – Let me see you before you go."

When Professor Dillard had returned upstairs, Markham took a turn up and down the room, his brows knit, his hands clasped behind him.

"What do you make of Drukker?" he asked, halting before Vance.

"Decidedly not a pleasant character. Diseased physically and mentally. A congenital liar. But canny – oh, deuced canny. An abnormal brain – you often find it in cripples of his type. Sometimes it runs to real constructive genius, as with Steinmetz; but too often it takes to abstruse speculation along impractical lines, as with Drukker. Still, our little verbal give-and-take has not been without fruit. He's hiding something that he'd like to tell but doesn't dare."

"That's possible, of course," returned Markham doubtfully. "He's touchy on the subject of that hour between eleven and noon. And he was watching you all the time like a cat."

"A weasel," Vance corrected him. "Yes, I was aware of his flatterin' scrutiny."

"Anyway, I can't see that he's helped us very much."

"No," agreed Vance. "We're not exactly forrader. But we're at least getting some luggage aboard. Our excitable mathematical wizard has opened up some very interestin' lines of speculation. And Mrs. Drukker is fairly teemin' with possibilities. If we knew what both of 'em together know we might find the key to this silly business."

Heath had been sullen for the past hour, and had looked on at the proceedings with bored disdain. But now he drew himself up combatively.

"I'm here to tell you, Mr. Markham, that we're wasting our time. What's the good of all these parleys? Sperling's the boy we want, and when my men bring him in and put him through a little sweating, we'll have enough material for an indictment. He was in love with the Dillard girl and was jealous of Robin – not only on account of the girl, but because Robin could shoot those red sticks straighter than he could. He had a scrap with Robin in this here room – the professor heard 'em at it; and he was down-stairs with Robin, according to the evidence, a few mintues before the murder. . . ."

"And," added Vance ironically, "his name means 'sparrow.' *Quod erat demonstrandum.* – No, Sergeant; it's much too easy. It works out like a game of Canfield with the cards stacked; whereas this thing was planned much too carefully for suspicion to fall directly on the guilty person."

"I can't see any careful planning about it," persisted Heath. "This Sperling gets sore, picks up a bow, grabs an arrow off of the wall, follows Robin outside, shoots him through the heart, and beats it."

Vance sighed.

"You're far too forthright for this wicked world, Sergeant. If only things happened with such naïve dispatch, life would be very simple – and depressin'. But such was not the *modus operandi* of the Robin's murder. First, no archer could shoot at a moving human target and strike just between the ribs over the vital spot of the heart. Secondly, there's that fracture of Robin's skull. He may have acquired it in falling, but it's not likely. Thirdly, his hat was at his feet, where it wouldn't have been if he had fallen naturally. Fourthly, the nock on the arrow is so bruised that I doubt if it would hold a string. Fifthly, Robin was facing the arrow, and during the drawing and aiming of the bow he would have had time to call out and cover himself. Sixthly. . . ."

Vance paused in the act of lighting a cigarette.

"*By Jove,* Sergeant! I've overlooked something. When a man's stabbed in the heart there's sure to be an immediate flow of blood, especially when the end of the weapon is larger than the shaft and there's no adequate plug for the hole. I say! It's quite possible that you'll find some blood spots on the floor of the archery-room – somewhere near the door most likely."

Heath hesitated, but only momentarily. Experience had long since taught him that Vance's suggestions were not to be treated cavalierly; and with a good-natured grunt he got up and disappeared toward the rear of the house.

"I think, Vance, I begin to see what you mean," observed Markham, with a troubled look. "But, good God! If Robin's apparent death with a bow and arrow was merely an *ex-post-facto* stage-setting, then we're confronted by something almost too diabolical to contemplate."

"It was the work of a maniac," declared Vance with unwonted sobriety. "Oh, not the conventional maniac who imagines he's Napoleon, but a madman with a brain so colossal that he has carried sanity to a, humanly speaking, *reductio ad absurdum* – to a point, that is, where humor itself becomes a formula in four dimensions."

Markham smoked vigorously, lost in speculation.

"I hope Heath doesn't find anything," he said at length.

"Why – in Heaven's name?" returned

Vance. "If there's no material evidence that Robin met his end in the archery room, it'll only make the problem more difficult legally."

But the material evidence was forthcoming. The Sergeant returned a few minutes later, crestfallen but excited.

"Damn it, Mr. Vance!" he blurted. "You had the dope all right." He made no attempt to keep the admiration out of his look. "There isn't any actual blood on the floor; but there's a dark place on the cement where somebody's scrubbed it with a wet rag to-day some time. It ain't dry yet; and the place is right near the door, where you said. And what makes it more suspicious is that one of those rugs has been pulled over it. – But that don't let Sperling out altogether," he added pugnaciously. "He mighta shot Robin indoors."

"And then cleaned up the blood, wiped off the bow and arrow, and placed the boy and the bow on the range, before making his departure? . . . Why? . . . Archery, to begin with, isn't an indoor sport, Sergeant. And Sperling knows too much about it to attempt murder with a bow and arrow. A hit such as the one that ended Robin's uneventful career would have been a pure fluke. Teucer himself couldn't have achieved it with any degree of certainty – and, according to Homer, Teucer was the champion archer of the Greeks."

As he spoke Pardee passed down the hall on his way out. He had nearly reached the front door when Vance rose suddenly and went to the archway.

"Oh, I say, Mr. Pardee. Just a moment, please."

The man turned with an air of gracious compliance.

"There is one other question we'd like to ask you," said Vance. "You mentioned seeing Mr. Sperling and Beedle leave here this morning by the wall gate. Are you sure you saw no one else use the gate?"

"Quite sure. That is, I don't recall any one else."

"I was thinking particularly of Mr. Drukker."

"Oh, Drukker?" Pardee shook his head with mild emphasis. "No, I would have remembered him. But you realize a dozen people might have entered and left this house without my noticing them."

"Quite – quite," Vance murmured indifferently. "How good a chess player, by the by, is Mr. Drukker?"

Pardee showed a flicker of suprise.

"He's not a player in the practical sense at all," he explained with careful precision. "He's an excellent analyst, however, and understands the theory of the game amazingly well. But he's had little practice at actual over-the-board play."

When Pardee had gone Heath cocked a triumphant eye at Vance.

"I notice, sir," he remarked good-naturedly, "that I'm not the only one who'd like to check the hunchback's alibi."

"Ah, but there's a difference between checking an alibi, and demanding that the person himself prove it."

At this moment the front door was thrown open. There were heavy footsteps in the hall, and three men appeared in the archway. Two were obviously detectives, and between them stood a tall, clean-cut youth of about thirty.

"We got him, Sergeant," announced one of the detectives, with a grin of vicious satisfaction. "He beat it straight home from here, and was packing up when we walked in on him."

Sperling's eyes swept the room with angry apprehension. Heath had planted himself before the man, and stood looking him up and down triumphantly.

"Well, young fella, you thought you'd get away, did you?" The Sergeant's cigar bobbed up and down between his lips as he spoke.

The color mounted to Sperling's cheeks, and he set his mouth stubbornly.

"So! You've got nothing to say?" Heath went on, squaring his jaw ferociously. "You're one of these silent lads, are you? Well, we'll make you talk." He turned to Markham. "How about it, sir? Shall I take him to Headquarters?"

"Perhaps Mr. Sperling will not object to answering a few questions here," said Markham quietly.

Sperling studied the District Attorney a moment; then his gaze moved to Vance, who nodded to him encouragingly.

"Answer questions about what?" he asked, with an obvious effort at self-control. "I was preparing to go away for the week-end when these ruffians forced their way into my room; and I was brought here without a word of explanation or even an opportunity to communicate with my family. Now you talk of taking me to Police Headquarters." He gave Heath a defiant glare. "All right, take me to Police Headquarters – and be damned to you!"

"What time did you leave here this morning, Mr. Sperling?" Vance's tone was soft and ingratiating, and his manner reassuring.

"About a quarter past eleven," the man answered. "In time to catch the 11:40 Scarsdale train from Grand Central."

"And Mr. Robin?"

"I don't know what time Robin went. He said he was going to wait for Belle – Miss Dillard. I left him in the archery-room."

"You saw Mr. Drukker?"

"For a minute – yes. He was in the archery-room when Robin and I went down-stairs; but he left immediately."

"Through the wall gate? Or did he walk down the range?"

"I don't remember – in fact, I didn't notice. . . . Say, look here: what's all this about anyway?"

"Mr. Robin was killed this morning," said Vance, "– at some time near eleven o'clock."

Sperling's eyes seemed to start from his head.

"Robin killed? My God! . . . Who – who killed him?" The man's lips were dry, and he wetted them with his tongue.

"We don't know yet," Vance answered. "He was shot through the heart with an arrow."

This news left Sperling stunned. His eyes traveled vaguely from side to side, and he fumbled in his pocket for a cigarette.

Heath stepped nearer to him, and thrust out his chin.

"Maybe *you* can tell us who killed him – *with a bow and arrow!*"

"Why – why do you – think I know?" Sperling managed to stammer.

"Well," returned the Sergeant relentlessly, "you were jealous of Robin, weren't you? You had a hot argument with him about the girl, right in this room, didn't you? And you were alone with him just before he was croaked, weren't you? And you're a pretty good shot with the bow and arrow, aren't you? – That's why I think that maybe you know something." He narrowed his eyes and drew his upper lip over his teeth. "Say! Come clean. Nobody else but you coulda done it. You had a fight with him over the girl, and you were the last person seen with him – *only a few minutes before he was killed.* And who else woulda shot him with a bow and arrow except a champeen archer – huh? . . . Make it easy for yourself, and spill the story. We've got you."

A strange light had gathered in Sperling's eyes, and his body became rigid.

"Tell me," – he spoke in a strained, unnatural voice – "did you find the bow?"

"Sure we found it." Heath laughed unpleasantly. "Right where you left it – in the alley."

"What kind of a bow was it?" Sperling's gaze had not moved from some distant point.

"What kind of a bow?" repeated Heath.

"A regular bow –"

Vance, who had been watching the youth closely, interrupted.

"I think I understand the question, Sergeant. – It was a woman's bow, Mr. Sperling. About five-feet-six, and rather light – under thirty pounds, I should say."

Sperling drew a slow, deep breath, like a man steeling himself for some bitter resolution. Then his lips parted in a faint, grim smile.

"What's the use?" he asked listlessly. "I thought I'd have time to get away. . . . Yes, I killed him."

Heath grunted with satisfaction, and his belligerent manner at once disappeared.

"You got more sense than I thought you had," he said, in an almost paternal tone, nodding in a businesslike manner to the two detectives. "Take him along, boys. Use my buggy – it's outside. And lock him up without booking him. I'll prefer the charge when I get to the office."

"Come along, bo," ordered one of the detectives, turning toward the hall.

But Sperling did not at once obey. Instead he looked appealingly at Vance.

"Could I – might I –" he began.

Vance shook his head.

"No, Mr. Sperling. It would be best if you

didn't see Miss Dillard. No use of harrowin' her feelings just now. . . . Cheerio."

The man turned without another word and went out between his captors.

CHAPTER VII

VANCE REACHES A CONCLUSION

(Saturday, April 2; 3.30 p.m.)

When we were again alone in the drawing-room Vance rose and, stretching himself, went to the window. The scene that had just been enacted, with its startling climax, had left us all somewhat dazed. Our minds were busy, I think, with the same idea; and when Vance spoke it was as if he were voicing our thoughts.

"We're back in the nursery, it seems. . . .

" 'I,' said the Sparrow,
'With my bow and arrow,
I killed Cock Robin.' . . .

I say, Markham; this thing is getting a bit thick."

He came slowly back to the centre-table and crushed out his cigarette. From the corner of his eye he looked at Heath.

"Why so pensive, Sergeant? You should be

singing roundelays and doing a joyous tarantella. Has not your villain confessed to the dark deed? Does it not fill you with gladness to know that the culprit will soon be languishin' in an oubliette?"

"To tell you the truth, Mr. Vance," Heath admitted sullenly, "I'm not satisfied. That confession came too easy, and – well, I've seen a lot of guys come across, but this one somehow didn't act like he was guilty. And that's a fact, sir."

"At any rate," submitted Markham hopefully, "his preposterous confession will damp the newspapers' curiosity and give us a free field to push our investigation. This case is going to make an ungodly noise; but as long as the reporters think the guilty person is jailed, they won't be bothering us for news of 'developments.' "

"I'm not saying he ain't guilty," asserted Heath pugnaciously, obviously arguing against his own convictions. "We certainly had the goods on him, and he mighta realized it and spilled the works, thinking it would go easier with him at the trial. Maybe he's not so dumb, after all."

"It won't do, Sergeant," said Vance. "The lad's mental workin's were deucedly simple. He knew Robin was waiting to see Miss

Dillard, and he also knew she'd non-suited him, so to speak, last night. Sperling evidently didn't have a high opinion of Robin; and when he heard of the gentleman's death at the hands of some one who wielded a short, light bow, he jumped to the conclusion that Robin had overstepped the bounds of propriety in his wooing, and received a righteous shaft through the heart. There was then nothing for our noble, mid-Victorian sparrow to do but slap his own manly bosom and proclaim: *'Ecce homo!'* It's most distressin'."

"Well, anyhow," grumbled Heath, "I'm not going to turn him loose. If Mr. Markham don't want to prosecute, that's up to him."

Markham looked at the Sergeant tolerantly. He realized the strain the man was under, and it was in keeping with his bigness of nature that he took no offence at the other's words.

"Perhaps, however, Sergeant," he said kindly, "you'll not object to continuing the investigation with me, even if I don't decide to prosecute Sperling."

Heath was at once contrite. He got up briskly and, going to Markham, held out his hand.

"You know it, sir!"

Markham took the offered hand, and rose with a gracious smile.

"I'll leave things with you, then, for the time being. I've some work to do at the office, and I told Swacker to wait for me."* He moved dispiritedly toward the hall. "I'll explain the situation to Miss Dillard and the professor before I go. – Anything special in mind, Sergeant?"

"Well, sir, I think I'll take a good look for that rag that was used to wipe up the floor down-stairs. And while I'm at it I'll go over the archery-room with a fine tooth comb. Also, I'll put the screws to the cook and the butler again – especially the cook. She musta been mighty close at hand when the dirty work was going on. . . . Then the regular routine stuff – inquiries in the neighborhood and that sorta thing."

"Let me know the results. I'll be at the Stuyvesant Club later to-day and to-morrow afternoon."

Vance had joined Markham in the archway.

"I say, old man," he remarked, as we went toward the stairs; "don't minimize the importance of that cryptic note left in the mail-box. I've a strong psychic suspicion that it may be the key to the nursery. You'd better ask Pro-

*Saturday was a "half day" at the District Attorney's office. Swacker was Markham's secretary.

fessor Dillard and his niece if 'Bishop' has any provocative significance for them. That diocesan signature has a meaning."

"I'm not so sure," returned Markham dubiously. "It appears utterly meaningless to me. But I'll follow your suggestion."

Neither the professor nor Miss Dillard, however, could recall any personal association with the word *Bishop;* and the professor was inclined to agree with Markham that the note was without any significant bearing on the case.

"It strikes me," he said, "as a piece of juvenile melodrama. It isn't likely that the person who killed Robin would adopt a vague pseudonym and write notes about his crime. I'm not acquainted with criminals, but such conduct doesn't impress me as logical."

"But the crime itself was illogical," ventured Vance pleasantly.

"One can't speak of a thing being illogical, sir," returned the professor tartly, "when one is ignorant of the very premises of a syllogism."

"Exactly." Vance's tone was studiously courteous. "Therefore, the note itself may not be without logic."

Markham tactfully changed the subject.

"What I came particularly to tell you, professor, is that Mr. Sperling called a short time ago and, when informed of Mr. Robin's death, confessed to having done it himself. . . ."

"Raymond confessed!" gasped Miss Dillard.

Markham looked at the girl sympathetically.

"To be quite frank, I didn't believe Mr. Sperling. Some mistaken idea of chivalry undoubtedly led him to admit the crime."

" 'Chivalry'?" she repeated, leaning forward tensely. "What exactly do you mean by that, Mr. Markham?"

It was Vance who answered.

"The bow that was found on the range was a woman's bow."

"Oh!" The girl covered her face with her hands, and her body shook with sobs.

Professor Dillard regarded her helplessly; and his impotency took the form of irritation.

"What flummery is this, Markham?" he demanded. "Any archer can shoot with a woman's bow. . . . That unutterable young idiot! Why should he make Belle miserable by his preposterous confession! . . . Markham, my friend, do what you can for the boy."

Markham gave his assurances, and we rose to go.

"By the by, Professor Dillard," said Vance, pausing at the door; "I trust you won't misunderstand me, but there's a bare possibility that it was some one with access to this house who indulged in the practical joke of typing that note. Is there, by any chance, a typewriter on the premises?"

It was patent that the professor resented Vance's question, but he answered civilly enough.

"No, – nor has there ever been one to my knowledge. I threw my own machine away ten years ago when I left the university. An agency does whatever typing I need."

"And Mr. Arnesson?"

"He never uses a typewriter."

As we descended the stairs we met Arnesson returning from Drukker's.

"I've placated our local Leipnitz," he announced, with an exaggerated sigh. "Poor old Adolph! The world is too much with him. When he's wallowing in the relativist formulas of Lorentz and Einstein he's serene. But when he's dragged down to actuality he disintegrates."

"It may interest you to know," said Vance casually, "that Sperling has just confessed to the murder."

"Ha!" Arnesson chuckled. "Quite in keeping. 'I,' said the Sparrow. . . . Very neat. Still, I don't know how it'll work out mathematically."

"And since we agreed to keep you posted," continued Vance, "it may help your calculations to know that we have reason to believe that Robin was killed in the archery-room and placed on the range afterwards."

"Glad to know it." Arnesson became momentarily serious. "Yes, that may affect my problem." He walked with us to the front door. "If there's any way I can be of service to you, call on me."

Vance had paused to light a cigarette, but I knew, by the languid look in his eyes, that he was making a decision. Slowly he turned to Arnesson.

"Do you know if Mr. Drukker or Mr. Pardee has a typewriter?"

Arnesson gave a slight start, and his eyes twinkled shrewdly.

"Aha! That Bishop note. . . . I see. Merely a matter of being thorough. Quite right." He nodded with satisfaction. "Yes; both have typewriters. Drukker types incessantly – thinks to the keyboard, so he says. And Pardee's chess correspondence is as voluminous as a movie hero's. Types it all himself, too."

"Would it be any great trouble to you," asked Vance, "to secure a specimen of the typing of each machine, and also a sample of the paper these two gentlemen use?"

"None whatever." Arnesson appeared delighted with the commission. "Have them for you this afternoon. Where'll you be?"

"Mr. Markham will be at the Stuyvesant Club. You might phone him there, and he can arrange –"

"Why bother to arrange anything? I'll bring my findings to Mr. Markham personally. Only too glad. Fascinating game, being a sleuth."

Vance and I returned home in the District Attorney's car, and Markham continued to the office. At seven o'clock that night the three of us met at the Stuyvesant Club for dinner; and at half past eight we were sitting in Markham's favorite corner of the lounge-room smoking and having our coffee.

During the meal no mention of the case had been made. The late editions of the afternoon papers had carried brief accounts of Robin's death. Heath had evidently succeeded in curbing the reporters' curiosity and clipping the wings of their imagination. The District Attorney's office being closed, the newspaper men were unable to bombard Markham with questions, and so the late press was inadequately supplied with information. The Sergeant had guarded the Dillard house well, for the reporters had not succeeded in reaching any member of the household.

Markham had picked up a late *Sun* on his way from the dining-room, and glanced through it carefully as he sipped his coffee.

"This is the first faint echo," he commented ruefully. "I shudder to think what the morning papers will contain."

"There's nothing to do but bear it," smiled Vance unfeelingly. "The moment some bright journalistic lad awakes to the robin-sparrow-arrow combination the city editors will go mad with joy, and every front page in the country will look like a Mother-Goose hoarding."

Markham lapsed into despondency. Finally he struck the arm of his chair angrily with his fist.

"Damn it, Vance! I won't let you inflame my imagination with this idiocy about nursery rhymes." Then he added, with the ferocity of uncertainty: "It's a sheer coincidence, I tell you. There simply couldn't be anything in it."

Vance sighed. "Convince yourself against your will; you're of the same opinion still – to paraphrase Butler." He reached into his pocket and took out a sheet of paper. "Putting all juvenilia to one side *pro tempore*, here's an edifyin' chronology I drew up before dinner. . . . Edifyin'? Well, it might be if we knew how to interpret it."

Markham studied the paper for several minutes. What Vance had written down was this:

9.00 a.m. Arnesson left house to go to university library.

9.15 a.m. Belle Dillard left house for the tennis courts.

9.30 a.m. Drukker called at house to see Arnesson.

9.50 a.m. Drukker went down-stairs to archery-room.

10.00 a.m. Robin and Sperling called at house and remained in drawing-room for half an hour.

10.30 a.m. Robin and Sperling went down to archery-room.

10.32 a.m. Drukker says he went out for a walk, by the wall gate.

10.35 a.m. Beedle went marketing.

10.55 a.m. Drukker says he returned to his own house.

11.15 a.m. Sperling went away by wall gate.

11.30 a.m. Drukker says he heard a scream in his mother's room.

11.35 a.m. Professor Dillard went on balcony of Arnesson's room.

11.40 a.m. Professor Dillard saw Robin's body on archery range.

11.45 a.m. Professor Dillard telephoned to District Attorney's office.

12.25 p.m. Belle Dillard returned from tennis.

12.30 p.m. Police arrived at Dillard house.

12.35 p.m. Beedle returned from market.

2.00 p.m. Arnesson returned from university.

Ergo: Robin was killed at some time between 11.15 (when Sperling departed) and 11.40 (when Professor Dillard discovered body).

The only other persons known to have been in the house during this time were Pyne and Professor Dillard.

The disposition of all other persons connected in any way with the murder was as follows (according to statements and evidence now in hand):

1. Arnesson was at the university library between 9 a.m. and 2 p.m.
2. Belle Dillard was at the tennis courts between 9.15 a.m. and 12.25 p.m.
3. Drukker was walking in the park between 10.32 a.m. and 10.55 a.m.; and was in his study from 10.55 a.m. on.
4. Pardee was in his house the entire morning.
5. Mrs. Drukker was in her room the entire morning.

6. Beedle was marketing between 10.35 a.m. and 12.35 p.m.

7. Sperling was on his way to the Grand Central Station between 11.15 a.m. and 11.40 a.m., at which hour he took a train for Scarsdale.

Conclusion: Unless at least one of these seven alibis is shaken, the whole weight of suspicion, and indeed the actual culpability, must rest upon either Pyne or Professor Dillard.

When Markham finished reading the paper, he made a gesture of exasperation.

"Your entire implication is preposterous," he said irritably; "and your conclusion is a *non-sequitur.* The chronology helps set the time of Robin's death, but your assumption that one of the persons we've seen to-day is necessarily guilty is arrant nonsense. You completely ignore the possibility that any outsider could have committed the crime. There were three ways of reaching the range and the archery-room without entering the house – the wall gate on 75th Street, the other wall gate on 76th Street, and the alleyway between the two apartment houses, leading to Riverside Drive."

"Oh, it's highly probable that one of these

three entrances was used," returned Vance. "But don't overlook the fact that the most secluded, and therefore the most likely, of these three means of entry – to wit, the alleyway – is guarded by a locked door to which no one would be apt to have a key except some member of the Dillard household. I can't picture a murderer walking into the range from either of the street gates: he would be taking too many chances of being seen."

Vance leaned forward seriously.

"And, Markham, there are other reasons why we may eliminate strangers or casual prowlers. The person who sent Robin to his Maker must have been privy to the exact state of affairs in the Dillard house this morning between a quarter past eleven and twenty minutes to twelve. He knew that Pyne and the old professor were alone there. He knew that Belle Dillard was not roaming about the premises. He knew that Belle was away and could neither hear him nor surprise him. He knew that Robin – his victim – was there, and that Sperling had departed. Moreover, he knew something of the lie of the land – the situation of the archery-room, for instance; for it's only too plain that Robin was killed in that room. No one who wasn't familiar with all these details would have dared enter the grounds and staged a spectacular murder. I tell you, Markham, it was some one very close to the Dillard ménage – some one who was able to find out just what conditions obtained in that household this morning."

"What about that scream of Mrs. Drukker's?"

"Ah, what about it, indeed? Mrs. Drukker's window may have been a factor that the murderer overlooked. Or perhaps he knew about it and decided to take that one chance of being seen. On the other hand, we don't know whether the lady screamed or not. She says No; Drukker says Yes. They both have an ulterior motive for what they poured into our trustin' ears. Drukker may have told of the scream by way of proving he was at home between eleven and twelve; and Mrs. Drukker may have denied it for fear he wasn't home. It's very much of an *olla podrida.* But it doesn't matter. The main point I'm trying to make is that only an intimate of the Dillard house could have done this devilish business."

"We have too few facts to warrant that conclusion," asserted Markham. "Chance may have played a part –"

"Oh, I say, old man! Chance may work out to a few permutations, but not to twenty. – And there is that note left in the mail-box. The murderer even knew Robin's middle name."

"Assuming, of course, that the murderer wrote the note."

"Do you prefer to assume that some balmy joker found out about the crime through telepathy or crystal-gazing, hied to a typewriter, composed a dithyramb, returned hot-footed to the house, and, for no good reason, took the terrific risk of being seen putting the paper in the mail-box?"

Before Markham could answer Heath entered the lounge room and hurried to our corner. That he was worried and uneasy was obvious. With scarcely a word of greeting he handed a typewritten envelope to Markham.

"That was received by the *World* in the late afternoon mail. Quinan, the police reporter of the *World*, brought it to me a little while ago; and he says that the *Times* and the *Herald* also got copies of it. The letters were stamped at one o'clock to-day, so they were probably posted between eleven and twelve. What's more, Mr. Markham, they were mailed in the neighborhood of the Dillard house, for they went through Post Office Station 'N' on West 69th Street."

Markham withdrew the enclosure from the envelope. Suddenly his eyes opened wide, and the muscles about his mouth tightened. Without looking up he handed the letter to Vance. It consisted of a single sheet of typewriting paper, and the words printed on it were identical to those on the note left in the Dillard mail-box. Indeed, the communication was an exact duplicate of the other: – "Joseph Cochrane Robin is dead. Who Killed Cock Robin? Sperling means sparrow. – THE BISHOP."

Vance scarcely glanced at the paper.

"Quite in keeping, don't y' know," he said indifferently. "The Bishop was afraid the public might miss the point of his joke; so he explained it to the press."

"Joke, did you say, Mr. Vance?" asked Heath bitterly. "It ain't the kind of joke I'm used to. This case gets crazier –"

"Exactly, Sergeant. A crazy joke."

A uniformed boy stepped up to the District Attorney and, bending over his shoulder discreetly, whispered something.

"Bring him here right away," ordered Markham. Then to us: "It's Arnesson. He'll probably have those specimens of typing." A shadow had settled on his face; and he glanced again at the note Heath had brought him. "Vance," he said in a low voice, "I'm beginning to believe that this case may turn out to be as terrible as you think. I wonder if the typing will correspond. . . ."

But when the note was compared with the specimens Arnesson brought, no similarity whatever could be discerned. Not only were the typing and the ink different from those of either Pardee's or Drukker's machine, but the paper did not match any one of the samples that Arnesson had secured.

CHAPTER VIII

ACT TWO

(Monday, April 11; 11.30 a.m.)

There is no need to recall here the nation-wide sensation caused by Robin's murder. Every one remembers how that startling tragedy was featured in the country's press. It was referred to by various designations. Some newspapers called it the Cock Robin murder. Others, more alliterative but less accurate,* termed it the Mother Goose murder. But the signature of the typewritten notes appealed strongly to the journalists sense of mystery; and in time the killing of Robin came to be known as the Bishop murder case. Its strange and fearful combination of horror and nursery jargon inflamed the public's imagination; and the sinister and

*The old anonymous nursery rhyme, "The Death and Burial of Cock Robin," is not, as is commonly supposed, one of the original "Mother Goose Melodies," although it has often been included in modern editions of that famous work.

insane implications of its details affected the entire country like some grotesque nightmare whose atmosphere could not be shaken off.

During the week following the discovery of Robin's body, the detectives of the Homicide Bureau, as well as the detectives connected with the District Attorney's office, were busy night and day pushing their inquiries. The receipt of the duplicate Bishop notes by the leading New York morning papers had dissipated whatever ideas Heath may have held as to Sperling's guilt; and though he refused to put his official imprimatur on the young man's innocence he threw himself, with his usual gusto and pertinacity into the task of finding another and more plausible culprit. The investigation which he organized and superintended was as complete as had been that of the Greene murder case. No avenue which held the meagrest hope of results was overlooked; and the report he drew up would have given joy even to those meticulous criminologists of the University of Lausanne.

On the afternoon of the day of the murder he and his men had searched for the cloth that had been used to wipe up the blood in the archery-room; but no trace of it was found. Also, a thorough examination of the Dillard basement was made in the hope of finding other clews;

but although Heath had put the task in the hands of experts, the result was negative. The only point brought to light was that the fibre rug near the door had recently been moved so as to cover the cleansed spot on the cement floor. This fact, however, merely substantiated the Sergeant's earlier observation.

The *post-mortem* report of Doctor Doremus lent color to the now officially accepted theory that Robin had been killed in the archery-room and then placed on the range. The autopsy showed that the blow on the back of his skull had been a particularly violent one and had been made with a heavy rounded instrument, resulting in a depressed fracture quite different from the fissured fracture caused by striking a flat surface. A search was instituted for the weapon with which the blow had been dealt; but no likely instrument was turned up.

Though Beedle and Pyne were questioned by Heath several times, nothing new was learned from them. Pyne insisted that he had been up-stairs the entire morning in Arnesson's room, except for a few brief absences to the linen-closet and the front door, and clung tenaciously to his denial that he had touched either the body or the bow when sent by Professor Dillard to find Sperling. The Sergeant, however, was not entirely satisfied with the man's testimony.

"That bleary-eyed old cormorant has got something up his sleeve," he told Markham disgustedly. "But it would take the rubber hose and the water cure to make him spill it."

A canvass of all the houses in 75th Street between West End Avenue and Riverside Drive was made in the hope of finding a tenant who had noticed some one entering or emerging from the Dillard wall gate during the forenoon. But nothing was gained by this tedious campaign. Pardee, it seemed, was the only resident within view of the Dillard house who had observed any one in the neighborhood that morning. In fact, after several days of arduous inquiries along this line the Sergeant realized that he would have to proceed without any outside or fortuitous assistance.

The various alibis of the seven persons whom Vance had tabulated in his notation for Markham, were gone into as thoroughly as circumstances would permit. It was obviously impossible to check them completely, for, in the main, they were based solely on the statements of the individuals involved. Moreover the investigation had to be made with the utmost care lest suspicion be aroused. The results of these inquiries were as follows:

1. Arnesson had been seen in the university library by various people, including an assistant librarian and two students. But the time covered by their evidence was neither consecutive nor specific as to the hour.

2. Belle Dillard had played several sets of tennis at the public courts at 119th Street and Riverside Drive, but because there had been more than four in her party she had twice relinquished her place to a friend; and none of the players could state positively that she had remained at the courts during these periods.

3. The time that Drukker departed from the archery-room was definitely determined by Sperling; but no one could be found who had seen him thereafter. He admitted he had met no one he knew in the park, but insisted he had stopped for a few minutes to play with some strange children.

4. Pardee had been alone in his study. His old cook and his Japanese valet had been in the rear of the house, and had not seen him until lunch time. His alibi therefore was purely a negative one.

5. Mrs. Drukker's word had to be accepted as to her whereabouts that morning, for no one had seen her between nine-thirty, when Drukker went to call on Arnesson, and

one o'clock, when the cook brought up her luncheon.

6. Beedle's alibi was checked with fairly satisfactory completeness. Pardee had seen her leave the house at 10.35; and she was remembered by several of the hucksters at the Jefferson Market between eleven and twelve.

7. The fact that Sperling had taken the 11.40 train to Scarsdale was verified; therefore he would have had to leave the Dillard house at the time he stated – namely: 11.15. The determination of this point, however, was merely a matter of routine, for he had been practically eliminated from the case. But if, as Heath explained, it had been found that he had not taken the 11.40 train, he would have again become an important possibility.

Pursuing his investigations along more general lines, the Sergeant went into the histories and associations of the various persons involved. The task was not a difficult one. All were well known, and information concerning them was readily accessible; but not one item was unearthed that could be regarded as even remotely throwing any light on Robin's murder. Nothing transpired to give so much as a hint to the motive for the crime; and after a week's intensive inquiry and speculation the case was still cloaked in seemingly impenetrable mystery.

Sperling had not been released. The *prima facie* evidence against him, combined with his absurd confession, made impossible such a step on the part of the authorities. Markham, however, had held an unofficial conference with the attorneys whom Sperling's father had engaged to handle the case, and some sort of a "gentleman's agreement" had, I imagine, been reached; for although the State made no move to apply for an indictment (despite the fact that the Grand Jury was sitting at the time), the defense lawyers did not institute *habeas corpus* proceedings. All the indications pointed to the supposition that both Markham and Sperling's attorneys were waiting for the real culprit to be apprehended.

Markham had had several interviews with the members of the Dillard household, in a persistent effort to bring out some trivial point that might lead to a fruitful line of inquiry; and Pardee had been summoned to the District Attorney's office to make an affidavit as to what he had observed from his window on the morning of the tragedy. Mrs. Drukker had been interrogated again; but not only did she emphatically deny having looked out of her window that morning, but she scoffed at the idea that she had screamed.

Drukker, when re-questioned, modified somewhat his former testimony. He explained that he might have been mistaken as to the source of the scream, and suggested that it could have come from the street or from one of the court windows of the apartment house. In fact, he said, it was highly unlikely that his mother had uttered the scream, for when he went to her door a moment later she was humming an old German nursery song from Humperdinck's "Hänsel und Gretel." Markham, convinced that nothing further was to be learned from either him or Mrs. Drukker, finally concentrated on the Dillard house itself.

Arnesson attended the informal conferences held in Markham's office; but for all his voluble and cynical observations, he appeared to be as much at sea as the rest of us. Vance chaffed him good-naturedly about the mathematical formula that was to solve the case, but Arnesson insisted that a formula could not be worked out until all the factors of the theorem were available. He appeared to regard the entire affair as a kind of Juvenalian lark; and Markham on several occasions gave vent to his exasperation. He reproached Vance for having made Arnesson an unofficial confrère in the investigation, but Vance defended himself on the ground that sooner or later Arnesson would supply some piece of seemingly irrelevant information that could be used as an advantageous *point de départ*.

"His crimino-mathematical theory is of course rubbish," said Vance. "Psychology – not abstract science – will eventually reduce this conundrum to its elements. But we need material to go on, and Arnesson knows the inwardness of the Dillard home better than we can ever know it. He knows the Drukkers, and he knows Pardee; and it goes without saying that a man who has had the academic honors heaped on him that he has, possesses an unusually keen mind. As long as he gives his thought and attention to the case, there's the chance that he'll hit upon something of vital importance to us."

"You may be right," grumbled Markham. "But the man's derisive attitude gets on my nerves."

"Be more catholic," urged Vance. "Consider his ironies in relation to his scientific speculations. What could be more natural than that a man who projects his mind constantly into the vast interplanet'ry reaches, and deals with light-years and infinities and hyperphysical dimensions, should sniff derisively at the infinitesimals of this life? . . . Stout fella, Arnesson. Not homey and comfortable perhaps, but dashed interestin'."

Vance himself had taken the case with unwonted seriousness. His Menander translations had been definitely put aside. He became moody and waspish – a sure sign that his mind was busy with an absorbing problem. After dinner each night he went into his library and read for hours – not the classic and æsthetic volumes on which he generally spent his time, but such books as Bernard Hart's "The Psychology of Insanity," Freud's "Der Witz und seine Beziehung zum Unbewussten," Coriat's "Abnormal Psychology" and "Repressed Emotions," Lippo's "Komik und Humor," Daniel A. Heubsch's "The Murder Complex," Janet's "Les Obsessions et la Psychasthènie," Donath's "Über Arithmomanie," Riklin's "Wish Fulfillment and Fairy Tales," Leppman's "Die forensische Bedeutung der Zwangsvorstellungen," Kuno Fischer's "Über den Witz," Erich Wulffen's "Kriminalpsychologie," Hollenden's "The Insanity of Genius," and Groos's "Die Spiele des Menschen."

He spent hours going over the police reports. He called twice at the Dillards', and on one occasion visited Mrs. Drukker in company with Belle Dillard. He had a long discussion one night with Drukker and Arnesson on de Sitter's conception of physical space as a Lobatchewskian pseudosphere, his object being, I surmised, to acquaint himself with Drukker's mentality. He read Drukker's book, "World Lines in Multidimensional Continua"; and spent nearly an entire day studying Janowski's and Tarrasch's analyses of the Pardee gambit.

On Sunday – eight days after the murder of Robin – he said to me:

"*Eheu,* Van! This problem is unbelievedly subtle. No ordin'ry investigation will ever probe it. It lies in a strange territ'ry of the brain; and its superficial childishness is its most terrible and bafflin' aspect. Nor is the perpetrator going to be content with a single coup. Cock Robin's death serves no definitive end. The perverted imagination that concocted this beastly crime is insatiable; and unless we can expose the abnormal psychological mechanism back of it there will be more grim jokes to contend with. . . ."

The very next morning his prognostication was verified. We went to Markham's office at eleven o'clock to hear Heath's report and to discuss further lines of action. Though nine days had passed since Robin had been found murdered, no progress had been made in the case, and the newspapers had grown bitter in their criticisms of the police and the District Attorney's office. It was therefore with considerable depression that Markham greeted us that Monday morning. Heath had not yet arrived; but when he came a few minutes later it was obvious that he, too, was discouraged.

"We run up against a brick wall, sir, every way we turn," he repined, when he had outlined the results of his men's activities. "There ain't a sign of a motive, and outside of Sperling there's nobody on the landscape that we can hang anything on. I'm coming to the conclusion that it was some stick-up man who ambled into the archery-room that morning and messed things up."

" 'Stick-up' men, Sergeant," countered Vance, "are deuced unimaginative, and they're without a sense of humor; whereas the johnny who sent Robin on the long, long trail had both imagination and humor. He wasn't content merely to kill Robin: he had to turn the act into an insane joke. Then, lest the public wouldn't see the point, he wrote explanat'ry letters to the press. – Does that sound like the procedure of an itinerant thug?"

Heath smoked unhappily for several minutes without speaking, and at length turned a gaze of exasperated dismay upon Markham.

"There's no sense in anything that's breaking round this town lately," he complained. "Just this morning a guy named Sprigg was shot in Riverside Park, up near 84th Street. Money in his pocket – nothing taken. Just shot. Young fella – student at Columbia. Lived with his parents; no enemies. Went out to take his usual walk before going to class. Found dead half an hour later by a bricklayer." The Sergeant chewed viciously on his cigar. "Now we got that homicide to worry about; and we'll probably get hell from the newspapers if we don't clear it up *pronto.* And there's nothing – absolutely nothing – to go on."

"Still, Sergeant," said Vance consolingly, "shooting a man is an ordin'ry event. There are numerous commonplace reasons for that sort of crime. It's the scenic and dramatic appurtenances of Robin's murder that play havoc with all our processes of deduction. If only it wasn't a nursery affair –"

Suddenly he stopped speaking, and his eyelids drooped slightly. Leaning forward he very deliberately crushed out his cigarette.

"Did you say, Sergeant, that this chap's name was Sprigg?"

Heath nodded gloomily.

"And I say," – despite Vance's effort, there

was a note of eagerness in his tone – "what was his first name?"

Heath gave Vance a look of puzzled surprise; but after a brief pause he drew forth his battered notebook and riffled the pages.

"John Sprigg," he answered. "John E. Sprigg."

Vance took out another cigarette, and lighted it with great care.

"And tell me: was he shot with a .32?"

"Huh?" Heath's eyes rounded, and his chin shot forward. "Yes, a .32. . . ."

"And was he shot through the top of his head?"

The Sergeant sprang to his feet, and stared at Vance with ludicrous bewilderment. Slowly his head moved up and down.

"That's right. – But how in hell, sir –?"

Vance held up a silencing hand. It was, however, the look on his face, rather than his gesture, that cut short the query.

"Oh, my precious aunt!" He rose like a man in a daze and gazed fixedly before him. Had I not known him so well I would have sworn he was frightened. Then going to the tall window behind Markham's desk he stood looking down on the gray stone walls of the Tombs.

"I can't credit it," he murmured. "It's too ghastly. . . . But of course it's so! . . ."

Markham's impatient voice sounded.

"What's all the mumbling about, Vance? Don't be so damned mysterious! How did you happen to know that Sprigg was shot through the crown with a .32? And what's the point, anyway?"

Vance turned and met Markham's eyes.

"Don't you see?" he asked softly. "It's the second act of this devilish parody! . . . Have you forgotten your 'Mother-Goose'?" And in a hushed voice that brought a sense of unutterable horror into that dingy old office he recited:

" 'There was a little man,
  And he had a little gun,
And his bullets were made of lead, lead, lead;
  He shot Johnny Sprig
  Through the middle of his wig,
And knocked it right off of his head, head, head.' "

CHAPTER IX

THE TENSOR FORMULA

(Monday, April 11; 11.30 a.m.)

Markham sat staring at Vance like a man hypnotized. Heath stood rigid, his mouth partly open, his cigar held a few inches from his lips. There was something almost comic in the Sergeant's attitude, and I had a nervous inclination to laugh; but for the moment my blood seemed frozen, and all muscular movement was impossible.

Markham was the first to speak. Jerking his head backward, he brought his hand down violently on the desk-top.

"What new lunacy of yours is this?" He was fighting desperately against Vance's dumbfounding suggestion. "I'm beginning to think the Robin case has affected your mind. Can't a man with the commonplace name of Sprigg be shot without your trying to turn it into some grotesque hocus-pocus?"

"Still, you must admit, Markham old dear,"

returned Vance mildly, "this particular Johnny Sprigg was shot with 'a little gun', through 'the middle of his wig', so to speak."

"What if he was?" A dull flush had crept into Markham's face. "Is that any reason for your going about babbling Mother-Goose rhymes?"

"Oh, I say! I never babble, don't y' know." Vance had dropped into a chair facing the District Attorney's desk. "I may not be a thrillin' elocutionist; but really, now, I don't babble." He gave Heath an ingratiating smile. "Do I, Sergeant?"

But Heath had no opinion to express. He still held his astonished pose, though his eyes had now become mere slits in his broad, pugnacious face.

"Are you seriously suggesting –?" began Markham; but Vance interrupted him.

"Yes! I'm seriously suggesting that the person who killed Cock Robin with an arrow has vented his grim humor upon the hapless Sprigg. Coincidence is out of the question. Such repetitive parallels would knock the entire foundation out from all sanity and reason. 'Pon my soul, the world is mad enough; but such madness would dissipate all science and rational thinking. Sprigg's death is rather hideous: but it must be faced. And however much you may force yourself to protest against its incredible implications you'll eventually have to accept them."

Markham had risen, and was pacing nervously up and down.

"I'll grant there are inexplicable elements in this new crime." His combativeness had gone, and his tone had moderated. "But if we assume, even tentatively, that some maniac is at large reconstructing the rhymes of his nursery days, I can't see how it will help us. It would practically close all routine lines of investigation."

"I shouldn't say that, don't y' know." Vance was smoking meditatively. "I'm inclined to think that such an assumption would supply us with a definite basis of inquiry."

"Sure!" snapped Heath with ponderous sarcasm. "All we gotta do is to go out and find one bug among six million people. A cinch!"

"Don't let the fumes of discouragement overcome you, Sergeant. Our elusive jester is a rather distinctive entomological specimen. Moreover, we have certain clews as to his exact habitat. . . ."

Markham swung round. "What do you mean by that?"

"Merely that this second crime is related to the first not only psychologically, but geographically. Both murders were committed within a few blocks of each other, – our destructive demon at least has a weakness for the neighborhood in which the Dillard house is situated. Furthermore, the very factors of the two murders preclude the possibility of his having come from afar to give rein to his distorted humor in unfamiliar surroundings. As I learnedly pointed out to you, Robin was translated into the Beyond by some one who knew all the conditions obtaining at the Dillard house at the exact hour the grisly drama was performed; and surely it's obvious that this second crime could not have been so tidily staged had not the impresario been acquainted with Sprigg's ambulat'ry intentions this morning. Indeed, the entire mechanism of these weird playlets proves that the operator was intimately cognizant of all the circumstances surrounding his victims."

The heavy silence that followed was broken by Heath.

"If you're right, Mr. Vance, then that lets Sperling out." The Sergeant made even this qualified admission reluctantly: but it showed that Vance's argument had not been without its effect on him. He turned desperately to the District Attorney. "What do you think we'd better do, sir?"

Markham was still battling against the

acceptance of Vance's theory, and he did not answer. Presently, however, he reseated himself at his desk and drummed with his fingers upon the blotter. Then, without looking up, he asked:

"Who's in charge of the Sprigg case, Sergeant?"

"Captain Pitts. The local men at the 68th-Street Station grabbed it first; but when the news was relayed to the Bureau, Pitts and a couple of our boys went up to look into it. Pitts got back just before I came over here. Says it's a washout. But Inspector Moran* told him to stay with it."

Markham pressed the buzzer beneath the edge of his desk, and Swacker, his youthful secretary, appeared at the swinging door that led to the clerical room between the District Attorney's private office and the main waiting-room.

"Get Inspector Moran on the wire," he ordered.

When the connection had been made he drew the telephone toward him and spoke for several minutes. When he had replaced the receiver, he gave Heath a weary smile.

*Inspector William M. Moran, who died two years ago, was, at the time of the Bishop case, the Commanding Officer of the Detective Bureau.

"You're now officially handling the Sprigg case, Sergeant. Captain Pitts will be here presently, and then we'll know where we stand." He began looking through a pile of papers before him. "I've got to be convinced," he added half-heartedly, "that Sprigg and Robin are tied up in the same sack."

Pitts, a short, stocky man, with a lean, hard face and a black tooth-brush moustache, arrived ten minutes later. He was, I learned afterwards, one of the most competent men in the Detective Division. His specialty was "white-collar" gangsters. He shook hands with Markham and gave Heath a companionable leer. When introduced to Vance and me he focussed suspicious eyes on us and bowed grudgingly. But as he was about to turn away his expression suddenly changed.

"Mr. Philo Vance, is it?" he asked.

"Alas! So it seems, Captain," Vance sighed.

Pitts grinned and, stepping forward, held out his hand.

"Glad to meet you, sir. Heard the Sergeant speak of you often."

"Mr. Vance is helping us unofficially with the Robin case, Captain," explained Markham; "and since this man Sprigg was killed in the same neighborhood we thought we'd like to hear your preliminary report on the affair." He took out a box of Corona *Perfectos*, and pushed it across the desk.

"You needn't put the request that way, sir." The Captain smiled, and selecting a cigar held it to his nose with a kind of voluptuous satisfaction. "The Inspector told me you had some ideas about this new case, and wanted to take it on. To tell you the truth, I'm glad to get rid of it." He sat down leisurely, and lighted his cigar. "What would you like to know, sir?"

"Let us have the whole story," said Markham.

Pitts settled himself comfortably.

"Well, I happened to be on hand when the case came through – a little after eight this morning – and I took a couple of the boys and beat it up-town. The local men were on the job, and an assistant Medical Examiner arrived the same time I did. . . ."

"Did you hear his report, Captain?" asked Vance.

"Sure. Sprigg was shot through the top of the head with a .32. No signs of a struggle – no bruises or anything. Nothing fancy. Just a straight shooting."

"Was he lying on his back when found?"

"That's right. Stretched out nice and pretty, right in the middle of the walk."

"And wasn't his skull fractured where he'd

fallen on the asphalt?" The question was put negligently.

Pitts took his cigar from his mouth and gave Vance a sly look.

"I guess maybe you fellows over here do know something about this case." He nodded his head sagaciously. "Yes, the back of the guy's skull was all bashed in. He sure had a tough fall. But I guess he didn't feel it – not with that bullet in his brain. . . ."

"Speaking of the shot, Captain, didn't anything about it strike you as peculiar?"

"Well . . . yes," Pitts admitted, rolling his cigar meditatively between his thumb and forefinger. "The top of a guy's head isn't where I'd ordinarily look for a bullet-hole. And his hat wasn't touched, – it must have fallen off before he was potted. You might call those facts peculiar, Mr. Vance."

"Yes, Captain, they're dashed peculiar. . . . And I take it the pistol was held at close range."

"Not more'n a couple of inches away. The hair was singed round the hole." He made a broad gesture of inconsequence. "Still and all, the guy might have seen the other fellow draw the gun, and ducked forward, spilling his hat. That would account for his getting the shot at close range in the top of the head."

"Quite, quite. Except that, in that case, he wouldn't have fallen over back, but would have pitched forward on his face. . . . But go on with the story, Captain."

Pitts gave Vance a look of crafty agreement, and continued.

"The first thing I did was to go through the fellow's pockets. He had a good gold watch on him and about fifteen dollars in bills and silver. So it didn't look like a robbery – unless the guy that shot him got panicky and beat it. But that didn't seem likely, for there's never any one round that part of the park early in the morning; and the walk there dips under a stone bluff, so that the view is cut off. The bird that did the job certainly picked a swell place for it. . . . Anyhow, I left a couple of men to guard the body till the wagon came for it, and went up to Sprigg's house in 93rd Street, – I'd got his name and address from a couple of letters in his pocket. I found out he was a student at Columbia, living with his parents, and that it was his habit to take a walk in the park after breakfast. He left home this morning about half past seven. . . ."

"Ah! It was his habit to promenade in the park each morning," murmured Vance. "Most interestin'."

"Even so, that don't get us anywheres,"

returned Pitts. "Plenty of fellows take an early constitutional. And there was nothing unusual about Sprigg this morning. He wasn't worried about anything, his folks told me; and was cheerful enough when he said good-bye to 'em. – After that I hopped up to the university and made inquiries; talked to a couple of the students that knew him, and also to one of the instructors. Sprigg was a quiet sort of chap. Didn't make friends and kept pretty much to himself. Serious bird – always working at his studies. Stood high in his classes, and was never seen going around with Janes. Didn't like women, in fact. Wasn't what you'd call sociable. From all reports he was the last man to get in a mess of any kind. That's why I can't see anything special in his getting shot. It must have been an accident of some kind. Might have been taken for somebody else."

"And he was found at what time?"

"About quarter to eight. A bricklayer on the new 79th-Street dock was cutting across the embankment toward the railway tracks, and saw him. He notified one of the post officers on the Drive, who phoned in to the local station."

"And Sprigg left his home in 93rd Street at half past seven." Vance gazed at the ceiling meditatively. "Therefore he would have had just enough time to reach this point in the park before being killed. It looks as if some one who knew his habits was waiting for him. Neatness and dispatch, what? . . . It doesn't appear exactly fortuitous, does it, Markham?"

Ignoring the jibe Markham addressed Pitts.

"Was there nothing found that could possibly be used as a lead?"

"No, sir. My men combed the spot pretty thoroughly, but nothing showed up."

"And in Sprigg's pockets – among his papers. . . ?"

"Not a thing. I've got all the stuff at the Bureau – a couple of ordinary letters, a few odds and ends of the usual kind. . . ." He paused as if suddenly remembering something, and pulled out a dog-eared note-book. "There was this," he said unenthusiastically, handing a torn, triangular scrap of paper to Markham. "It was found under the fellow's body. It don't mean anything, but I stuck it in my pocket – force of habit."

$$\text{Bikst} = \frac{\lambda}{3}\ (\text{gik gst} - \text{gis gkt})$$

$$\text{Bikst} = 0\ (\text{flat at } \infty)$$

The paper was not more than four inches long, and appeared to have been torn from the corner of an ordinary sheet of unruled stationery. It contained part of a typewritten mathematical formula, with the lambda, the equals and the infinity sign marked in with pencil. I reproduce the paper here, for despite its seeming irrelevancy, it was to play a sinister and amazing part in the investigation of Sprigg's death.

Vance glanced only casually at the exhibit, but Markham held it in his hand frowning at it for several moments. He was about to make some comment when he caught Vance's eye; and, instead, he tossed the paper to the desk carelessly with a slight shrug.

"Is this everything you found?"

"That's all, sir."

Markham rose.

"We're very grateful to you, Captain. I don't know what we'll be able to make out of this Sprigg case, but we'll look into it." He pointed to the box of *Perfectos*. "Put a couple in your pocket before you go."

"Much obliged, sir." Pitts selected the cigars, and placing them tenderly in his waistcoat pocket, shook hands with all of us.

When he had gone Vance got up with

alacrity, and bent over the scrap of paper on Markham's desk.

"My word!" He took out his monocle and studied the symbols for several moments. "Most allurin'. Now where have I seen that formula recently? . . . Ah! The Riemann-Christoffel tensor – of course! Drukker uses it in his book for determining the Gaussian curvature of spherical and homaloidal space. . . . But what was Sprigg doing with it? The formula is considerably beyond the college curricula. . . ." He held the paper up to the light. "It's the same stock as that on which the Bishop notes are written. And you probably observed that the typing is also similar."

Heath had stepped forward, and now scrutinized the paper.

"It's the same, all right." The fact seemed to nonplus him. "That's a link anyway between the two crimes."

Vance's eyes took on a puzzled look.

"A link – yes. But the presence of the formula under Sprigg's body appears as irrational as the murder itself. . . ."

Markham moved uneasily.

"You say it is a formula that Drukker uses in his book?"

"Yes. But the fact doesn't necessarily involve him. The tensor is known to all advanced mathematicians. It is one of the technical expressions used in non-Euclidean geometry; and though it was discovered by Riemann in connection with a concrete problem in physics,* it has now become of widespread importance in the mathematics of relativity. It's highly scientific in the abstract sense, and can have no direct bearing on Sprigg's murder." He sat down again. "Arnesson will be delighted with the find. He may be able to work out some astonishing conclusion from it."

"I see no reason," protested Markham, "to inform Arnesson of this new case. My idea would be to keep it under cover as much as possible."

"The Bishop won't let you, I fear," returned Vance.

Markham set his jaw.

"Good God!" he burst out. "What damnable sort of thing are we facing? I expect every minute to wake up and discover I've been living a nightmare."

"No such luck, sir," growled Heath. He took a resolute breath like a man preparing for combat. "What's on the cards? Where do we go

*This expression was actually developed by Christoffel for a problem on the conductivity of heat, and published by him in 1869 in the "Crelle Journal für reine und angewandte Mathematik."

from here? I need action."

Markham appealed to Vance.

"You seem to have some idea about this affair. What's your suggestion? I frankly admit I'm floundering about in a black chaos."

Vance inhaled deeply on his cigarette. Then he leaned forward as if to give emphasis to his words.

"Markham old man, there's only one conclusion to be drawn. These two murders were engineered by the same brain; both sprang from the same grotesque impulse; and since the first of them was committed by some one intimately familiar with conditions inside the Dillard house, it follows that we must now look for a person who, in addition to that knowledge, had definite information that a man named John Sprigg was in the habit of taking a walk each morning in a certain part of the Riverside Park. Having found such a person, we must check up on the points of time, place, opportunity, and possible motive. There's some interrelation between Sprigg and the Dillards. What it is I don't know. But our first move should be to find out. What better starting-point than the Dillard house itself?"

"We'll get some lunch first," said Markham wearily. "Then we'll run out there."

CHAPTER X

A REFUSAL OF AID

(Monday, April 11; 2 p.m.)

It was shortly after two o'clock when we reached the Dillard house. Pyne answered our ring; and if our visit caused him any surprise he succeeded admirably in hiding it. In the look he gave Heath, however, I detected a certain uneasiness; but when he spoke his voice had the flat, unctuous quality of the well-trained servant.

"Mr. Arnesson has not returned from the university," he informed us.

"Mind-reading, I see," said Vance, "is not your *forte*, Pyne. We called to see you and Professor Dillard."

The man looked ill at ease; but before he could answer Miss Dillard appeared in the archway of the drawing-room.

"I thought I recognized your voice, Mr. Vance." She included us all in a smile of wistful welcome. "Please come in. . . . Lady

Mae dropped in for a few minutes, – we're going riding together this afternoon," she explained, as we entered the room.

Mrs. Drukker stood by the centre-table, one bony hand on the back of the chair from which she had evidently just risen. There was fear in her eyes as she stared at us unblinkingly; and her lean features seemed almost contorted. She made no effort to speak, but stood rigidly as if waiting for some dread pronouncement, like a convicted prisoner at the bar about to receive sentence.

Belle Dillard's pleasant voice relieved the tensity of the situation.

"I'll run up and tell uncle you're here."

She had no sooner quitted the room than Mrs. Drukker leaned over the table and said to Markham in a sepulchral, awe-stricken whisper: "I know why you've come! It's about that fine young man who was shot in the park this morning."

So amazing and unexpected were her words that Markham could make no immediate answer; and it was Vance who replied.

"You have heard of the tragedy, then, Mrs. Drukker? How could the news have come to you so soon?"

A look of canniness came into the woman's expression, giving her the appearance of an evil old witch.

"Every one is talking about it in the neighborhood," she answered evasively.

"Indeed? That's most unfortunate. But why do you assume we have come here to make inquiries about it?"

"Wasn't the young man's name Johnny Sprigg?" A faint, terrible smile accompanied the question.

"So it was. John E. Sprigg. Still, that does not explain his connection with the Dillards."

"Ah, but it does!" Her head moved up and down with a sort of horrible satisfaction. "It's a game – a child's game. First Cock Robin . . . then Johnny Sprigg. Children must play – all healthy children must play." Her mood suddenly changed. A softness shone on her face, and her eyes grew sad.

"It's a rather diabolical game, don't you think, Mrs. Drukker?"

"And why not? Isn't life itself diabolical?"

"For some of us – yes." A curious sympathy informed Vance's words as he gazed at this strange tragic creature before us. "Tell me," he went on quickly, in an altered tone; "do you know who the Bishop is?"

"The Bishop?" She frowned perplexedly. "No, I don't know him. Is that another child's game?"

"Something of that kind, I imagine. At any rate, the Bishop is interested in Cock Robin and Johnny Sprigg. In fact, he may be the person who is making up these fantastic games. And we're looking for him, Mrs. Drukker. We hope to learn the truth from him."

The woman shook her head vaguely. "I don't know him." Then she glared vindictively at Markham. "But it's not going to do you any good to try to find out who killed Cock Robin and shot Johnny Sprigg through the middle of his wig. You'll never learn – never – *never*. . . ." Her voice had risen excitedly, and a fit of trembling seized her.

At this moment Belle Dillard re-entered the room, and going quickly to Mrs. Drukker put her arm about her.

"Come," she said soothingly; "we'll have a long drive in the country, Lady Mae." Reproachfully she turned to Markham, and said coldly: "Uncle wishes you to come to the library." With that she led Mrs. Drukker from the room and down the hall.

"Now that's a queer one, sir," commented Heath, who had stood looking on with bewildered amazement. "She had the dope on this Johnny-Sprigg stuff all the time!"

Vance nodded.

"And our appearance here frightened her.

Still, her mind is morbid and sensitive, Sergeant; and dwelling as she does constantly on her son's deformity and the early days when he was like other children, it's quite possible she merely hit accidentally upon the Mother-Goose significance of Robin's and Sprigg's death. . . . I wonder." He looked toward Markham. "There are strange undercurrents in this case – incredible and terrifying implications. It's like being lost in the Dovrë-Troll caverns of Ibsen's 'Peer Gynt,' where only monstrosities and abnormalities exist." He shrugged his shoulders, though I knew he had not wholly escaped the pall of horror cast on us by Mrs. Drukker's words. "Perhaps we can find a little solid footing with Professor Dillard."

The professor received us without enthusiasm and with but scant cordiality. His desk was littered with papers, and it was obvious that we had disturbed him in the midst of his labors.

"Why this unexpected visit, Markham?" he asked, after we had seated ourselves. "Have you something to report on Robin's death?" He marked a page in Weyl's "Space, Time and Matter" and, settling back reluctantly, regarded us with impatience. "I'm very busy working on a problem of Mach's mechanics. . . ."

"I regret," said Markham, "I have nothing to report on the Robin case. But there has been another murder in this neighborhood to-day, and we have reason to believe that it may be connected with Robin's death. What I wanted particularly to ask you, sir, is whether or not the name of John E. Sprigg is familiar to you."

Professor Dillard's expression of annoyance changed quickly.

"Is that the name of the man who was killed?" There was no longer any lack of interest in his attitude.

"Yes. A man named John E. Sprigg was shot in Riverside Park, near 84th Street, this morning shortly after half past seven."

The professor's eyes wandered to the mantelpiece, and he was silent for several moments. He seemed to be debating inwardly some point that troubled him.

"Yes," he said at length, "I – we – do know a young man of that name – though it's wholly unlikely he's the same one."

"Who is he?" Markham's voice was eagerly insistent.

Again the professor hesitated.

"The lad I have in mind is Arnesson's prize student in mathematics – what they'd call at Cambridge a senior wrangler."

"How do you happen to know him, sir?"

"Arnesson has brought him to the house here several times. Wanted me to see him and talk to him. Arnesson was quite proud of the boy; and I must admit he showed unusual talent."

"Then he was known to all the members of the household?"

"Yes. Belle met him, I think. And if by 'the household' you include Pyne and Beedle, I should say the name was probably familiar to them too."

Vance asked the next question.

"Did the Drukkers know Sprigg, Professor Dillard?"

"It's quite possible. Arnesson and Drukker see each other a great deal. . . . Come to think of it, I believe Drukker was here one night when Sprigg called."

"And Pardee: did he also know Sprigg?"

"As to that I couldn't say." The professor tapped impatiently on the arm of his chair, and turned back to Markham. "See here" – his voice held a worried petulance – "what's the point of these questions? What has our knowing a student named Sprigg to do with this morning's affair? Surely you don't mean to tell me that the man who was killed was Arnesson's pupil."

"I'm afraid it's true," said Markham.

There was a note of anxiety – of fear almost,

I thought – in the professor's voice when he next spoke.

"Even so, what can that fact have to do with us? And how can you possibly connect his death with Robin's?"

"I admit we have nothing definite to go on," Markham told him. "But the purposelessness of both crimes – the total lack of any motive in either case – seems to give them a curious unity of aspect."

"You mean, of course, that you have found no motive. But if all crimes without apparent motive were assumed to be connected –"

"Also there are the elements of time and proximity in these two cases," Markham amplified.

"Is that the basis of your assumption?" The professor's manner was benevolently contemptuous. "You never were a good mathematician, Markham, but at least you should know that no hypothesis can be built on such a flimsy premise."

"Both names," interposed Vance, "– Cock Robin and Johnny Sprigg – are the subjects of well-known nursery rhymes."

The old man stared at him with undisguised astonishment; and gradually an angry flush mounted to his face.

"Your humor, sir, is out of place."

"It is not *my* humor, alas!" replied Vance sadly. "The jest is the Bishop's."

"The Bishop?" Professor Dillard strove to curb his irritation. "Look here, Markham; I won't be played with. That's the second mention of a mysterious Bishop that's been made in this room; and I want to know the meaning of it. Even if a crank did write an insane letter to the papers in connection with Robin's death, what has this Bishop to do with Sprigg?"

"A paper was found beneath Sprigg's body bearing a mathematical formula typed on the same machine as the Bishop notes."

"What!" The professor bent forward. "The same machine, you say? And a mathematical formula? . . . What was the formula?"

Markham opened his pocketbook, and held out the triangular scrap of paper that Pitts had given him.

"The Riemann-Christoffel tensor. . . ." Professor Dillard sat for a long time gazing at the paper; then he handed it back to Markham. He seemed suddenly to have grown older; and there was a weary look in his eyes as he lifted them to us. "I don't see any light in this matter." His tone was one of hopeless resignation. "But perhaps you are right in following your present course. – What do you want of me?"

Markham was plainly puzzled by the other's altered attitude.

"I came to you primarily to ascertain if there was any link between Sprigg and this house; but, to be quite candid, I don't see how that link, now that I have it, fits into the chain – I would, however, like your permission to question Pyne and Beedle in whatever way I think advisable."

"Ask them anything you like, Markham. You shall never be able to accuse me of having stood in your way." He glanced up appealingly. "But you will, I hope, advise me before you take any drastic steps."

"That I can promise you, sir." Markham rose. "But I fear we are a long way from any drastic measures at present." He held out his hand, and from his manner it was evident he had sensed some hidden anxiety in the old man and wanted to express his sympathy without voicing his feelings.

The professor walked with us to the door.

"I can't understand that typed tensor," he murmured, shaking his head. "But if there's anything I can do. . . ."

"There *is* something you can do for us, Professor Dillard," said Vance, pausing at the door. "On the morning Robin was killed we interviewed Mrs. Drukker –"

"Ah!"

"And though she denied having sat at her window during the forenoon there is a possibility she saw something happen on the archery range between eleven and twelve."

"She gave you that impression?" There was an undertone of suppressed interest in the professor's question.

"Only in a remote way. It was Drukker's statement that he had heard his mother scream, and her denial of having screamed, that led me to believe that she might have seen something she preferred to keep from us. And it occurred to me that you would probably have more influence with her than any one else, and that, if she did indeed witness anything, you might prevail upon her to speak."

"No!" Professor Dillard spoke almost harshly; but he immediately placed his hand on Markham's arm, and his tone changed. "There are some things you must not ask me to do for you. If that poor harassed woman saw anything from her window that morning, you must find it out for yourself. I'll have no hand in torturing her; and I sincerely hope you'll not worry her either. There are other ways of finding out what you want to know." He looked straight into Markham's eyes. "*She* must not be the one to tell you. You yourself would be sorry afterwards."

"We must find out what we can," Markham answered resolutely but with kindliness. "There's a fiend loose in this city, and I cannot stay my hand to save any one from suffering – however tragic that suffering may be. But I assure you I shall not unnecessarily torture any one."

"Have you thought," asked Professor Dillard quietly, "that the truth you seek may be more frightful even than the crimes themselves?"

"That I shall have to risk. But even if I knew it to be a fact, it would not deter me in any degree."

"Certainly not. But, Markham, I'm much older than you. I had gray hair when you were a lad struggling with your logs and antilogs; and when one gets old one learns the true proportions in the universe. The ratios all change. The estimates we once placed on things lose their meaning. That's why the old are more forgiving: they know that no man-made values are of any importance."

"But as long as we must live by human values," argued Markham, "it is my duty to uphold them. And I cannot, through any personal sense of sympathy, refuse to take any avenue that may lead to the truth."

"You are perhaps right," the professor

sighed. "But you must not ask me to help you in this instance. If you learn the truth, be charitable. Be sure your culprit is accountable before you demand that he be sent to the electric chair. There are diseased minds as well as diseased bodies; and often the two go together."

When we had returned to the drawing-room Vance lighted a cigarette with more than his usual care.

"The professor," he said, "is not at all happy about Sprigg's death; and, though he won't admit it, that tensor formula convinced him that Sprigg and Robin belong to the same equation. But he was convinced dashed easily. Now, why? – Moreover, he didn't care to admit that Sprigg was known hereabouts. I don't say he has suspicions, but he has fears. . . . Deuced funny, his attitude. He apparently doesn't want to obstruct the legal justice which you uphold with such touchin' zeal, Markham; but he most decidedly doesn't care to abet your crusade where the Drukkers are concerned. I wonder what's back of his consideration for Mrs. Drukker. I shouldn't say, offhand, that the professor was of a sentimental nature. – And what was that platitude about a diseased mind and a diseased body? Sounded like a prospectus for a physical culture class, what? . . . Lackaday! Let's put a few questions to Pyne and kin."

Markham sat smoking moodily. I had rarely seen him so despondent.

"I don't see what we can hope for from them," he commented. "However, Sergeant, get Pyne in here."

When Heath had stepped out Vance gave Markham a waggish look.

"Really, y' know, you shouldn't repine. Let Terence console you: – *Nil tam difficile est, quin quærendo investigari possit.* And, 'pon my soul, this is a difficult problem. . . ." He became suddenly sober. "We're dealing with unknown quantities here. We're pitted against some strange, abnormal force that doesn't operate according to the accepted laws of conduct. It's at once subtle – oh, no end subtle – and unfamiliar. But at least we know that it emanates from somewhere in the environs of this old house; and we must search in every psychological nook and cranny. Somewhere about us lies the invisible dragon. So don't be shocked at the questions I shall put to Pyne. We must look in the most unlikely places. . . ."

Footsteps were heard approaching the archway, and a moment later Heath entered with the old butler in tow.

CHAPTER XI

THE STOLEN REVOLVER

(Monday, April 11; 3 p.m.)

"Sit down, Pyne," said Vance, with peremptory kindness. "We have permission from Professor Dillard to question you; and we shall expect answers to all our questions."

"Certainly, sir," the man answered. "I'm sure there's nothing that Professor Dillard has any reason to hide."

"Excellent." Vance lay back lazily. "To begin with, then; what hour was breakfast served here this morning?"

"At half past eight, sir – the same as always."

"Were all the members of the family present?"

"Oh, yes, sir."

"Who calls the family in the morning? And at what time?"

"I do myself – at half past seven. I knock on the doors –"

"And wait for an answer?"

"Yes, sir – always."

"Now think, Pyne: did every one answer you this morning?"

The man inclined his head emphatically. "Yes, sir."

"And no one was late to breakfast?"

"Every one was on time promptly – as usual, sir."

Vance leaned over and deposited his cigarette ash in the grate.

"Did you happen to see any one leaving the house or returning to it this morning before breakfast?"

The question was put casually, but I noted a slight quiver of surprise in the butler's thin drooping eyelids.

"No, sir."

"Even though you saw no one," pursued Vance, "would it not have been possible for some member of the household to have gone out and returned without your knowing it?"

Pyne for the first time during the interview appeared reluctant to answer.

"Well, sir, the fact is," he said uneasily, "any one might have used the front door this morning without my knowing it, as I was in the dining-room setting table. And, for the matter of that, any one might have used the archery-room door, for my daughter generally keeps the kitchen door closed while preparing breakfast."

Vance smoked thoughtfully a moment. Then in an even, matter-of-fact tone he asked: "Does any one in the house own a revolver?"

The man's eyes opened wide.

"Not that I – know of, sir," he answered haltingly.

"Ever hear of the Bishop, Pyne?"

"Oh, no, sir!" His face blanched. "You mean the man who wrote those letters to the papers?"

"I merely mean the Bishop," said Vance carelessly. "But tell me: have you heard anything about a man being killed in Riverside Park this morning?"

"Yes, sir. The janitor next door was telling me about it."

"You knew young Mr. Sprigg, didn't you?"

"I'd seen him at the house here once or twice, sir."

"Was he here recently?"

"Last week, sir. Thursday I think it was."

"Who else was here at the time?"

Pyne frowned as if trying to remember.

"Mr. Drukker, sir," he said after a moment. "And, as I recall, Mr. Pardee came too. They were together in Mr. Arnesson's room talking until late."

"In Mr. Arnesson's room, eh? Is it custom'ry for Mr. Arnesson to receive callers in his room?"

"No, sir," Pyne explained; "but the professor was working in the library, and Miss Dillard was with Mrs. Drukker in the drawing-room here."

Vance was silent a while.

"That will be all, Pyne," he said at length. "But please send Beedle to us at once."

Beedle came and stood before us with sullen aggressiveness. Vance questioned her along the same lines as he had taken with Pyne. Her answers, for the most part monosyllabic, added nothing to what had already been learned. But at the end of the brief interview Vance asked her if she had happened to look out of the kitchen window that morning before breakfast.

"I looked out once or twice," she answered defiantly. "Why shouldn't I look out?"

"Did you see any one on the archery range or in the rear yard?"

"No one but the professor and Mrs. Drukker."

"No strangers?" Vance strove to give the impression that the fact of Professor Dillard's and Mrs. Drukker's presence in the rear yard that morning was of no importance; but, by the slow, deliberate way in which he reached into his pocket for his cigarette-case, I knew the information had interested him keenly.

"No," the woman replied curtly.

"What time did you notice the professor and Mrs. Drukker?"

"Eight o'clock maybe."

"Were they talking together?"

"Yes. – Anyway," she emended, "they were walking up and down near the arbor."

"Is it custom'ry for them to stroll in the yard before breakfast?"

"Mrs. Drukker often comes out early and walks about the flower beds. And I guess the professor has a right to walk in his own yard any time he wants to."

"I'm not questioning his rights in the matter, Beedle," said Vance mildly. "I was merely wondering if he was in the habit of exercising those rights at such an early hour."

"Well, he was exercising 'em this morning."

Vance dismissed the woman and, rising, went to the front window. He was patently puzzled, and he stood several minutes looking down the street toward the river.

"Well, well," he murmured. "It's a nice day for communin' with nature. At eight this morning the lark was on the wing no doubt, and – who knows? – maybe there was a snail on the thorn. But – my word! – all wasn't right with the world."

Markham recognized the signs of Vance's perplexity.

"What do you make of it?" he asked. "I'm inclined to ignore Beedle's information."

"The trouble is, Markham, we can't afford to ignore anything in this case." Vance spoke softly, without turning. "I'll admit, though, that at present Beedle's revelation is meaningless. We've merely learned that two of the actors in our melodrama were up and about this morning shortly after Sprigg was snuffed out. The al-fresco rendezvous between the professor and Mrs. Drukker may, of course, be just one of your beloved coincidences. On the other hand, it may have some bearing on the old gentleman's sentimental attitude toward the lady. . . . I think we'll have to make a few discreet inquiries of him about his ante-prandial tryst, what? . . ."

He leaned suddenly toward the window.

"Ah! Here comes Arnesson. Looks a bit excited."

A few moments later there was the sound of a key in the front door, and Arnesson strode down the hall. When he saw us he came quickly into the drawing-room and, without a word of greeting, burst forth:

"What's this I hear about Sprigg being shot?"

His eager eyes darted from one to the other of us. "I suppose you're here to ask me about him. Well, fire away." He threw a bulky brief-case on the centre-table and sat down abruptly on the edge of a straight chair. "There was a detective up at college this morning asking fool questions and acting like a burlesque sleuth in a comic opera. Very mysterious. . . . Murder – horrible murder! What did we know about a certain John E. Sprigg? And so on. . . . Scared a couple of juniors out of an entire semester's mental growth, and sent a harmless young English instructor into incipient nervous collapse. I didn't see the Dogberry myself – was in class at the time. But he had the cheek to ask what women Sprigg went around with. Sprigg and women! That boy didn't have a thought in his head but his work. Brightest man in senior math. Never missed a class. When he didn't answer roll-call this morning I knew something serious was the matter. At the lunch hour every one was buzzing about murder. . . . What's the answer?"

"We haven't the answer, Mr. Arnesson." Vance had been watching him closely. "However, we have another determinant for your formula. Johnny Sprig was shot this morning with a little gun through the middle of his wig."

Arnesson stared at Vance for some time without moving. Then he threw his head back and gave a sardonic laugh.

"Some more mumbo-jumbo, eh? – like the death of Cock Robin. . . . Read me the rune."

Vance gave him briefly the details of the crime.

"That's all we know at present," he concluded. "Could *you,* Mr. Arnesson, add any suggestive details?"

"Good Lord, no!" The man appeared genuinely amazed. "Not a thing. Sprigg . . . one of the keenest students I ever had. Something of a genius, by Gad! Too bad his parents named him John – plenty of other names. It sealed his doom apparently; got him shot through the head by a maniac. Obviously the same merry-andrew who did Robin in with an arrow." He rubbed his hands together, – the abstract philosopher in him had become uppermost. "A nice problem. You've told me everything? I'll need every known integer. Maybe I'll hit upon a new mathematical method in the process – like Kepler." He chuckled over the conceit. "Remember Kepler's 'Doliometrie'? It became the foundation of Infinitesimal Calculus. He arrived at it trying to construct a cask for his wine – a cask with a minimum amount of wood and a maximum cubical content. Maybe the formulas I work out to solve these crimes will open up new fields of scientific research. Ha! Robin and Sprigg will then become martyrs."

The man's humor, even taking into consideration his life's passion for abstractions, struck me as particularly distasteful. But Vance seemed not to mind his cold-blooded cynicism.

"There's one item," he said, "that I omitted to mention." Turning to Markham he asked for the piece of paper containing the formula, and handed it to Arnesson. "This was found beneath Sprigg's body."

The other scrutinized it superciliously.

"The Bishop, I see, is again involved. Same paper and typing as the notes. . . . But where did he get that Riemann-Christoffel tensor? Now, if it had been some other tensor – like the G-sigma-tau, for instance – any one interested in practical physics might have hit on it. But this one isn't common; and the statement of it here is arbitrary and unusual. Certain terms omitted. . . . *By George!* I was talking to Sprigg about this only the other night. He wrote it down, too."

"Pyne mentioned the fact that Sprigg had called here Thursday night," put in Vance.

"Oh, he did, did he? . . . Thursday – that's right. Pardee was here, too. And Drukker. We had a discussion on Gaussian co-ordinates. This tensor came up – Drukker mentioned it first, I think. And Pardee had some mad notion of applying the higher mathematics to chess. . . ."

"Do you play chess, by the by?" asked Vance.

"Used to. But no more. A beautiful game, though – if it wasn't for the players. Queer crabs, chess players."

"Did you ever make any study of the Pardee gambit?" (At the time I could not understand the seeming irrelevance of Vance's questions; and I noticed that Markham too was beginning to show signs of impatience.)

"Poor old Pardee!" Arnesson smiled unfeelingly. "Not a bad elementary mathematician. Should have been a high-school teacher. Too much money, though. Took to chess. I told him his gambit was unscientific. Even showed him how it could be beaten. But he couldn't see it. Then Capablanca, Vidmar and Tartakower came along and knocked it into a cocked hat. Just as I told him they would. Wrecked his life. He's been fussing around with another gambit for years, but can't make it cohere. Reads Weyl, Silberstein, Eddington and Mach in the hope of getting inspiration."

"That's most interestin'." Vance extended his

match-case to Arnesson, who had been filling his pipe as he talked. "Was Pardee well acquainted with Sprigg?"

"Oh, no. Met him here twice – that's all. Pardee knows Drukker well, though. Always asking him about potentials and scalars and vectors. Hopes to hit on something that'll revolutionize chess."

"Was he interested in the Riemann-Christoffel tensor when you discussed it the other night?"

"Can't say that he was. A bit out of his realm. You can't hitch the curvature of space-time to a chess-board."

"What do you make of this formula being found on Sprigg?"

"Don't make anything of it. If it had been in Sprigg's handwriting I'd say it dropped out of his pocket. But who'd go to the trouble of trying to type a mathematical formula?"

"The Bishop apparently."

Arnesson took his pipe from his mouth and grinned.

"Bishop X. We'll have to find him. He's full of whimsies. Perverted sense of values."

"Obviously." Vance spoke languidly. "And, by the by, I almost forgot to ask you: does the Dillard house harbor any revolvers?"

"Oho!" Arnesson chuckled with unrestrained

delight. "Sits the wind there? . . . Sorry to disappoint you. No revolvers. No sliding doors. No secret stairways. All open and above-board."

Vance sighed theatrically.

"Sad . . . sad! And I had such a comfortin' theory."

Belle Dillard had come silently down the hall, and now stood in the archway. She had evidently heard Vance's question and Arnesson's answer.

"But there *are* two revolvers in the house, Sigurd," she declared. "Don't you remember the old revolvers I used for target practice in the country?"

"Thought you'd thrown 'em away long ago." Arnesson rose and drew up a chair for her. "I told you when we returned from Hopatcong that summer that only burglars and bandits are allowed to own guns in this benevolent State. . . ."

"But I didn't believe you," the girl protested. "I never know when you're jesting and when you're serious."

"And you kept them, Miss Dillard?" came Vance's quiet voice.

"Why – yes." She shot an apprehensive glance at Heath. "Shouldn't I have done so?"

"I believe it was technically illegal.

However" – Vance smiled reassuringly – "I don't think the Sergeant will invoke the Sullivan law against you. – Where are they now?"

"Down-stairs – in the archery-room. They're in one of the drawers of the tool-chest."

Vance rose.

"Would you be so good, Miss Dillard, as to show us where you put them? I have a gnawin' curiosity to see 'em, don't y' know."

The girl hesitated and looked to Arnesson for guidance. When he nodded she turned without a word and led the way to the archery-room.

"They're in that chest by the window," she said.

Going to it she drew out a small deep drawer in one end. At the rear, beneath a mass of odds and ends, was a .38 Colt automatic.

"Why!" she exclaimed. "There's only one here. The other is gone."

"It was a smaller pistol, wasn't it?" asked Vance.

"Yes. . . ."

"A .32?"

The girl nodded and turned bewildered eyes on Arnesson.

"Well, it's gone, Belle," he told her, with a shrug. "Can't be helped. Probably one of your young archers took it to blow out his brains with after he'd foozled at shooting arrows up the alley."

"Do be serious, Sigurd," she pleaded, a little frightened. "Where could it have gone?"

"Ha! Another dark mystery," scoffed Arnesson. "Strange disappearance of a discarded .32."

Seeing the girl's uneasiness Vance changed the subject.

"Perhaps, Miss Dillard, you'd be good enough to take us to Mrs. Drukker. There are one or two matters we want to speak to her about; and I assume, by your presence here, that the ride in the country has been postponed."

A shadow of distress passed over the girl's face.

"Oh, you mustn't bother her to-day." Her tone was tragically appealing. "Lady Mae is very ill. I can't understand it – she seemed so well when I was talking with her up-stairs. But after she'd seen you and Mr. Markham she changed: she became weak and . . . oh, something terrible seemed to be preying on her mind. After I'd put her to bed she kept repeating in an awful whisper: 'Johnny Sprig, Johnny Sprig.' . . . I phoned her doctor and he came right over. He said she had to be kept very quiet. . . ."

"It's of no importance," Vance assured her. "Of course we shall wait. – Who is her doctor, Miss Dillard?"

"Whitney Barstead. He's attended her as long as I can remember."

"A good man," nodded Vance. "There's no better neurologist in the country. We'll do nothing without his permission."

Miss Dillard gave him a grateful look. Then she excused herself.

When we were again in the drawing-room Arnesson stationed himself before the fireplace and regarded Vance satirically.

" 'Johnny Sprig, Johnny Sprig.' Ha! Lady Mae got the idea at once. She may be cracked, but certain lobes of her brain are over-active. Unaccountable piece of machinery, the human brain. Some of the greatest mental computers of Europe are morons. And I know a couple of chess masters who need nurses to dress and feed 'em."

Vance appeared not to hear him. He had stopped by a small cabinet near the archway and was apparently absorbed in a set of jade carvings of ancient Chinese origin.

"That elephant doesn't belong there," he remarked casually, pointing to a tiny figure in the collection. "It's a *bunjinga* – decadent, don't y' know. Clever, but not authentic. Probably a copy of a Manchu piece." He stifled a yawn and turned toward Markham. "I say, old man, there's nothing more we can do. Suppose we toddle. We might have a brief word with the professor before we go, though. . . . Mind waiting for us here, Mr. Arnesson?"

Arnesson lifted his eyebrows in some surprise, but immediately crinkled his face into a disdainful smile.

"Oh, no. Go ahead." And he began refilling his pipe.

Professor Dillard was much annoyed at our second intrusion.

"We've just learned," said Markham, "that you were speaking to Mrs. Drukker before breakfast this morning. . . ."

The muscles of Professor Dillard's cheeks worked angrily.

"Is it any concern of the District Attorney's office if I speak to a neighbor in my garden?"

"Certainly not, sir. But I am in the midst of an investigation which seriously concerns your house, and I assumed that I had the privilege of seeking help from you."

The old man spluttered a moment.

"Very well," he acquiesced irritably. "I saw no one except Mrs. Drukker – if that's what you're after."

Vance projected himself into the conversation.

"That's not what we came to you for, Professor Dillard. We wanted merely to ask you if Mrs. Drukker gave you the impression this morning that she suspected what had taken place earlier in Riverside Park."

The professor was about to make a sharp retort, but checked himself. After a moment he said simply:

"No, she gave me no such impression."

"Did she appear in any way uneasy or, let us say, excited?"

"She did not!" Professor Dillard rose and faced Markham. "I understand perfectly what you are driving at; and I won't have it. I've told you, Markham, that I'll take no part in spying or tale-bearing where this unhappy woman is concerned. That's all I have to say to you." He turned back to his desk. "I regret I'm very busy to-day."

We descended to the main floor and made our adieus to Arnesson. He waved his hand to us cordially as we went out; but his smile held something of contemptuous patronage, as if he had witnessed, and was gloating over, the rebuff we had just received.

When we were on the sidewalk Vance paused

to light a fresh cigarette.

"Now for a brief *causerie* with the sad and gentlemanly Mr. Pardee. I don't know what he can tell us, but I have a yearnin' to commune with him."

Pardee, however, was not at home. His Japanese servant informed us that his master was most likely at the Manhattan Chess Club.

"To-morrow will be time enough," Vance said to Markham, as we turned away from the house. "I'll get in touch with Doctor Barstead in the morning and try to arrange to see Mrs. Drukker. We'll include Pardee in the same pilgrimage."

"I sure hope," grumbled Heath, "that we learn more to-morrow than we did to-day."

"You overlook one or two consolin' windfalls, Sergeant," returned Vance. "We've found out that every one connected with the Dillard house was acquainted with Sprigg and could easily have known of his early morning walks along the Hudson. We've also learned that the professor and Mrs. Drukker were ramblin' in the garden at eight o'clock this morning. And we discovered that a .32 revolver has disappeared from the archery-room – Not an embarrassment of riches, but something – oh, decidedly something."

As we drove down-town Markham roused

himself from gloomy abstraction, and looked apprehensively at Vance.

"I'm almost afraid to go on with this case. It's becoming too sinister. And if the newspapers get hold of that Johnny-Sprig nursery rhyme and connect the two murders, I hate to think of the gaudy sensation that'll follow."

"I fear you're in for it, old man," sighed Vance. "I'm not a bit psychic – never had dreams that came true, and don't know what a telepathic seizure feels like – but something tells me that the Bishop is going to acquaint the press with that bit of Mother-Goose verse. The point of his new joke is even obscurer than his Cock-Robin comedy. He'll see to it that no one misses it. Even a grim humorist who uses corpses for his cap-and-bells must have his audience. Therein lies the one weakness of his abominable crimes. It's about our only hope, Markham."

"I'll give Quinan a ring," said Heath, "and find out if anything has been received."

But the Sergeant was saved the trouble. The *World* reporter was waiting for us at the District Attorney's office, and Swacker ushered him in at once.

"Howdy, Mr. Markham." There was a breezy impudence in Quinan's manner, but withal he showed signs of nervous excitement.

"I've got something here for Sergeant Heath. They told me at Headquarters that he was handling the Sprigg case, and said he was parleying with you. So I blew over." He reached in his pocket and, taking out a sheet of paper, handed it to Heath. "I'm being mighty high, wide and handsome with you, Sergeant, and I expect a little inside stuff by way of reciprocity. . . . Cast your eye on that document. Just received by America's foremost family journal."

It was a plain piece of typewriting paper, and it contained the Mother-Goose melody of Johnny Sprig, typed in élite characters with a pale-blue ribbon. In the lower right-hand corner was the signature in capitals: THE BISHOP.

"And here's the envelope, Sergeant." Quinan again dug down into his pocket.

The official cancellation bore the hour of 9 a.m., and, like the first note, it had been mailed in the district of Post Office Station "N."

CHAPTER XII

A MIDNIGHT CALL

(Tuesday, April 12; 10 a.m.)

The following morning the front pages of the metropolitan press carried sensational stories which surpassed Markham's worst fears. In addition to the *World* two other leading morning journals had received notes similar to the one shown us by Quinan; and the excitement created by their publication was tremendous. The entire city was thrown into a state of apprehension and fear; and though half-hearted attempts were made here and there to dismiss the maniacal aspect of the crimes on the ground of coincidence, and to explain away the Bishop notes as the work of a practical joker, all the newspapers and the great majority of the public were thoroughly convinced that a new and terrible type of killer was preying upon the community.*

*A similar state of panic obtained in London in 1888 when Jack-the-Ripper was engaged in his grisly, abnormal debauch; and again in Hanover in 1923 when Haarmann, the werwolf, was busy with his anthropophagous slaughters. But I can recall no other modern parallel for the atmosphere of gruesome horror that settled over New York during the Bishop murders.

Markham and Heath were beset by reporters, but a veil of secrecy was sedulously maintained. No intimation was given that there was any reason to believe that the solution lay close to the Dillard household; and no mention was made of the missing .32 revolver. Sperling's status was sympathetically dealt with by the press. The general attitude now was that the young man had been the unfortunate victim of circumstances; and all criticism of Markham's procrastination in prosecuting him was instantly dropped.

On the day that Sprigg was shot Markham called a conference at the Stuyvesant Club. Both Inspector Moran of the Detective Bureau and Chief Inspector O'Brien* attended. The two murders were gone over in detail, and Vance outlined his reasons for believing that the answer to the problem would eventually be found either in the Dillard house or in some quarter directly connected with it.

"We are now in touch," he ended, "with every person who could possibly have had sufficient knowledge of the conditions surrounding the two victims to perpetrate the crimes successfully; and our only course is to concentrate on these persons."

*Chief Inspector O'Brien was then in command of the entire Police Department.

Inspector Moran was inclined to agree. "Except," he qualified, "that none of the *dramatis personæ* you have mentioned strikes me as a bloodthirsty maniac."

"The murderer is not a maniac in the conventional sense," returned Vance. "He's probably normal on all other points. His brain, in fact, may be brilliant except for this one lesion – too brilliant, I should say. He has lost all sense of proportion through sheer exalted speculation."

"But does even a perverted superman indulge in such hideous jests without a motive?" asked the Inspector.

"Ah, but there is a motive. Some tremendous impetus is back of the monstrous conception of these murders – an impetus which, in its operative results, takes the form of satanic humor."

O'Brien took no part in this discussion. Though impressed by its vague implications, he became nettled by its impractical character.

"That sort of talk," he rumbled ponderously, "is all right for newspaper editorials, but it ain't workable." He shook his fat black cigar at Markham. "What we gotta do is to run down every lead and get some kind of legal evidence."

It was finally decided that the Bishop notes

were to be turned over to an expert analyst, and an effort made to trace both the typewriter and the stationery. A systematic search was to be instituted for witnesses who might have seen some one in Riverside Park between seven and eight that morning. Sprigg's habits and associations were to be the subject of a careful report; and a man was to be detailed to question the mail collector of the district in the hope that, when taking the letters from the various boxes, he had noticed the envelopes addressed to the papers and could say in which box they had actually been posted.

Various other purely routine activities were outlined; and Moran suggested that for a time three men be stationed day and night in the vicinity of the murders to watch for any possible developments or for suspicious actions on the part of those involved. The Police Department and the District Attorney's office were to work hand in hand. Markham, of course, in tacit agreement with Heath, assumed command.

"I have already interviewed the members of the Dillard and Drukker homes in connection with the Robin murder," Markham explained to Moran and O'Brien: "and I've talked the Sprigg case over with Professor Dillard and Arnesson. To-morrow I shall see Pardee and the Drukkers."

The next morning Markham, accompanied by Heath, called for Vance a little before ten o'clock.

"This thing can't go on," he declared, after the meagrest of greetings. "If any one knows anything, we've got to find it out. I'm going to put the screws on – and damn the consequences!"

"By all means, chivy 'em." Vance himself appeared despondent. "I doubt if it'll help though. No ordin'ry procedure is going to solve this riddle. However, I've phoned Barstead. He says we may talk with Mrs. Drukker this morning. But I've arranged to see him first. I have a hankerin' to know more of the Drukker pathology. Hunchbacks, d' ye see, are not usually produced by falls."

We drove at once to the doctor's home and were received without delay. Doctor Barstead was a large comfortable man, whose pleasantness of manner impressed me as being the result of schooled effort.

Vance went straight to the point.

"We have reason to believe, doctor, that Mrs. Drukker and perhaps her son are indirectly concerned in the recent death of Mr. Robin at the Dillard house; and before we question either of them further we should like to have you tell us – as far as professional etiquette will permit – something of the neurological situation we are facing."

"Please be more explicit, sir." Doctor Barstead spoke with defensive aloofness.

"I am told," Vance continued, "that Mrs. Drukker regards herself as responsible for her son's kyphosis; but it is my understanding that such malformations as his do not ordinarily result from mere physical injuries."

Doctor Barstead nodded his head slowly.

"That is quite true. Compression paraplegia of the spinal cord may follow a dislocation or injury, but the lesion thus produced is of the focal transverse type. Osteitis or caries of the vertebræ – what we commonly call Pott's disease – is usually of tubercular origin; and this tuberculosis of the spine occurs most frequently in children. Often it exists at birth. True, an injury may precede the onset by determining the site of infection or exciting a latent focus; and this fact no doubt gives rise to the belief that the injury itself produces the disease. But both Schmaus and Horsley have exposed the true pathological anatomy of spinal caries. Drukker's deformity is unquestionably of tubercular origin. Even his curvature is of the marked rounded type, denoting an extensive involvement of vertebræ; and there is no scholiosis whatever. Moreover, he has all the local symptoms of osteitis."

"You have, of course, explained the situation to Mrs. Drukker."

"On many occasions. But I have had no success. The fact is, a terrific instinct of perverted martyrdom bids her cling to the notion that she is responsible for her son's condition. This erroneous idea has become an *idée fixe* with her. It constitutes her entire mental outlook, and gives meaning to the life of service and sacrifice she has lived for forty years."

"To what extent," asked Vance, "would you say this psychoneurosis has affected her mind?"

"That would be difficult to say; and it is not a question I would care to discuss. I may say this, however: she is undoubtedly morbid; and her values have become distorted. At times there have been – I tell you this in strictest confidence – signs of marked hallucinosis centring upon her son. His welfare has become an obsession with her. There is practically nothing she would not do for him."

"We appreciate your confidence, doctor. . . . And would it not be logical to assume that her upset condition yesterday resulted from some fear or shock connected with his welfare?"

"Undoubtedly. She has no emotional or mental life outside of him. But whether her temporary collapse was due to a real or imaginary fear, one cannot say. She has lived too long on the borderland between reality and fantasy."

There was a short silence, and then Vance asked:

"As to Drukker himself: would you regard him as wholly responsible for his acts?"

"Since he is my patient," returned Doctor Barstead, with frigid reproach, "and since I have taken no steps to sequester him, I consider your question an impertinence."

Markham leaned over and spoke peremptorily.

"We haven't time to mince words, doctor. We're investigating a series of atrocious murders. Mr. Drukker is involved in those murders – to what extent we don't know. But it is our duty to find out."

The doctor's first impulse was to combat Markham; but he evidently thought better of it, for when he answered, it was in an indulgently matter-of-fact voice.

"I have no reason, sir, to withhold any information from you. But to question Mr. Drukker's responsibility is to impute negligence to me in the matter of public safety.

Perhaps, however, I misunderstand this gentleman's question." He studied Vance for a brief moment. "There are, of course, degrees of responsibility," he went on, in a professional tone. "Mr. Drukker's mind is overdeveloped, as is often the case with kyphotic victims. All mental processes are turned inward, as it were; and the lack of normal physical reactions often tends to produce inhibitions and aberrancies. But I've noted no indications of this condition in Mr. Drukker. He is excitable and prone to hysteria; but, then, psychokinesia is a common accompaniment of his disease."

"What form do his recreations take?" Vance was politely casual.

Doctor Barstead thought a moment.

"Children's games, I should say. Such recreations are not unusual with cripples. In Mr. Drukker's case it is what we might term a waking wish-fulfilment. Having had no normal childhood, he grasps at whatever will give him a sense of youthful rehabilitation. His juvenile activities tend to balance the monotony of his purely mental life."

"What is Mrs. Drukker's attitude toward his instinct for play?"

"She very correctly encourages it. I've often seen her leaning over the wall above the playground in Riverside Park watching him. And she always presides at the children's parties and dinners which he holds in his home."

We took our leave a few minutes later. As we turned into 76th Street, Heath, as if arousing himself from a bad dream, drew a deep breath and sat upright in the car.

"Did you get that about the kid games?" he asked, in an awe-stricken voice. "Good God, Mr. Vance! What's this case going to turn into?"

A curious sadness was in Vance's eyes as he gazed ahead toward the misty Jersey cliffs across the river.

Our ring at the Drukker house was answered by a portly German woman, who planted herself stolidly before us and informed us suspiciously that Mr. Drukker was too busy to see any one.

"You'd better tell him, however," said Vance, "that the District Attorney wishes to speak to him immediately."

His words produced a strange effect on the woman. Her hands went to her face, and her massive bosom rose and fell convulsively. Then, as though panic-stricken, she turned and ascended the stairs. We heard her knock on a door; there was a sound of voices; and a few moments later she came back to inform us that Mr. Drukker would see us in his study.

As we passed the woman Vance suddenly turned and, fixing his eyes on her ominously, asked:

"What time did Mr. Drukker get up yesterday morning?"

"I – don't know," she stammered, thoroughly frightened. "*Ja, ja,* I know. At nine o'clock – like always."

Vance nodded and moved on.

Drukker received us standing by a large table covered with books and sheets of manuscript. He bowed sombrely, but did not ask us to have chairs.

Vance studied him a moment as if trying to read the secret that lay behind his restless, hollow eyes.

"Mr. Drukker," he began, "it is not our desire to cause you unnecess'ry trouble; but we have learned that you were acquainted with Mr. John Sprigg, who, as you probably know, was shot near here yesterday morning. Now, could you suggest any reason that any one might have had for killing him?"

Drukker drew himself up. Despite his effort at self-control there was a slight tremor in his voice as he answered.

"I knew Mr. Sprigg but slightly. I can suggest nothing whatever in regard to his death. . . ."

"There was found on his body a piece of paper bearing the Riemann-Christoffel tensor which you introduce in your book in the chapter on the finiteness of physical space." As Vance spoke he moved one of the typewritten sheets of papers on the table toward him, and glanced at it casually.

Drukker seemed not to notice the action. The information contained in Vance's words had rivetted his attention.

"I can't understand it," he said vaguely. "May I see the notation?"

Markham complied at once with his request. After studying the paper a moment Drukker handed it back; and his little eyes narrowed malevolently.

"Have you asked Arnesson about this? He was discussing this very subject with Sprigg last week."

"Oh, yes," Vance told him carelessly. "Mr. Arnesson recalled the incident, but couldn't throw any light on it. We thought perhaps you could succeed where he had failed."

"I regret I can't accommodate you." There was the suggestion of a sneer in Drukker's reply. "Any one might use the tensor. Weyl's and Einstein's works are full of it. It isn't copyrighted. . . ." He leaned over a revolving book case and drew out a thin octavo pamphlet.

"Here it is in Minkowski's 'Relativitätsprinzip,' only with different symbols – a T for the B, for instance; and Greek letters for the indices." He reached for another volume. "Poincaré also uses it in his 'Hypothèses Cosmogoniques,' with still other symbolic equivalents." He tossed the books on the table contemptuously. "Why come to me about it?"

"It wasn't the tensor formula alone that led our roving footsteps to your door," said Vance lightly. "For instance, we have reason to believe that Sprigg's death is connected with Robin's murder. . . ."

Drukker's long hands caught the edge of the table, and he leaned forward, his eyes glittering excitedly.

"Connected – Sprigg and Robin? You don't believe that newspaper talk, do you? . . . It's a damned lie!" His face had begun to twitch, and his voice rose shrilly. "It's insane nonsense. . . . There's no proof, I tell you – not a shred of proof!"

"Cock Robin and Johnny Sprig, don't y' know," came Vance's soft insistent voice.

"That rot! That crazy rot! – Oh, good God! Has the world gone mad! . . ." He swayed back and forth as he beat on the table with one hand, sending the papers flying in all directions.

Vance looked at him with mild surprise.

"Aren't you acquainted with the Bishop, Mr. Drukker?"

The man stopped swaying and, steadying himself, stared at Vance with terrible intensity. His mouth was drawn back at the corners, resembling the transverse laugh of progressive muscular dystrophy.

"You, too! You've gone mad!" He swept his eyes over us. "You damned, unutterable fools! There's no such person as the Bishop! There wasn't any such person as Cock Robin or Johnny Sprig. And here you are – men grown – trying to frighten me – *me*, a mathematician – with nursery tales! . . ." He began to laugh hysterically.

Vance went to him quickly, and taking his arm led him to his chair. Slowly his laughter died away, and he waved his hand wearily.

"Too bad Robin and Sprigg were killed." His tone was heavy and colorless. "But children are the only persons that matter. . . . You'll probably find the murderer. If you don't, maybe I'll help you. But don't let your imaginations run away with you. Keep to facts . . . facts. . . ."

The man was exhausted, and we left him.

"He's scared, Markham – deuced scared," observed Vance, when we were again in the hall. "I could bear to know what is hidden in that shrewd warped mind of his."

He led the way down the hall to Mrs. Drukker's door.

"This method of visiting a lady doesn't accord with the best social usage. Really, y' know, Markham, I wasn't born to be a policeman. I abhor snooping."

Our knock was answered by a feeble voice. Mrs. Drukker, paler than usual, was lying back on her chaise-longue by the window. Her white prehensile hands lay along the arms of the chair, slightly flexed; and more than ever she recalled to my mind the pictures I had seen of the ravening Harpies that tormented Phineus in the story of the Argonauts.

Before we could speak she said in a strained terrified voice: "I knew you would come – I knew you were not through torturing me. . . ."

"To torture you, Mrs. Drukker," returned Vance softly, "is the furthest thing from our thoughts. We merely want your help."

Vance's manner appeared to alleviate her terror somewhat, and she studied him calculatingly.

"If only I could help you!" she muttered. "But there's nothing to be done – nothing. . . ."

"You might tell us what you saw from your window on the day of Mr. Robin's death,"

Vance suggested kindly.

"No – no!" Her eyes stared horribly. "I saw nothing – I wasn't near the window that morning. You may kill me, but my dying words would be No – no – *no!*"

Vance did not press the point.

"Beedle tells us," he went on, "that you often rise early and walk in the garden."

"Oh, yes." The words came with a sigh of relief. "I don't sleep well in the mornings. I often wake up with dull boring pains in my spine, and the muscles of my back feel rigid and sore. So I get up and walk in the yard whenever the weather is mild enough."

"Beedle saw you in the garden yesterday morning."

The woman nodded absently.

"And she also saw Professor Dillard with you."

Again she nodded, but immediately afterward she shot Vance a combative inquisitive glance.

"He sometimes joins me," she hastened to explain. "He feels sorry for me, and he admires Adolph; he thinks he's a great genius. And he *is* a genius! He'd be a great man – as great as Professor Dillard – if it hadn't been for his illness. . . . And it was all my fault. I let him fall when he was a baby. . . ." A dry sob shook her emaciated body, and her fingers worked spasmodically.

After a moment Vance asked: "What did you and Professor Dillard talk about in the garden yesterday?"

A sudden wiliness crept into the woman's manner.

"About Adolph mostly," she said, with a too obvious attempt at unconcern.

"Did you see any one else in the yard or on the archery range?" Vance's indolent eyes were on the woman.

"No!" Again a sense of fear pervaded her. "But somebody else was there, wasn't there? – somebody who didn't wish to be seen." She nodded her head eagerly. "Yes! Some one else was there – and they thought I saw them.... But I didn't! Oh, merciful God, I didn't!..." She covered her face with her hands, and her body shook convulsively. "If only I had seen them! If only I knew! But it wasn't Adolph – it wasn't my little boy. He was asleep – thank God, he was asleep!"

Vance went close to the woman.

"Why do you thank God that it wasn't your son?" he asked gently.

She looked up with some amazement.

"Why, don't you remember? A little man shot Johnny Sprig with a little gun yesterday morning – the same little man that killed Cock Robin with a bow and arrow. It's all a horrible game – and I'm *afraid.* . . . But I mustn't tell – I *can't* tell. The little man might do something awful. Maybe" – her voice became dull with horror – "maybe he has some insane idea that I'm *the old woman who lived in a shoe!* . . ."

"Come, come, Mrs. Drukker." Vance forced a consoling smile. "Such talk is nonsense. You've let these matters prey on your mind. There's a perfectly rational explanation for everything. And I have a feeling that you yourself can help us find that explanation."

"No – no! I can't – I mustn't! I don't understand it myself." She took a deep, resolute inspiration, and compressed her lips.

"Why can't you tell us?" persisted Vance.

"Because I don't know," she cried. "I wish to God I did! I only know that something horrible is going on here – that some awful curse is hanging over this house. . . ."

"How do you know that?"

The woman began to tremble violently, and her eyes roamed distractedly about the room.

"Because" – her voice was barely audible – "because the little man came here last night!"

A chill passed up my spine at this statement, and I heard even the imperturbable Sergeant's sharp intake of breath. Then

Vance's calm voice sounded.

"How do you know he was here, Mrs. Drukker? Did you see him?"

"No, I didn't see him; but he tried to get into this room – by that door." She pointed unsteadily toward the entrance to the hallway through which we had just come.

"You must tell us about it," said Vance; "or we will be driven to conclude that you manufactured the story."

"Oh, but I didn't manufacture it – may God be my witness!" There could be no doubt whatever of the woman's sincerity. Something had occurred which filled her with mortal fear. "I was lying in bed, awake. The little clock on the mantel had just struck midnight; and I heard a soft rustling sound in the hall outside. I turned my head toward the door – there was a dim night-light burning on the table here . . . and then I saw the door-knob turn slowly – silently – as if some one were trying to get in without waking me –"

"Just a moment, Mrs. Drukker," interrupted Vance. "Do you always lock your door at night?"

"I've never locked it until recently – after Mr. Robin's death. I've somehow felt insecure since then – I can't explain why. . . ."

"I quite understand. – Please go on with the

story. You say you saw the door-knob move. And then?"

"Yes – yes. It moved softly – back and forth. I lay there in bed, frozen with terror. But after a while I managed to call out – I don't know how loud; but suddenly the door-knob ceased to turn, and I heard footsteps moving rapidly away – down the hall. . . . Then I managed to get up. I went to the door and listened. I was afraid – afraid for Adolph. And I could hear those soft footsteps descending the stairs –"

"Which stairs?"

"At the rear – leading to the kitchen. . . . Then the door of the screen porch shut, and everything was silent again. . . . I knelt with my ear to the keyhole a long time, listening, waiting. But nothing happened, and at last I rose. . . . Something seemed to tell me I must open the door. I was in deadly terror – and yet I knew I had to open the door. . . ." A shudder swept her body. "Softly I turned the key, and took hold of the knob. As I pulled the door slowly inward, a tiny object that had been poised on the outside knob fell to the floor with a clatter. There was a light burning in the hall – I always keep one burning at night, – and I tried not to look down. I tried – I *tried* . . . but I couldn't keep my eyes away from the floor.

And there at my feet – oh, God in Heaven! – there lay *something!* . . ."

She was unable to go on. Horror seemed to paralyze her tongue. Vance's cool, unemotional voice, however, steadied her.

"What was it that lay on the floor, Mrs. Drukker?"

With difficulty the woman rose and, bracing herself for a moment at the foot of the bed, went to the dressing-table. Pulling out a small drawer she reached inside and fumbled among its contents. Then she extended her open hand to us. On the palm lay a small chessman – ebony black against the whiteness of her skin. It was the bishop!

CHAPTER XIII

IN THE BISHOP'S SHADOW

(Tuesday, April 12; 11 a.m.)

Vance took the bishop from Mrs. Drukker and slipped it into his coat pocket.

"It would be dangerous, madam," he said, with impressive solemnity, "if what happened here last night became known. Should the person who played this joke on you find out that you had informed the police, other attempts to frighten you might be made. Therefore, not one word of what you have told us must pass your lips."

"May I not even tell Adolph?" the woman asked distractedly.

"No one! You must maintain a complete silence, even in the presence of your son."

I could not understand Vance's emphasis on this point; but before many days had passed it was all too clear to me. The reason for his advice was revealed with tragic force; and I realized that even at the time of Mrs.

Drukker's disclosure his penetrating mind had worked out an uncannily accurate ratiocination, and foreseen certain possibilities unsuspected by the rest of us.

We took our leave a few moments later, and descended the rear stairs. The staircase made a sharp turn to the right at a landing eight or ten steps below the second floor, and led into a small dark passageway with two doors – one on the left, opening into the kitchen, and another, diagonally opposite, giving on the screen porch.

We stepped out immediately to the porch, now flooded in sunshine, and stood without a word trying to shake off the atmosphere cast about us by Mrs. Drukker's terrifying experience.

Markham was the first to speak.

"Do you believe, Vance, that the person who brought that chessman here last night is the killer of Robin and Sprigg?"

"There can be no doubt of it. The purpose of his midnight visit is hideously clear. It fits perfectly with what has already come to light."

"It strikes me merely as a ruthless practical joke," Markham rejoined, "– the act of a drunken fiend."

Vance shook his head.

"It's the only thing in this whole nightmare

that doesn't qualify as a piece of insane humor. It was a deadly serious excursion. The devil himself is never so solemn as when covering his tracks. Our particular devil's hand had been forced, and he made a bold play. 'Pon my soul, I almost prefer his jovial mood to the one that prompted him to break in here last night. However, we now have something definite to go on."

Heath, impatient of all theorizing, quickly picked up this last remark.

"And what might that be, sir?"

Imprimis, we may assume that our chess-playing troubadour was thoroughly familiar with the plan of this house. The night-light in the upper hall may have cast its gleam down the rear stairs as far as the landing, but the rest of the way must have been in darkness. Moreover, the arrangement of the rear of the house is somewhat complicated. Therefore, unless he knew the layout he couldn't have found his way about noiselessly in the dark. Obviously, too, the visitor knew in which room Mrs. Drukker slept. Also, he must have known what time Drukker turned in last night, for he wouldn't have chanced making his call unless he had felt sure that the coast was clear."

"That don't help us much," grumbled Heath. "We've been going on the theory right along that the murderer was wise to everything connected with these two houses."

"True. But one may be fairly intimate with a family and still not know at what hour each of its members retires on a certain night, or just how to effect a surreptitious entry to the house. Furthermore, Sergeant, our midnight caller was some one who knew that Mrs. Drukker was in the habit of leaving her door unlocked at night; for he had every intention of entering her room. His object wasn't merely to leave his little memento outside and then depart. The silent stealthy way he tried the knob proves that."

"He may simply have wanted to waken Mrs. Drukker so she would find it at once," suggested Markham.

"Then why did he turn the knob so carefully – as if trying *not* to waken any one? A rattling of the knob, or a soft tapping, or even throwing the chessman against the door, would have answered that purpose much better. . . . No, Markham; he had a far more sinister object in mind; but when he found himself thwarted by the locked door and heard Mrs. Drukker's cry of fright, he placed the bishop where she would find it, and fled."

"Still and all, sir," argued Heath, "any one mighta known she left her door unlocked at night; and any one coulda learned the lay of the house so's to find their way around in the dark."

"But who, Sergeant, had a key to the rear door? And who could have used it at midnight last night?"

"The door mighta been left unlocked," countered Heath; "and when we check up on the alibis of everybody we may get a lead."

Vance sighed.

"You'll probably find two or three people without any alibi at all. And if last night's visit here was planned, a convincing alibi may have been prepared. We're not dealing with a simpleton, Sergeant. We're playing a game to the death with a subtle and resourceful murderer, who can think as quickly as we can, and who has had long training in the subtleties of logic. . . ."

As if on a sudden impulse he turned and passed indoors, motioning us to follow. He went straight to the kitchen where the German woman who had admitted us earlier sat stolidly by a table preparing the midday meal. She rose as we entered and backed away from us. Vance, puzzled by her demeanor, studied her for several moments without speaking. Then his eyes drifted to the table where a large eggplant had been halved lengthwise and scooped out.

"Ah!" he exclaimed, glancing at the contents of the various dishes standing about. *"Aubergines à la Turque,* what? An excellent dish. But I'd mince the mutton a bit finer, if I were you. And not too much cheese: it detracts from the sauce *espagnole* which I see you're preparing." He looked up with a pleasant smile. "What's your name, by the by?"

His manner astonished the woman greatly, but it also had the effect of alleviating her fears.

"Menzel," she answered in a dull voice. "Grete Menzel."

"And how long have you been with the Drukkers?"

"Going on twenty-five years."

"A long time," Vance commented musingly. "Tell me: why were you frightened when we called here this morning?"

The woman became sullen, and her large hands closed tightly.

"I wasn't frightened. But Mr. Drukker was busy –"

"You thought perhaps we had come to arrest him," Vance broke in.

Her eyes dilated, but she made no answer.

"What time did Mr. Drukker rise yesterday morning?" Vance went on.

"I told you . . . nine o'clock – like always."

"What time did Mr. Drukker rise?" The insistent, detached quality of his voice was far more ominous than any dramatic intonation could have been.

"I told you –"

"Die Wahrheit, Frau Menzel! Um wie viel Uhr ist er aufgestanden?"

The psychological effect of this repetition of the question in German was instantaneous. The woman's hands went to her face, and a stifled cry, like a trapped animal's, escaped her.

"I don't – know," she groaned. "I called him at half past eight, but he didn't answer, and I tried the door. . . . It wasn't locked and – *Du lieber Gott!* – he was gone."

"When did you next see him?" asked Vance quietly.

"At nine. I went up-stairs again to tell him breakfast was ready. He was in the study – at his desk – working like mad, and all excited. He told me to go away."

"Did he come down to breakfast?"

"Ja – ja. He came down – half an hour later."

The woman leaned heavily against the drain-board of the sink, and Vance drew up a chair for her.

"Sit down, Mrs. Menzel," he said kindly. When she had obeyed, he asked: "Why did you tell me this morning that Mr. Drukker rose at nine?"

"I had to – I was told to." Her resistance was gone, and she breathed heavily like a person exhausted. "When Mrs. Drukker came back from Miss Dillard's yesterday afternoon she told me that if any one asked me that question about Mr. Drukker I was to say 'Nine o'clock.' She made me swear I'd say it. . . ." Her voice trailed off, and her eyes took on a glassy stare. "I was afraid to say anything else."

Vance still seemed puzzled. After several deep inhalations on his cigarette he remarked:

"There's nothing in what you've told us to affect you this way. It's not unnatural that a morbid woman like Mrs. Drukker should have taken such a fantastic measure to protect her son from possible suspicion, when a murder had been committed in the neighborhood. You've surely been with her long enough to realize how she might exaggerate every remote possibility where her son is concerned. In fact, I'm surprised you take it so seriously. . . . Have you any other reason to connect Mr. Drukker with this crime?"

"No – no!" The woman shook her head distractedly.

Vance strolled to the rear window, frowning. Suddenly he swung about. He had become stern and implacable.

"Where were you, Mrs. Menzel, the

morning Mr. Robin was killed?"

An astounding change came over the woman. Her face paled; her lips trembled; and she clinched her hands with a spasmodic gesture. She tried to take her staring eyes from Vance, but some quality in his gaze held her.

"Where were you, Mrs. Menzel?" The question was repeated sharply.

"I was – here –" she began; then stopped abruptly and cast an agitated glance at Heath, who was watching her fixedly.

"You were in the kitchen?"

She nodded. The power of speech seemed to have deserted her.

"And you saw Mr. Drukker return from the Dillards'?"

Again she nodded.

"Exactly," said Vance. "And he came in the rear way, by the screen porch, and went upstairs. . . . And he didn't know that you saw him through the kitchen door. . . . And later he inquired regarding your whereabouts at that hour. . . . And when you told him you had been in the kitchen he warned you to keep silent about it. . . . And then you learned of Mr. Robin's death a few minutes before you saw him enter here. . . . And yesterday, when Mrs. Drukker told you to say he had not risen until nine, and you heard that some one else had been killed near here, you became suspicious and frightened. . . . That's correct, is it not, Mrs. Menzel?"

The woman was sobbing audibly in her apron. There was no need for her to reply, for it was obvious that Vance had guessed the truth.

Heath took his cigar from his mouth and glared at her ferociously.

"So! You were holding out on me," he bellowed, thrusting forward his jaw. "You lied to me when I questioned you the other day. Obstructing justice, were you?"

She gave Vance a look of frightened appeal.

"Mrs. Menzel, Sergeant," he said, "had no intention of obstructing justice. And now that she has told us the truth, I think we may overlook her perfectly natural deception in the matter." Then before Heath had time to reply he turned to the woman and asked in a matter-of-fact tone: "Do you lock the door leading to the screen porch every night?"

"*Ja* – every night." She spoke listlessly: the reaction from her fright had left her apathetic.

"You are sure you locked it last night?"

"At half past nine – when I went to bed."

Vance stepped across the little passageway and inspected the lock.

"It's a snap-lock," he observed, on returning.

"Who has a key to the door?"

"I have a key. And Mrs. Drukker – she has one, too."

"You're sure no one else has a key?"

"No one except Miss Dillard. . . ."

"Miss Dillard?" Vance's voice was suddenly resonant with interest. "Why should she have one?"

"She's had it for years. She's like a member of the family – over here two and three times a day. When I go out I lock the back door; and her having a key saves Mrs. Drukker the trouble of coming down and letting her in."

"Quite natural," Vance murmured. Then: "We sha'n't bother you any more, Mrs. Menzel." He strolled out on the little rear porch.

When the door had been closed behind us he pointed to the screen door that opened into the yard.

"You'll note that this wire mesh has been forced away from the frame, permitting one to reach inside and turn the latch. Either Mrs. Drukker's key or Miss Dillard's – probably the latter – was used to open the door of the house."

Heath nodded: this tangible aspect of the case appealed to him. But Markham was not paying attention. He stood in the background smoking with angry detachment. Presently he turned resolutely and was about to re-enter the house when Vance caught his arm.

"No – no, Markham! That would be abominable technique. Curb your ire. You're so dashed impulsive, don't y' know."

"But, damn it, Vance!" Markham shook off the other's hand. "Drukker lied to us about going out the Dillard gate before Robin's murder –"

"Of course he did. I've suspected all along that the account he gave us of his movements that morning was a bit fanciful. But it's useless to go upstairs now and hector him about it. He'll simply say that the cook is mistaken."

Markham was unconvinced.

"But what about yesterday morning? I want to know where he was when the cook called him at half past eight. Why should Mrs. Drukker be so anxious to have us believe he was asleep?"

"She, too, probably went to his room and saw that he was gone. Then when she heard of Sprigg's death her febrile imagination became overheated, and she proceeded to invest him with an alibi. But you're only inviting trouble when you plan to chivy him about the discrepancies in his tale."

"I'm not so sure." Markham spoke with significative gravity. "I may be inviting a solution to this hideous business."

Vance did not reply at once. He stood gazing down at the quivering shadows cast on the lawn by the willow trees. At length he said in a low voice:

"We can't afford to take that chance. If what you're thinking should prove to be true, and you should reveal the information you've just received, the little man who was here last night might prowl about the upper hall again. And this time he might not be content to leave his chessman *outside the door!*"

A look of horror came into Markham's eyes.

"You think I might be jeopardizing the cook's safety if I used her evidence against him at this time?"

"The terrible thing about this affair is that, until we know the truth, we face danger at every turn." Vance's voice was heavy with discouragement. "We can't risk exposing any one. . . ."

The door leading to the porch opened, and Drukker appeared on the threshold, his little eyes blinking in the sunlight. His gaze came to rest on Markham, and a crafty, repulsive smile contorted his mouth.

"I trust I am not disturbing you," he apologized, with a menacing squint; "but the cook has just informed me that she told you she saw me enter here by the rear door on the morning of Mr. Robin's unfortunate death."

"Oh, my aunt!" murmured Vance, turning away and busying himself with the selection of a fresh cigarette. "That tears it."

Drukker shot him an inquisitive look, and drew himself up with a kind of cynical fortitude.

"And what about it, Mr. Drukker?" demanded Markham.

"I merely desired to assure you," the man replied, "that the cook is in error. She has obviously confused the date, – you see, I come and go so often by this rear door. On the morning of Mr. Robin's death, as I explained to you, I left the range by the 75th-Street gate and, after a brief walk in the park, returned home by the front way. I have convinced Grete that she is mistaken."

Vance had been listening to him closely. Now he turned and met the other's smile with a look of blank ingenuousness.

"Did you convince her with a chessman, by any chance?"

Drukker jerked his head forward and sucked in a rasping breath. His twisted frame became taut; the muscles about his eyes and mouth began to twitch; and the ligaments of his neck stood out like whipcord. For a moment I thought he was going to lose his self-control; but with a great effort he steadied himself.

"I don't understand you, sir." There was the vibrancy of an intense anger in his words. "What has a chessman to do with it?"

"Chessmen have various names," suggested Vance softly.

"Are *you* telling *me* about chess?" A venomous contempt marked Drukker's manner, but he managed to grin. "Various names, certainly. There's king and queen, the rook, the knight –" He broke off. *"The bishop!* . . ." He lay his head against the casement of the door and began to cackle mirthlessly. "So! That's what you mean? *The bishop!* . . . You're a lot of imbecile children playing a nonsense game."

"We have excellent reason to believe," said Vance, with impressive calmness, "that the game is being played by some one else – with the chess bishop as the principal symbol."

Drukker sobered.

"Don't take my mother's vagaries too seriously," he admonished. "Her imagination often plays tricks on her."

"Ah! And why do you mention your mother in this connection?"

"You've just been talking to her, haven't you? And your comments, I must say, sound very much like some of her harmless hallucinations."

"On the other hand," Vance rejoined mildly, "your mother may have perfectly good grounds for her beliefs."

Drukker's eyes narrowed, and he looked swiftly at Markham.

"Rot!"

"Ah, well," sighed Vance; "we sha'n't debate the point." Then in an altered tone he added: "It might help us though, Mr. Drukker, if we knew where you were between eight and nine yesterday morning."

The man opened his mouth slightly as if to speak, but quickly his lips closed again, and he stood staring calculatingly at Vance. At length he answered in a high-pitched insistent voice.

"I was working – in my study – from six o'clock until half past nine." He paused, but evidently felt that further explanation was desirable. "For several months I've been working on a modification of the ether-string theory to account for the interference of light, which the quantum theory is unable to explain. Dillard told me I couldn't do it"; – a fanatical light came into his eyes – "but I awoke early yesterday morning with certain factors of the problem clarified; and I got up and went to my study. . . ."

"So that's where you were." Vance spoke carelessly. "It's of no great importance. Sorry we discommoded you to-day." He beckoned with his head to Markham, and moved toward the screen door. As we stepped upon the range he turned back and, smiling, said almost dulcetly: "Mrs. Menzel is under our protection. It would pain us deeply if anything should happen to her."

Drukker looked after us with sort of hypnotized fascination.

The moment we were out of hearing Vance moved to Heath's side.

"Sergeant," he said in a troubled voice, "that forthright German *Hausfrau* may have put her head unwittingly in a noose. And – my word! – I'm afraid. You'd better have a good man watch the Drukker house to-night – from the rear, under those willow trees. And tell him to break in at the first scream or call. . . . I'll sleep better if I know there's a plain-clothes angel guarding Frau Menzel's slumbers."

"I get you, sir." Heath's face was grim. "There won't be no chess players worrying her to-night."

CHAPTER XIV

A GAME OF CHESS

(Tuesday, April 12; 11.30 a. m.)

As we walked slowly toward the Dillard house it was decided that immediate inquiries should be made regarding the whereabouts the night before of every person connected in any way with this gruesome drama.

"We must be careful, however, to drop no hint of what befell Mrs. Drukker," warned Vance. "Our midnight bishop-bearer did not intend that we should learn of his call. He believed that the poor lady would be too frightened to tell us."

"I'm inclined to think," objected Markham, "that you're attaching too much importance to the episode."

"Oh, my dear fellow!" Vance stopped short and put both hands on the other's shoulders. "You're much too effete – that's your great shortcomin'. You don't feel – you are no child of nature. The poetry of your soul has run to prose. Now I, on the other hand, give my imagination full sway; and I tell you that the leaving of that bishop at Mrs. Drukker's door was no Hallowe'en prank, but the desperate act of a desperate man. It was meant as a warning."

"You think she knows something?"

"I think she saw Robin's body placed on the range. And I think she saw something else – something she would give her life not to have seen."

In silence we moved on. It was our intention to pass through the wall gate into 75th Street and present ourselves at the Dillards' front door; but as we passed the archery-room the basement door opened, and Belle Dillard confronted us anxiously.

"I saw you coming down the range," she said, with troubled eagerness, addressing her words to Markham. "For over an hour I've been waiting to get in touch with you – phoning your office. . . ." Her manner became agitated. "Something strange has happened. Oh, it may not mean anything . . . but when I came through the archery-room here this morning, intending to call on Lady Mae, some impulse made me go to the tool-chest again and look in the drawer, – it seemed so – so queer that the little revolver should have been stolen

. . . . And there it lay – in plain sight – beside the other pistol!" She caught her breath. "Mr. Markham, some one returned it to the drawer last night!"

This information acted electrically on Heath. "Did you touch it?" he asked excitedly.

"Why – no. . . ."

He brushed past her unceremoniously and, going to the tool-chest, yanked open the drawer. There, beside the larger automatic that we had seen the day before, lay a small pearl-handled .32. The Sergeant's eyes glistened as he ran his pencil through the trigger-guard and lifted it gingerly. He held it to the light and sniffed at the end of the barrel.

"One empty chamber," he announced, with satisfaction. "And it's been shot off recently. . . . This oughta get us somewheres." He wrapped the revolver tenderly in a handkerchief and placed it in his coat pocket. "I'll get Dubois busy on this for finger-prints; and I'll have Cap Hagedorn* check up on the bullets."

"Really now, Sergeant," said Vance banter-

*Captain Hagedorn was the fire-arms expert of the New York Police Department. It was he who, in the Benson murder case, gave Vance the data with which to establish the height of the murderer; and who made the examination of the three bullets fired from the old Smith & Wesson revolver in the Greene murder case.

ingly; "do you imagine that the gentleman we're looking for would wipe a bow and arrow clean and then leave his digital monogram on a revolver?"

"I haven't got your imagination, Mr. Vance," returned Heath surlily. "So I'm going ahead doing the things that oughta be done."

"You're quite right." Vance smiled with good-natured admiration at the other's dogged thoroughness. "Forgive me for trying to damp your zeal."

He turned to Belle Dillard.

"We came here primarily to see the professor and Mr. Arnesson. But there's also a matter we'd like to speak about to you. – We understand you have a key to the rear door of the Drukker house."

She gave him a puzzled nod.

"Yes; I've had one for years. I run back and forth so much; and it saves Lady Mae a lot of bother. . . ."

"Our only interest in the key is that it might have been used by some one who had no right to it."

"But that's impossible. I've never lent it to any one. And I always keep it in my handbag."

"Is it generally known you have a key to the Drukkers'?"

"Why – I suppose so." She was obviously perplexed. "I've never made a secret of it. The family certainly know about it."

"And you may perhaps have mentioned or revealed the fact when there were outsiders present?"

"Yes – though I can't recall any specific instance."

"Are you sure you have the key now?"

She gave Vance a startled look, and without a word picked up a small lizard-skin hand-bag which lay on the wicker table. Opening it she felt swiftly in one of its inner compartments.

"Yes!" she announced, with relief. "It's where I always keep it. . . . Why do you ask me about it?"

"It's important that we know who had access to the Drukker house," Vance told her. Then, before she could question him further, he asked: "Could the key possibly have left your possession last night? – that is, could it have been extracted from your bag without your knowledge?"

A look of fright came into her face.

"Oh, what has happened – ?" she began; but Vance interrupted her.

"Please, Miss Dillard! There's nothing for you to worry about. We're merely striving to eliminate certain remote possibilities in connection with our investigation. – Tell me: could any one have taken your key last night?"

"No one," she answered uneasily. "I went to the theatre at eight o'clock, and had my bag with me the entire time."

"When did you last make use of the key?"

"After dinner last night. I ran over to see how Lady Mae was and to say good-night."

Vance frowned slightly. I could see that this information did not square with some theory he had formed.

"You made use of the key after dinner," he recapitulated, "and kept it with you in your hand-bag the rest of the evening, without letting it once go out of your sight. – Is that right, Miss Dillard?"

The girl nodded.

"I even held the bag in my lap during the play," she amplified.

Vance regarded the hand-bag thoughtfully.

"Well," he said lightly, "so ends the romance of the key. – And now we're going to bother your uncle again. Do you think you'd better act as our *avant-courier;* or shall we storm the citadel unannounced?"

"Uncle is out," she informed us. "He went for a walk along the Drive."

"And Mr. Arnesson, I suppose, has not yet returned from the university."

"No; but he'll be here for lunch. He has no classes Tuesday afternoons."

"In the meantime, then, we'll confer with Beedle and the admirable Pyne. – And I might suggest that it would do Mrs. Drukker no end of good if you'd pay her a visit."

With a troubled smile and a little nod the girl passed out through the basement door.

Heath at once went in search of Beedle and Pyne and brought them to the drawing-room, where Vance questioned them about the preceding night. No information, however, was obtained from them. They had both gone to bed at ten o'clock. Their rooms were on the fourth floor at the side of the house; and they had not even heard Miss Dillard when she returned from the theatre. Vance asked them about noises on the range, and intimated that the screen-porch door of the Drukkers might have slammed shut at about midnight. But apparently both of them had been asleep at that hour. Finally they were dismissed with a warning not to mention to any one the questions that had just been asked them.

Five minutes later Professor Dillard came in. Though surprised to see us, he greeted us amiably.

"For once, Markham, you've chosen an hour for your visit when I am not absorbed in work.

– More questions, I suppose. Well, come along to the library for the inquisition. It'll be more comfortable there." He led the way upstairs, and when we were seated he insisted that we join him in a glass of port which he himself served from the sideboard.

"Drukker should be here," he remarked. "He has a fondness for my 'Ninety-six,' though he'll drink it only on rare occasions. I tell him he should take more port; but he imagines it's bad for him, and points to my gout. But there's no connection between gout and port – the notion is sheer superstition. Sound port is the most wholesome of wines. Gout is unknown in Oporto. A little physical stimulation of the right kind would be good for Drukker. . . . Poor fellow. His mind is like a furnace that's burning his body up. A brilliant man, Markham. If he had sufficient bodily energy to keep pace with his brain, he'd be one of the world's great physicists."

"He tells me," commented Vance, "that you twitted him on his inability to work out a modification of the quantum theory in regard to light-interference."

The old man smiled ruefully.

"Yes. I knew that such a criticism would spur him to a maximum effort. The fact is, Drukker is on the track of something revolutionary. He has already worked out some very interesting theorems. . . . But I'm sure this isn't what you gentlemen came here to discuss. What can I do for you, Markham? Or, perhaps you came to give me news."

"Unfortunately we have no news. We have come to solicit aid again. . . ." Markham hesitated as if uncertain how to proceed; and Vance assumed the role of questioner.

"The situation has changed somewhat since we were here yesterday. One or two new matters have arisen, and there is a possibility that our investigation would be facilitated if we knew the exact movements of the members of your household last night. These movements, in fact, may have influenced certain factors in the case."

The professor lifted his head in some surprise, but made no comment. He said merely; "That information is very easily given. To what members do you refer?"

"To no member specifically," Vance hastened to assure him.

"Well, let me see. . . ." He took out his old meerschaum pipe and began filling it. "Belle and Sigurd and I had dinner alone at six o'clock. At half past seven Drukker dropped in, and a few minutes later Pardee called. Then at eight Sigurd and Belle went to the theatre, and at half past ten Drukker and Pardee went away. I myself turned in shortly after eleven, after locking up the house – I'd let Pyne and Beedle go to bed early. – And that's about all I can tell you."

"Do I understand that Miss Dillard and Mr. Arnesson went to the theatre together?"

"Yes. Sigurd rarely patronizes the theatre, but whenever he does he takes Belle along. He attends Ibsen's plays, for the most part. He's a devout disciple of Ibsen's, by the way. His American upbringing hasn't in the least tempered his enthusiasm for things Norwegian. At heart he's quite loyal to his native country. He's as well grounded in Norwegian literature as any professor at the University of Oslo; and the only music he really cares for is Grieg's. When he goes to concerts or the theatre you're pretty sure to find that the programs are liberally Norwegian."

"It was an Ibsen play, then, he attended last night?"

" 'Rosmersholm,' I believe. There's a revival of Ibsen's dramas at present in New York."

Vance nodded. "Walter Hampden's doing them. – Did you see either Mr. Arnesson or Miss Dillard after they returned from the theatre?"

"No; they came in rather late, I imagine. Belle told me this morning they went to the Plaza for supper after the play. However, Sigurd will be here at any minute, and you can learn the details from him." Though the professor spoke with patience, it was plain that he was annoyed by the apparently irrelevant nature of the interrogation.

"Will you be good enough, sir," pursued Vance, "to tell us the circumstances connected with Mr. Drukker's and Mr. Pardee's visit here after dinner?"

"There was nothing unusual about their call. They often drop in during the evening. The object of Drukker's visit was to discuss with me the work he had done on his modification of the quantum theory; but when Pardee appeared the discussion was dropped. Pardee is a good mathematician, but advanced physics is beyond his depth."

"Did either Mr. Drukker or Mr. Pardee see Miss Dillard before she went to the theatre?"

Professor Dillard took his pipe slowly from his mouth, and his expression became resentful.

"I must say," he replied testily, "that I can see no valid object in my answering such questions. – However," he added, in a more indulgent tone, "if the domestic trivia of my household can be of any possible assistance to you, I will of course be glad to go into detail." He regarded Vance a moment. "Yes, both Drukker and Pardee saw Belle last night. All of us, including Sigurd, were together in this room for perhaps half an hour before theatre time. There was even a casual discussion about Ibsen's genius, in which Drukker annoyed Sigurd greatly by maintaining Hauptmann's superiority."

"Then at eight o'clock, I gather, Mr. Arnesson and Miss Dillard departed, leaving you and Mr. Pardee and Mr. Drukker alone here."

"That is correct."

"And at half past ten, I think you said, Mr. Drukker and Mr. Pardee went away. Did they go together?"

"They went down-stairs together," the professor answered, with more than a suggestion of tartness. "Drukker, I believe, went home; but Pardee had an appointment at the Manhattan Chess Club."

"It seems a bit early for Mr. Drukker to have gone home," mused Vance, "especially as he had come to discuss an important matter with you and had had no adequate opportunity to do so up to the time of his departure."

"Drukker is not well." The professor's voice

was again studiously patient. "As I've told you, he tires easily. And last night he was unusually played out. In fact, he complained to me of his fatigue and said he was going immediately to bed."

"Yes . . . quite in keeping," murmured Vance. "He told us a little while ago that he was up working at six yesterday morning."

"I'm not surprised. Once a problem has posed itself in his mind he works on it incessantly. Unfortunately he has no normal reactions to counterbalance his consuming passion for mathematics. There have been times when I've feared for his mental stability."

Vance, for some reason, steered clear of this point.

"You spoke of Mr. Pardee's engagement at the Chess Club last night," he said, when he had carefully lighted a fresh cigarette. "Did he mention the nature of it to you?"

Professor Dillard smiled with patronizing lenity.

"He talked about it for fully an hour. It appears that a gentleman named Rubinstein – a genius of the chess world, I understand, who is now visiting this country – had taken him on for three exhibition games. The last one was yesterday. It began at two o'clock, and was postponed at six. It should have been played off at eight, but Rubinstein was the lion of some dinner down-town; so the hour set for the play-off was eleven. Pardee was on tenterhooks, for he had lost the first game and drawn the second; and if he could have won last night's game he would have broken even with Rubinstein. He seemed to think he had an excellent chance according to the way the game stood at six o'clock; although Drukker disagreed with him. . . . He must have gone directly from here to the club, for it was fully half past ten when he and Drukker went out."

"Rubinstein's a strong player," observed Vance. A new note of interest, which he strove to conceal, had come into his voice. "He's one of the grand masters of the game. He defeated Capablanca at San Sebastian in 1911, and between 1907 and 1912 was considered the logical contender for the world's title held by Doctor Lasker.* . . . Yes, it would have been a great feather in Pardee's cap to have beaten him. Indeed, it was no small compliment to him that he should have been matched with Rubinstein. Pardee, despite the fame of his

*Akiba Rubinstein was then, and is to-day, the chess champion of Poland and one of the great international masters of the game. He was born in Stavisk, near Lodz, in 1882, and made his debut in international chess at the Ostend tournament in 1906. His recent visit to America resulted in a series of new triumphs.

gambit, has never been ranked as a master. – Have you heard the result of last night's game, by the by?"

Again I noted a faint tolerant smile at the corners of the professor's mouth. He gave the impression of looking down benevolently on the foolish capers of children from some great intellectual height.

"No," he answered; "I didn't inquire. But my surmise is that Pardee lost; for when Drukker pointed out the weakness of his adjourned position, he was more positive than usual. Drukker by nature is cautious, and he rarely expresses a definite opinion on a problem without have excellent grounds for so doing."

Vance raised his eyebrows in some astonishment.

"Do you mean to tell me that Pardee analyzed his unfinished game with Drukker and discussed the possibilities of its ending? Not only is such a course unethical, but any player would be disqualified for doing such a thing."

"I'm unfamiliar with the punctilio of chess," Professor Dillard returned acidly; "but I am sure Pardee would not be guilty of a breach of ethics in that regard. And, as a matter of fact, I recall that when he was engaged with the chessmen at the table over there and Drukker stepped up to look on, Pardee requested him to offer no advice. The discussion of the position took place some time later, and was kept entirely to generalities. I don't believe there was a mention of any specific line of play."

Vance leaned slowly forward and crushed out his cigarette with that taut deliberation which I had long since come to recognize as a sign of repressed excitement. Then he rose carelessly and moved to the chess table in the corner. He stood there, one hand resting on the exquisite marquetry of the alternating squares.

"You say that Mr. Pardee was analyzing his position on this board when Mr. Drukker came over to him?"

"Yes, that is right." Professor Dillard spoke with forced politeness. "Drukker sat down facing him and studied the layout. He started to make some remark, and Pardee requested him to say nothing. A quarter of an hour or so later Pardee put the men away; and it was then that Drukker told him that his game was lost – that he had worked himself into a position which, though it looked favorable, was fundamentally weak."

Vance had been running his fingers aimlessly over the board; and he had taken two or three of the men from the box and tossed them back, as if toying with them.

"Do you remember just what Mr. Drukker

said?" he asked without looking up.

"I didn't pay very close attention – the subject was not exactly one of burning moment to me." There was an unescapable note of irony in the answer. "But, as nearly as I can recall, Drukker said that Pardee could have won provided it had been a rapid-transit game, but that Rubinstein was a notoriously slow and careful player and would inevitably find the weak spot in Pardee's position."

"Did Pardee resent this criticism?" Vance now strolled back to his chair and selected another cigarette from his case; but he did not sit down again.

"He did – very much. Drukker has an unfortunately antagonistic manner. And Pardee is hypersensitive on the subject of his chess. The fact is, he went white with anger at Drukker's strictures. But I personally changed the subject; and when they went away the incident had apparently been forgotten."

We remained but a few minutes longer. Markham was profuse in his apologies to the professor and sought to make amends for the patent annoyance our visit had caused him. He was not pleased with Vance for his seemingly garrulous insistence on the details of Pardee's chess game, and when we had descended to the drawing-room he expressed his displeasure.

"I could understand your questions relating to the whereabouts of the various occupants of this house last night, but I could see no excuse for your harping on Pardee's and Drukker's disagreement over a game of chess. We have other things to do besides gossip."

"A hate of gossip parlance also crown'd Tennyson's Isabel thro' all her placid life," Vance returned puckishly. "But – my word, Markham! – our life is not like Isabel's. Speakin' seriously, there was method in my gossip. I prattled – and I learned."

"You learned what?" Markham demanded sharply.

With a cautious glance into the hall Vance leaned forward and lowered his voice.

"I learned, my dear Lycurgus, that a black bishop is missing from that set in the library, and that the chessman left at Mrs. Drukker's door matches the other pieces up-stairs!"

CHAPTER XV

AN INTERVIEW WITH PARDEE

(Tuesday, April 12; 12.30 p.m.)

This piece of news had a profound effect on Markham. As was his habit when agitated, he rose and began pacing back and forth, his hands clasped behind him. Heath, too, though slower to grasp the significance of Vance's revelation, puffed vigorously on his cigar – an indication that his mind was busy with a difficult adjustment of facts.

Before either had formulated any comment the rear door of the hall opened and light footsteps approached the drawing-room. Belle Dillard, returning from Mrs. Drukker's, appeared in the archway. Her face was troubled, and letting her eyes rest on Markham, she asked:

"What did you say to Adolph this morning? He's in an awful state of funk. He's going about testing all the door-locks and window-catches as if he feared burglars; and he has frightened poor Grete by telling her to be sure to bolt herself in at night."

"Ah! He has warned Mrs. Menzel, has he?" mused Vance. "Very interestin'."

The girl's gaze turned swiftly to him.

"Yes; but he will give me no explanation. He's excited and mysterious. And the strangest thing about his attitude is that he refuses to go near his mother. . . . What does it mean, Mr. Vance? I feel as though something terrible were impending."

"I don't know just what it does mean." Vance spoke in a low, distressed voice. "And I'm afraid even to try to interpret it. If I should be wrong. . . ." He became silent for a moment. "We must wait and see. To-night perhaps we'll know. – But there's no cause for alarm on your part, Miss Dillard." He smiled comfortingly. "How did you find Mrs. Drukker?"

"She seemed much better. But there's still something worrying her; and I think it has to do with Adolph, for she talked about him the whole time I was there, and kept asking me if I'd noticed anything unusual in his manner lately."

"That's quite natural in the circumstances," Vance returned. "But you mustn't let her morbid attitude affect you. – And now, to change the subject: I understand that you were in the library for half an hour or so last night just before you went to the theatre. Tell me, Miss Dillard: where was your hand-bag during that time?"

The question startled her; but after a momentary hesitation she answered: "When I came into the library I placed it with my wrap on the little table by the door."

"It was the lizard-skin bag containing the key?"

"Yes. Sigurd hates evening dress, and when we go out together I always wear my day clothes."

"So you left the bag on the table during that half-hour, and then kept it with you the rest of the evening. – And what about this morning?"

"I went out for a walk before breakfast and carried it with me. Later I put it on the hat-rack in the hall for an hour or so; but when I started for Lady Mae's at about ten I took it with me. It was then I discovered that the little pistol had been returned, and I postponed my call. I left the bag down-stairs in the archery-room until you and Mr. Markham came; and I've had it with me ever since."

Vance thanked her whimsically.

"And now that the peregrinations of the bag have been thoroughly traced, please try to forget all about it." She was on the point of asking a question, but he anticipated her curiosity and said quickly: "You went to the Plaza for supper last night, your uncle told us. You must have been late in getting home."

"I never stay out very late when I go anywhere with Sigurd," she answered, with a maternal note of complaint. "He has a constitutional aversion to any kind of night life. I begged him to stay out longer, but he looked so miserable I hadn't the heart to remain. We actually got home at half past twelve."

Vance rose with a gracious smile.

"You've been awfully good to bear with our foolish questions so patiently. . . . Now we're going to drop in on Mr. Pardee and see if he has any illuminatin' suggestions to offer. He's generally in at this time, I believe."

"I'm sure he's in now." The girl walked with us to the hall. "He was here only a little while before you came, and he said he was returning home to attend to some correspondence."

We were about to go out when Vance paused.

"Oh, I say, Miss Dillard; there's one point I forgot to ask you about. When you came home last night with Mr. Arnesson, how did you know it was just half past twelve? I notice you don't wear a watch."

"Sigurd told me," she explained. "I was rather mean to him for bringing me home so early, and as we entered the hall here I asked him spitefully what time it was. He looked at his watch and said it was half past twelve. . . ."

At that moment the front door opened and Arnesson came in. He stared at us in mock astonishment; then he caught sight of Belle Dillard.

"Hallo, sis," he called to her pleasantly. "In the hands of the *gendarmerie*, I see." He flashed us an amused look. "Why the conclave? This house is becoming a regular police station. Hunting for clews of Sprigg's murderer? Ha! Bright youth done away with by his jealous professor, and that sort of thing, eh? . . . Hope you chaps haven't been putting Diana the Huntress through a third degree."

"Nothing of the kind," the girl spoke up. "They've been most considerate. And I've been telling them what an old fogy you are – bringing me home at half past twelve."

"I think I was very indulgent," grinned Arnesson. "Much too late for a child like you to be out."

"It must be terrible to be senile and – and mathematically inclined," she retorted with some heat, and ran up-stairs.

Arnesson shrugged his shoulders and looked

after her until she had disappeared. Then he fixed a cynical eye on Markham.

"Well, what glad tidings do you bring? Any news about the latest victim?" He led ths way back to the drawing-room. "You know, I miss that lad. He'd have gone far. Rotten shame he had to be named Johnny Sprigg. Even 'Peter Piper' would have been safer. Nothing happened to Peter Piper aside from the pepper episode; and you couldn't very well work that up into a murder. . . ."

"We have nothing to report, Arnesson," Markham broke in, nettled by the man's flippancy. "The situation remains unchanged."

"Just dropped in for a social call, I presume. Staying for lunch?"

"We reserve the right," said Markham coldly, "to investigate the case in whatever manner we deem advisable. Nor are we accountable to you for our actions."

"So! Something *has* happened that irks you." Arnesson spoke with sarcasm. "I thought I had been accepted as a coadjutor; but I see I am to be turned forth into the darkness." He sighed elaborately and took out his pipe. "Dropping the pilot! – Bismarck and me. Alas!"

Vance had been smoking dreamily near the archway, apparently oblivious of Arnesson's complaining. Now he stepped into the room.

"Really, y'know, Markham, Mr. Arnesson is quite right. We agreed to keep him posted; and if he's to be of any help to us he must know all the facts."

"It was you yourself," protested Markham, "who pointed out the possible danger of mentioning last night's occurrence. . . ."

"True. But I had forgotten at the time our promise to Mr. Arnesson. And I'm sure his discretion can be relied on." Then Vance related in detail Mrs. Drukker's experience of the night before.

Arnesson listened with rapt attention. I noticed that his sardonic expression gradually disappeared, and that in its place came a look of calculating sombreness. He sat for several minutes in contemplative silence, his pipe in his hand.

"That's certainly a vital factor in the problem," he commented at length. "It changes our constant. I can see that this thing has got to be calculated from a new angle. The Bishop, it appears, is in our midst. But why should he come to haunt Lady Mae?"

"She is reported to have screamed at almost the exact moment of Robin's death."

"Aha!" Arnesson sat up. "I grasp your implication. She saw the Bishop from her window on the morning of Cock Robin's dissolution, and later he returned and perched on her doorknob as a warning for her to keep mum."

"Something like that, perhaps. . . . Have you enough integers now to work out your formula?"

"I'd like to cast an eye on this black bishop. Where is it?"

Vance reached in his pocket, and held out the chessman. Arnesson took it eagerly. His eyes glittered for a moment. He turned the piece over in his hand, and then gave it back.

"You seem to recognize this particular bishop," said Vance dulcetly. "You're quite correct. It was borrowed from your chess set in the library."

Arnesson nodded a slow affirmative.

"I believe it was." Suddenly he turned to Markham, and an ironic leer came over his lean features. "Was that why I was to be kept in the dark? Under suspicion, am I? Shades of Pythagoras! What penalty attaches to the heinous crime of distributing chessmen among one's neighbors?"

Markham got up and walked toward the hall.

"You are not under suspicion, Arnesson," he answered, with no attempt to conceal his ill-humor. "The bishop was left at Mrs. Drukker's at exactly midnight."

"And I was half an hour too late to qualify.

Sorry to have disappointed you."

"Let us hear if your formula works out," said Vance, as we passed out of the front door. "We've a little visit to pay to Mr. Pardee now."

"Pardee? Oho! Calling in a chess expert on the subject of bishops, eh? I see your reasoning – it at least has the virtue of being simple and direct. . . ."

He stood on the little porch and watched us, like a japish gargoyle, as we crossed the street.

Pardee received us with his customary quiet courtesy. The tragic, frustrated look which was a part of his habitual expression was even more pronounced than usual; and when he drew up chairs for us in his study his manner was that of a man whose interest in life had died, and who was merely going through the mechanical motions of living.

"We have come here, Mr. Pardee," Vance began, "to learn what we can of Sprigg's murder in Riverside Park yesterday morning. We have excellent reasons for every question we are about to ask you."

Pardee nodded resignedly.

"I shall not be offended at any line of interrogation you take. After reading the papers I realize just how unusual a problem you are facing."

"First, then, please inform us where you

were yesterday morning between seven and eight."

A faint flush overspread Pardee's face, but he answered in a low, even voice.

"I was in bed. I did not rise until nearly nine."

"Is it not your habit to take a walk in the park before breakfast?" (I knew this was sheer guesswork on Vance's part, for the subject of Pardee's habits had not come up during the investigation.)

"That is quite true," the man replied, without a moment's hesitation. "But yesterday I did not go, – I had worked rather late the night before."

"When did you first hear of Sprigg's death?"

"At breakfast. My cook repeated the gossip of the neighborhood. I read the official account of the tragedy in the early edition of the evening *Sun.*"

"And you saw the reproduction of the Bishop note, of course, in this morning's paper. – What is your opinion of the affair, Mr. Pardee?"

"I hardly know." For the first time his lacklustre eyes showed signs of animation. "It's an incredible situation. The mathematical chances are utterly opposed to such a series of interrelated events being coincidental."

"Yes," Vance concurred. "And speaking of mathematics: are you at all familiar with the Riemann-Christoffel tensor?"

"I know of it," the man admitted. "Drukker uses it in his book on world lines. My mathematics, however, are not of the physicist's type. Had I not become enamored of chess" – he smiled sadly – "I would have been an astronomer. Next to manœuvering the factors in a complicated chess combination, the greatest mental satisfaction one can get, I think, is plotting the heavens and discovering new planets. I even keep a five-inch equatorial telescope in a pent-house on my roof for amateur observations."

Vance listened to Pardee with close attention; and for several minutes discussed with him Professor Pickering's recent determination of the trans-Neptunean *O*,* much to Markham's bewilderment and to the Sergeant's annoyance. At length he brought the conversation back to the tensor formula.

"You were, I understand, at the Dillards last Thursday when Mr. Arnesson was discussing this tensor with Drukker and Sprigg."

"Yes, I recall that the subject came up then."

*Since this discussion took place Professor Pickering has posited from the perturbations of Uranus, two other outer planets beyond Neptune: *P* and *S*.

"How well did you know Sprigg?"

"Only casually. I had met him with Arnesson once or twice."

"Sprigg, also, it seems, was in the habit of walking in Riverside Park before breakfast," observed Vance negligently. "Ever run into him there, Mr. Pardee?"

The man's eyelids quivered slightly, and he hesitated before answering.

"Never," he said finally.

Vance appeared indifferent to the denial. He rose and, going to the front window, looked out.

"I thought one might be able to see into the archery range from here. But I note that the angle cuts off the view entirely."

"Yes, the range is quite private. There's even a vacant lot opposite the wall, so that no one can see over it. . . . Were you thinking of a possible witness to Robin's death?"

"That, and other things." Vance returned to his chair. "You don't go in for archery, I take it."

"It's a trifle too strenuous for me. Miss Dillard once tried to interest me in the sport, but I was not a very promising acolyte. I've been to several tournaments with her, however."

An unusually soft note had crept into

Pardee's voice, and for some reason which I could not exactly explain I got the feeling that he was fond of Belle Dillard. Vance, too, must have received the same impression, for after a brief pause he said:

"You will realize, I trust, that it is not our intention to pry unnecessarily into any one's private affairs; but the question of motive in the two murders we are investigating still remains obscure, and as Robin's death was at first superficially attributed to a rivalry for Miss Dillard's affections, it might help us to know, in a general way, what the true situation is concerning the young lady's preference. . . . As a friend of the family you probably know; and we'd appreciate your confidence in the matter."

Pardee's gaze travelled out of the window, and the suggestion of a sigh escaped him.

"I've always had the feeling that she and Arnesson would some day be married. But that is only conjecture. She once told me quite positively that she was not going to consider matrimony until she was thirty." (One could easily guess in what connection Belle Dillard had made this pronouncement to Pardee. His emotional, as well as his intellectual life, had apparently met with failure.)

"You do not believe then," pursued Vance,

"that her heart is seriously concerned with young Sperling?"

Pardee shook his head. "However," he qualified, "martyrdom such as he is undergoing at present has a tremendous sentimental appeal for women."

"Miss Dillard tells me you called on her this morning."

"I generally drop over during the day." He was obviously uncomfortable and, I thought, a little embarrassed.

"Do you know Mrs. Drukker well?"

Pardee gave Vance a quick, inquisitive look.

"Not particularly," he said. "I've naturally met her several times."

"You've called at her house?"

"On many occasions, but always to see Drukker. I've been interested for years in the relation of mathematics to chess. . . ."

Vance nodded.

"How did your game with Rubinstein come out last night, by the by? I didn't see the papers this morning."

"I resigned on the forty-fourth move." The man spoke hopelessly. "Rubinstein found a weakness in my attack which I had entirely overlooked when I sealed my move at the adjournment."

"Drukker, Professor Dillard tells us, foresaw

the outcome when you and he were discussing the situation last night."

I could not understand why Vance referred so pointedly to this episode, knowing as he did how sore a point it was with Pardee. Markham, also, frowned at what appeared to be an unforgivably tactless remark on Vance's part.

Pardee colored, and shifted in his chair.

"Drukker talked too much last night." The statement was not without venom. "Though he's not a tournament player, he should know that such discussions are taboo during unfinished games. Frankly, though, I put little stock in his prophecy. I thought my sealed move had taken care of the situation, but Drukker saw farther ahead than I did. His analysis was uncannily profound." There was the jealousy of self-pity in his tone, and I felt that he hated Drukker as bitterly as his seemingly mild nature would permit.

"How long did the game last?" Vance asked casually.

"It was over a little after one o'clock. There were only fourteen moves in last night's session."

"Were there many spectators?"

"An unusually large number, considering the late hour."

Vance put out his cigarette and got up.

When we were in the lower hall on our way to the front door he halted suddenly and, fixing Pardee with a gaze of sardonic amusement, said:

"Y' know, the black bishop was at large again last night around midnight."

His words produced an astonishing effect. Pardee drew himself up as if he had been struck in the face; and his cheeks went chalky white. For a full half-minute he stared at Vance, his eyes like live coals. His lips moved with a slight tremor, but no word came from them. Then, as if with superhuman effort, he turned stiffly away and went to the door. Jerking it open he held it for us to pass out.

As we walked up Riverside Drive to the District Attorney's car, which had been left in front of the Drukker house in 76th Street, Markham questioned Vance sharply in regard to the final remark he had made to Pardee.

"I was in hopes," explained Vance, "of surprising some look of recognition or understanding from him. But, 'pon my soul, Markham, I didn't expect any effect like the one I produced. Astonishin' how he reacted. I don't grasp it – I don't at all grasp it. . . ."

He became engrossed in his thoughts. But as the car swung into Broadway at 72nd Street he roused himself and directed the chauffeur to the Sherman Square Hotel.

"I have a gaspin' desire to know more of that chess game between Pardee and Rubinstein. No reason for it – sheer vagary on my part. But the idea has been workin' in me ever since the professor mentioned it. . . . From eleven until past one – that's a deuced long time to play off an unfinished game of only forty-four moves."

We had drawn up to the curb at the corner of Amsterdam Avenue and 71st Street, and Vance disappeared into the Manhattan Chess Club. It was fully five minutes before he returned. In his hand he carried a sheet of paper filled with notations. There was, however, no sign of jubilance in his expression.

"My far-fetched but charmin' theory," he said with a grimace, "has run aground on base prosaic facts. I just talked to the secret'ry of the club; and last night's session consumed two hours and nineteen minutes. It seems to have been a coruscatin' battle full of esoteric quirks and strategical soul-searchin's. Along about half past eleven the onlooking genii had Pardee picked for the winner; but Rubinstein then staged a masterly piece of sustained analysis, and proceeded to tear Pardee's tactics to smithereens – just as Drukker had prognosticated. Astonishin' mind, Drukker's. . . ."

It was plain that even now he was not entirely satisfied with what he had learned; and his next words voiced his dissatisfaction.

"I thought while I was at it I'd take a page from the Sergeant's book, so to speak, and indulge in a bit of routine thoroughness. So I borrowed the score sheet of last night's game and copied down the moves. I may run over the game some day when time hangs heavy."

And, with what I thought unusual care, he folded the score and placed it in his wallet.

CHAPTER XVI

ACT THREE

(Tuesday, April 12 — Saturday, April 16.)

After lunch at the Elysée Markham and Heath continued down-town. A hard afternoon lay before them. Markham's routine work had accumulated; and the Sergeant, having taken on the Sprigg case in addition to the Robin investigation, had to keep two separate machines working, co-ordinate all his reports, answer innumerable questions from his superiors, and attempt to satisfy the voraciousness of an army of reporters. Vance and I went to an exhibition of modern French art at Knoedler's, had tea at the St. Regis, and met Markham at the Stuyvesant Club for dinner. Heath and Inspector Moran joined us at half past eight for an informal conference; but though it lasted until nearly midnight nothing of a tangible nature came out of it.

Nor did the following day bring anything but

discouragement. The report from Captain Dubois stated that the revolver given him by Heath contained no sign of a finger-print. Captain Hagedorn identified the weapon as the one used in the shooting of Sprigg; but this merely substantiated our already positive belief. The man set to guard the rear of the Drukker residence spent an uneventful night. No one had entered or departed from the house; and by eleven o'clock every window had been dark. Nor had a sound of any kind come from the house until the next morning when the cook set about her chores for the day. Mrs. Drukker had appeared in the garden a little after eight; and at half past nine Drukker went out the front door and sat for two hours in the park reading.

Two days went by. A watch was kept on the Dillard house; Pardee was put under strict surveillance; and a man was stationed each night under the willow trees behind the Drukker house. But nothing unusual happened; and, despite the Sergeant's tireless activities, all promising lines of investigation seemed to be automatically closed. Both Heath and Markham were deeply worried. The newspapers were outdoing themselves in gaudy rhetoric; and the inability of the Police Department and the District Attorney's office to make the slightest headway against the mystery of the two spectacular murders was rapidly growing into a political scandal.

Vance called on Professor Dillard and discussed the case along general lines. He also spent over an hour on Thursday afternoon with Arnesson in the hope that the working out of the proposed formula had brought to light some detail that could be used as a starting-point for speculation. But he was dissatisfied with the interview, and complained to me that Arnesson had not been wholly frank with him. Twice he dropped in at the Manhattan Chess Club and attempted to lead Pardee into conversation; but each time he was met with the reticence of cold courtesy. I noticed that he made no effort to communicate with either Drukker or Mrs. Drukker; and when I asked him his reason for ignoring them, he answered:

"The truth cannot be learned from them now. Each is playing a game; and both are thoroughly frightened. Until we have some definite evidence, more harm than good will result from any attempt to cross-examine them."

This definite evidence was to come the very next day from a most unexpected quarter; and it marked the beginning of the last phase of our investigation – a phase fraught with such sinister, soul-stirring tragedy and unspeakable horror, with such wanton cruelty and monstrous humor, that even now, years later, as I set down this reportorial record of it, I find it difficult to believe that the events were not, after all, a mere grotesque dream of fabulous wickedness.

Friday afternoon Markham, in a mood of desperation, called another conference. Arnesson asked permission to attend; and at four o'clock we all met, including Inspector Moran, in the District Attorney's private room in the old Criminal Courts Building. Arnesson was unwontedly silent during the discussion, and not once did he indulge in his usual flippancy. He listened with close attention to all that was said, and seemed purposely to avoid expressing an opinion, even when directly appealed to by Vance.

We had been in conference perhaps half an hour when Swacker entered quietly and placed a memorandum on the District Attorney's desk. Markham glanced at it and frowned. After a moment he initialed two printed forms and handed them to Swacker.

"Fill these in right away and give them to Ben,"* he ordered. Then when the man had

*Colonel Benjamin Hanlon, commanding officer of the Detective Division attached to the District Attorney's office.

gone out through the outer-hall door, he explained the interruption. "Sperling has just sent a request to speak to me. He says he has information that may be of importance. I thought, in the circumstances, it might be well to see him now."

Ten minutes later Sperling was brought in by a deputy sheriff from the Tombs. He greeted Markham with a friendly boyish smile, and nodded pleasantly to Vance. He bowed – a bit stiffly, I thought – to Arnesson, whose presence seemed both to surprise and disconcert him. Markham motioned him to a chair, and Vance offered him a cigarette.

"I wanted to speak to you, Mr. Markham," he began, a bit diffidently, "about a matter which may be of help to you. . . . You remember, when you were questioning me about my being in the archery-room with Robin, you wanted to know which way Mr. Drukker went when he left us. I told you I didn't notice, except that he went out by the basement door. . . . Well, sir, I've had a lot of time to think lately; and I've naturally gone over in my mind all that happened that morning. I don't know just how to explain it, but everything has become a lot clearer now. Certain – what you might call impressions – have come back to me. . . ."

He paused and looked down at the carpet. Then lifting his head, he went on:

"One of these impressions has to do with Mr. Drukker – and that's why I wanted to see you. Just this afternoon I was – well, sort of pretending I was in the archery-room again, talking to Robin; and all of a sudden the picture of the rear window flashed across my mind. And I remembered that when I had glanced out of the window that morning to see how the weather was for my trip, I had seen Mr. Drukker sitting in the arbor behind the house. . . ."

"At what time was this?" Markham demanded brusquely.

"Only a few seconds before I went to catch my train."

"Then you imply that Mr. Drukker, instead of leaving the premises, went to the arbor and remained there until you departed."

"It looks that way, sir." Sperling was reluctant to make the admission.

"You're quite sure you saw him?"

"Yes, sir. I remember distinctly now. I even recall the peculiar way he had his legs drawn up under him."

"You would swear to it," asked Markham gravely, "knowing that a man's life might rest on your testimony?"

"I'd swear to it, sir," Sperling returned simply.

When the sheriff had escorted his prisoner from the room, Markham looked at Vance.

"I think that gives us a foothold."

"Yes. The cook's testimony was of little value, since Drukker merely denied it; and she's the type of loyal stubborn German who'd back up his denial if any real danger threatened him. Now we're armed with an effective weapon."

"It seems to me," Markham said, after a few moments of speculative silence, "that we have a good circumstantial case against Drukker. He was in the Dillard yard only a few seconds before Robin was killed. He could easily have seen when Sperling went away; and, as he had recently come from Professor Dillard, he knew that the other members of the family were out. Mrs. Drukker denied she saw anyone from her window that morning, although she screamed at the time of Robin's death and then went into a panic of fear when we came to question Drukker. She even warned him against us and called us 'the enemy.' My belief is she saw Drukker returning home immediately after Robin's body had been placed on the range. – Drukker was not in his room at the time Sprigg was killed, and both he and his mother have been at pains to cover up the fact. He has become excited whenever we broached the subject of the murders, and has ridiculed the idea that they were connected. In fact, many of his actions have been highly suspicious. Also, we know he is abnormal and unbalanced, and that he is given to playing children's games. It's quite possible – in view of what Doctor Barstead told us – that he has confused fantasy and reality, and perpetrated these crimes in a moment of temporary insanity. The tensor formula is not only familiar to him, but he may have associated it in some crazy way with Sprigg as a result of Arnesson's discussion with Sprigg about it. – As for the Bishop notes, they may have been part of the unreality of his insane games, – children all want an approving audience when they invent any new form of amusement. His choice of the word 'bishop' was probably the result of his interest in chess – a playful signature intended to confuse. And this supposition is further borne out by the actual appearance of a chess bishop on his mother's door. He may have feared that she saw him that morning, and thus sought to silence her without openly admitting to her that he was guilty. He could easily have slammed the screen-porch door from the inside, without having had a key, and thereby given the impression that the bearer of the bishop had entered and departed by the rear door. Furthermore, it would have been a simple matter for him to take the bishop from the library the night Pardee was analyzing his game. . . ."

Markham continued for some time building up his case against Drukker. He was thorough and detailed, and his summation accounted for practically all of the evidence that had been adduced. The logical and relentless way in which he pieced his various factors together was impressively convincing; and a long silence followed his résumé.

Vance at length stood up, as if to break the tension of his thoughts, and walked to the window.

"You may be right, Markham," he admitted. "But my chief objection to your conclusion is that the case against Drukker is too good. I've had him in mind as a possibility from the first; but the more suspiciously he acted and the more the indications pointed toward him, the more I felt inclined to dismiss him from consideration. The brain that schemed these abominable murders is too competent, too devilishly shrewd, to become entangled in any such net of circumstantial evidence as you've drawn about Drukker. Drukker has an amazing mentality – his intelligence and intellect are supernormal, in fact; and it's difficult to conceive of him, if guilty, leaving so many loopholes."

"The law," returned Markham with acerbity, "can hardly be expected to throw out cases because they're too convincing."

"On the other hand," pursued Vance, ignoring the comment, "it is quite obvious that Drukker, even if not guilty, knows something that has a direct and vital bearing on the case; and my humble suggestion is that we attempt to prise this information out of him. Sperling's testimony has given us the lever for the purpose. . . . I say, Mr. Arnesson, what's your opinion?"

"Haven't any," the man answered. "I'm a disinterested onlooker. I'd hate, however, to see poor Adolph in durance vile." Though he would not commit himself it was plain that he agreed with Vance.

Heath thought, characteristically, that immediate action was advisable, and expressed himself to that effect.

"If he's got anything to tell he'll tell it quick enough after he's locked up."

"It's a difficult situation," Inspector Moran demurred, in a soft judicial voice. "We can't afford to make an error. If Drukker's evidence should convict some one else, we'd be a laughing-stock if we had arrested the wrong man."

Vance looked toward Markham and nodded agreement.

"Why not have him on the tapis first, and see if he can't be persuaded to unburden his soul. You might dangle a warrant over his head, don't y' know, as a kind of moral inducement. Then, if he remains coy and reticent, bring out the gyves and have the doughty Sergeant escort him to the bastille."

Markham sat tapping indecisively on the desk, his head enveloped in smoke as he puffed nervously on his cigar. At last he set his chin firmly and turned to Heath.

"Bring Drukker here at nine o'clock to-morrow morning. You'd better take a wagon and a John-Doe warrant in case he offers any objection." His face was grim and determined. "Then I'll find out what he knows – and act accordingly."

The conference broke up immediately. It was after five o'clock, and Markham and Vance and I rode up-town together to the Stuyvesant Club. We dropped Arnesson at the subway, and he took leave of us with scarcely a word. His garrulous cynicism seemed entirely to have deserted him. After dinner Markham pleaded fatigue, and Vance and I went to the Metropolitan and heard Geraldine Farrar in "Louise."*

The next morning broke dark and misty. Currie called us at half past seven, for Vance intended to be present at the interview with Drukker; and at eight o'clock we had breakfast in the library before a light grate fire. We were held up in the traffic on our way down-town, and though it was quarter after nine when we reached the District Attorney's office, Drukker and Heath had not yet arrived.

Vance settled himself comfortably in a large leather-upholstered chair and lighted a cigarette.

"I feel rather bucked this morning," he remarked. "If Drukker tells his story, and if the tale is what I think it is, we'll know the combination to the lock."

His words had scarcely been uttered when Heath burst into the office and, facing Markham without a word of greeting, lifted both arms and let them fall in a gesture of hopeless resignation.

"Well, sir, we ain't going to question Drukker this morning – or no other time," he blurted. "He fell offa that high wall in River-

*"Louise" was Vance's favorite modern opera, but he greatly preferred Mary Garden to Farrar in the title rôle.

side Park right near his house last night, and broke his neck. Wasn't found till seven o'clock this morning. His body's down at the morgue now. . . . Fine breaks we get!" He sank disgustedly into a chair.

Markham stared at him unbelievingly.

"You're sure?" he asked, with startled futility.

"I was up there before they removed the body. One of the local men phoned me about it just as I was leaving the office. I stuck around and got all the dope I could."

"What did you learn?" Markham was fighting against an overwhelming sense of discouragement.

"There wasn't much to find out. Some kids in the park found the body about seven o'clock this morning – lots of kids around, it being Saturday; and the local men hopped over and called a police surgeon. The doc said Drukker musta fallen off the wall about ten o'clock last night – killed instantly. The wall at that spot – right opposite 76th Street – is all of thirty feet above the playground. The top of it runs along the bridle path; and it's a wonder more people haven't broke their necks there. Kids are all the time walking along the stone ledge."

"Has Mrs. Drukker been notified?"

"No. I told 'em I'd attend to it. But I thought

I'd come here first and see what you wanted done about it."

Markham leaned back dejectedly.

"I don't see that there's much of anything we can do."

"It might be well," suggested Vance, "to inform Arnesson. He'll probably be the one who'll have to look after things. . . . My word, Markham! I'm beginning to think that this case is a nightmare, after all. Drukker was our principal hope, and at the very moment when there's a chance of our forcing him to speak, he tumbled off of a wall –" Abruptly he stopped. "Off of a wall! . . ." As he repeated these words he leapt to his feet. *"A hunchback falls off of a wall! . . . A hunchback! . . ."*

We stared at him as if he had gone out of his mind; and I admit that the look on his face sent a chill over me. His eyes were fixed, like those of a man gazing at a malignant ghost. Slowly he turned to Markham, and said in a voice that I hardly recognized:

"It's another mad melodrama – another Mother-Goose rhyme. . . . 'Humpty Dumpty' this time!"

The astonished silence that followed was broken by a strained harsh laugh from the Sergeant.

"That's stretching things, ain't it, Mr. Vance?"

"It's preposterous!" declared Markham, studying Vance with genuine concern. "My dear fellow, you've let this case prey on your mind too much. Nothing has happened except that a man with a hump has fallen from the coping of a wall in the park. It's unfortunate, I know; and it's doubly unfortunate at just this time." He went to Vance and put his hand on his shoulder. "Let the Sergeant and me run this show – we're used to these things. Take a trip and get a good rest. Why not go to Europe as you generally do in the spring –?"

"Oh, quite – quite." Vance sighed and smiled wearily. "The sea air would do me worlds of good, and all that. Bring me back to normal, what? – build up the wreck of this once noble brain. . . . I give up! The third act in this terrible tragedy is played almost before your eyes, and you serenely ignore it."

"Your imagination has got the better of you," Markham returned, with the patience of a deep affection. "Don't worry about it any more. Have dinner with me to-night. We'll talk it over then."

At this moment Swacker looked in, and spoke to the Sergeant.

"Quinan of the *World* is here. Wants to see you."

Markham swung about.

"Oh, my God! . . . Bring him in here!"

Quinan entered, waved us a cheery salutation, and handed the Sergeant a letter.

"Another *billet-doux* – received this morning. – What privileges do I get for being so big-hearted?"

Heath opened the letter as the rest of us looked on. At once I recognized the paper and the faint blue characters of the élite type. The note read:

Humpty Dumpty sat on a wall,
Humpty Dumpty had a great fall;
All the king's horses and all the king's men
Cannot put Humpty Dumpty together again.

Then came that ominous signature, in capitals: THE BISHOP.

CHAPTER XVII

AN ALL–NIGHT LIGHT

(Saturday, April 16; 9.30 a.m.)

When Heath had got rid of Quinan with promises such as would have gladdened any reporter's heart,* there were several minutes of tense silence in the office. "The Bishop" had been at his grisly work again; and the case had now become a terrible triplicate affair, with the solution apparently further off than ever. It was not, however, the insolubility of these incredible crimes that primarily affected us; rather was it the inherent horror that emanated, like a miasma, from the acts themselves.

Vance, who was pacing sombrely up and

*It may be recalled that the *World's* accounts of the Bishop case were the envy of the other metropolitan newspapers. Sergeant Heath, though impartial in his statements of facts to the press, nevertheless managed to save several picturesque *bonnesbouches* for Quinan, and permitted himself certain speculations which, while having no news value, gave the *World's* stories an added interest and color.

down, gave voice to his troubled emotions.

"It's damnable, Markham – it's the essence of unutterable evil. . . . Those children in the park – up early on their holiday in search of dreams – busy with their play and make-believe . . . and then the silencing reality – the awful, overpowering disillusion. . . . Don't you see the wickedness of it? Those children found Humpty Dumpty – *their* Humpty Dumpty, with whom they had played – lying dead at the foot of the famous wall – a Humpty Dumpty they could touch and weep over, broken and twisted and never more to be put together. . . ."

He paused by the window and looked out. The mist had lifted, and a faint diffusion of spring sunlight lay over the gray stones of the city. The golden eagle on the New York Life Building glistened in the distance.

"I say; one simply mustn't get sentimental," he remarked with a forced smile, turning back to the room. "It decomposes the intelligence and stultifies the dialectic processes. Now that we know Drukker was not the capricious victim of the law of gravity, but was given a helpin' hand in his departure from this world, the sooner we become energetic, the better, what?"

Though his change of mood was an obvious

tour de force, it roused the rest of us from our gloomy apathy. Markham reached for the telephone and made arrangements with Inspector Moran for Heath to handle the Drukker case. Then he called the Medical Examiner's office and asked for an immediate *post-mortem* report. Heath got up vigorously, and after taking three cups of ice-water, stood with legs apart, his derby pulled far down on his forehead, waiting for the District Attorney to indicate a line of action.

Markham moved restlessly.

"Several men from your department, Sergeant, were supposed to be keeping an eye on the Drukker and Dillard houses. Did you talk to any of them this morning?"

"I didn't have time, sir; and, anyway, I figured it was only an accident. But I told the boys to hang around until I got back."

"What did the Medical Examiner have to say?"

"Only that it looked like an accident; and that Drukker had been dead about ten hours. . . ."

Vance interpolated a question.

"Did he mention a fractured skull in addition to the broken neck?"

"Well, sir, he didn't exactly say the skull was fractured, but he did state that Drukker had landed on the back of his head." Heath nodded understandingly. "I guess it'll prove to be a fracture all right – same like Robin and Sprigg."

"Undoubtedly. The technique of our murderer seems to be simple and efficacious. He strikes his victims on the vault, either stunning them or killing them outright, and then proceeds to cast them in the rôles he has chosen for them in his puppet-plays. Drukker was no doubt leaning over the wall, perfectly exposed for such an attack. It was misty, and the setting was somewhat obscured. Then came the blow on the head, a slight heave, and Drukker fell noiselessly over the parapet – the third sacrificial offering on the altar of old Mother Goose."

"What gets me," declared Heath with surly anger, "is why Guilfoyle,* the fellow I set to watch the rear of the Drukker house, didn't report the fact that Drukker was out all night. He returned to the Bureau at eight o'clock, and I missed him. – Don't you think, sir, it might be a good idea to find out what he knows before we go up-town?"

Markham agreed, and Heath bawled an

*Guilfoyle, it may be remembered, was one of the detectives who shadowed Tony Skeel in the Canary murder case.

order over the telephone. Guilfoyle made the distance between Police Headquarters and the Criminal Courts Building in less than ten minutes. The Sergeant almost pounced on him as he entered.

"What time did Drukker leave the house last night?" he bellowed.

"About eight o'clock – right after he'd had dinner." Guilfoyle was ill at ease, and his tone had the wheedling softness of one who had been caught in a dereliction of duty.

"Which way did he go?"

"He came out the back door, walked down the range, and went into the Dillard house through the archery-room."

"Paying a social visit?"

"It looked that way, Sergeant. He spends a lot of time at the Dillards'."

"Huh! And what time did he come back home?"

Guilfoyle moved uneasily.

"It don't look like he came back home, Sergeant."

"Oh, it don't?" Heath's retort was ponderous with sarcasm. "I thought maybe after he'd broke his neck he mighta come back and passed the time of day with you."

"What I meant was, Sergeant –"

"You meant that Drukker – the bird you

were supposed to keep an eye on – went to call on the Dillards at eight o'clock, and then you set down in the arbor, most likely, and took a little beauty nap. . . . What time did you wake up?"

"Say, listen!" Guilfoyle bristled. "I didn't take no nap. I was on the job all night. Just because I didn't happen to see this guy come back home don't mean I was laying down on the watch."

"Well, if you didn't see him come back, why didn't you phone in that he was spending his week-end out of town or something?"

"I thought he musta come in by the front door."

"Thinking again, were you? Ain't your brain worn out this morning?"

"Have a heart, Sergeant. My job wasn't to tail Drukker. You told me to watch the house and see who went in and out, and that if there was any sign of trouble to bust in. – Now, here's what happened. Drukker went to the Dillards' at eight o'clock, and I kept my eye on the windows of the Drukker house. Along about nine o'clock the cook goes up-stairs and turns on the light in her room. Half an hour later the light goes out, and says I: 'She's put to bed.' Then along about ten o'clock the lights are turned on in Drukker's room –"

"What's this?"

"Yeh – you heard me. The lights go on in Drukker's room about ten o'clock; and I can see a shadow of somebody moving about. – Now, I ask you, Sergeant: wouldn't you yourself have took it for granted that the hunchback had come in by the front door?"

Heath grunted.

"Maybe so," he admitted. "You're sure it was ten o'clock?"

"I didn't look at my watch; but I'm here to tell you it wasn't far off of ten."

"And what time did the lights go out in Drukker's room?"

"They didn't go out. They stayed on all night. He was a queer bird. He didn't keep regular hours, and twice before his lights were on till nearly morning."

"That's quite understandable," came Vance's lazy voice. "He has been at work on a difficult problem lately. – But tell us, Guilfoyle: what about the light in Mrs. Drukker's room?"

"Same as usual. The old dame always keeps a light burning in her room all night."

"Was there any one on guard in front of the Drukker house last night?" Markham asked Heath.

"Not after six o'clock, sir. We've had a man tailing Drukker during the day, but he goes off duty at six when Guilfoyle takes up his post in the rear."

There was a moment's silence. Then Vance turned to Guilfoyle.

"How far away were you last night from the door of the alleyway between the two apartment houses?"

The man paused to visualize the scene.

"Forty or fifty feet, say."

"And between you and the alleyway were the iron fence and some tree branches."

"Yes, sir. The view was more or less cut off, if that's what you mean."

"Would it have been possible for any one, coming from the direction of the Dillard house, to have gone out and returned by that door without your noticing him?"

"It mighta been done," the detective admitted: "provided, of course, the guy didn't want me to see him. It was foggy and dark last night, and there's always a lot of traffic noises from the Drive that woulda drowned out his movements if he was being extra cautious."

When the Sergeant had sent Guilfoyle back to the Bureau to await orders, Vance gave voice to his perplexity.

"It's a dashed complicated situation. Drukker called on the Dillards at eight o'clock, and at ten o'clock he was shoved over the wall in the park. As you observed, the note that Quinan just showed us was postmarked 11 p.m. – which means that it was probably typed *before the crime.* The Bishop therefore had planned his comedy in advance and prepared the note for the press. The audacity of it is amazin'. But there's one assumption we can tie to – namely, that the murderer was some one who knew of Drukker's exact whereabouts and proposed movements between eight and ten."

"I take it," said Markham, "your theory is that the murderer went and returned by the apartment-house alley."

"Oh, I say! I have no theory. I asked Guilfoyle about the alley merely in case we should learn that no one but Drukker was seen going to the park. In that event we could assume, as a tentative hypothesis, that the murderer had managed to avoid detection by taking the alleyway and crossing to the park in the middle of the block."

"With that possible route open to the murderer," Markham observed gloomily, "it wouldn't matter much who was seen going out with Drukker."

"That's just it. The person who staged this farce may have walked boldly into the park under the eyes of an alert myrmidon, or he may have hied stealthily through the alley."

Markham nodded an unhappy agreement.

"The thing that bothers me most, however," continued Vance, "is that light in Drukker's room all night. It was turned on at about the time the poor chap was tumbling into eternity. And Guilfoyle says that he could see some one moving about there after the light went on –"

He broke off, and stood for several seconds in an attitude of concentration.

"I say, Sergeant; I don't suppose you know whether or not Drukker's front-door key was in his pocket when he was found."

"No, sir; but I can find out in no time. The contents of his pockets are being held till after the autopsy."

Heath stepped to the telephone, and a moment later he was talking to the desk sergeant of the 68th-Street Precinct Station. Several minutes of waiting passed; then he grunted and banged down the receiver.

"Not a key of any kind on him."

"Ah!" Vance drew a deep puff on his cigarette and exhaled the smoke slowly. "I'm beginnin' to think that the Bishop purloined Drukker's key and paid a visit to his room after the murder. Sounds incredible, I know; but for that matter, so does everything else that's happened in this fantastic business."

"But what, in God's name, would have been

his object?" protested Markham incredulously.

"We don't know yet. But I have an idea that when we learn the motive of these astonishin' crimes, we'll understand why that visit was paid."

Markham, his face set austerely, took his hat from the closet.

"We'd better be getting out there."

But Vance made no move. He remained standing by the desk smoking abstractedly.

"Y' know, Markham," he said, "it occurs to me that we should see Mrs. Drukker first. There was tragedy in that house last night: something strange took place there that needs explaining; and now perhaps she'll tell us the secret that has been locked up in her brain. Moreover, she hasn't been notified of Drukker's death, and with all the rumor and gossip in the neighborhood, word of some kind is sure to leak through to her before long. I fear the result of the shock when she hears the news. In fact, I'd feel better if we got hold of Barstead right away and took him with us. What do you say to my phoning him?"

Markham assented, and Vance briefly explained the situation to the doctor.

We drove up-town immediately, called for Barstead, and proceeded at once to the Drukker house. Our ring was answered by

Mrs. Menzel, whose face showed plainly that she knew of Drukker's death. Vance, after one glance at her, led her into the drawing-room away from the stairs, and asked in a low tone:

"Has Mrs. Drukker heard the news?"

"Not yet," she answered, in a frightened, quavering voice. "Miss Dillard came over an hour ago, but I told her the mistress had gone out. I was afraid to let her up-stairs. Something's wrong. . . ." She began to tremble violently.

"What's wrong, Mrs. Menzel?" Vance placed a quieting hand on her arm.

"I don't know. But she hasn't made a sound all morning. She didn't come down for breakfast . . . and I'm afraid to go and call her."

"When did you hear of the accident?"

"Early – right after eight o'clock. The paper boy told me; and I saw all the people down on the Drive."

"Don't be frightened," Vance consoled her. "We have the doctor here, and we'll attend to everything."

He turned back to the hall and led the way upstairs. When we came to Mrs. Drukker's room he knocked softly and, receiving no answer, opened the door. The room was empty. The night-light still burned on the table, and I noticed that the bed had not been slept in.

Without a word Vance retraced his steps down the hall. There were only two other main doors, and one of them, we knew, led to Drukker's study. Unhesitatingly Vance stepped to the other and opened it without knocking. The window shades were drawn, but they were white and semi-transparent, and the gray daylight mingled with the ghastly yellow radiation from the old-fashioned chandelier. The lights which Guilfoyle had seen burning all night had not been extinguished.

Vance halted on the threshold, and I saw Markham, who was just in front of me, give a start.

"Mother o' God!" breathed the Sergeant, and crossed himself.

On the foot of the narrow bed lay Mrs. Drukker, fully clothed. Her face was ashen white; her eyes were set in a hideous stare; and her hands were clutching her breast.

Barstead sprang forward and leaned over. After touching her once or twice he straightened up and shook his head slowly.

"She's gone. Been dead probably most of the night." He bent over the body again and began making an examination. "You know, she's suffered for years from chronic nephritis, arteriosclerosis, and hypertrophy of the heart. . . . Some sudden shock brought on an acute dilatation. . . Yes, I'd say she died about the same time as Drukker . . . round ten o'clock."

"A natural death?" asked Vance.

"Oh, undoubtedly. A shot of adrenalin in the heart might have saved her if I'd been here at the time. . . ."

"No signs of violence?"

"None. As I told you, she died from dilatation of the heart brought on by shock. A clear case – true to type in every respect."

CHAPTER XVIII

THE WALL IN THE PARK

(Saturday, April 16; 11 a.m.)

When the doctor had straightened Mrs. Drukker's body on the bed and covered it with a sheet, we returned down-stairs. Barstead took his departure at once after promising to send the death certificate to the Sergeant within an hour.

"It's scientifically correct to talk of natural death from shock," said Vance, when we were alone; "but our immediate problem, d' ye see, is to ascertain the cause of that sudden shock. Obviously it's connected with Drukker's death. Now, I wonder. . . ."

Turning impulsively, he entered the drawing-room. Mrs. Menzel was sitting where we had left her, in an attitude of horrified expectancy. Vance went to her and said kindly:

"Your mistress died of heart failure during the night. And it's much better that she should not have outlived her son."

"Gott geb' ihr die ewige Ruh'!" the woman murmured piously. *"Ja,* it is best. . . ."

"The end came at about ten last night. – Were you awake at that time, Mrs. Menzel?"

"All night I was awake." She spoke in a low, awed voice.

Vance contemplated her with eyes half shut. "Tell us what you heard?"

"Somebody came here last night!"

"Yes, some one came at about ten o'clock – by the front door. Did you hear him enter?"

"No; but after I had gone to bed I heard voices in Mr. Drukker's room."

"Was it unusual to hear voices in his room at ten o'clock at night?"

"But it wasn't *him!* He had a high voice, and this one was low and gruff." The woman looked up in bewildered fright. "And the other voice was Mrs. Drukker's . . . and she never went in Mr. Drukker's room at night!"

"How could you hear so plainly with your door shut?"

"My room is right over Mr. Drukker's," she explained. "And I was worried – what with all these awful things going on; so I got up and listened at the top of the steps."

"I can't blame you," said Vance. "What did you hear?"

"At first it was like as though the mistress

was moaning, but right away she began to laugh, and then the man spoke angry-like. But pretty soon I heard him laugh, too. After that it sounded like the poor lady was praying – I could hear her saying 'Oh, God – oh, God!' Then the man talked some more – very quiet and low. . . . And in a little while it seemed like the mistress was – reciting – a poem. . . ."

"Would you recognize the poem if you heard it again? . . . Was it

> Humpty Dumpty sat on a wall;
> Humpty Dumpty had a great fall. . . .?"

"Bei Gott, das ist's! It sounded just like that!" A new horror came into the woman's expression. "And Mr. Drukker fell from the wall last night. . . !"

"Did you hear anything else, Mrs. Menzel?" Vance's matter-of-fact voice interrupted her confused correlation of Drukker's death to the verse she had heard.

Slowly she shook her head.

"No. Everything was quiet after that."

"Did you hear any one leave Mr. Drukker's room?"

She gave Vance a panic-stricken nod.

"A few minutes later some one opened and shut the door, very soft; and I heard steps moving down the hall in the dark. Then the stairs creaked, and pretty soon the front door shut."

"What did you do after that?"

"I listened a little while, and then I went back to bed. But I couldn't sleep. . . ."

"It's all over now, Mrs. Menzel," Vance told her comfortingly. "There's nothing for you to fear. – You'd best go to your room and wait till we need you."

Reluctantly the woman went up-stairs.

"I think now," said Vance, "we can make a pretty close guess as to what happened here last night. The murderer took Drukker's key and let himself in by the front door. He knew Mrs. Drukker's quarters were at the rear, and he no doubt counted on accomplishing his business in Drukker's room and departing as he had come. But Mrs. Drukker heard him. It may be she associated him with 'the little man' who had left the black bishop at her door, and feared that her son was in danger. At any rate, she went at once to Drukker's room. The door may have been slightly open, and I think she saw the intruder and recognized him. Startled and apprehensive, she stepped inside and asked him why he was there. He may have answered that he had come to inform her of Drukker's death – which would account for her moans and her hysterical laughter. But that was only a prelimin'ry on his part – a play for time. He was devising some means of meeting the situation – he was planning how he would kill her! Oh, there can be no doubt of that. He couldn't afford to let her leave that room alive. Maybe he told her so in as many words – he spoke 'angry-like,' you recall. And then he laughed. He was torturing her now – perhaps telling her the whole truth in a burst of insane egoism; and she could say only 'Oh God – oh God!' He explained how he had pushed Drukker over the wall. And did he mention Humpty Dumpty? I think he did; for what more appreciative audience could he have had for his monstrous jest than the victim's own mother? That last revelation proved too much for her hypersensitive brain. She repeated the nursery rhyme in a spell of horror; and then the accumulated shock dilated her heart. She fell across the bed, and the murderer was saved the necessity of sealing her lips with his own hands. He saw what had happened, and went quietly away."

Markham took a turn up and down the room.

"The least comprehensible part of last night's tragedy," he said, "is why this man should have come here after Drukker's death."

Vance was smoking thoughtfully.

"We'd better ask Arnesson to help us explain that point. Maybe he can throw some light on it."

"Yeh, maybe he can," chimed in Heath. Then after rolling his cigar between his lips for a moment, he added sulkily: "There's several people around here, I'm thinking, that could do some high-class explaining."

Markham halted before the Sergeant.

"The first thing we'd better do is to find out what your men know about the movements of the various persons hereabouts last night. Suppose you bring them here and let me question them. – How many were there, by the way? – and what were their posts?"

The Sergeant had risen, alert and energetic.

"There were three, sir, besides Guilfoyle. Emery was set to tail Pardee; Snitkin was stationed at the Drive and 75th Street to watch the Dillard house; and Hennessey was posted on 75th Street up near West End Avenue. – They're all waiting down at the place where Drukker was found. I'll get 'em up here *pronto.*"

He disappeared through the front door, and in less than five minutes returned with the three detectives. I recognized them all, for each had worked on one or more of the cases in which Vance had figured.* Markham questioned Snitkin first as the one most likely to have information bearing directly on the previous night's affair. The following points were brought out by his testimony:

> Pardee had emerged from his house at 6.30 and gone straight to the Dillards'.
>
> At 8.30 Belle Dillard, in an evening gown, had got into a taxi and been driven up West End Avenue. (Arnesson had come out of the house with her and helped her into the taxicab, but had immediately returned indoors.)
>
> At 9.15 Professor Dillard and Drukker had left the Dillard house and walked slowly toward Riverside Drive. They had crossed the Drive at 74th Street, and turned up the bridle path.
>
> At 9.30 Pardee had come out of the Dillard house, walked down to the Drive, and turned up-town.

*Hennessey had kept watch with Doctor Drumm over the Greene mansion from the Narcoss Flats, in the Greene murder case. Snitkin also had taken part in the Greene investigation, and had played a minor rôle in both the Benson and the Canary case. The dapper Emery was the detective who had unearthed the cigarette stubs from beneath the fire-logs in Alvin Benson's living-room.

At a little after 10.00 Professor Dillard had returned to his house alone, recrossing the Drive at 74th Street.

At 10.20 Pardee had returned home, coming from the same direction he had taken when going out.

Belle Dillard had been brought home at 12.30 in a limousine filled with young people.

Hennessey was interrogated next; but his evidence merely substantiated Snitkin's. No one had approached the Dillard house from the direction of West End Avenue; and nothing of a suspicious nature had happened.

Markham then turned his attention to Emery, who reported that, according to Santos whom he had relieved at six, Pardee had spent the early part of the afternoon at the Manhattan Chess Club and had returned home at about four o'clock.

"Then, like Snitkin and Hennessey said," Emery continued, "he went to the Dillards' at half past six, and stayed till half past nine. When he came out I followed, keeping half a block or so behind him. He walked up the Drive to 79th Street, crossed to the upper park, and walked round the big grass bowl, past the rocks, and on up toward the Yacht Club. . . ."

"Did he take the path where Sprigg was shot?" Vance asked.

"He had to. There ain't any other path up that way unless you walk along the Drive."

"How far did he go?"

"The fact is, he stopped right about where Sprigg was bumped off. Then he came back the same way he'd gone and turned into the little park with the playground on the south side of 79th Street. He went slowly down the walk under the trees along the bridle path; and as he passed along the top of the wall under the drinking fountain, who should he run into but the old man and the hunchback, resting up against the ledge and talking. . . ."

"You say he met Professor Dillard and Drukker at the very spot where Drukker fell over the wall?" Markham leaned forward hopefully.

"Yes, sir. Pardee stopped to visit with them; and I naturally kept on going. As I passed 'em I heard the hunchback say: 'Why ain't you practising chess this evening?' And it sounded to me like he was sore at Pardee for stopping, and was hinting that he wasn't wanted. Anyhow, I ambled along the wall till I got to 74th Street where there was a couple of trees to hide under. . . ."

"How well could you see Pardee and

Drukker after you'd reached 74th Street?" interrupted Markham.

"Well, sir, to tell you the truth, I couldn't see 'em at all. It was getting pretty misty about that time, and there isn't any lamp-post at that part of the walk where they were confabulating. But I figured Pardee would be along pretty soon, so I waited for him."

"This must have been well on toward ten o'clock."

"About a quarter of, I should say, sir."

"Were there any people on the walk at that time?"

"I didn't see anybody. The fog musta driven 'em indoors – it wasn't no warm balmy evening. And it was on account of there being nobody around that I went as far ahead as I did. Pardee's nobody's fool, and I'd already caught him looking at me once or twice as though he suspected I was tailing him."

"How long was it before you picked him up again?"

Emery shifted his position.

"My figuring wasn't so good last night," he confessed, with a weak grin. "Pardee musta gone back the way he came and recrossed the Drive at 79th Street; for a half-hour or so later I saw him heading home in front of the apartment-house light on the corner of 75th Street."

"But," interposed Vance, "if you were at the 74th-Street entrance to the park until a quarter past ten you must have seen Professor Dillard pass you. He returned home about ten o'clock by that route."

"Sure, I saw him. I'd been waiting for Pardee about twenty minutes when the Professor came strolling along all alone, crossed the Drive, and went home. I naturally thought Pardee and the hunchback were still gabbing, – that's why I took it easy and didn't go back to check up."

"Then, as I understand, about fifteen minutes after Professor Dillard passed you, you saw Pardee returning home from the opposite direction along the Drive."

"That's right, sir. And, of course, I took up my post again on 75th Street."

"You realize, Emery," said Markham gravely, "that it was during the time you waited at 74th Street that Drukker fell over the wall."

"Yes, sir. But you're not blaming me, are you? Watching a man on a foggy night on an open path when there ain't anybody around to screen you, is no easy job. You gotta take a few chances and do a little figuring if you don't want to get spotted."

"I realize your difficulty," Markham told him; "and I'm not criticizing you."

The Sergeant dismissed the three detectives gruffly. He was obviously dissatisfied with their reports.

"The farther we go," he complained, "the more gummed up this case gets."

"*Sursum corda,* Sergeant," Vance exhorted him. "Let not dark despair o'ercome you. When we have Pardee's and the Professor's testimony as to what took place while Emery was watchfully waiting beneath the trees at 74th Street, we may be able to fit some very interestin' bits together."

As he spoke Belle Dillard entered the front hall from the rear of the house. She saw us in the drawing-room and came in at once.

"Where's Lady Mae?" she asked in a troubled voice. "I was here an hour ago, and Grete told me she was out. And she's not in her room now."

Vance rose and gave her his chair.

"Mrs. Drukker died last night of heart failure. When you were here earlier Mrs. Menzel was afraid to let you go up-stairs."

The girl sat very quiet for some time. Presently the tears welled to her eyes.

"Perhaps she heard of Adolph's terrible accident."

"Possibly. But it's not quite clear what happened here last night. Doctor Barstead thinks Mrs. Drukker died at about ten o'clock."

"Almost the same time Adolph died," she murmured. "It seems too terrible. . . . Pyne told me of the accident when I came down to breakfast this morning, – every one in the quarter was talking about it, – and I came over at once to be with Lady Mae. But Grete said she had gone out, and I didn't know what to think. There's something very strange about Adolph's death. . . ."

"What do you mean by that, Miss Dillard?" Vance stood by the window watching her covertly.

"I – don't know – what I mean," she answered brokenly. "But only yesterday afternoon Lady Mae spoke to me about Adolph and the – wall. . . ."

"Oh, did she, now?" Vance's tone was more indolent than usual, but every nerve in his body was, I knew, vigilantly alert.

"On my way to the tennis courts," the girl went on, in a low, hushed voice, "I walked with Lady Mae along the bridle path above the playground – she often went there to watch Adolph playing with the children, – and we stood for a long time leaning over the stone balustrade of the wall. A group of children were gathered around Adolph: he had a toy aeroplane and was showing them how to fly it.

And the children seemed to regard him as one of themselves; they didn't look upon him as a grown-up. Lady Mae was very happy and proud about it. She watched him with shining eyes, and then she said to me: 'They're not afraid of him, Belle, because he's a hunchback. they call him Humpty Dumpty – he's their old friend of the story-book. My poor Humpty Dumpty! It was all my fault for letting him fall when he was little.' . . ." The girl's voice faltered, and she put her handkerchief to her eyes.

"So she mentioned to you that the children called Drukker Humpty Dumpty." Vance reached slowly in his pocket for his cigarette-case.

She nodded, and a moment later lifted her head as if forcing herself to face something she dreaded.

"Yes! And that's what was so strange; for after a little while she shuddered and drew back from the wall. I asked her what was the matter, and she said in a terrified voice: 'Suppose, Belle – suppose that Adolph should ever fall off of this wall – the way the real Humpty Dumpty did!' I was almost afraid myself; but I forced a smile, and told her she was foolish. It didn't do any good, though. She shook her head and gave me a look that sent a chill through me. 'I'm not foolish,' she said. 'Wasn't Cock Robin killed with a bow and arrow, and wasn't Johnny Sprig shot with a little gun – *right here in New York?*' " The girl turned a frightened gaze upon us. "And it *did* happen, didn't it – just as she foresaw?"

"Yes, it happened," Vance nodded. "But we mustn't be mystical about it. Mrs. Drukker's imagination was abnormal. All manner of wild conjectures went through her tortured mind; and with these two other Mother-Goose deaths so vivid in her memory, it's not remarkable that she should have turned the children's sobriquet for her son into a tragic speculation of that kind. That he should actually have been killed in the manner she feared is nothing more than a coincidence. . . ."

He paused and drew deeply on his cigarette.

"I say, Miss Dillard," he asked negligently; "did you, by any chance, repeat your conversation with Mrs. Drukker to any one yesterday?"

She regarded him with some surprise before answering.

"I mentioned it at dinner last night. It worried me all the afternoon, and – somehow – I didn't want to keep it to myself?"

"Were any comments made about it?"

"Uncle told me I shouldn't spend so much time with Lady Mae – that she was unhealthily morbid. He said the situation was very tragic, but that there was no need for me to share Lady Mae's suffering. Mr. Pardee agreed with uncle. He was very sympathetic, and asked if something could not be done to help Lady Mae's mental condition."

"And Mr. Arnesson?"

"Oh, Sigurd never takes anything seriously, – I hate his attitude sometimes. He laughed as though it was a joke; and all he said was: 'It would be a shame if Adolph took his tumble before he got his new quantum problem worked out.' "

"Is Mr. Arnesson at home now, by the by?" asked Vance. "We want to ask him about the necess'ry arrangements in regard to the Drukkers."

"He went to the university early this morning; but he'll be back before lunch. He'll attend to everything, I am sure. We were about the only friends Lady Mae and Adolph had. I'll take charge in the meantime and see that Grete gets the house in order."

A few minutes later we left her and went to interview Professor Dillard.

CHAPTER XIX

THE RED NOTE-BOOK

(Saturday, April 16; noon)

The professor was plainly perturbed when we entered the library that noon. He sat in an easy chair with his back to the window, a glass of his precious port on the table beside him.

"I've been expecting you, Markham," he said, before we had time to speak. "There's no need to dissemble. Drukker's death was no accident. I'll admit I felt inclined to discount the insane implications arising from the deaths of Robin and Sprigg; but the moment Pyne related the circumstances of Drukker's fall I realized that there was a definite design behind these deaths: the probabilities of their being accidental would be incalculable. You know it, as well as I; otherwise you wouldn't be here."

"Very true." Markham had seated himself facing the professor. "We're confronted by a terrific problem. Moreover, Mrs. Drukker died of shock last night at almost the same time her son was killed."

"That at least," returned the old man after a pause. "may be regarded as a blessing. It's better she didn't survive him – her mind unquestionably would have collapsed." He looked up. "In what way can I help?"

"You were probably the last person, with the exception of the actual murderer, to see Drukker alive; and we would like to know everything you can tell us of what took place last night."

Professor Dillard nodded.

"Drukker came here after dinner – about eight, I should say. Pardee had dined with us; and Drukker was annoyed at finding him here – in fact, he was openly hostile. Arnesson twitted him good-naturedly about his irascibility – which only made him more irritable; and, knowing that Drukker was anxious to thrash out a problem with me, I finally suggested that he and I stroll down to the park. . . ."

"You were not gone very long," suggested Markham.

"No. An unfortunate episode occurred. We walked up the bridle path to almost the exact spot where, I understand, the poor fellow was killed. We had been there for perhaps half an hour, leaning against the stone balustrade of the wall, when Pardee walked up. He stopped to speak to us, but Drukker was so antagonistic in his remarks that, after a few minutes, Pardee turned and walked away in the direction he had come. Drukker was very much upset, and I suggested we postpone the discussion. Furthermore, a damp mist had fallen, and I was beginning to get some twinges in my foot. Drukker straightway became morose, and said he didn't care to go indoors just yet. So I left him alone by the wall, and came home."

"Did you mention the episode to Arnesson?"

"I didn't see Sigurd after I got back. I imagine he'd gone to bed."

Later as we rose to take our leave, Vance asked casually: "Can you tell us where the key to the alley door is kept?"

"I know nothing about it, sir," the professor replied irritably, but added in a more equable tone: "However, as I remember, it used to hang on a nail by the archery-room door."

From Professor Dillard we went straight to Pardee, and were received at once in his study. His manner was rigid and detached, and even after we had seated ourselves he remained standing by the window, staring at us with unfriendly eyes.

"Do you know, Mr. Pardee," asked Markham, "that Mr. Drukker fell from the wall in the park at ten o'clock last night – shortly after you stopped and spoke to him?"

"I heard of the accident this morning." The man's pallor became more noticeable, and he toyed nervously with his watch chain. "It's very unfortunate." His eyes rested vacantly for a while on Markham. "Have you asked Professor Dillard about it? He was with Drukker –"

"Yes, yes; we've just come from him," interrupted Vance. "He said there was a ruffled atmosphere between you and Mr. Drukker last night."

Pardee slowly walked to the desk and sat down stiffly.

"Drukker was displeased for some reason to find me at the Dillards' when he came over after dinner. He hadn't the good taste to hide his displeasure, and created a somewhat embarrassing situation. But, knowing him as I did, I tried to pass the matter off. Soon, however Professor Dillard took him out for a walk."

"You didn't remain long afterward," observed Vance indolently.

"No – about a quarter of an hour. Arnesson was tired and wanted to turn in, so I went for a walk myself. On my return I took the bridle path instead of the Drive, and came on Professor Dillard and Drukker standing by the wall talking. Not wishing to appear rude, I stopped for a moment. But Drukker was in a beastly mood and made several sneering remarks. I turned and walked back to 79th Street, crossed the Drive, and came home."

"I say; didn't you loiter a bit by the wayside?"

"I sat down near the 79th-Street entrance and smoked a cigarette."

For nearly half an hour Markham and Vance interrogated Pardee, but nothing more could be learned from him. As we came out into the street Arnesson hailed us from the front porch of the Dillard house and stalked forward to meet us.

"Just heard the sad news. Got home from the university a little while ago, and the professor told me you'd gone to rag Pardee. Learn anything?" Without waiting for an answer he ran on: "Frightful mess. I understand the entire Drukker family is wiped out. Well, well. And more story-book mumbo-jumbo to boot. . . . Any clews?"

"Ariadne has not yet favored us," responded Vance. "Are you an ambassador from Crete?"

"One never knows. Bring out your questionnaire."

Vance had led the way toward the wall gate, and we now stepped down on the range.

"We'll repair to the Drukker house first," he said. "There'll be a number of things to settle. I suppose you'll look after Drukker's affairs and the funeral arrangements."

Arnesson made a grimace.

"Elected! I refuse, however, to attend the funeral. Obscene spectacles, funerals. But Belle and I will see to everything. Lady Mae probably left a will. We'll have to find it. Now, where do women generally hide their wills? . . ."

Vance halted by the Dillards' basement door and stepped into the archery-room. After glancing along the door's moulding he rejoined us on the range.

"The alley key isn't there. – By the by, what do you know about it, Mr. Arnesson?"

"You mean the key to yon wooden door in the fence? . . . Haven't an idea on the subject. Never use the alley myself – much simpler going out the front door. No one uses it, as far as I know. Belle locked it up years ago: thought some one might sneak in off the Drive and get an arrow in the eye. I told her, let 'em get popped – serve 'em right for being interested in archery."

We entered the Drukker house by the rear door. Belle Dillard and Mrs. Menzel were busy in the kitchen.

"Hallo, sis," Arnesson greeted the girl. His

cynical manner had been dropped. "Hard lines for a young 'un like you. You'd better run home now. I'll assume command." And taking her arm in a jocularly paternal fashion, he led her to the door.

She hesitated and looked back at Vance.

"Mr. Arnesson is right," he nodded. "We'll carry on for the present. – But just one question before you go. Did you always keep the key to the alley door hanging in the archery-room?"

"Yes – always. Why? Isn't it there now?"

It was Arnesson who answered, with burlesque irony.

"Gone! Disappeared! – Most tragic. Some eccentric key-collector has evidently been snooping around." When the girl had left us, he cocked an eye at Vance. "What, in the name of all that's unholy, has a rusty key to do with the case?"

"Perhaps nothing," said Vance carelessly. "Let's go to the drawin'-room. It's more comfortable there." He led the way down the hall. "We want you to tell us what you can about last night."

Arnesson took an easy chair by the front window, and drew out his pipe.

"Last night, eh? . . . Well, Pardee came to dinner – it's a sort of habit with him on

Fridays. Then Drukker, in the throes of quantum speculation, dropped in to pump the professor; and Pardee's presence galled him. Showed his feelings too, by Gad! No control. The professor broke up the *contretemps* by taking Drukker for an airing. Pardee moped for fifteen minutes or so, while I tried to keep awake. Then he had the goodness to depart. I looked over a few test papers . . . and so to bed." He lighted his pipe. "How does that thrilling recital explain the end of poor Drukker?"

"It doesn't," said Vance. "But it's not without interest. – Did you hear Professor Dillard when he returned home?"

"Hear him?" Arnesson chuckled. "When he hobbles about with his gouty foot, thumping his stick down and shaking the banisters, there's no mistaking his arrival on the scene. Fact is, he was unusually noisy last night."

"Offhand, what do you make of these new developments?" asked Vance, after a short pause.

"I'm somewhat foggy as to the details. The professor was not exactly phosphorescent. Sketchy, in fact. Drukker fell from the wall, like Humpty Dumpty, round ten o'clock, and was found this morning – that's all plain. But under what conditions did Lady Mae succumb to shock? Who, or what, shocked her? And how?"

"The murderer took Drukker's key and came here immediately after the crime. Mrs. Drukker caught him in her son's room. There was a scene, according to the cook, who listened from the head of the stairs; and during it Mrs. Drukker died from dilatation of the heart."

"Thereby relieving the gentleman of the bother of killing her."

"That seems clear enough," agreed Vance. "But the reason for the murderer's visit here is not so lucid. Can you suggest an explanation?"

Arnesson puffed thoughtfully on his pipe.

"Incomprehensible," he muttered at length. "Drukker had no valuables, or no compromising documents. Straightforward sort of cuss – not the kind to mix in any dirty business. . . . No possible reason for any one prowling about his room."

Vance lay back and appeared to relax.

"What was this quantum theory Drukker was working on?"

"Ha! Big thing!" Arnesson became animated. "He was on the path of reconciling the Einstein-Bohr theory of radiation with the facts of interference, and of overcoming the inconsistencies inherent in Einstein's hypothesis.

His research had already led him to an abandonment of causal space-time coordination of atomic phenomena, and to its replacement by a statistical description.* . . . Would have revolutionized physics – made him famous. Shame he was told off before he'd put his data in shape."

"Do you happen to know where Drukker kept the records of these computations?"

"In a loose-leaf note-book – all tabulated and indexed. Methodical and neat about everything. Even his chirography was like copperplate."

"You know, then, what the note-book looked like?"

"I ought to. He showed it to me often enough. Red limp-leather cover – thin yellow pages – two or three clips on every sheet holding notations – his name gold-stamped in large letters on the binding . . . Poor devil! *Sic transit. . . .*"

"Where would this note-book be now?"

"One of two places – either in the drawer of his desk in the study or else in the escritoire in

*An important step toward the solution of these complex problems was taken a few years later by the de Broglie-Schrödinger theory as laid down in de Broglie's "Ondes et Mouvements" and Schrödinger's "Abhandlungen zur Wellenmechanik."

his bedroom. In the daytime, of course, he worked in the study; but he fussed day and night when wrapped up in a problem. Kept an escritoire in his bedroom, where he put his current records when he retired, in case he got an inspiration to monkey with 'em during the night. Then, in the morning, back they'd go to the study. Regular machine for system."

Vance had been gazing lazily out of the window as Arnesson rambled on. The impression he gave was that he had scarcely heard the description of Drukker's habits; but presently he turned and fixed Arnesson with a languid look.

"I say," he drawled; "would you mind toddling up-stairs and fetching Drukker's notebook? Look in both the study and the bedroom."

I thought I noticed an almost imperceptible hesitation on Arnesson's part; but straightway he rose.

"Good idea. Too valuable a document to be left lying round." And he strode from the room.

Markham began pacing the floor, and Heath revealed his uneasiness by puffing more energetically on his cigar. There was a tense atmosphere in the little drawing-room as we waited for Arnesson's return. Each of us was in a state of expectancy, though just what we hoped for or feared would have been difficult to define.

In less than ten minutes Arnesson reappeared at the door. He shrugged his shoulders and held out empty hands.

"Gone!" he announced. "Looked in every likely place – couldn't find it." He threw himself into a chair and relighted his pipe. "Can't understand it. . . . Perhaps he hid it."

"Perhaps," murmured Vance.

CHAPTER XX

THE NEMESIS

(Saturday, April 16; 1 p.m.)

It was past one o'clock, and Markham, Vance and I rode to the Stuyvesant Club. Heath remained at the Drukker house to carry on the routine work, to draw up his report, and to deal with the reporters who would be swarming there shortly.

Markham was booked for a conference with the Police Commissioner at three o'clock; and after lunch Vance and I walked to Stieglitz's Intimate Gallery and spent an hour at an exhibition of Georgia O'Keefe's floral abstractions. Later we dropped in at Aeolian Hall and sat through Debussy's G-minor quartette. There were some Cézanne water-colors at the Montross Galleries; but by the time we had pushed our way through the late-afternoon traffic of Fifth Avenue the light had begun to fail, and Vance ordered the chauffeur to the Stuyvesant Club, where we joined

Markham for tea.

"I feel so youthful, so simple, so innocent," Vance complained lugubriously. "So many things are happenin', and they're bein' manipulated so ingeniously that I can't grasp 'em. It's very disconcertin', very confusin'. I don't like it – I don't at all like it. Most wearin'." He sighed drearily and sipped his tea.

"Your sorrows leave me cold," retorted Markham. "You've probably spent the afternoon inspecting arquebuses and petronels at the Metropolitan Museum. If you'd had to go through what I've suffered –"

"Now, don't be cross," Vance rebuked him. "There's far too much emotion in the world. Passion is not going to solve this case. Cerebration is our only hope. Let us be calm and thoughtful." His mood became serious. "Markham, this comes very near being the perfect crime. Like one of Morphy's great chess combinations, it has been calculated a score of moves ahead. There are no clews; and even if there were, they'd probably point in the wrong direction. And yet . . . and yet there's something that's trying to break through. I feel it: sheer intuition – that is to say, nerves. There's an inarticulate voice that wants to speak, and can't. A dozen times I've sensed the presence of some struggling force, like an invisible ghost trying to make contact without revealing its identity."

Markham gave an exasperated sigh.

"Very helpful. Do you advise calling in a medium?"

"There's something we've overlooked," Vance went on, disregarding the sarcasm. "The case is a cipher, and the key-word is somewhere before us, but we don't recognize it. 'Pon my soul, it's dashed annoyin'. . . . Let's be orderly. Neatness – that's our desideratum. First, Robin is killed. Next, Sprigg is shot. Then Mrs. Drukker is frightened with a black bishop. After that, Drukker is shoved over a wall. Makin' four distinct episodes in the murderer's extravaganza. Three of 'em were carefully planned. One – the leaving of the bishop at Mrs. Drukker's door – was forced on the murderer, and was therefore decided on without preparation. . . ."

"Clarify your reasoning on that point."

"Oh, my dear fellow! The conveyor of the black bishop was obviously acting in self-defence. An unexpected danger developed along his line of campaign, and he took this means of averting it. Just before Robin's death Drukker departed from the archery-room and installed himself in the arbor of the yard, where he could look into the archery-room through the rear window. A little later he saw some one in the room talking to Robin. He returned to his house, and at that moment Robin's body was thrown on the range. Mrs. Drukker saw it, and at the same time she probably saw Drukker. She screamed – very natural, what? Drukker heard the scream, and told us of it later in an effort to establish an alibi for himself after we'd informed him that Robin had been killed. Thus the murderer learned that Mrs. Drukker had seen something – how much, he didn't know. But he wasn't taking any chances. He went to her room at midnight to silence her, and took the bishop to leave beside her body as a signature. But he found the door locked, and left the bishop outside, by way of warning her to say nothing on pain of death. He didn't know that the poor woman suspected her own son."

"But why didn't Drukker tell us whom he saw in the archery-room with Robin?"

"We can only assume that the person was some one whom he couldn't conceive of as being guilty. And I'm inclined to believe he mentioned the fact to this person and thus sealed his own doom."

"Assuming the correctness of your theory, where does it lead us?"

"To the one episode that wasn't elaborately

prepared in advance. And when there has been no preparation for a covert act there is pretty sure to be a weakness in one or more of the details. – Now, please note that at the time of each of the three murders any one of the various persons in the drama could have been present. No one had an alibi. That, of course, was cleverly calculated: the murderer chose an hour when all of the actors were, so to speak, waiting in the wings. But that midnight visit! Ah! That was a different matter. There was no time to work out a perfect set of circumstances, – the menace was too immediate. And what was the result? Drukker and Professor Dillard were, apparently, the only persons on hand at midnight. Arnesson and Belle Dillard were supping at the Plaza and didn't return home until half past twelve. Pardee was hornlocked with Rubinstein over a chess-board from eleven to one. Drukker is now of course eliminated. . . . What's the answer?"

"I could remind you," returned Markham irritably, "that the alibis of the others have not been thoroughly checked."

"Well, well, so you could." Vance lay back indolently and sent a long regular series of smoke-rings toward the ceiling. Suddenly his body tensed, and with meticulous care he leaned over and put out his cigarette. Then he glanced at his watch and got to his feet. He fixed Markham with a quizzical look.

"*Allons, mon vieux*. It's not yet six. Here's where Arnesson makes himself useful."

"What now?" expostulated Markham.

"Your own suggestion," Vance replied, taking him by the arm and leading him toward the door. "We're going to check Pardee's alibi."

Half an hour later we were seated with the professor and Arnesson in the Dillard library.

"We've come on a somewhat unusual errand," explained Vance; "but it may have a vital bearing on our investigation." He took out his wallet, and unfolded a sheet of paper. "Here's a document, Mr. Arnesson, I wish you'd glance over. It's a copy of the official scoresheet of the chess game between Pardee and Rubinstein. Very interestin'. I've toyed with it a bit, but I'd like your expert analysis of it. The first part of the game is usual enough, but the play after the adjournment rather appeals to me."

Arnesson took the paper and studied it with cynical amusement.

"Aha! The inglorious record of Pardee's Waterloo, eh?"

"What's the meaning of this, Markham?" asked Professor Dillard contemptuously. "Do you hope to run a murderer to earth by dilly-dallying over a chess game?"

"Mr. Vance hoped something could be learned from it."

"Fiddlesticks!" The professor poured himself another glass of port and, opening a book, ignored us completely.

Arnesson was absorbed in the notations of the chess score.

"Something a bit queer here," he muttered. "The time's askew. Let's see. . . . The scoresheet shows that, up to the time of adjournment, White – that is, Pardee – had played one hour and forty-five minutes, and Black, or Rubinstein, one hour and fifty-eight minutes. So far, so good. Thirty moves. Quite in order. But the time at the end of the game, when Pardee resigned, totals two hours and thirty minutes for White, and three hours and thirty-two minutes for Black – which means that, during the second session of the game, White consumed only forty-five minutes whereas Black used up one hour and thirty-four minutes."

Vance nodded.

"Exactly. There were two hours and nineteen minutes of play beginning at 11 p.m., which carried the game to 1.19 a.m. And Rubinstein's moves during that time took forty-nine minutes longer than Pardee's. – Can you make out what happened?"

Arnesson pursed his lips and squinted at the notations.

"It's not clear. I'd need time."

"Suppose," Vance suggested, "we set up the game in the adjourned position and play it through. I'd like your opinion on the tactics."

Arnesson rose jerkily and went to the little chess table in the corner.

"Good idea." He emptied the men from the box. "Let's see now. . . . Oho! A black bishop is missing. When do I get it back, by the way?" He gave Vance a plaintive leer. "Never mind. We don't need it here. One black bishop was swapped." And he proceeded to arrange the men to accord with the position of the game at the time of adjournment. Then he sat down and studied the set-up.

"It doesn't strike me as a particularly unfavorable position for Pardee," ventured Vance.

"Me either. Can't see why he lost the game. Looks drawish to me." After a moment Arnesson referred to the scoresheet. "We'll run through the play and find out where the trouble lay." He made half a dozen moves; then, after several minutes' study, gave a grunt. "Ha! This is rather deep stuff of Rubinstein's. Amazing combination he began working up here. Subtle, by Gad! As I know Rubinstein, it took him a long time to figure it out. Slow, plodding chap."

"It's possible, isn't it," suggested Vance, "that the working out of that combination explains the discrepancy in time between Black and White?"

"Oh, undoubtedly. Rubinstein must have been in good form not to have made the discrepancy greater. Planning the combination took him all of forty-five minutes – or I'm a duffer."

"At what hour, would you say," asked Vance carelessly, "did Rubinstein use up that forty-five minutes?"

"Well, let's see. The play began at eleven: six moves before the combination started. . . . Oh, say, somewhere between half past eleven and half past twelve. . . . Yes, just about. Thirty moves before the adjournment: six moves beginning at eleven – that makes thirty-six: then on the forty-fourth move Rubinstein moved his pawn to Bishop-7-check, and Pardee resigned. . . . Yes – the working out of the combination was between eleven-thirty and twelve-thirty."

Vance regarded the men on the board, which were now in the position they had occupied at the time of Pardee's resignation.*

*For the benefit of the expert chess-player who may be academically interested I append the exact position of the game when Pardee resigned: – WHITE: King at QKtsq; Rook at QB8; Pawns at QR2 and Q2. BLACK: King at Q5; Knight at QKt5; Bishop at QR6; Pawns at QKt7 and QB7.

"Out of curiosity," he said quietly, "I played the game through to the checkmate the other night. – I say, Mr. Arnesson; would you mind doin' the same. I could bear to hear your comment on it."

Arnesson studied the position closely for a few minutes. Then he turned his head slowly and lifted his eyes to Vance. A sardonic grin overspread his face.

"I grasp the point. Gad! What a situation! Five moves for Black to win through. And an almost unheard-of finale in chess. Can't recall a similar instance. The last move would be Bishop to Knight-7, mating. In other words, Pardee was beaten by the black bishop! Incredible!"*

Professor Dillard put down his book.

"What's this?" he exclaimed, joining us at the chess table. "Pardee was defeated by the bishop?" He gave Vance a shrewd, admiring look. "You evidently had good reason, sir, for investigating that chess game. Pray overlook an old man's temper." He stood gazing down at the board with a sad, puzzled expression.

Markham was frowning with deep perplexity.

*The final five unplayed moves for Black to mate, as I later obtained them from Vance, were: – *45.* RxP; KtxR. *46.* KxKt; P – Kt8 (Queen). *47.* KxQ; K–Q6. *48.* K – Rsq; K – B7. *49.* P – Q3; B – Kt7 mate.

"You say it's unusual for a bishop alone to mate?" he asked Arnesson.

"Never happens – almost unique situation. And that it should happen to Pardee of all people! Incomprehensible!" He gave a short ironic laugh. "Inclines one to believe in a nemesis. You know, the bishop has been Pardee's *bête noir* for twenty years – it's ruined his life. Poor beggar! The black bishop is the symbol of his sorrow. Fate, by Gad! It's the one chessman that defeated the Pardee gambit. Bishop-to-Knight-5 always broke up his calculations – disqualified his pet theory – made a hissing and a mocking of his life's work. And now, with a chance to break even with the great Rubinstein, the bishop crops up again and drives him back into obscurity."

A few minutes later we took our departure and walked to West End Avenue, where we hailed a taxicab.

"It's no wonder, Vance," commented Markham, as we rode down-town, "that Pardee went white the other afternoon when you mentioned the black bishop's being at large at midnight. He probably thought you were deliberately insulting him – throwing his life's failure in his face."

"Perhaps. . . ." Vance gazed dreamily out into the gathering shadows. "Dashed queer about the bishop being his incubus all these years. Such recurring discouragements affect the strongest minds sometimes; create a desire for revenge on the world, with the cause of one's failure exalted to an Astræan symbol."

"It's difficult to picture Pardee in a vindictive rôle," objected Markham. Then, after a moment: "What was your point about the discrepancy in time between Pardee's and Rubinstein's playing? Suppose Rubinstein did take forty-five minutes or so to work out his combination. The game wasn't over until after one. I don't see that your visit to Arnesson put us ahead in any way."

"That's because you're unacquainted with the habits of chess players. In a clock game of that kind no player sits at the table all the time his opponent is figuring out moves. He walks about, stretches his muscles, takes the air, ogles the ladies, imbibes ice-water, and even indulges in food. At the Manhattan Square Masters Tournament last year there were four tables, and it was a common sight to see as many as three empty chairs at one time. Pardee's a nervous type. He wouldn't sit through Rubinstein's protracted mental speculations."

Vance lighted a cigarette slowly.

"Markham, Arnesson's analysis of that game reveals the fact that Pardee had three-quarters of an hour to himself around midnight."

CHAPTER XXI

MATHEMATICS AND MURDER

(Saturday, April 16; 8.30 p.m.)

Little was said about the case during dinner, but when we had settled ourselves in a secluded corner of the club lounge-room Markham again broached the subject.

"I can't see," he said, "that finding a loophole in Pardee's alibi helps us very much. It merely complicates an already intolerable situation."

"Yes," sighed Vance. "A sad and depressin' world. Each step appears to tangle us a little more. And the amazin' part of it is, the truth is staring us in the face; only, we can't see it."

"There's no evidence pointing to any one. There's not even a suspect against whose possible culpability reason doesn't revolt."

"I wouldn't say that, don't y' know. It's a mathematician's crime; and the landscape has been fairly cluttered with mathematicians."

Throughout the entire investigation no one had been indicated by name as the possible murderer. Yet each of us realized in his own heart that one of the persons with whom we had talked was guilty; and so hideous was this knowledge that we instinctively shrank from admitting it. From the first we had cloaked our true thoughts and fears with generalities.

"A mathematician's crime?" repeated Markham. "The case strikes me as a series of senseless acts committed by a maniac running amuck."

Vance shook his head.

"Our criminal is supersane, Markham. And his acts are not senseless: they're hideously logical and precise. True, they have been conceived with a grim and terrible humor, with a tremendously cynical attitude; but within themselves they are exact and rational."

Markham regarded Vance thoughtfully.

"How can you reconcile these Mother-Goose crimes with the mathematical mind?" he asked. "In what way can they be regarded as logical? To me they're nightmares, unrelated to sanity."

Vance settled himself deeper in his chair, and smoked for several minutes. Then he began an analysis of the case, which not only clarified the seeming madness of the crimes themselves, but brought all the events and the characters into a uniform focus. The accuracy of this analysis was brought home to us with tragic and overwhelming force before many days had passed.*

"In order to understand these crimes," he began, "we must consider the stock-in-trade of the mathematician, for all his speculations and computations tend to emphasize the relative insignificance of this planet and the unimportance of human life. – Regard, first, the mere scope of the mathematician's field. On the one hand he attempts to measure infinite space in terms of parsees and light-years, and, on the other, to measure the electron which is so infinitely small that he has to invent the Rutherford unit – a millionth of a millimicron. His vision is one of transcendental perspectives, in which this earth and its people sink almost to the vanishing point. Some of the stars – such as Arcturus, Canopus and Betelgeuse – which he regards merely as minute and insignificant units, are many times more massive than our entire solar system. Shapleigh's estimate of the diameter of the Milky Way is 300,000 light-years; yet we must place 10,000 Milky Ways together to get the

*I am obviously unable to set down Vance's exact words, despite the completeness of my notes; but I sent him a proof of the following passages with a request that he revise and edit them; so that, as they now stand, they represent an accurate paraphrase of his analysis of the psychological factors of the Bishop murders.

diameter of the universe – which gives us a cubical content a thousand milliard times greater than the scope of astronomical observation. Or, to put it relatively in terms of mass: – the sun's weight is 324,000 times greater than the weight of the earth; and the weight of the universe is postulated as that of a trillion* – a milliard times a milliard – suns. . . . Is it any wonder that workers in such stupendous magnitudes should sometimes lose all sense of earthly proportions?"

Vance made an insignificant gesture.

"But these are element'ry figures – the every-day facts of journeyman calculators. The higher mathematician goes vastly further. He deals in abstruse and apparently contradict'ry speculations which the average mind can not even grasp. He lives in a realm where time, as we know it, is without meaning save as a fiction of the brain, and becomes a fourth co-ordinate of three-dimensional space; where distance also is meaningless except for neighboring points, since there are an infinite number of shortest routes between any two given points; where the language of cause and

*Vance was here using the English connotation of "trillion," which is the third power of a million, as opposed to the American and French system of numeration which regards a trillion as a mere million millions.

effect becomes merely a convenient shorthand for explanat'ry purposes; where straight lines are non-existent and insusceptible of definition; where mass grows infinitely great when it reaches the velocity of light; where space itself is characterized by curvatures; where there are lower and higher orders of infinities; where the law of gravitation is abolished as an acting force and replaced by a characteristic of space – a conception that says, in effect, that the apple does not fall because it is attracted by the earth, but because it follows a geodesic, or world-line. . . .

"In this realm of the modern mathematician, curves exist without tangents. Neither Newton nor Leibnitz nor Bernoulli even dreamed of a continuous curve without a tangent – that is, a continuous function without a differential coefficient. Indeed, no one is able to picture such a contradiction, – it lies beyond the power of imagination. And yet it is a commonplace of modern mathematics to work with curves that have no tangents. – Moreover, *pi* – that old friend of our school-days, which we regarded as immutable – is no longer a constant; and the ratio between diameter and circumference now varies according to whether one is measuring a circle at rest or a rotating circle. . . . Do I bore you?"

"Unquestionably," retorted Markham. "But pray continue, provided your observations have an earthly direction."

Vance sighed and shook his head hopelessly, but at once became serious again.

"The concepts of modern mathematics project the individual out of the world of reality into a pure fiction of thought, and lead to what Einstein calls the most degenerate form of imagination – pathological individualism. Silberstein, for instance, argues the possibility of five- and six-dimensional space, and speculates on one's ability to see an event before it happens. The conclusions contingent on the conception of Flammarion's Lumen – a fictive person who travels faster than the velocity of light and is therefore able to experience time extending in a reverse direction – are in themselves enough to distort any natural and sane point of view.* But there

*Lumen was invented by the French astronomer to prove the possibility of the reversal of time. With a speed of 250,000 miles per second, he was conceived as soaring into space at the end of the battle of Waterloo, and catching up all the light-rays that had left the battlefield. He attained a gradually increasing lead, until at the end of two days he was witnessing, not the end, but the beginning of the battle; and in the meantime he had been viewing events in reverse order. He had seen projectiles leaving the objects they had penetrated and returning to the cannon; dead men coming to life and arranging themselves in battle formation. Another hypothetical adventure of Lumen was jumping to the moon, turning about instantaneously, and seeing himself leaping from the moon to the earth backwards.

is another conceptual Homunculus even weirder than Lumen from the standpoint of rational thinking. This hypothetical creature can traverse all worlds at once with infinite velocity, so that he is able to behold all human history at a glance. From Alpha Centauri he can see the earth as it was four years ago; from the Milky Way he can see it as it was 4,000 years ago; and he can also choose a point in space where he can witness the ice-age and the present day simultaneously! . . ."

Vance settled himself more deeply in his chair.

"Toying with the simple idea of infinity is enough to unhinge the average man's mind. But what of the well-known proposition of modern physics that we cannot take a straight and ever-advancing path into space without returning to our point of departure? This proposition holds, in brief, that we may go straight to Sirius and a million times further without changing direction, but we can never leave the universe: we at last return to our starting-point *from the opposite direction!* Would you say, Markham, that this idea is conducive to what we quaintly call normal thinking? But however paradoxical and incomprehensible it may seem, it is almost rudiment'ry when compared with other theorems advanced by mathematical physics. Consider, for example, what is called the problem of the twins. One of two twins starts to Arcturus at birth – that is, with accelerated motion in a gravitational field – and, on returning, discovers that he is much younger than his brother. If, on the other hand, we assume that the motion of the twins is Galilean and that they are therefore travelling with uniform motion relative to each other, then each twin will find that his brother is younger than himself! . . .

"These are not paradoxes of logic, Markham: they're only paradoxes of feeling. Mathematics accounts for them logically and scientifically.* The point I'm trying to make is that things which seem inconsistent and even absurd to the lay mind, are commonplace to the mathematical intelligence. A mathematico-physicist like Einstein announces that the diameter of space – of *space*, mind you – is 100,000,000 light-years, or 700 trillion miles; and considers the calculation abecedarian. When we ask what is beyond this diameter, the answer is: 'There is no beyond: these limitations include everything.' To wit, infinity is finite! Or, as the

*Vance requested me to mention here A. d'Abro's recent scholarly work, "The Evolution of Scientific Thought," in which there is an excellent discussion of the paradoxes associated with space-time.

scientist would say, space is unbounded but finite. – Let your mind meditate on this idea for half an hour, Markham, and you'll have a sensation that you're going mad."

He paused to light a cigarette.

"Space and matter – that's the mathematician's speculative territ'ry. Eddington conceives matter as a characteristic of space – a bump in nothingness; whereas Weil conceives space as a characteristic of matter, – to him empty space is meaningless. Thus Kant's noumenon and phenomenon become interchangeable; and even philosophy loses all significance. But when we come to the mathematical conceptions of finite space all rational laws are abrograted. De Sitter's conception of the shape of space is globular, or spherical. Einstein's space is cylindrical; and matter approaches zero at the periphery, or 'border condition.' Weyl's space, based on Mach's mechanics, is saddle-shaped. . . . Now, what becomes of nature, of the world we live in, of human existence, when we weigh them against such conceptions? Eddington suggests the conclusion that there are no natural laws – namely, that nature is not amenable to the law of sufficient reason. Alas, poor Schopenhauer!* And Bertrand Russell sums

*Vance's M.A. thesis, I recall, dealt with Schopenhauer's "Ueber die vierfache Wurzel des Satzes vom zureichenden Grunde."

up the inevitable results of modern physics by suggesting that matter is to be interpreted merely as a group of occurrences, and that matter itself need not be existent! . . . Do you see what it all leads to? If the world is non-causative and non-existent, what is a mere human life? – or the life of a nation? – or, for that matter, existence itself? . . ."

Vance looked up, and Markham nodded dubiously.

"So far I follow you, of course," he said. "But your point seems vague – not to say esoteric."

"Is it surprising," asked Vance, "that a man dealing in such colossal, incommensurable concepts, wherein the individuals of human society are infinitesimal, might in time lose all sense of relative values on earth, and come to have an enormous contempt for human life? The comparatively insignificant affairs of this world would then become mere petty intrusions on the macrocosmos of his mental consciousness. Inevitably such a man's attitude would become cynical. In his heart he would scoff at all human values, and sneer at the littleness of the visual things about him. Perhaps there would be a sadistic element in his attitude; for cynicism is a form of sadism. . . ."

"But deliberate, planned murder!" objected Markham.

"Consider the psychological aspects of the case. With the normal person, who takes his recreations daily, a balance is maintained between the conscious and the unconscious activities: the emotions, being constantly dispersed, are not allowed to accumulate. But with the abnormal person, who spends his entire time in intense mental concentration and who rigorously suppresses all his emotions, the loosening of the subconscious is apt to result in a violent manifestation. This long inhibition and protracted mental application, without recreation or outlet of any kind, causes an explosion which often assumes the form of deeds of unspeakable horror. No human being, however intellectual, can escape the results. The mathematician who repudiates nature's laws is nevertheless amenable to those laws. Indeed, his rapt absorption in hyperphysical problems merely increases the pressure of his denied emotions. And outraged nature, in order to maintain her balance, produces the most grotesque fulminations – reactions which, in their terrible humor and perverted gaiety, are the exact reverse of the grim seriousness of abstruse mathematical theories. The fact that Sir William Crookes and Sir Oliver Lodge – both great mathematical physicists – became confirmed spiritists, constitutes a similar psychological phenomenon."

Vance took several deep inhalations on his cigarette.

"Markham, there's no escaping the fact: these fantastic and seemingly incredible murders were planned by a mathematician as forced outlets to a life of tense abstract speculation and emotional repression. They fulfill all the indicated requirements: they are neat and precise, beautifully worked out, with every minute factor fitting snugly in place. No loose ends, no remainders, apparently no motive. And aside from their highly imaginative precision, all their indications point unmistakably to an abstrusely conceptive intelligence on the loose – a devotee of pure science having his fling."

"But why their grisly humor?" asked Markham. "How do you reconcile the Mother-Goose phase of them with your theory?"

"The existence of inhibited impulses," explained Vance, "always produces a state favorable to humor. Dugas designates humor as a '*détente*' – a release from tension; and Bain, following Spencer, calls humor a relief from restraint. The most fertile field for a manifestation of humor lies in accumulated potential energy – what Freud calls *Besetzungsenergie* – which in time demands a free discharge. In these Mother-Goose crimes we have the mathematician reacting to the most fantastic of frivolous acts in order to balance his superserious logical speculations. It's as if he were saying cynically: 'Behold! This is the world that you take so seriously because you know nothing of the infinitely larger abstract world. Life on earth is a child's game – hardly important enough to make a joke about.' . . . And such an attitude would be wholly consistent with psychology; for after any great prolonged mental strain one's reactions will take the form of reversals – that is to say, the most serious and dignified will seek an outlet in the most childish games. Here, incidentally, you have the explanation for the practical joker with his sadistic instincts. . . .

"Moreover, all sadists have an infantile complex. And the child is totally amoral. A man, therefore, who experiences these infantile psychological reversals is beyond good and evil. Many modern mathematicians even hold that all convention, duty, morality, good, and the like, could not exist except for the fiction of free will. To them the science of ethics is a field haunted by conceptual ghosts; and they even arrive at the disintegrating doubt as to whether truth itself is not merely a figment of the imagination. . . . Add to these considerations the sense of earthly distortion and the contempt for human life which might easily result from the speculations of higher mathematics, and you have a perfect set of conditions for the type of crimes with which we are dealing."

When Vance had finished speaking Markham sat silent for a long time. Finally he moved restively.

"I can understand," he said, "how these crimes might fit almost any of the persons involved. But, on the basis of your argument, how do you account for the notes to the press?"

"Humor must be imparted," returned Vance. " 'A jest's prosperity lies in the ear of him who hears it.' Also, the impulse toward exhibitionism enters into the present case."

"But the 'Bishop' alias?"

"Ah! That's a most vital point. The *raison d'être* of this terrible orgy of humor lies in that cryptic signature."

Markham turned slowly.

"Does the chess player and the astronomer fulfil the conditions of your theory as well as the mathematical physicist?"

"Yes," Vance replied. "Since the days of Philidor, Staunton and Kieseritzki, when chess was something of a fine art, the game has degenerated almost into an exact science; and during Capablanca's régime it has become largely a matter of abstract mathematical speculation. Indeed, Maroczy, Doctor Lasker and Vidmar are all well-known mathematicians. . . . And the astronomer, who actually views the universe, may get an even more intense impression of the unimportance of this earth than the speculative physicist. Imagination runs riot through a telescope. The mere theory of existing life on distant planets tends to reduce earthly life to second'ry consideration. For hours after one has looked at Mars, for instance, and dallied with the notion that its inhabitants outnumber and surpass in intelligence our own population, one has difficulty in readjusting oneself to the petty affairs of life here on earth. Even a reading of Percival Lowell's romantic book* temporarily takes away from the imaginative person all consciousness of the significance of any single planet'ry existence."

There was a long silence. Then Markham asked:

"Why should Pardee have taken Arnesson's black bishop that night instead of one from the club where it would not have been missed?"

"We don't know enough of the motive to say.

*I do not know whether Vance was here referring to "Mars and Its Canals" or "Mars as the Abode of Life."

He may have taken it with some deliberate purpose in view. – But what evidence have you of his guilt? All the suspicions in the world would not permit you to take any step against him. Even if we knew indubitably who the murderer was, we'd be helpless. . . . I tell you, Markham, we're facing a shrewd brain – one that figures out every move, and calculates all the possibilities. Our only hope is to create our own evidence by finding a weakness in the murderer's combination."

"The first thing in the morning," declared Markham grimly, "I'm going to put Heath to work on Pardee's alibi that night. There'll be twenty men checking it up by noon, questioning every spectator at that chess game, and making a door-to-door canvass between the Manhattan Chess Club and the Drukker house. If we can find some one who actually saw Pardee in the vicinity of the Drukkers' around midnight, then we'll have a very suspicious piece of circumstantial evidence against him."

"Yes," agreed Vance; "that would give us a definite starting-point. Pardee would have considerable difficulty in explaining why he was six blocks away from the club during his set-to with Rubinstein at the exact hour a black bishop was being left at Mrs. Drukker's door. . . . Yes, yes. By all means have Heath and his minions tackle the problem. It may lead us forward."

But the Sergeant was never called upon to check the alibi. Before nine o'clock on the following morning Markham called at Vance's house to inform him that Pardee had committed suicide.

CHAPTER XXII

THE HOUSE OF CARDS

(Sunday, April 17; 9 a.m.)

The astounding news of Pardee's death had a curiously disturbing effect on Vance. He stared at Markham unbelievingly. Then he rang hastily for Currie and ordered his clothes and a cup of coffee. There was an eager impatience in his movements as he dressed.

"My word, Markham!" he exclaimed. "This is most extr'ordin'ry. . . . How did you hear of it?"

"Professor Dillard phoned me at my apartment less than half an hour ago. Pardee killed himself in the archery-room of the Dillard home some time last night. Pyne discovered the body this morning and informed the professor. I relayed the news to Sergeant Heath, and then came here. In the circumstances I thought we ought to be on hand." Markham paused to light his cigar. "It looks as if the Bishop case was over. . . . Not an entirely satisfactory ending, but perhaps the best for every one concerned."

Vance made no immediate comment. He sipped his coffee abstractedly, and at length got up and took his hat and stick.

"Suicide. . . ," he murmured, as we went down the stairs. "Yes, that would be wholly consistent. But, as you say, unsatisfact'ry – dashed unsatisfact'ry. . . ."

We rode to the Dillard house, and were admitted by Pyne. Professor Dillard had no more than joined us in the drawing-room when the door-bell rang, and Heath, pugnacious and dynamic, bustled in.

"This'll clean things up, sir," he exulted to Markham, after the usual ritualistic hand-shake. "Those quiet birds . . . you never can tell. Yet, who'd've thought. . . ?"

"Oh, I say, Sergeant," Vance drawled; "let's not think. Much too wearin'. An open mind – arid like a desert – is indicated."

Professor Dillard led the way to the archery-room. The shades at all the windows were drawn, and the electric lights were still burning. I noticed, too, that the windows were closed.

"I left everything exactly as it was," explained the professor.

Markham walked to the large wicker centre-table. Pardee's body was slumped in a chair facing the range door. His head and shoulders had fallen forward over the table; and his right arm hung at his side, the fingers still clutching an automatic pistol. There was an ugly wound in his right temple; and on the table beneath his head was a pool of coagulated blood.

Our eyes rested but a moment on the body, for a startling and incongruous thing diverted our attention. The magazines on the table had been pushed aside, leaving an open space in front of the body; and in this cleared area rose a tall and beautifully constructed house of playing cards. Four arrows marked the boundaries of the yard, and matches had been laid side by side to represent the garden walks. It was a reproduction that would have delighted a child's heart; and I recalled what Vance had said the night before about serious minds seeking recreation in children's games. There was something unutterably horrible in the juxtaposition of this juvenile card structure and violent death.

Vance stood looking down at the scene with sad, troubled eyes.

"Hic jacet John Pardee," he murmured, with a sort of reverence. "And this is the house that Jack built . . . a house of cards. . . ."

He stepped forward as if to inspect it more

closely; but as his body struck the edge of the table there was a slight jar, and the flimsy edifice of cards toppled over.

Markham drew himself up and turned to Heath.

"Have you notified the Medical Examiner?"

"Sure." The Sergeant seemed to find it difficult to take his eyes from the table. "And Burke's coming along, in case we need him." He went to the windows and threw up the shades, letting in the bright daylight. Then he returned to Pardee's body and stood regarding it appraisingly. Suddenly he knelt down and leaned over.

"That looks to me like the .38 that was in the tool-chest," he remarked.

"Undoubtedly," nodded Vance, taking out his cigarette-case.

Heath rose and, going to the chest, inspected the contents of its drawer. "I guess that's it, all right. We'll get Miss Dillard to identify it after the doc has been here."

At this moment Arnesson, clothed in a brilliant red-and-yellow dressing-gown, burst excitedly into the room.

"By all the witches!" he exclaimed. "Pyne just told me the news." He came to the table and stared at Pardee's body. "Suicide, eh? . . . But why didn't he choose his own house for the performance? Damned inconsiderate of him to muss up some one else's house this way. Just like a chess player." He lifted his eyes to Markham. "Hope this won't involve us in more unpleasantness. We've had enough notoriety. Distracts the mind. When'll you be able to take the beggar's remains away? Don't want Belle to see him."

"The body will be removed as soon as the Medical Examiner has seen it," Markham told him in a tone of frosty rebuke. "And there will be no necessity to bring Miss Dillard here."

"Good." Arnesson still stood staring at the dead man. Slowly a look of cynical wistfulness came over his face. "Poor devil! Life was too much for him. Hypersensitive – no psychic stamina. Took things too seriously. Brooded over his fate ever since his gambit went up in smoke. Couldn't find any other diversion. The black bishop haunted him; probably tipped his mind from its axis. By Gad! Wouldn't be surprised if the idea drove him to self-destruction. Might have imagined he was a chess bishop – trying to get back at the world in the guise of his nemesis."

"Clever idea," returned Vance. "By the by, there was a house of cards on the table when we first saw the body."

"Ha! I wondered what the cards were doing

there. Thought he might have sought solace in solitaire during his last moments. . . . A card house, eh? Sounds foolish. Do you know the answer?"

"Not all of it. 'The house that Jack built' might explain something."

"I see." Arnesson looked owlish. "Playing children's games to the end – even on himself. Queer notion." He yawned cavernously. "Guess I'll get some clothes on." And he went up-stairs.

Professor Dillard had stood watching Arnesson with a look at once distressed and paternal. Now he turned to Markham with a gesture of annoyance.

"Sigurd's always protecting himself against his emotions. He's ashamed of his feelings. Don't take his careless attitude too seriously."

Before Markham could make a reply Pyne ushered Detective Burke into the room; and Vance took the opportunity of questioning the butler about his discovery of Pardee.

"How did it happen you entered the archery-room this morning?" he asked.

"It was a bit close in the pantry, sir," the man returned, "and I opened the door at the foot of the stairs to get a little more air. Then I noticed that the shades were down –"

"It's not custom'ry to draw the shades

at night, then?"

"No, sir – not in this room."

"How about the windows?"

"I always leave them slightly open from the top at night."

"Were they left open last night?"

"Yes, sir."

"Very good. – And after you opened the door this morning?"

"I started to put out the lights, thinking Miss Dillard had forgotten to turn the switch last night; but just then I saw the poor gentleman there at the table, and went straight up and informed Professor Dillard."

"Does Beedle know about the tragedy?"

"I told her of it right after you gentlemen arrived."

"What time did you and Beedle retire last night?"

"At ten o'clock, sir."

When Pyne had left us Markham addressed Professor Dillard.

"It might be well for you to give us what details you can while we're waiting for Doctor Doremus. – Shall we go up-stairs?"

Burke remained in the archery-room, and the rest of us went to the library.

"I'm afraid there's little I can tell you," the professor began, settling himself and taking out his pipe. There was a noticeable reserve in his manner – a kind of detached reluctance. "Pardee came here last night after dinner, ostensibly to chat with Arnesson, but actually, I imagine, to see Belle. Belle, however, excused herself early and went to bed – the child had a bad headache – and Pardee remained until about half past eleven. Then he went out; and that was the last I saw of him until Pyne brought me the terrible news this morning. . . ."

"But if," put in Vance, "Mr. Pardee came to see your niece, how do you account for his staying so late after she had retired?"

"I don't account for it." The old man exhibited perplexity. "He gave the impression, though, that there was something on his mind and that he desired a sense of human contact. The fact is, I had to hint rather broadly about being tired before he finally got up to go."

"Where was Mr. Arnesson during the evening?"

"Sigurd remained here talking with us for an hour or so after Belle had retired, and then went to bed. He'd been busy with Drukker's affairs all afternoon, and was played out."

"What time would that have been?"

"About half past ten."

"And you say," continued Vance, "that Mr.

Pardee impressed you as being under a mental strain?"

"Not a strain exactly." The professor drew on his pipe, frowning. "He appeared depressed, almost melancholy."

"Did it strike you that he was in fear of something?"

"No; not in the least. He was more like a man who had suffered a great sorrow and couldn't shake the effects of it."

"When he went out did you go with him into the hall – that is, did you note which direction he took?"

"No. We always treated Pardee very informally here. He said good-night and left the room. I took it for granted he went to the front door and let himself out."

"Did you go to your own room at once?"

"In about ten minutes. I stayed up only long enough to arrange some papers I'd been working on."

Vance lapsed into silence – he was obviously puzzled over some phase of the episode; and Markham took up the interrogation.

"I suppose," he said, "that it is useless to ask if you heard any sound last night that might have been a shot."

"Everything in the house was quiet," Professor Dillard replied. "And anyway no sound of a shot would carry from the archery-room to this floor. There are two flights of stairs, the entire length of the lower hall and a passageway, and three heavy doors between. Moreover, the walls of this old house are very thick and solid."

"And no one," supplemented Vance, "could have heard the shot from the street, for the archery-room windows were carefully closed."

The professor nodded and gave him a searching look.

"That is true. I see you, too, noticed that peculiar circumstance. I don't quite understand why Pardee should have shut the windows."

"The idiosyncrasies of suicides have never been satisfactorily explained," returned Vance casually. Then, after a short pause, he asked: "What were you and Mr. Pardee talking about during the hour preceding his departure?"

"We talked very little. I was more or less engaged with a new paper of Millikan's in the *Physics Review* on alkali doublets, and I tried to interest him in it; but his mind, as I've said, was noticeably preoccupied, and he amused himself at the chess-board for the best part of the hour."

"Ah! Did he, now? That's most interestin'."

Vance glanced at the board. A number of pieces were still standing on the squares; and he rose quickly and crossed the room to the little table. After a moment he came back and reseated himself.

"Most curious," he murmured, and very deliberately lighted a cigarette. "He was evidently pondering over the end of his game with Rubinstein just before he went downstairs last night. The pieces are set up exactly as they were at the time he resigned the contest – with the inevitable black-bishop-mate only five moves off."

Professor Dillard's gaze moved to the chess table wonderingly.

"The black bishop," he repeated in a low tone. "Could that have been what was preying on his mind last night? It seems unbelievable that so trivial a thing could affect him so disastrously."

"Don't forget, sir," Vance reminded him, "that the black bishop was the symbol of his failure. It represented the wreckage of his hopes. Less potent factors have driven men to take their own lives."

A few minutes later Burke informed us that the Medical Examiner had arrived. Taking leave of the professor we descended again to the archery-room, where Doctor Doremus was busy with his examination of Pardee's body.

He looked up as we entered and waved one

hand perfunctorily. His usual jovial manner was gone.

"When's this business going to stop?" he grumbled. "I don't like the atmosphere round here. Murders – death from shock – suicides. Enough to give any one the creeps. I'm going to get a nice uneventful job in a slaughter house."

"We believe," said Markham, "that this is the end."

Doremus blinked. "So! That's it, is it? – the Bishop suicides after running the town ragged. Sounds reasonable. Hope you're right." He again bent over the body, and, unflexing the fingers, tossed the revolver to the table.

"For your armory, Sergeant."

Heath dropped the weapon in his pocket.

"How long's he been dead, doc?"

"Oh, since midnight, or thereabouts. Maybe earlier, maybe later. – Any other fool questions?"

Heath grinned. "Is there any doubt about it being suicide?"

Doremus glared passionately at the Sergeant. "What does it look like? A black-hand bombing?" Then he became professional. "The weapon was in his hand. Powder marks on the temple. Hole the right size for the gun, and in the right place. Position of the body natural.

Can't see anything suspicious. – Why? Got any doubts?"

It was Markham who answered.

"To the contrary, doctor. Everything from our angle of the case points to suicide."

"It's suicide all right, then. I'll check up a little further, though. – Here, Sergeant, give me a hand."

When Heath had helped to lift Pardee's body to the divan for a more detailed examination, we went to the drawing-room where we were joined shortly by Arnesson.

"What's the verdict?" he asked, dropping into the nearest chair. "I suppose there's no question that the chap committed the act himself."

"Why should you raise the point, Mr. Arnesson?" Vance parried.

"No reason. An idle comment. Lots of queer things going on hereabouts."

"Oh, obviously." Vance blew a wreath of smoke upward. "No; the Medical Examiner seems to think there's no doubt in the matter. Did Pardee, by the by, impress you as bent on self-destruction last night?"

Arnesson considered. "Hard to say," he concluded. "He was never a gay soul. But suicide? . . . I don't know. However, you say there's no question about it; so there you are."

"Quite, quite. And how does this new situation fit into your formula?"

"Dissipates the whole equation, of course. No more need for speculation." Despite his words, he appeared uncertain. "What I can't understand," he added, "is why he should choose the archery-room. Lot of space in his own house for a *felo-de-se.*"

"There was a convenient gun in the archery-room," suggested Vance. "And that reminds me: Sergeant Heath would like to have Miss Dillard identify the weapon, as a matter of form."

"That's easy. Where is it?"

Heath handed it to him, and he started from the room.

"Also" – Vance halted him – "you might ask Miss Dillard if she kept playing cards in the archery-room."

Arnesson returned in a few minutes and informed us that the gun was the one which had been in the tool-chest drawer, and that not only were playing cards kept in the table drawer of the archery-room but that Pardee knew of their presence there.

Doctor Doremus appeared soon afterwards and iterated his conclusion that Pardee had shot himself.

"That'll be my report," he said. "Can't see

any way out of it. To be sure, lots of suicides are fakes – but that's *your* province. Nothing in the least suspicious here."

Markham nodded with undisguised satisfaction.

"We've no reason to question your findings, doctor. In fact, suicide fits perfectly with what we already know. It brings this whole Bishop orgy to a logical conclusion." He got up like a man from whose shoulders a great burden had been lifted. "Sergeant, I'll leave you to arrange for the removal of the body for the autopsy; but you'd better drop in at the Stuyvesant Club later. Thank Heaven today is Sunday! It gives us time to turn round."

That night at the club Vance and Markham and I sat alone in the lounge-room. Heath had come and gone, and a careful statement had been drawn up for the press announcing Pardee's suicide and intimating that the Bishop case was thereby closed. Vance had said little all day. He had refused to offer any suggestion as to the wording of the official statement, and had appeared reluctant even to discuss the new phase of the case. But now he gave voice to the doubts that had evidently been occupying his mind.

"It's too easy, Markham – much too easy. There's an aroma of speciousness about it. It's perfectly logical, d' ye see, but it's not satisfyin'. I can't exactly picture our Bishop terminating his debauch of humor in any such banal fashion. There's nothing witty in blowin' one's brain out – it's rather commonplace, don't y' know. Shows a woeful lack of originality. It's not worthy of the artificer of the Mother-Goose murders."

Markham was digruntled.

"You yourself explained how the crimes accorded with the psychological possibilities of Pardee's mentality; and to me it appears highly reasonable that, having perpetrated his gruesome jokes and come to the end of his rope, he should have done away with himself."

"You're probably right," sighed Vance. "I haven't any coruscatin' arguments to combat you with. Only, I'm disappointed. I don't like anticlimaxes, especially when they don't jibe with my idea of the dramatist's talent. Pardee's death at this moment is too deuced neat – it clears things up too tidily. There's too much utility in it, and too little imagination."

Markham felt that he could afford to be tolerant.

"Perhaps his imagination was exhausted on the murders. His suicide might be regarded merely as a lowering of the curtain when the play was over. In any event, it was by no means an incredible act. Defeat and disappointment and discouragement – a thwarting of all one's ambitions – have constituted cause for suicide since time immemorial."

"Exactly. We have a reasonable motive, or explanation, for his suicide, but no motive for the murders."

"Pardee was in love with Belle Dillard," argued Markham; "and he probably knew that Robin was a suitor for her hand. Also, he was intensely jealous of Drukker."

"And Sprigg's murder?"

"We have no data on that point."

Vance shook his head.

"We can't separate the crimes as to motive. They all sprang from one underlying impulse: they were actuated by a single urgent passion."

Markham sighed impatiently.

"Even if Pardee's suicide is unrelated to the murders, we're at a dead end, figuratively and literally."

"Yes, yes. A dead end. Very distressin'. Consolin' for the police, though. It lets them out – for a while, anyway. But don't misinterpret my vagaries. Pardee's death is unquestionably related to the murders. Rather intimate relationship, too, I'd say."

Markham took his cigar slowly from his mouth and scrutinized Vance for several moments.

"Is there any doubt in your mind," he asked, "that Pardee committed suicide?"

Vance hesitated before answering.

"I could bear to know," he drawled, "why that house of cards collapsed so readily when I deliberately leaned against the table –"

"Yes?"

"– and why it didn't topple over when Pardee's head and shoulders fell forward on the table after he'd shot himself."

"Nothing to that," said Markham. "The first jar may have loosened the cards –" Suddenly his eyes narrowed. "Are you implying that the card-house was built *after* Pardee was dead?"

"Oh, my dear fellow! I'm not indulgin' in implications. I'm merely givin' tongue to my youthful curiosity, don't y' know."

CHAPTER XXIII

A STARTLING DISCOVERY

(Monday, April 25; 8.30 p.m.)

Eight days went by. The Drukker funeral was held in the little house on 76th Street, attended only by the Dillards and Arnesson and a few men from the university who came to pay a last tribute of respect to a scientist for whose work they had a very genuine admiration.

Vance and I were at the house on the morning of the funeral when a little girl brought a small cluster of spring flowers she had picked herself, and asked Arnesson to give them to Drukker. I almost expected a cynical response from him, and was surprised when he took the flowers gravely and said in a tone almost tender:

"I'll give them to him at once, Madeleine. And Humpty Dumpty thanks you for remembering him." When the child had been led away by her governess, he turned to us. "She was Drukker's favorite. . . . Funny fellow.

Never went to the theatre. Detested travel. His only recreation was entertaining youngsters."

I mention this episode because, in spite of its seeming unimportance, it was to prove one of the most vital links in the chain of evidence that eventually cleared up, beyond all question of doubt, the problem of the Bishop murders.

The death of Pardee had created a situation almost unique in the annals of modern crime. The statement given out by the District Attorney's office had only intimated that there was a possibility of Pardee's being guilty of the murders. Whatever Markham may have personally believed, he was far too honorable and just to cast any direct doubt on another's character without overwhelming proofs. But the wave of terror arising from these strange murders had reached such proportions that he could not, in view of the duty he owed to the community, refrain from saying that he believed the case to be closed. Thus, while no open accusation of guilt was made against Pardee, the Bishop murders were no longer regarded as a source of menace to the city, and a sigh of relief went up from all quarters.

In the Manhattan Chess Club there was probably less discussion of the case than anywhere else in New York. The members felt perhaps that the club's honor was in some way involved. Or there may have been a sense of loyalty toward a man who had done as much for chess as Pardee. But whatever the cause of the club's avoidance of the subject, the fact remained that its members attended, almost to a man, Pardee's funeral. I could not help admiring this tribute to a fellow chess player; for, whatever his personal acts, he had been one of the great sustaining patrons of the royal and ancient game to which they were devoted.*

Markham's first official act on the day after Pardee's death was to secure Sperling's release. The same afternoon the Police Department moved all its records of the Bishop murders to the file marked "shelved cases," and withdrew the guards from the Dillard house. Vance protested mildly against this latter step; but in view of the fact that the Medical Examiner's *post-mortem* report had substantiated in every particular the theory of suicide, there was little that Markham could do in the matter. Furthermore, he was thoroughly convinced that the death of Pardee had terminated the case; and he scoffed at Vance's wavering doubts.

During the week following the finding of

*Pardee left in his will a large sum for the futherance of chess; and in the autumn of that same year, it will be remembered, the Pardee Memorial Tournament was held at Cambridge Springs.

Pardee's body Vance was restive and more distrait than usual. He attempted to interest himself in various matters, but without any marked success. He showed signs of irritability; and his almost miraculous equanimity seemed to have deserted him. I got the impression that he was waiting for something to happen. His manner was not exactly expectant, but there was a watchfulness in his attitude amounting at times almost to apprehension.

On the day following the Drukker funeral Vance called on Arnesson, and on Friday night accompanied him to a performance of Ibsen's "Ghosts" – a play which, I happened to know, he disliked. He learned that Belle Dillard had gone away for a month's visit to the home of a relative in Albany. As Arnesson explained, she had begun to show the effects of all she had been through, and needed a change of scene. The man was plainly unhappy over her absence, and confided to Vance that they had planned to be married in June. Vance also learned from him that Mrs. Drukker's will had left everything to Belle Dillard and the professor in the event of her son's death – a fact which appeared to interest Vance unduly.

Had I known, or even suspected, what astounding and terrible things were hanging over us that week, I doubt if I could have stood the strain. For the Bishop murder case was not ended. The climactic horror was still to come; but even that horror, terrific and staggering as it proved, was only a shadow of what it might have been had not Vance reasoned the case out to two separate conclusions, only one of which had been disposed of by Pardee's death. It was this other possibility, as I learned later, that had kept him in New York, vigilant and mentally alert.

Monday, April 25, was the beginning of the end. We were to dine with Markham at the Bankers Club and go afterwards to a performance of "Die Meistersinger"*; but we did not witness the triumphs of *Walther* that night. I noticed that when we met Markham in the rotunda of the Equitable Building he seemed troubled; and we were no more than seated in the club grill when he told us of a phone call he had received from Professor Dillard that afternoon.

"He asked me particularly to come to see him to-night," Markham explained; "and when I tried to get out of it he became urgent. He

*Of the Wagnerian operas this was Vance's favorite. He always asserted that it was the only opera that had the structural form of a symphony; and more than once he expressed the regret that it had not been written as an orchestral piece instead of as a conveyance for an absurd drama.

made a point of the fact that Arnesson would be away the entire evening, and said that a similar opportunity might not present itself until it was too late. I asked him what he meant by that; but he refused to explain, and insisted that I come to his house after dinner. I told him I'd let him know if I could make it."

Vance had listened with the intensest interest.

"We must go there, Markham. I've been rather expecting a call of this kind. It's possible we may at last find the key to the truth."

"The truth about what?"

"Pardee's guilt."

Markham said no more, and we ate our dinner in silence.

At half past eight we rang the bell of the Dillard house, and were taken by Pyne direct to the library.

The old professor greeted us with nervous reserve.

"It's good of you to come, Markham," he said, without rising. "Take a chair and light a cigar. I want to talk to you – and I want to take my time about it. It's very difficult. . . ." His voice trailed off as he began filling his pipe.

We settled ourselves and waited. A sense of expectancy invaded me for no apparent reason, except perhaps that I caught some of the radiations of the professor's obviously distraught mood.

"I don't know just how to broach the subject," he began; "for it has to do, not with physical facts, but with the invisible human consciousness. I've struggled all week with certain vague ideas that have been forcing themselves upon me; and I see no way to rid myself of them but by talking with you. . . ."

He looked up hesitantly.

"I preferred to discuss these ideas with you when Sigurd was not present, and as he has gone to-night to see Ibsen's 'Pretenders' – his favorite play, by the way – I took the opportunity to ask you here."

"What do these ideas concern?" asked Markham.

"Nothing specifically. As I have said, they're very vague; but they have nevertheless grown fairly insistent. . . . So insistent, in fact," he added, "that I thought it best to send Belle away for a while. It's true that she was in a tortured state of mind as a result of all these tragedies; but my real reason for shipping her north was that I was beset by intangible doubts."

"Doubts?" Markham leaned forward. "What sort of doubts?"

Professor Dillard did not reply at once.

"Let me answer that question by asking another," he countered presently. "Are you wholly satisfied in your mind that the situation in regard to Pardee is exactly as it appears?"

"You mean the authenticity of his suicide?"

"That and his presumptive culpability."

Markham settled back contemplatively.

"Are *you* not wholly satisfied?" he asked.

"I can't answer that question." Professor Dillard spoke almost curtly. "You have no right to ask me. I merely wanted to be sure that the authorities, having all the data in their hands, were convinced that this terrible affair was a closed book." A look of deep concern came over his face. "If I knew that to be a fact, it would help me to repulse the vague misgivings that have haunted me day and night for the past week."

"And if I were to say that I am not satisfied?"

The old professor's eyes took on a distant, distressed look. His head fell slightly forward, as if some burden of sorrow had suddenly weighed him down. After several moments he lifted his shoulders and drew a deep breath.

"The most difficult thing in this world," he said, "is to know where one's duty lies; for duty is a mechanism of the mind, and the heart is forever stepping in and playing havoc with one's resolutions. Perhaps I did wrong to ask you here; for, after all, I have only misty suspicions and nebulous ideas to go on. But there was the possibility that my mental uneasiness was based on some deep hidden foundation of whose existence I was unaware. . . . Do you see what I mean?" Evasive as were his words, there was no doubt as to the disturbing mien of the shadowy image that lurked at the back of his mind.

Markham nodded sympathetically.

"There is no reason whatever to question the findings of the Medical Examiner." He made the statement in a forced matter-of-fact voice. "I can understand how the proximity of these tragedies might have created an atmosphere conducive to doubts. But I think you need have no further misgivings."

"I sincerely hope you're right," the professor murmured; but it was clear he was not satisfied. "Suppose, Markham –" he began, and then stopped. "Yes, I hope you're right," he repeated.

Vance had sat through this unsatisfactory discussion smoking placidly; but he had been listening with unwonted concentration, and now he spoke.

"Tell me, Professor Dillard, if there has been anything – no matter how indefinite – that may have given birth to your uncertainty."

"No – nothing." The answer came quickly and with a show of spirit. "I have merely been wondering – testing every possibility. I dared not be too sanguine without some assurance. Pure logic is all very well for principles that do not touch us personally. But where one's own safety is concerned the imperfect human mind demands visual evidence."

"Ah, yes." Vance looked up, and I thought I detected a flash of understanding between these two disparate men.

Markham rose to make his adieu; but Professor Dillard urged him to remain a while.

"Sigurd will be here before long. He'd enjoy seeing you again. As I said, he's at 'The Pretenders,' but I'm sure he will come straight home. . . . By the way, Mr. Vance," he went on, turning from Markham; "Sigurd tells me you accompanied him to 'Ghosts' last week. Do you share his enthusiasm for Ibsen?"

A slight lift of Vance's eyebrows told me that he was somewhat puzzled by this question; but when he answered there was no hint of perplexity in his voice.

"I have read Ibsen a great deal; and there can be little doubt that he was a creative genius of a high order, although I've failed to find in him either the aesthetic form or the philosophic depth that characterizes Goethe's 'Faust,' for instance."

"I can see that you and Sigurd would have a permanent basis of disagreement."

Markham declined the invitation to stay longer, and a few minutes later we were walking down West End Avenue in the brisk April air.

"You will please take note, Markham old dear," observed Vance, with a touch of waggishness, as we turned into 72nd Street and headed for the park, "that there are others than your modest collaborator who are hag-ridden with doubts as to the volition of Pardee's taking-off. And I might add that the professor is not in the least satisfied with your assurances."

"His suspicious state of mind is quite understandable," submitted Markham. "These murders have touched his house pretty closely."

"That's not the explanation. The old gentleman has fears. And he knows something which he will not tell us."

"I can't say that I got that impression."

"Oh, Markham – my dear Markham! Weren't you listening closely to his halting, reluctant tale? It was as if he were trying to convey some suggestion to us without actually putting it into words. We were supposed to guess. Yes! That was why he insisted that you visit him when Arnesson was safely away at an Ibsen revival –"

Vance ceased speaking abruptly and stood stock-still. A startled look came in his eyes.

"Oh, my aunt! Oh, my precious aunt! So that was why he asked me about Ibsen! . . . My word! How unutterably dull I've been!" He stared at Markham, and the muscles of his jaw tightened. "The truth at last!" he said with impressive softness. "And it is neither you nor the police nor I who has solved this case: it is a Norwegian dramatist who has been dead for twenty years. In Ibsen is the key to the mystery."

Markham regarded him as though he had suddenly gone out of his mind; but before he could speak Vance hailed a taxicab.

"I'll show you what I mean when we reach home," he said, as we rode east through Central Park. "It's unbelievable, but it's true. And I should have guessed it long ago; but the connotation of the signature on those notes was too clouded with other possible meanings. . . ."

"If it were midsummer instead of spring," commented Markham wrathfully, "I'd suggest that the heat had affected you."

"I knew from the first there were three possible guilty persons," continued Vance. "Each was psychologically capable of the murders, provided the impact of his emotions had upset his mental equilibrium. So there was nothing to do but to wait for some indication that would focus suspicion. Drukker was one of my three suspects, but he was murdered; and that left two. Then Pardee to all appearances committed suicide, and I'll admit that his death made reasonable the assumption that he had been the guilty one. But there was an eroding doubt in my mind. His death was not conclusive; and that house of cards troubled me. We were stalemated. So again I waited, and watched my third possibility. Now I know that Pardee was innocent, and that he did not shoot himself. He was murdered – just as were Robin and Sprigg and Drukker. His death was another grim joke – he was a victim thrown to the police in the spirit of diabolical jest. And the murderer has been chuckling at our gullibility ever since."

"By what reasoning do you arrive at so fantastic a conclusion?"

"It's no longer a question of reasoning. At last I have the explanation for the crimes; and I know the meaning of the 'Bishop' signature to the notes. I'll show you a piece of amazing and incontrovertible evidence very soon."

A few minutes later we reached his apartment, and he led us straight to the library.

"The evidence has been here within arm's reach all the time."

He went to the shelves where he kept his dramas, and took down Volume II of the collected works of Henrik Ibsen.* The book contained "The Vikings at Helgeland" and "The Pretenders"; but with the first of these plays Vance was not concerned. Turning to "The Pretenders" he found the page where the *dramatis personæ* were given, and laid the book on the table before Markham.

"Read the cast of characters of Arnesson's favorite play," he directed.

Markham, silent and puzzled, drew the volume toward him; and I looked over his shoulder. This is what we saw:

HÅKON HÅKONSSON, *the King elected by the Birchlegs.*
INGA OF VARTEIG, *his mother.*
EARL SKULE.
LADY RAGNHILD, *his wife.*
SIGRID, *his sister.*
MARGRETE, *his daughter.*

*Vance's set was the William Archer copyright edition, published by Charles Scribner's Sons.

GUTHORM INGESSON.
SIGURD RIBBUNG.
NICHOLAS ARNESSON, *Bishop of Oslo.*
DAGFINN THE PEASANT, *Hakon's marshal.*
IVAR BODDE, *his chaplain.*
VEGARD VÆRADAL, *one of his guard.*
GREGORIUS JONSSON, *a nobleman.*
PAUL FLIDA, *a nobleman.*
INGEBORG, *Andres Skialdarband's wife.*
PETER, *her son, a young priest.*
SIRA VILIAM, *Bishop Nicholas's chaplain.*
MASTER SIGARD OF BRABANT, *a physician.*
JATGEIR SKALD, *an Icelander.*
*B*ÅRD BRATTE, *a chieftain from the Trondhiem district.*

But I doubt if either of us read beyond the line:

NICHOLAS ARNESSON, *Bishop of Oslo.*

My eyes became riveted on that name with a set and horrified fascination. And then I remembered. . . . *Bishop Arnesson* was one of the most diabolical villains in all literature – a cynical, sneering monster who twisted all the sane values of life into hideous buffooneries.

CHAPTER XXIV

THE LAST ACT

(Tuesday, April 26; 9 a. m.)

With this astounding revelation the Bishop murder case entered its final and most terrible phase. Heath had been informed of Vance's discovery; and it was arranged that we should meet in the District Attorney's office early the following day for a counsel of war.

Markham, when he took leave of us that night, was more troubled and despondent than I had ever seen him.

"I don't know what can be done," he said hopelessly. "There's no legal evidence against the man. But we may be able to devise some course of action that will give us the upper hand. . . . I never believed in torture, but I almost wish we had access to-day to the thumbscrew and the rack."

Vance and I arrived at his office a few minutes after nine the next morning. Swacker intercepted us and asked us to wait in the reception room for a little while. Markham, he explained, was engaged for the moment. We had no more than seated ourselves when Heath appeared, grim, pugnacious and sullen.

"I gotta hand it to you, Mr. Vance," he proclaimed. "You sure got a line on the situation. But what good it's going to do us I don't see. We can't arrest a guy because his name's in a book."

"We may be able to force the issue some way," Vance rejoined. "In any event, we now know where we stand."

Ten minutes later Swacker beckoned to us and indicated that Markham was free.

"Sorry to have kept you waiting," Markham apologized. "I had an unexpected visitor." His voice had a despairing ring. "More trouble. And, curiously enough, it's connected with the very section of Riverside Park where Drukker was killed. However, there's nothing I can do about it. . . ." He drew some papers before him. "Now to business."

"What's the new trouble in Riverside Park?" asked Vance casually.

Markham frowned.

"Nothing that need bother us now. A kidnapping, in all likelihood. There's a brief account of it in the morning papers, in case you're interested. . . ."

"I detest reading the papers." Vance spoke blandly, but with an insistence that puzzled me. "What happened?"

Markham drew a deep breath of impatience. "A child disappeared from the playground yesterday after talking with an unknown man. Her father came here to solicit my help. But it's a job for the Bureau of Missing Persons; and I told him so. – Now, if your curiosity is appeased –"

"Oh, but it isn't," persisted Vance. "I simply must hear the details. That section of the park fascinates me strangely."

Markham shot him a questioning glance through lowered lids.

"Very well," he acquiesced. "A five-year-old girl, named Madeleine Moffat, was playing with a group of children at about half past five last evening. She crawled up on a high mound near the retaining wall, and a little later, when her governess went to get her, thinking she had descended the other side, the child was nowhere to be found. The only suggestive fact is that two of the other children say they saw a man talking to her shortly before she disappeared; but, of course, they can give no description of him. The police were notified, and are investigating. And that's all there is to the case so far."

" 'Madeleine.' " Vance repeated the name musingly. "I say, Markham; do you know if this child knew Drukker?"

"Yes!" Markham sat up a little straighter. "Her father mentioned that she often went to parties at his house. . . ."

"I've seen the child." Vance rose and stood, hands in pockets, gazing down at the floor. "An adorable little creature . . . golden curls. She brought a handful of flowers for Drukker the morning of his funeral. . . . And now she has disappeared after having been seen talking with a strange man. . . ."

"What's going on in your mind?" demanded Markham sharply.

Vance appeared not to have heard the question.

"Why should her father appeal to you?"

"I've known Moffat slightly for years – he was at one time connected with the city administration. He's frantic – grasping at every straw. The proximity of the affair to the Bishop murders has made him morbidly apprehensive. . . . But see here, Vance; we didn't come here to discuss the Moffat child's disappearance. . . ."

Vance lifted his head: there was a look of startled horror on his face.

"Don't speak – oh, don't speak. . . ." He

began pacing up and down, while Markham and Heath watched him in mute amazement. "Yes – yes; that would be it," he murmured to himself. "The time is right . . . it all fits. . . ."

He swung about, and going to Markham seized his arm.

"Come – quickly! It's our only chance – we can't wait another minute." He fairly dragged Markham to his feet and led him toward the door. "I've been fearing something like this all week –"

Markham wrenched his arm free from the other's grip.

"I won't move from this office, Vance, until you explain."

"It's another act in the play – the last act! Oh, take my word for it." There was a look in Vance's eyes I had never seen before. "It's 'Little Miss Muffet' now. The name isn't identical, but that doesn't matter. It's near enough for the Bishop's jest; he'll explain it all to the press. He probably beckoned the child to the tuffet, and sat down beside her. And now she's gone – frightened away. . . ."

Markham moved forward in a sort of daze; and Heath, his eyes bulging, leapt to the door. I have often wondered what went on in their minds during those few seconds of Vance's importunate urgings. Did they believe in his interpretation of the episode? Or were they merely afraid not to investigate, in view of the remote possibility that another hideous joke had been perpetrated by the Bishop? Whatever their convictions or doubts, they accepted the situation as Vance saw it; and a moment later we were in the hall, hastening toward the elevator. At Vance's suggestion we picked up Detective Tracy from the branch office of the Detective Bureau in the Criminal Courts Building.

"This affair is serious," he explained. "Anything may happen."

We emerged through the Franklin-Street entrance, and in a few minutes were on our way up-town in the District Attorney's car, breaking speed regulations and ignoring traffic signals. Scarcely a word was spoken on that momentous ride; but as we swung through the tortuous roads of Central Park Vance said:

"I may be wrong, but we will have to risk it. If we wait to see whether the papers get a note, it'll be too late. We're not supposed to know yet; and that's our one chance. . . ."

"What do you expect to find?" Markham's tone was husky and a little uncertain.

Vance shook his head despondently.

"Oh, I don't know. But it'll be something devilish."

When the car drew up with a lurch in front of the Dillard house Vance leapt out and ran up the steps ahead of us. Pyne answered his insistent ring.

"Where's Mr. Arnesson?" he demanded.

"At the university, sir," the old butler replied; and I imagined there was fright in his eyes. "But he'll be home for an early lunch."

"Then take us at once to Professor Dillard."

"I'm sorry sir," Pyne told him; "but the professor is also out. He went to the Public Library –"

"Are you alone here?"

"Yes, sir. Beedle's gone to market."

"So much the better." Vance took hold of the butler and turned him toward the rear stairs. "We're going to search the house, Pyne. You lead the way."

Markham came forward.

"But, Vance, we can't do that!"

Vance wheeled round.

"I'm not interested in what you can do or can't do. I'm going to search this house. . . . Sergeant, are you with me?" There was a strange look on his face.

"You bet your sweet life!" (I never liked Heath as much as at that moment.)

The search was begun in the basement. Every hallway, every closet, every cupboard and waste space was inspected. Pyne, completely cowed by Heath's vindictiveness, acted as guide. He brought keys and opened doors for us, and even suggested places we might otherwise have overlooked. The Sergeant had thrown himself into the hunt with energy, though I am sure he had only a vague idea as to its object. Markham followed us disapprovingly; but he, too, had been caught in the sweep of Vance's dynamic purposefulness; and he must have realized that Vance had some tremendous justification for his rash conduct.

Gradually we worked our way upward through the house. The library and Arnesson's room were gone over carefully. Belle Dillard's apartment was scrutinized, and close attention was given to the unused rooms on the third floor. Even the servants' quarters on the fourth floor were overhauled. But nothing suspicious was discovered. Though Vance suppressed his eagerness I could tell what a nervous strain he was under by the tireless haste with which he pushed the search.

Eventually we came to a locked door at the rear of the upper hall.

"Where does that lead?" Vance asked Pyne.

"To a little attic room, sir. But it's never used –"

"Unlock it."

The man fumbled for several moments with his bunch of keys.

"I don't seem to find the key, sir. It's supposed to be here. . . ."

"When did you have it last?"

"I couldn't say, sir. To my knowledge no one's been in the attic for years."

Vance stepped back and crouched.

"Stand aside, Pyne."

When the butler had moved out of the way Vance hurled himself against the door with terrific force. There was a creaking and straining of wood; but the lock held.

Markham rushed forward and caught him round the shoulders.

"Are you mad!" he exclaimed. "You're breaking the law."

"The law!" There was scathing irony in Vance's retort. "We're dealing with a monster who sneers at all law. You may coddle him if you care to, but I'm going to search that attic if it means spending the rest of my life in jail. – Sergeant, open that door!"

Again I experienced a thrill of liking for Heath. Without a moment's hesitation he poised himself on his toes and sent his shoulders crashing against the door's panel just above the knob. There was a splintering of wood as the lock's bolt tore through the moulding. The door swung inward.

Vance, freeing himself from Markham's hold, ran stumbling up the steps with the rest of us at his heels. There was no light in the attic, and we paused for a moment at the head of the stairs to accustom our eyes to the darkness. Then Vance struck a match and, groping forward, sent up the window shade with a clatter. The sunlight poured in, revealing a small room, scarcely ten feet square, cluttered with all manner of discarded odds and ends. The atmosphere was heavy and stifling, and a thick coating of dust lay over everything.

Vance looked quickly about him, and an expression of disappointment came over his face.

"This is the only place left," he remarked, with the calmness of desperation.

After a more careful scrutiny of the room, he stepped to the corner by the little window and peered down at a battered suit-case which lay on its side against the wall. I noticed that it was unlatched and that its straps hung free. Leaning over he threw the cover back.

"Ah! here, at least, is something for you, Markham."

We crowded about him. In the suit-case was an old Corona typewriter. A sheet of paper was in the carriage; and on it had already been typed, in pale blue élite characters, the two lines:

> Little Miss Muffet
> Sat on a tuffet

At this point the typist had evidently been interrupted, or for some other reason had not completed the Mother-Goose rhyme.

"The new Bishop note for the press," observed Vance. Then reaching into the suitcase he lifted out a pile of blank paper and envelopes. At the bottom, beside the machine, lay a red-leather note-book with thin yellow leaves. He handed it to Markham with the terse announcement:

"Drukker's calculations for the quantum theory."

But there was still a look of defeat in his eyes; and again he began inspecting the room. Presently he went to an old dressing-table which stood against the wall opposite to the window. As he bent over to peer behind it he suddenly drew back and, lifting his head, sniffed several times. At the same moment he caught sight of something on the floor at his feet, and kicked it toward the centre of the room. We looked down at it with astonishment. It was a gas-mask of the kind used by chemists.

"Stand back, you chaps!" he ordered; and holding one hand to his nose and mouth he swung the dressing-table away from the wall. Directly behind it was a small cupboard door about three feet high, set into the wall. He wrenched it open and looked inside, then slammed it shut immediately.

Brief as was my view of the interior of the cupboard, I was able to glimpse its contents clearly. It was fitted with two shelves. On the lower one were several books lying open. On the upper shelf stood an Erlenmeyer flask clamped to an iron support, a spirit-lamp, a condenser tube, a glass beaker, and two small bottles.

Vance turned and gave us a despairing look.

"We may as well go: there's nothing more here."

We returned to the drawing-room, leaving Tracy to guard the door to the attic.

"Perhaps, after all, you were justified in your search," acknowledged Markham, studying Vance gravely. "I don't like such methods, however. If we hadn't found the typewriter –"

"Oh, that!" Vance, preoccupied and restless, went to the window overlooking the archery range. "I wasn't hunting for the typewriter – or the note-book, either. What do they matter?" His chin fell forward on his breast, and his eyes closed in a kind of lethargy of defeat. "Everything's gone wrong – my logic has failed. We're too late."

"I don't pretend to know what you're grumbling about," said Markham. "But at least you've supplied me with evidence of a sort. I'll now be able to arrest Arnesson when he returns from the university."

"Yes, yes; of course. But I wasn't thinking of Arnesson, or the arrest of the culprit, or the triumph of the District Attorney's office. I was hoping –"

He broke off and stiffened.

"We're *not* too late! I didn't think far enough. . . ." He went swiftly to the archway. "It's the Drukker house we must search. . . . Hurry!" He was already half-running down the hall, Heath behind him, and Markham and I bringing up the rear.

We followed him down the rear stairs, across the archery-room, and out on the range. We did not know, and I doubt if any of us even guessed, what was in his mind; but some of his inner excitation had been communicated to us, and we realized that only a vital urgency could have shaken him so completely out of his usual attitude of disinterest and calm.

When we came to the screen-porch of the Drukker house he reached through the broken wire-netting and released the catch. The kitchen door, to my astonishment, was unlocked; but Vance seemed to expect this, for he unhesitatingly turned the knob and threw it open.

"Wait!" he directed, pausing in the little rear hallway. "There's no need to search the entire house. The most likely place. . . . Yes! Come along . . . up-stairs . . . somewhere in the centre of the house . . . a closet most likely . . . where no one could hear. . . ." As he spoke he led the way up the rear stairs, past Mrs. Drukker's room and the study, and thence to the third floor. There were but two doors on this upper hall – one at the extreme end, and a smaller door set midway in the right wall.

Vance went straight to the latter. There was a key protruding from the lock, and, turning it, he drew open the door. Only a shadowy blackness met our eyes. Vance was on his knees in a second, groping inside.

"Quick, Sergeant. Your flash-light."

Almost before he had uttered the words a luminous circle fell on the floor of the closet. What I saw sent a chill of horror over me. A choked exclamation burst from Markham; and a soft whistle told me that Heath too was appalled by the sight. Before us on the floor, in a limp, silent heap, lay the little girl who had brought flowers to her broken Humpty

Dumpty on the morning of his funeral. Her golden hair was dishevelled; her face was deathly pale, and there were streaks down her cheeks where the futile tears had welled forth and dried.

Vance bent over and put his ear to her heart. Then he gathered her tenderly in his arms.

"Poor little Miss Muffet," he whispered, and rising went toward the front stairs. Heath preceded him, flashing his light all the way so there would be no chance of his stumbling. In the main lower hall he paused.

"Unbolt the door, Sergeant."

Heath obeyed with alacrity, and Vance stepped out on the sidewalk.

"Go to the Dillards' and wait for me there," he flung back over his shoulder. And with the child clasped closely to his breast he started diagonally across 76th Street to a house on which I could make out a doctor's brass name-plate.

CHAPTER XXV

THE CURTAIN FALLS

(Tuesday, April 26; 11 a.m.)

Twenty minutes later Vance rejoined us in the Dillard drawing-room.

"She's going to be all right," he announced, sinking into a chair and lighting a cigarette. "She was only unconscious, had fainted from shock and fright; and she was half-suffocated." His face darkened. "There were bruises on her little wrist. She probably struggled in that empty house when she failed to find Humpty Dumpty; and then the beast forced her into the closet and locked the door. No time to kill her, d' ye see. Furthermore, killing wasn't in the book. 'Little Miss Muffet' wasn't killed – merely frightened away. She'd have died, though, from lack of air. And *he* was safe: no one could hear her crying. . . ."

Markham's eyes rested on Vance affectionately.

"I'm sorry I tried to hold you back," he said

simply. (For all his conventionally legal instincts, there was a fundamental bigness to his nature.) "You were right in forcing the issue, Vance. . . . And you, too, Sergeant. We owe a great deal to your determination and faith."

Heath was embarrassed.

"Oh, that's all right, sir. You see, Mr. Vance had me all worked up about the kid. And I like kids, sir."

Markham turned an inquisitive look on Vance.

"You expected to find the child alive?"

"Yes; but drugged or stunned perhaps. I didn't think of her as dead, for that would have contravened the Bishop's joke."

Heath had been pondering some troublous point.

"What I can't get through my head," he said, "is why this Bishop, who's been so damn careful about everything else, should leave the door of the Drukker house unlocked."

"We were expected to find the child," Vance told him. "Everything was made easy for us. Very considerate of the Bishop, what? But we weren't supposed to find her till to-morrow – after the papers had received the Little-Miss-Muffet notes. They were to have been our clew. But we anticipated the gentleman."

"But why weren't the notes sent yesterday?"

"It was no doubt the Bishop's original intention to post his poetry last night; but I imagine he decided it was best for his purpose to let the child's disappearance attract public attention first. Otherwise the relationship between Madeleine Moffat and little Miss Muffet might have been obscured."

"Yeh!" snarled Heath through his teeth. "And by to-morrow the kid woulda been dead. No chance then of her identifying him."

Markham looked at his watch and rose with determination.

"There's no point in waiting for Arnesson's return. The sooner we arrest him the better." He was about to give Heath an order when Vance intervened.

"Don't force the issue, Markham. You haven't any real evidence against the man. It's too delicate a situation for aggression. We must go carefully or we'll fail."

"I realize that the finding of the typewriter and the note-book is not conclusive," concurred Markham. "But the identification by the child –"

"Oh, my dear fellow! What weight would a jury attach to a frightened five-year-old girl's identification without powerful contribut'ry evidence? A clever lawyer could nullify it in five minutes. And even assuming you could make the identification hold, what would it boot you? It wouldn't connect Arnesson in any way with the Bishop murders. You could only prosecute him for attempted kidnapping, – the child's unharmed, remember. And if you should, through a legal miracle, get a doubtful conviction, Arnesson would receive at most a few years in the bastille. That wouldn't end this horror. . . . No, no. You mustn't be precipitate."

Reluctantly Markham resumed his seat. He saw the force of Vance's argument.

"But we can't let this thing go," he declared ferociously. "We must stop this maniac some way."

"Some way – yes." Vance began pacing the room restlessly. "We may be able to wangle the truth out of him by subterfuge: he doesn't know yet that we've found the child. . . . It's possible Professor Dillard could assist us –" He halted and stood looking down at the floor. "Yes! That's our one chance. We must confront Arnesson with what we know when the professor is present. The situation is sure to force an issue of some kind. The professor now will do all in his power to help convict Arnesson."

"You believe he knows more than he had told us?"

"Undoubtedly. I've told you so from the first. And when he hears of the Little Miss Muffet episode, it's not unlikely he'll supply us with the evidence we need."

"It's a long chance." Markham was pessimistic. "But it can do no harm to try. In any event, I shall arrest Arnesson before I leave here, and hope for the best."

A few moments later the front door opened and Professor Dillard appeared in the hall opposite the archway. He scarcely acknowledged Markham's greeting – he was scanning our faces as if trying to read the meaning of our unexpected visit. Finally he put a question.

"You have, perhaps, thought over what I said last night?"

"Not only have we thought it over," said Markham, "but Mr. Vance has found the thing that was disturbing you. After we left here he showed me a copy of 'The Pretenders.' "

"Ah!" The exclamation was like a sigh of relief. "For days that play has been in my mind, poisoning every thought. . . ." He looked up fearfully. "What does it mean?"

Vance answered the question.

"It means, sir, that you've led us to the truth. We're waiting now for Mr. Arnesson. – And I think it would be well if we had a talk with you in the meantime. You may be able to help us."

The old man hesitated.

"I had hoped not to be made an instrument in the boy's conviction." His voice held a tragic paternal note. But presently his features hardened; a vindictive light shone in his eyes; and his hand tightened over the knob of his stick. "However, I can't consider my own feelings now. Come; I will do what I can."

On reaching the library he paused by the side-board and poured himself a glass of port. When he had drunk it he turned to Markham with a look of apology.

"Forgive me. I'm not quite myself." He drew forward the little chess table and placed glasses on it for all of us. "Please overlook my discourtesy." He filled the glasses and sat down.

We drew up chairs. There was none of us, I think, who did not feel the need of a glass of wine after the harrowing events we had just passed through.

When we had settled ourselves the professor lifted heavy eyes to Vance, who had taken a seat opposite to him.

"Tell me everything," he said. "Don't try to spare me."

Vance drew out his cigarette-case.

"First, let me ask you a question. Where was Mr. Arnesson between five and six yesterday afternoon?"

"I – don't know." There was a reluctance in the words. "He had tea here in the library; but he went out about half past four, and I didn't see him again until dinner time."

Vance regarded the other sympathetically for a moment, then he said:

"We've found the typewriter on which the Bishop notes were printed. It was in an old suit-case hidden in the attic of this house."

The professor showed no sign of being startled.

"You were able to identify it?"

"Beyond any doubt. Yesterday a little girl named Madeleine Moffat disappeared from the playground in the park. There was a sheet of paper in the machine, and on it had already been typed: 'Little Miss Muffet sat on a tuffet.' "

Professor Dillard's head sank forward.

"Another insane atrocity! If only I hadn't waited till last night to warn you – !"

"No great harm has been done," Vance hastened to inform him. "We found the child in time: she's out of danger now."

"Ah!"

"She had been locked in the hall-closet on the top floor of the Drukker house. We had thought she was here somewhere – which is how we came to search your attic."

There was a silence; then the professor asked:

"What more have you to tell me?"

"Drukker's note-book containing his recent quantum researches was stolen from his room the night of his death. We found this note-book in the attic with the typewriter."

"He stooped even to that?" It was not a question, but an exclamation of incredulity. "Are you sure of your conclusions? Perhaps if I had made no suggestion last night – had not sowed the seed of suspicion. . . ."

"There can be no doubt," declared Vance softly. "Mr. Markham intends to arrest Mr. Arnesson when he returns from the university. But to be frank with you, sir: we have practically no legal evidence, and it is a question in Mr. Markham's mind whether or not the law can even hold him. The most we can hope for is a conviction for attempted kidnapping through the child's identification."

"Ah, yes . . . the child would know." A bitterness crept into the old man's eyes. "Still, there should be some means of obtaining justice for the other crimes."

Vance sat smoking pensively, his eyes on the wall beyond. At last he spoke with quiet gravity.

"If Mr. Arnesson were convinced that our

case against him was a strong one, he might choose suicide as a way out. That perhaps would be the most humane solution for every one."

Markham was about to make an indignant protest, but Vance anticipated him.

"Suicide is not an indefensible act *per se.* The Bible, for instance, contains many accounts of heroic suicide. What finer example of courage than Rhazis', when he threw himself from the tower to escape the yoke of Demetrius?* There was gallantry, too, in the death of Saul's sword-bearer, and in the self-hanging of Ahithophel. And surely the suicides of Samson and Judas Iscariot had virtue. History is filled with notable suicides – Brutus and Cato of Utica, Hannibal, Lucretia, Cleopatra, Seneca. . . . Nero killed himself lest he fall into the hands of Otho and the Pretorian guards. In Greece we have the famous self-destruction of Demosthenes; and Empedocles threw himself in the crater of Etna. Aristotle was the first great thinker to advance the dictum that suicide is an anti-social act, but, according to

*I admit that the name of Rhazis was unfamiliar to me; and when I looked it up later I found that the episode to which Vance referred does not appear in the Anglican bible, but in the second book of Maccabees in the Apocrypha.

tradition, he himself took poison after the death of Alexander. And in modern times let us not forget the sublime gesture of Baron Nogi. . . ."

"All that is no justification of the act," Markham retorted. "The law –"

"Ah, yes – the law. In Chinese law every criminal condemned to death has the option of suicide. The Codex adopted by the French National Assembly at the end of the eighteenth century abolished all punishments for suicide; and in the *Sachsenspiegel* – the principal foundation of Teuton law – it is plainly stated that suicide is not a punishable act. Moreover, among the Donatists, Circumcellions and Patricians suicide was considered pleasing to the gods. And even in More's Utopia there was a synod to pass on the right of the individual to take his own life. . . . Law, Markham, is for the protection of society. What of a suicide that makes possible that protection? Are we to invoke a legal technicality, when, by so doing, we actually lay society open to continued danger? Is there no law higher than those on the statute books?"

Markham was sorely troubled. He rose and walked the length of the room and back, his face dark with anxiety. When he sat down again he looked at Vance a long while, his fingers drumming with nervous indecision on the table.

"The innocent of course must be considered," he said in a voice of discouragement. "As morally wrong as suicide is, I can see your point that at times it may be theoretically justified." (Knowing Markham as I did, I realized what this concession had cost him; and I realized, too, for the first time, how utterly hopeless he felt in the face of the scourge of horror which it was his duty to wipe out.)

The old professor nodded understandingly.

"Yes, there are some secrets so hideous that it is well for the world not to know them. A higher justice may often be achieved without the law taking its toll."

As he spoke the door opened, and Arnesson stepped into the room.

"Well, well. Another conference, eh?" He gave us a quizzical leer, and threw himself into a chair beside the professor. "I thought the case had been adjudicated, so to speak. Didn't Pardee's suicide put *finis* to the affair?"

Vance looked straight into the man's eyes.

"We've found little Miss Muffet, Mr. Arnesson."

The other's eyebrows went up with sardonic amusement.

"Sounds like a charade. What am I supposed

to answer: 'How's little Jack Horner's thumb?' Or, should I inquire into the health of Jack Sprat?"

Vance did not relax his steady gaze.

"We found her in the Drukker house, locked in a closet," he amplified, in a low, even tone.

Arnesson became serious, and an involuntary frown gathered on his forehead. But his slackening of pose was only transient. Slowly his mouth twisted into a smirk.

"You policemen are so efficient. Fancy finding little Miss Muffet so soon. Remarkable." He wagged his head in mock admiration. "However, sooner or later it was to be expected. – And what, may I ask, is to be the next move?"

"We also found the typewriter," pursued Vance, ignoring the question. "And Drukker's stolen notebook."

Arnesson was at once on his guard.

"Did you really?" He gave Vance a canny look. "Where were these tell-tale objects?"

"Up-stairs – in the attic."

"Aha! Housebreaking?"

"Something like that."

"Withal," Arnesson scoffed, "I can't see that you have a cast-iron case against any one. A typewriter is not like a suit of clothes that fits only one person. And who can say how

Drukker's note-book found its way into our attic? – You must do better than that, Mr. Vance."

"There is, of course, the factor of opportunity. The Bishop is a person who could have been on hand at the time of each murder."

"That is the flimsiest of contributory evidence," the man countered. "It would not help much toward a conviction."

"We might be able to show why the murderer chose the sobriquet of Bishop."

"Ah! That unquestionably would help." A cloud settled on Arnesson's face, and his eyes became reminiscent. "I'd thought of that, too."

"Oh, had you, now?" Vance watched him closely. "And there's another piece of evidence I haven't mentioned. Little Miss Muffet will be able to identify the man who led her to the Drukker house and forced her into the closet."

"So! The patient has recovered?"

"Oh, quite. Doing nicely, in fact. We found her, d' ye see, twenty-four hours before the Bishop intended us to."

Arnesson was silent. He was staring down at his hands which, though folded, were working nervously. Finally he spoke.

"And if, in spite of everything, you were wrong. . . ."

"I assure you, Mr. Arnesson," said Vance

quietly, "that I *know* who is guilty."

"You positively frighten me!" The man had got a grip on himself, and he retorted with biting irony. "If, by any chance, I myself were the Bishop, I'd be inclined to admit defeat. . . . Still, it's quite obvious that it was the Bishop who took the chessman to Mrs. Drukker at midnight; and I didn't return home with Belle until half past twelve that night."

"So you informed her. As I recall, you looked at your watch and told her what time it was. – Come, now: what time was it?"

"That's correct – half past twelve."

Vance sighed and tapped the ash from his cigarette.

"I say, Mr. Arnesson; how good a chemist are you?"

"One of the best," the man grinned. "Majored in it. – What then?"

"When I was searching the attic this morning I discovered a little wall-closet in which some one had been distilling hydrocyanic acid from potassium ferrocyanide. There was a chemist's gas-mask on hand, and all the paraphernalia. Bitter-almond odor still lurking in the vicinity."

"Quite a treasure-trove, our attic. A sort of haunt of Loki, it would seem."

"It was just that," returned Vance gravely,

"– the den of an evil spirit."

"Or else the laboratory of a modern Doctor Faustus. . . . But why the cyanide, do you think?"

"Precaution, I'd say. In case of trouble the Bishop could step out of the picture painlessly. Everything in readiness, don't y' know."

Arnesson nodded.

"Quite a correct attitude on his part. Really decent of him, in fact. No use putting people to unnecessary bother if you're cornered. Yes, very correct."

Professor Dillard had sat during this sinister dialogue with one hand pressed to his eyes, as though in pain. Now he turned sorrowfully to the man he had fathered for so many years.

"Many great men, Sigurd, have justified suicide –" he began; but Arnesson cut him short with a cynical laugh.

"Faugh! Suicide needs no justification. Nietzsche laid the bugaboo of voluntary death. *'Auf eine stolze Art sterben, wenn es nicht mehr möglich ist, auf eine stolze Art zu leben. Der Tod unter den verächtlichsten Bedingungen, ein unfreier Tod, ein Tod zur unrechten Zeit ist ein Feiglings-Tod. Wir haben es nicht in der Hand, zu verhindern, geboren zu werden: aber wir können diesen Fehler – denn bisweilen ist es ein Fehler – wieder gut machen. Wenn man sich abschafft, tut* *man die achtungswürdigste Sache, die es giebt: man verdient beinahe damit, zu leben.'** – Memorized that passage from 'Götzen-Dämmerung' in my youth. Never forgot it. A sound doctrine."

"Nietzsche had many famous predecessors who also upheld suicide," supplemented Vance. "Zeno the Stoic left us a passionate dithyramb defending voluntary death. And Tacitus, Epictetus, Marcus Aurelius, Cato, Kant, Fichte, Diderot, Voltaire and Rousseau, all wrote apologias for suicide. Schopenhauer protested bitterly against the fact that suicide was regarded as a crime in England. . . . And yet, I wonder if the subject can be formulated. Somehow I feel that it's too personal a matter for academic discussion."

The professor agreed sadly.

"No one can know what goes on in the human heart in that last dark hour."

During this discussion Markham had been

*"One should die proudly when it is no longer possible to live proudly. The death which takes place in the most contemptible circumstances, the death that is not free, the death which occurs at the wrong time, is the death of a coward. We have not the power to prevent ourselves from being born; but this error – for sometimes it is an error – can be rectified if we choose. The man who does away with himself, performs the most estimable of deeds; he almost deserves to live for having done so."

growing impatient and uneasy; and Heath, though at first rigid and watchful, had begun to unbend. I could not see that Vance had made the slightest progress; and I was driven to the conclusion that he had failed signally in accomplishing his purpose of ensnaring Arnesson. However, he did not appear in the least perturbed. I even got the impression that he was satisfied with the way things were going. But I did notice that, despite his outer calm, he was intently alert. His feet were drawn back and poised; and every muscle in his body was taut. I began to wonder what the outcome of this terrible conference would be.

The end came swiftly. A short silence followed the professor's remark. Then Arnesson spoke.

"You say you know who the Bishop is, Mr. Vance. That being the case, why all this palaver?"

"There was no great haste." Vance was almost casual. "And there was the hope of tying up a few loose ends, – hung juries are so unsatisfact'ry, don't y' know. . . . Then again, this port is excellent."

"The port? . . . Ah yes." Arnesson glanced at our glasses, and turned an injured look on the professor. "Since when have I been a teetotaler, sir?"

The other gave a start, hesitated, and rose.

"I'm sorry, Sigurd. It didn't occur to me . . . you never drink in the forenoon." He went to the sideboard and, filling another glass, placed it, with an unsteady hand, before Arnesson. Then he refilled the other glasses.

No sooner had he resumed his seat than Vance uttered an exclamation of surprise. He had half risen and was leaning forward, his hands resting on the edge of the table, his eyes fixed with astonishment on the mantel at the end of the room.

"My word! I never noticed that before. . . . Extr'ordin'ry!"

So unexpected and startling had been his action, and so tense was the atmosphere, that involuntarily we swung about and looked in the direction of his fascinated gaze.

"A Cellini plaque!" he exclaimed. "The Nymph of Fontainebleau! Berenson told me it was destroyed in the seventeenth century. I've seen its companion piece in the Louvre. . . ."

A red flush of angry indignation mounted to Markham's cheeks; and for myself I must say that, familiar as I was with Vance's idiosyncrasies and intellectual passion for rare antiques, I had never before known him to exhibit such indefensible bad taste. It seemed unbelievable that he would have let himself be distracted by an *objet d'art* in such a tragic hour.

Professor Dillard frowned at him with consternation.

"You've chosen a strange time, sir, to indulge your enthusiasm for art," was his scathing comment.

Vance appeared abashed and chagrined. He sank back in his seat, avoiding our eyes, and began turning the stem of his glass between his fingers.

"You are quite right, sir," he murmured. "I owe you an apology."

"The plaque, incidentally," the professor added, by way of mitigating the severity of his rebuke, "is merely a copy of the Louvre piece."

Vance, as if to hide his confusion, raised his wine to his lips. It was a highly unpleasant moment: every one's nerves were on edge; and, in automatic imitation of his action, we lifted our glasses too.

Vance gave a swift glance across the table and, rising, went to the front window, where he stood, his back to the room. So unaccountable was his hasty departure that I turned and watched him wonderingly. Almost at the same moment the edge of the table was thrust violently against my side, and simultaneously there came a crash of glassware.

I leapt to my feet and gazed down with horror at the inert body sprawled forward in the chair opposite, one arm and shoulder flung across the table. A short silence of dismay and bewilderment followed. Each of us seemed momentarily paralyzed. Markham stood like a graven image, his eyes fastened on the table; and Heath, staring and speechless, clung rigidly to the back of his chair.

"Good Gad!"

It was Arnesson's astonished ejaculation that snapped the tension.

Markham went quickly round the table and bent over Professor Dillard's body.

"Call a doctor, Arnesson," he ordered.

Vance turned wearily from the window and sank into a chair.

"Nothing can be done for him," he said, with a deep sigh of fatigue. "He prepared for a swift and painless death when he distilled his cyanide. – The Bishop case is over."

Markham was glaring at him with dazed incomprehension.

"Oh, I've half-suspected the truth ever since Pardee's death," Vance went on, in answer to the other's unspoken question. "But I wasn't sure of it until last night when he went out of his way to hang the guilt on Mr. Arnesson."

"Eh? What's that?" Arnesson turned from the telephone.

"Oh, yes," nodded Vance. "You were to pay the penalty. You'd been chosen from the first as the victim. He even suggested the possibility of your guilt to us."

Arnesson did not seem as surprised as one would have expected.

"I knew the professor hated me," he said. "He was intensely jealous of my interest in Belle. And he was losing his intellectual grip – I've seen that for months. I've done all the work on his new book, and he's resented every academic honor paid me. I've had an idea he was back of all this deviltry; but I wasn't sure. I didn't think, though, he'd try to send me to the electric chair."

Vance got up and, going to Arnesson, held out his hand.

"There was no danger of that. – And I want to apologize for the way I've treated you this past half hour. Merely a matter of tactics. Y' see, we hadn't any real evidence, and I was hopin' to force his hand."

Arnesson grinned sombrely.

"No apology necessary, old son. I knew you didn't have your eye on me. When you began riding me I saw it was only technique. Didn't know what you were after, but I followed your cues the best I could. Hope I didn't bungle the job."

"No, no. You turned the trick."

"Did I?" Arnesson frowned with deep perplexity. "But what I don't understand is why he should have taken the cyanide when he thought it was I you suspected."

"That particular point we'll never know," said Vance. "Maybe he feared the girl's identification. Or he may have seen through my deception. Perhaps he suddenly revolted at the idea of shouldering you with the onus. . . . As he himself said, no one knows what goes on in the human heart during the last dark hour."

Arnesson did not move. He was looking straight into Vance's eyes with penetrating shrewdness.

"Oh, well," he said at length; "we'll let it go at that. . . . Anyway, thanks!"

CHAPTER XXVI

HEATH ASKS A QUESTION

(Tuesday, April 26; 4 p.m.)

When Markham and Vance and I departed from the Dillard house an hour later, I thought the Bishop affair was over. And it was over as far as the public was concerned. But there was another revelation to come; and it was, in a way, the most astounding of all the facts that had been brought to light that day.

Heath joined us at the District Attorney's office after lunch, for there were several delicate official matters to be discussed; and later that afternoon Vance reviewed the entire case, explaining many of its obscure points.

"Arnesson has already suggested the motive for these insane crimes," he began. "The professor knew that his position in the world of science was being usurped by the younger man. His mind had begun to lose its force and penetration; and he realized that his new book on atomic structure was being made possible only through Arnesson's help. A colossal hate grew up in him for his foster son; Arnesson became in his eyes a kind of monster whom he himself, like Frankenstein, had created, and who was now rising to destroy him. And this intellectual enmity was augmented by a primitive emotional jealousy. For ten years he had centred in Belle Dillard the accumulated affection of a life of solit'ry bachelorhood – she represented his one hold on every-day existence – and when he saw that Arnesson was likely to take her from him, his hatred and resentment were doubled in intensity."

"The motive is understandable," said Markham. "But it does not explain the crimes."

"The motive acted as a spark to the dry powder of his pent-up emotions. In looking about for a means to destroy Arnesson, he hit upon the diabolical jest of the Bishop murders. These murders gave relief to his repressions; they met his psychic need for violent expression; and at the same time they answered the dark question in his mind how he could dispose of Arnesson and keep Belle Dillard for himself."

"But why," Markham asked, "didn't he merely murder Arnesson and have done with it?"

"You overlook the psychological aspects of

the situation. The professor's mind had disintegrated through long intense repression. Nature was demanding an outlet. And it was his passionate hatred of Arnesson that brought the pressure to an explosion point. The two impulses were thus combined. In committing the murders he was not only relieving his inhibitions, but he was also venting his wrath against Arnesson, for Arnesson, d' ye see, was to pay the penalty. Such a revenge was more potent, and hence more satisfying, than the mere killing of the man would have been, – it was the great grim joke behind the lesser jokes of the murders themselves. . . .

"However, this fiendish scheme had one great disadvantage, though the professor did not see it. It laid the affair open to psychological analysis; and at the outset I was able to postulate a mathematician as the criminal agent. The difficulty of naming the murderer lay in the fact that nearly every possible suspect was a mathematician. The only one I knew to be innocent was Arnesson, for he was the only one who consistently maintained a psychic balance – that is, who constantly discharged the emotions arising from his protracted abstruse speculations. A general sadistic and cynical attitude that is volubly expressed, and a violent homicidal outburst, are psychologically equivalent. Giving full rein to one's cynicism as one goes along produces a normal outlet and maintains an emotional equilibrium. Cynical, scoffing men are always safe, for they are farthest removed from sporadic physical outbreaks; whereas the man who represses his sadism and accumulates his cynicism beneath a grave and stoical exterior is always liable to dangerous fulminations. This is why I knew Arnesson was incapable of the Bishop murders and why I suggested your letting him help us with the investigation. As he admitted, he suspected the professor; and his request to assist us was, I believe, actuated by a desire to keep posted so that he could better protect Belle Dillard and himself in case his suspicions should prove correct."

"That sounds reasonable," acceded Markham. "But where did Dillard get his fantastic ideas for the murders?"

"The Mother-Goose motif was probably suggested to him when he heard Arnesson jestingly tell Robin to beware of an arrow from Sperling's bow. He saw in that remark a means of venting his hatred against the man who had made it; and he bided his time. The opportunity to stage the crime came shortly after. When he saw Sperling pass up the street that morning, he knew that Robin was alone in the archery-room. So he went below, engaged Robin in conversation, struck him over the head, drove a shaft into his heart, and shoved him out on the range. He then wiped up the blood, destroyed the cloth, posted his notes at the corner, put one in the house letter-box, returned to the library, and called up this office. One unforeseen factor cropped up, however: – Pyne was in Arnesson's room when the professor said he went out on the balcony. But no harm came of it, for though Pyne knew something was amiss when he caught the professor lying, he certainly didn't suspect the old gentleman of being a murderer. The crime was a decided success."

"Still and all," put in Heath, "you guessed that Robin hadn't been shot with a bow and arrow."

"Yes. I saw from the battered condition of the nock of the arrow that it had been hammered into Robin's body; and I concluded therefore that the chap had been killed indoors, after having first been stunned with a blow on the head. That was why I assumed that the bow had been thrown to the range from the window – I didn't know then that the professor was guilty. The bow of course was never on the range. – But the evidence on which I based my deductions cannot be held as an error or oversight on the professor's part. As long as his Mother-Goose joke was accomplished, the rest didn't matter to him."

"What instrument do you think he used?" Markham put the question.

"His walking stick, most likely. You may have noticed it has an enormous gold knob perfectly constructed as a lethal weapon.* Incidentally, I'm inclined to think he exaggerated his gout to attract sympathy and to shunt any possible suspicion from himself."

"And the suggestion for the Sprigg murder?"

"After Robin's death he may have deliberately looked about for Mother-Goose material for another crime. In any event, Sprigg visited the house the Thursday night preceding the shooting; and it was at that time, I imagine, that the idea was born. On the day chosen for the gruesome business he rose early and dressed, waited for Pyne's knock at half past seven, answered it, and then went to the park – probably through the archery-room and by way of the alley. Sprigg's habit of taking

*It was discovered later that the large weighted gold handle, which was nearly eight inches long, was loose and could be easily removed from the stick. The handle weighed nearly two pounds and, as Vance had observed, constituted a highly efficient "black jack." Whether or not it had been loosened for the purpose to which it was put, is of course wholly a matter of conjecture.

daily morning walks may have been casually mentioned by Arnesson, or even by the lad himself."

"But how do you explain the tensor formula?"

"The professor had heard Arnesson talking to Sprigg about it a few nights before; and I think he placed it under the body to call attention – through association – to Arnesson. Moreover, that particular formula subtly expressed the psychological impulse beneath the crimes. The Riemann-Christoffel tensor is a statement of the infinity of space – the negation of infinitesimal human life on this earth; and subconsciously it no doubt satisfied the professor's perverted sense of humor, giving added homogeneity to his monstrous conception. The moment I saw it I sensed its sinister significance; and it substantiated my theory that the Bishop murders were the acts of a mathematician whose values had become abstract and incommensurable."

Vance paused to light another cigarette, and after a moment's thoughtful silence continued.

"We come now to the midnight visit to the Drukker house. That was a grim *entr'acte* forced on the murderer by the report of Mrs. Drukker's scream. He feared the woman had seen Robin's body thrown to the range; and when, on the morning of Sprigg's murder she had been in the yard and met him returning from the kill, he was more worried than ever that she would put two and two together. No wonder he tried to prevent our questioning her! And at the earliest opportunity he attempted to silence her for all time. He took the key from Belle Dillard's handbag before the theatre that night, and replaced it the next morning. He sent Pyne and Beedle to bed early; and at half past ten Drukker complained of fatigue and went home. At midnight he figured that the coast was clear for his grisly visit. His taking the black bishop as a symbolic signature to the contemplated murder was probably suggested by the chess discussion between Pardee and Drukker. Then again, it was Arnesson's chessman, and I even suspect him of telling us of the chess discussion to call attention to Arnesson's chess set in case the black bishop should fall into our hands."

"Do you think he had any idea of involving Pardee at that time?"

"Oh, no. He was genuinely surprised when Arnesson's analysis of the Pardee-Rubinstein game revealed the fact that the bishop had long been Pardee's nemesis. . . . And you were undoubtedly right about Pardee's reaction to my mention of the black bishop the next day.

The poor chap thought I was deliberately ridiculing him as a result of his defeat at Rubinstein's hands. . . ."

Vance leaned over and tapped the ashes from his cigarette.

"Too bad," he murmured regretfully. "I owe him an apology, don't y' know." He shrugged his shoulders slightly, and, settling back in his chair, took up his narrative. "The professor got his idea for Drukker's murder from Mrs. Drukker herself. She expressed her imaginative fears to Belle Dillard, who repeated them at dinner that night; and the plan took shape. There were no complications to its execution. After dinner he went to the attic and typed the notes. Later he suggested a walk to Drukker, knowing Pardee wouldn't remain long with Arnesson; and when he saw Pardee on the bridle path he of course knew Arnesson was alone. As soon as Pardee had walked away, he struck Drukker and tipped him over the wall. Immediately he took the little path to the Drive, crossed to 76th Street, and went to Drukker's room, returning by the same route. The whole episode couldn't have occupied more than ten minutes. Then he calmly walked past Emery and went home with Drukker's note-book under his coat. . . ."

"But why," interposed Markham, "if you

were sure that Arnesson was innocent, did you make such a point of locating the key to the alley door? Only Arnesson could have used the alley on the night of Drukker's death. Dillard and Pardee both went out by the front door."

"I wasn't interested in the key from the standpoint of Arnesson's guilt. But if the key was gone, d' ye see, it would have meant that some one had taken it in order to throw suspicion on Arnesson. How simple it would have been for Arnesson to slip down the alley after Pardee had gone, cross the Drive to the little path and attack Drukker after the professor had left him. . . . And, Markham, that is what we were supposed to think. It was, in fact, the obvious explanation of Drukker's murder."

"What I can't get through my head, though," complained Heath, "is why the old gent should have killed Pardee. That didn't throw any suspicion on Arnesson, and it made it look like Pardee was guilty and had got disgusted and croaked himself."

"That spurious suicide, Sergeant, was the professor's most fantastic joke. It was at once ironical and contemptuous; for all during that comic interlude plans were being made for Arnesson's destruction. And, of course, the fact that we possessed a plausible culprit had the great advantage of relaxing our watchfulness and causing the guards to be removed from the house. The murder, I imagine, was conceived rather spontaneously. The professor invented some excuse to accompany Pardee to the archery-room, where he had already closed the windows and drawn the shades. Then, perhaps pointing out an article in a magazine, he shot his unsuspecting guest through the temple, placed the gun in his hand, and, as a bit of sardonic humor, built the house of cards. On returning to the library he set up the chessmen to give the impression that Pardee had been brooding over the black bishop. . . .

"But, as I say, this piece of grim grotesquerie was only a side-issue. The Little-Miss-Muffet episode was to be the *dénouement;* and it was carefully planned so as to bring the heavens crashing down on Arnesson. The professor was at the Drukker house the morning of the funeral when Madeleine Moffat brought the flowers for Humpty Dumpty; and he undoubtedly knew the child by name – she was Drukker's favorite and had been to the house on numerous occasions. The Mother-Goose idea being now firmly implanted in his mind, like a homicidal obsession, he very naturally associated the name Moffat with

Muffet. Indeed, it's not unlikely that Drukker or Mrs. Drukker had called the child 'Little Miss Muffat' in his presence. It was easy for him to attract her attention and summon her to the mound by the wall yesterday afternoon. He probably told her that Humpty Dumpty wanted to see her; and she came with him eagerly, following him under the trees by the bridle path, thence across the Drive, and through the alley between the apartment houses. No one would have noticed them, for the Drive is teeming with children at that hour. Then last night he planted in us the seed of suspicion against Arnesson, believing that when the Little-Miss-Muffet notes reached the press we would look for the child and find her, dead from lack of air, in the Drukker house. . . . A clever, devilish plan!"

"But did he expect us to search the attic of his own home?"

"Oh, yes; but not until to-morrow. By then he would have cleaned out the closet and put the typewriter in a more conspicuous place. And he would have removed the note-book, for there's little doubt that he intended to appropriate Drukker's quantum researches. But we came a day too soon, and upset his calculations."

Markham smoked moodily for a time.

"You say you were convinced of Dillard's guilt last night when you remembered the character of *Bishop Arnesson. . . .*"

"Yes – oh, yes. That gave me the motive. At the moment I realized that the professor's object was to shoulder Arnesson with the guilt, and that the signature to the notes had been chosen for that purpose."

"He waited a long time before he called our attention to 'The Pretenders,' " commented Markham.

"The fact is, he didn't expect to have to do it at all. He thought we'd discover the name for ourselves. But we were duller than he anticipated; and at last, in desperation, he sent for you and beat cleverly round the bush, accentuating 'The Pretenders.' "

Markham did not speak for several moments. He sat frowning reproachfully, his fingers tapping a tattoo on the blotter.

"Why," he asked at length, "did you not tell us last night that the professor and not Arnesson was the Bishop? You let us think –"

"My dear Markham! What else could I do? In the first place, you wouldn't have believed me, and would most likely have suggested another ocean trip, what? Furthermore, it was essential to let the professor think we suspected Arnesson. Otherwise, we'd have had no chance to force the issue as we did. Subterfuge was our only hope; and I knew that if you and the Sergeant suspected him you'd have to dissemble; and lo! it all worked out beautifully."

The Sergeant, I noticed, had, for the past half hour, been regarding Vance from time to time with a look of perplexed uncertainty; but for some reason he had seemed reluctant to give voice to his troubled thoughts. Now, however, he shifted his position uneasily and, taking his cigar slowly from his mouth, asked a startling question.

"I ain't complaining about your not putting us wise last night, Mr. Vance, but what I would like to know is: why, when you hopped up and pointed at that plate on the mantel, did you switch Arnesson's and the old gent's glasses?"

Vance sighed deeply and gave a hopeless wag of the head.

"I might have known that nothing could escape your eagle eye, Sergeant."

Markham thrust himself forward over the desk, and glared at Vance with angry bewilderment.

"What's this!" he spluttered, his usual self-restraint deserting him. "You changed the glasses? You deliberately –"

"Oh, I say!" pleaded Vance. "Let not your

wrathful passions rise." He turned to Heath with mock reproach. "Behold what you've got me in for, Sergeant."

"This is no time for evasion." Markham's voice was cold and inexorable. "I want an explanation."

Vance made a resigned gesture.

"Oh, well. Attend. My idea, as I've explained to you, was to fall in with the professor's plan and appear to suspect Arnesson. This morning I purposely let him see that we had no evidence, and that, even if we arrested Arnesson, it was doubtful if we could hold him. I knew that, in the circumstances, he would take some action – that he would try to meet the situation in some heroic way – for the sole object of the murders was to destroy Arnesson utterly. That he would commit some overt act and give his hand away, I was confident. What it would be I didn't know. But we'd be watching him closely. . . . Then the wine gave me an inspiration. Knowing he had cyanide in his possession, I brought up the subject of suicide, and thus planted the idea in his mind. He fell into the trap, and attempted to poison Arnesson and make it appear like suicide. I saw him surreptitiously empty a small phial of colorless fluid into Arnesson's glass at the sideboard when he poured the wine. *My* first intention was to halt the murder and have the wine analyzed. We could have searched him and found the phial, and I could have testified to the fact that I saw him poison the wine. This evidence, in addition to the identification by the child, might have answered our purpose. But at the last moment, after he had refilled all our glasses, I decided on a simpler course –"

"And so you diverted our attention and switched the glasses!"

"Yes, yes. Of course. I figured that a man should be willing to drink the wine he pours for another."

"You took the law in your own hands!"

"I took it in my arms – it was helpless. . . . But don't be so righteous. Do you bring a rattlesnake to the bar of justice? Do you give a mad dog his day in court? I felt no more compunction in aiding a monster like Dillard into the Beyond than I would have in crushing out a poisonous reptile in the act of striking."

"But it was murder!" exclaimed Markham in horrified indignation.

"Oh, doubtless," said Vance cheerfully. "Yes – of course. Most reprehensible. . . . I say, am I by any chance under arrest?"

The "suicide" of Professor Dillard terminated the famous Bishop murder case, and automatically cleared Pardee's reputation of all suspicion. The following year Arnesson and Belle Dillard were married quietly and sailed for Norway, where they made their home. Arnesson had accepted the chair of applied mathematics at the University of Oslo; and it will be remembered that two years later he was awarded the Nobel prize for his work in physics. The old Dillard house in 75th Street was torn down, and on the site now stands a modern apartment house on whose façade are two huge terra-cotta medallions strongly suggestive of archery targets. I have often wondered if the architect was deliberate in his choice of decoration.